THE DAYS
OF ETERNITY

Also by Gordon Glasco

SECOND NATURE

THE
DAYS OF
ETERNITY

Gordon Glasco

DOUBLEDAY & COMPANY, INC.
GARDEN CITY, NEW YORK

For my mother, Pauline,
with a lifetime of love and gratitude;
thanks to the support of
my editor, Susan Schwartz,
Jane Rotrosen, Steve Waterman, and
Martin J. Brickman, M.D.;
and the help of Juergen Striemer,
Marion Chambers, and Harriet Bara

Who can number the sand of the sea,
the drops of rain, or the days of eternity?
Who can fathom the height of heaven,
the breadth of the earth, or the depths
of the abyss? Wisdom was created before
all things else, and prudence from eternity.

Ecclesiasticus 1:2–4

PROLOGUE
1972

The monsignor reached the communion rail and removed a consecrated Host from the gold ciborium. The altar boy steadied the patent under the communicant's chin. "Body of Christ." The monsignor offered the Host.

"Amen."

He placed it on the woman's tongue and moved on to her husband. The two elderly Coggins were regular communicants at the Sunday noon Mass. "Body of Christ."

"Amen."

Removing a third Host, he glanced up to observe the number of waiting communicants. Fifty, at most. For a congregation of three hundred, fifty was a poor number. He had been right last night when he complained to Father Auden, his assistant, that Communions had fallen off since the Vietnam War. "Body of Christ."

"Amen," replied Matt Goff.

Matt was a regular communicant, but he was also middle-aged. He moved on, glancing up again to see if there were young people in line. He knew all his parishioners at a glance. Only a handful of young people. "Body of Christ," he said, taking a second glance toward the side aisle.

"Amen."

His eye rested for an instant on an elegantly dressed, foreign-looking woman in a brown suit, a stranger to St. Luke's. "Body of Christ."

"Amen."

He felt a chilling tingle of delayed recognition and glanced again. The dark hair, the large dark eyes: she was staring at him, knowingly. The Host fell from his fingers into the ciborium, and he quickly reached for another. "Body of Christ."

"Amen."

He dared not look again and moved on. Impossible, he thought, then remembered he had not eaten between the eight and the ten o'clock Masses. He had felt dizzy during his sermon. He was imagining things. "Body of Christ."

"Amen."

Despite himself, he looked again. The stare was cold and unblinking. The face—the eyes, the chin, the way she wore her hair knotted behind her head—the face was almost identical, only a little older. Impossible. He tried to grasp a Host, but his fingers were shaking. "Body of Christ."

"Amen."

He realized some of the waiting communicants were staring at him. He moved on, forcing himself to concentrate on the spiritual task at hand. *Faith, trust, commitment—if we doubt in everything outside ourselves, then moral responsibility for our failures to both man and to God becomes meaningless.* He recalled the words of his morning sermon, which were to prepare his parishioners for Ash Wednesday and the approaching season of Lent. "Body of Christ."

"Amen," replied Pete Callahan.

He placed the Host on Pete's tongue and moved on to Pete's wife, Virginia. "Body of Christ."

"Amen."

He thought for the second time that morning of the other young men in his parish who, unlike Pete, had come back from Vietnam broken in spirit and faith. Most of the communicants at all the Masses that morning had been middle-aged or elderly. "Body of Christ."

"Amen."

He was approaching the end of the communion rail. He would have to go back and begin again; this time, the woman would be there, waiting. "Body of Christ."

"Amen."

No, he thought, impossible—it was inconceivable she could have come halfway around the world to find him here in Los Angeles. How would she have known? It was merely one of those cases of resemblance. "Body of Christ."

"Amen."

He turned back across the sanctuary, followed by the altar boy, and saw the woman kneeling, four communicants from the end. Her head was lowered, but the profile—the nose, the chin, and the brown knotted hair—the face was just as . . . He drew a deep breath and passed the woman. Though her head was bowed, he saw that she was in her late thirties, at most. Either that, or she had aged very little over the years. At the end of the rail he began again, saying, "Body of Christ," feeling sweat break on his brow. And with the sweat came the dark memory of that other catastrophe.

"Amen."

He grasped a Host, remembering these past seventeen long years as a priest. God's Providence would not undo the work of a lifetime in a mere instant. "Body of Christ."

"Amen."

The altar boy stared at him, puzzled.

"Body of Christ," he said, but saw in his mind another body and instantly recoiled from its sacrilegious intrusion.

"Amen."

The altar boy placed the patent under the woman's lowered face.

The monsignor fumbled for a Host, sensing that the waiting parishioners were staring at him, seeing that the bowed head was beautiful: *still*. The word, with all its terrifying implications, fell in his mind like a judgment and a sentence. Removing the Host, he realized there was nothing he could do or say except what the ritual demanded. He would not know until she raised her head. His voice shook when he murmured, "Body of Christ," and remembered again that different body in that different place, and felt the edge of an inchoate grief slice into his heart.

The woman lifted her face and looked up at him.

I
1944

CHAPTER 1

I

This time the pleasure came with the force of pain, and under its power she whimpered, then caught and held her breath. It came again, rolling up like a terrific wave through her body. He went on moving, blinding her with pleasure. "Carlo!" she cried out before she could stop herself and gripped his shoulders, losing all awareness of anything but the joy of who they were together. He rolled her body with his, and she opened her eyes but saw only the shadow of his head above her against the sunlight: saw him rise up with his head thrust back. He made a sound—it could have been her name, Anna, or a foreign word in his own language—and held them both, just as they were, motionless, as the wave rolled up again, carrying them both and holding them on its crest. This time they both made a sound—sounds of pleasure driven beyond joy into pain. Suspended with him in the moment, she lost all the old familiar feelings of guilt and fear and knew only a new feeling of terrific completion, of having come to rest.

She shut her eyes as he came down and closed her up in his arms. She felt small under him, like an embryonic moth protected inside a cocoon, safe and secure. His breath beat against her neck. After a while she lifted the lids of her eyes and saw sweat trickle through his dark hair. She quickly closed them again against the intrusion of light into their private space. Under his uniform shirt she embraced him, wanting to hold him forever as he was now, wanting the world itself to remain like this forever, but knowing that this kind of perfection of the moment was an illusion and would pass away. She emptied her mind of the familiar dark thoughts of love's transience and listened to his breath against her ear, felt his heartbeat against her breast. His heart was faster than hers, but he was seven years older. In her schoolgirl dreams of lovers before the war she had always imagined an impossible good fortune for herself: A handsome foreigner would pass through her village, an older, worldly man from some big city beyond the mountains; they would meet by accident in the street or in her father's store; they would fall in love at first sight, and he would sweep her away with him to freedom. An older, wiser, man would know the world and shelter her from its dangers. Her sister Livia had herself imagined the same thrilling story, but the fulfillment of this dream had been Anna's alone. Except her handsome worldly savior had come to her from . . .

He whispered something in his own language.

She whispered "What?" in hers.

"I'm heavy, aren't I? You can't breathe."

She sensed he would move and pressed her hands against his back. "No. Don't."

He gave in and relaxed. She opened and closed her eyes, relishing the beat of his heart slowing with hers. In these last eight dangerous months together here in the Adele Ravine he had always thought of her first. That, too, was one of the virtues she had imagined in her childhood dream of a lover: Though worldly, strong, and commanding, he would be kind and solicitous. It would be known by the world that she alone occupied that soft center of his tough, manly heart.

He ran his fingers over her forehead, stroking away the sweat, as he was wont to do. She kept her eyes closed against the hot August sun slanting down on them through the trees.

People would be astonished to know the difference between the public and the private man. But she had seen his gentle kindness, his compassion, as long ago as January—that first time they met in Signore Fabbiani's bakery. Before that, like everyone else in Montefalco, she had judged him to be remote and cold, though very handsome with his brown hair peeking out from under his officer's cap and his startling blue-green eyes sheltered under the brim. When he came into the bakery and overheard her denouncing the Fabbianis for profiting from the war by unjustly raising the price of flour, he had at once ordered the bakers to reduce the price to its previous level. He had smiled at her and winked. That day she had begun to wonder if her fantasy lover might not have come to her in the person of this alien army commander with the forbidding uniform and serene demeanor—this man who had passed her in the streets and stirred forbidden desires in her body, but who, until then, had only chilled her blood.

He lifted his head, bringing her back to the present. "What are you thinking?" he murmured.

She smiled. He had always asked the same question after they made love. Even when they talked about marriage, until now, until today, she had sheltered her thoughts about commitment behind hints and allusions. Given the war, given who they were in that world beyond the ravine, given the uncertainty of their future, the words *I love you* had seemed dangerous and frightening, for they would fix them both for eternity in these uncertain days to come.

"Anna," he insisted, "tell me what you're thinking."

She hesitated, recalling the discussion two days before between her father and brother about the outcome of the war. Her brother Piero knew more than even Carlo about what was happening in the war south of their Reno Valley. Piero had bragged about the end of peace that was soon to come here in the Tuscan mountains. Time, she had realized that day, their eight months of secret happiness, might now, despite Carlo's assurances, run out for them. She opened her eyes to the blinding sunlight and, leaping out into that future darkness, said, "I love you, Carlo."

A question formed in his eyes. He saw the fear in her face. His response was immediate. He pressed his mouth to hers and kissed her —hard this time—affirming his own oft-repeated vow, *I love you,* with his tongue inside her mouth. She squirmed, glorying in the tingle of promise in her skin. After a moment he relaxed and pressed his face against hers. A realization came to her. They had made love here only six times before, and only after months of meeting innocently to talk and sometimes to hold hands. Sometimes to kiss. With a feeling of contentment she realized they had already learned the silent language of lovers: the language she had first discovered in the *romanzi* she and her sister kept hidden between the mattresses of their beds at home. For a while neither of them moved. But she knew what they both were thinking. They were both weighing the certainty of their love against the greater uncertainty of the future.

He drew himself up on his elbow, studied her face, and ran the tip of his finger over the graceful line of her mouth. A flush still lingered in the pale skin around her high cheekbones. Her long, rich brown hair—hints of reddish summer sheen in the sunlight—lay splayed out across the white tablecloth she had brought with her this time for them to lie on. He recalled the beautiful, modestly dressed schoolgirl he had seen in the streets of Montefalco when he first arrived back at the end of December. Obeying his own orders forbidding his men to associate with the local population, he had refrained from acknowledging the aloof young schoolgirl. Then came that first meeting two weeks later, when he went into the Fabbiani bakery to buy a *mistocca* and discovered not a shy frightened little beauty like the others he had seen in his long march up the Italian boot but a brave nineteen-year-old young woman of convictions, temperament, and fire—which was what, coming from a colder climate of repression and reserve, he had imagined all the girls of Italy would be. Moreover, as he saw at once, she was both intelligent and educated —far beyond that of other peasant girls.

"And now," she said, "it's your turn. What are you thinking?"

"I'm thinking that you're the woman I always imagined you were," he said, touching her delicate chin with his fingertip, "the kind of woman I would never find back home where I come from."

She thought of the mental list of his qualities she had made for herself during these months of hesitation and indecision. "What kind of woman do you imagine I am?" she asked, probing.

"I'm not going to tell you." He grinned. "If I told you what you are and why I love you, you'd stop wondering if you *are* those things to me. Then you'd stop trying. I'll tell you after the war is over, when we're married. You're too young to know all the good things now." He pinched her chin playfully. "You're vain enough already."

"Tell me this," she said. "Did you have a girl friend at home before me?"

"Girl friends, yes. But never one I could live with forever—day in and day out for the rest of my life. Anna"—he sat up higher— "when the war is over, I want you to come home with me. To my country. You'll like it there."

She appeared to be walking a mental tightrope for a moment. "Would they like me? I mean . . ."

He laughed. "Of course. There's nothing to be afraid of. You'll find we're just like everybody else in the world."

The world, she thought. Between adolescence and now those words had taken on a different, a frightening meaning. The foreign tourists, the handsome men who had visited Montefalco's hot water spas before the war, had come, she had imagined, from a magical world of rich and indulgent variety. But in these last five years since the war began she had seen for herself how cruel men from that other, different, world could be. More recently, she had discovered the bitter taste of fear. Except . . . except for this one man, her Carlo. She said, "I want us to be married here, though, in Italy."

"In Montefalco?"

"That's impossible. Somewhere else, but in Italy. I want us to be married in the Church, Carlo."

He chuckled. "I told you, I'm a Catholic, too. We have Catholic churches at home."

"I know, but I want to be married before we go there. Before we leave Italy."

"All right." He kissed the tip of her nose. "Anything you say."

"You promise?"

"I promise. Then I'll take you home and we'll have our first child there."

"Yes. I'd . . . I'd like that."

"Promise?" He smiled. They were once again playing their little game of promises for the future.

"I promise."

"A son?"

She grinned up at him. He had always talked of having a son before a daughter. "I'll try, but I can't promise that."

"The odds are fifty-fifty. Do you like to gamble?"

"I'll gamble for as long as you love me. Besides, how could I lose if you love me?"

"He'll be beautiful, too, like you, and he'll"—he touched it—"he'll have this dark brown hair and"—he ran his finger down its slender bridge—"this straight aristocratic nose."

She giggled.

"But not this pretty little mouth or this delicate chin."

"Okay. I'll give him your mouth and your man's stubborn chin, if you want," she said and laughed.

"And whose eyes?"

She had noticed his eyes long before they met, once in the Via Garibaldi and again in the Piazza Nazionale. Brown eyes had always been too common in her childhood dreams of lovers. She had seen his startling blue-green eyes in the streets and in Fabbiani's bakery, but it was not until two weeks later, when she met him walking alone on the road outside town and he took off his soldier's cap, that she saw them close up, felt them pass through her body and touch her blood. "He'll have your eyes, Carlo," she affirmed, knowing even now that it would be so.

"That's a very big gamble," he said.

In the next instant their contentment was cut short by a rustle of leaves nearby and the snap of a limb. "What is it?" she exclaimed before she could stop herself.

"Shhh!" He covered her mouth, lifted himself slowly, knelt astride her body, and drew his pistol from its holster. He scanned the darkening wedge-end of the ravine. There was a scratching noise of tiny claws on the bark of a nearby tree. "A squirrel." He relaxed and sat back on his haunches, relieved. She smiled to herself. His uniform trousers and his funny baggy army drawers were bunched down around the tops of his boots. In all the times they had made love here in the ravine, he had never dared to remove all his clothes for fear they would be surprised by an intruder. Knowing how meticulous he was about his military appearance, she thought he looked quite funny half-dressed.

He saw her amusement and lay back down beside her. She had not until now thought to cover herself as she had always done in the past after their lovemaking, and in a quick reflex of embarrassment she reached for the panels of her dress. He caught her hand and grinned. She knew what he was thinking—that she had, for the first time, abandoned her Catholic schoolgirl modesty. She had worn the buttoned dress that afternoon because it could be easily opened down the front, and she had further revealed her intentions by not wearing underclothes. He seemed amused and somehow pleased by her daring forethought. She gave in to the restraint of his hand, pleased by her little victory over the old guilts.

He kissed her, then sat up again and looked off through the trees toward the river, worried. It's the hour, she thought, observing him calculate the position of the sun against the rim of the mountains on the opposite side of the valley. It would be close to four. In August the sun always set behind the mountains a little after five. Even though they had again stayed too long, she wished he would lie back again with her. The short forelock of his brown hair was matted against his forehead. His cheekbones glistened with sweat. For the first time since they had begun to make love, she heard the noises around them: water spilling over the rocks at the river's edge; the chirp of birds high in the trees and the walls of the ravine overhead; the hiss of the slow, dry August wind in the pine needles. She was glad this time that she had stolen a tablecloth from home for them to lie on. Before this the pine needles had always pricked their skin and made them sit up too soon. She had brought the tablecloth hidden under napkins she had embroidered for the nuns at the convent of Santa Cecilia, a clever thing she would do again next time they met. "Carlo?" she asked.

"*Sì, mia bimba?*"

She tried to smile at his clumsy attempt to contrive an affectionate diminutive in Italian. Though he spoke her language well, he spoke it with bookish formality. "When will it be over? When will you take me away from here?"

"Soon. Be patient."

"I want us to have a house—a place of our own."

"I know the house. It's five kilometers from the city where my parents live. There's land enough for a lawn and a garden."

Over several months they had planned everything—the kind of life they would have, the number of children, even the style of their furniture. They had planned everything except the date of their wedding. That detail was not yet theirs to plan. This time the explicitness of his plan for them frightened her, for it sounded too sure to be either real or possible. She thought of the chaotic madness they would be trapped in between now and then. With a sudden inpouring of dread and helplessness, she sat up and said, "I'm so afraid, Carlo!"

"There's nothing to be afraid of. Trust me."

A bell began to ring somewhere up the valley, the dull, leaden clank of the cast-iron bell in the tower of the church of San Tommaso in Montefalco, the same clank that had sounded every day of her life for nineteen years. A bell of this world, she thought, poor and rural and monotonous, not the heavenly bronze toll of that other childhood world—from the great worldly bells of Florence she had once heard years before. "The Angelus," she said and thought of poor Don Alessandro in the tower, pulling the rope.

"We should go." He sighed. "I told them I would be back in an hour and a half." He stood and pulled up his underwear and trousers. They had been there well over two hours. He thought of the dangerous suspicions his absence would have aroused back at headquarters. It had been like this for months, though, since that afternoon in March when he went walking on the Spedaletto road south of town and saw Anna wandering alone across the field next to the ridge of the Adele Ravine. She had walked up the crest and vanished down the other side into the ravine. He had debated his choices for but a moment: to obey his own military orders or, for the first time in his life, to follow the rebellion welling up in his blood and renounce all reason, logic, and responsibility. Before Montefalco he had only imagined what passion of this kind was like, for he had grown up thinking the only worthy and honorable passions were those that drove the mind to excel in ideals. Forsaking duty that afternoon, following this blind pull of the blood and the body's heart, he had followed Anna down into the ravine and found her in the pine grove near the riverside. Though startled, she had seemed less frightened of his sudden appearance than he had anticipated, explaining that she had come there to look for wild mushrooms. By the end of their awkward conversation together, he had known they would meet again in this safe seclusion, for she had said she often came here to gather *funghi* and even told him exactly when. "Next time," he said while dressing, "we'll meet earlier. The days are getting shorter now."

"When?"

"I don't know. We have to be careful, Anna."

She began buttoning her dress from the collar down. This, the dressing part, had always embarrassed her, bringing to mind thoughts of the confessional and the sins she had compounded these last three months since June when they first made love. She had gone to confession each week since then, but had never confessed these mortal sins of fornication, thereby making a mockery of the Sacrament. Worse, there were eleven sacrilegious Communions to answer for. She had never dared miss Communion on Sunday when she went to Mass with her family, for they would have known she was in mortal sin. She knelt up and saw that he was having trouble fastening his holster belt. She got up and put her shoes on. It was she who had left the usual signal in the church that afternoon for them to meet, a candle lit under the statue of the Sacred Heart. "Where do your men think you go when you come here?"

"Walking."

"Don't they ask questions?"

He grinned. "It's not their place to ask me questions. Who do you think's in charge here?"

She could never think of Carlo and his office at the same time. Duty, she knew, was something he took for granted, as inseparable from him as his soul. Funny, it was his exacting fidelity to duty that had been one of the qualities that attracted her to him when they first met. It was one of the virtues she had imagined in that childhood dream of a perfect lover: Her lover would be a man to depend on, not like the deceitful young men of her village who played games with girls merely to seduce them and then betrayed themselves by bragging about their faithlessness. When the war was over and his duties as a soldier came to an end, Carlo would, thank God, have only her to be faithful to, and that would be worth all these patient concessions. She gathered the tablecloth from the pine needles. "Yesterday," she said, "my mother asked questions. She and Papa argued about my visits to the convent. Mamma says it's too dangerous for me to walk alone outside the town, but Papa says we need the money I get for my sewing. Mamma compromised. She says my sister will have to come with me from now on."

"Your sister knows about us, doesn't she?"

"She knows I see you here. She knows we're going to be married when the war's over. But she doesn't know what we've been doing here."

"I see."

Anna left it at that, thinking of the danger of Carlo knowing too much about her family. She shook the needles from the cloth and folded it. "Papa says they'll try to break through the Gothic Line before the autumn rains come."

"It's the Green Line now," he corrected. "Of course, they'll try."

She tucked the tablecloth under the bundle of men's shirts in the basket. The nuns had given her shirts to mend in exchange for the napkins. "Papa says they'll do it."

"Impossible. I've already explained all that to you."

When she turned, he was fully dressed, except that his jacket, as always, needed buttoning. "If they did—just suppose they did— what would happen to us?" She walked toward him.

"It would depend on when and where they broke through."

Dreading his knowledge more than her own ignorance, she left the subject behind and, as she always had in the past, began to button his jacket for him.

He read her thoughts and said, "Listen to me, Anna. Whatever happens, nothing between us is going to change." He took hold of her shoulders. "Do you understand? I love you. And nothing will ever change that."

She started to say *your duty,* but the conviction in his voice stopped her. Her gaze rested on the tiny metal emblem pinned to the ribbon on his jacket. The little crisscrossed silver arms inside the silver circle glinted in the sunlight. In recent months she had come to hate the symbol and what it stood for. Carlo (she had used the Italian form of his name to mask her guilt)—Karl called it the *Hakenkreuz,* but her brother Piero had told her another name for it that sounded evil and sinister: swastika. She finished his buttons, wondering to herself how it was possible to love a man so much and, at the same time, so hate the things he believed in and fought for.

He seemed to read her mind, for he drew her close to him and held her firmly. "Oh, Anna, Anna—believe me, I hate this war. I hate it as much as you hate it."

"I know, Carlo." She held onto him and gave in to the impulse to cry.

"Please . . . please don't blame me for what I can't change. Some things are just *given,* Anna. You didn't choose to be Italian, and I . . . I didn't choose to be German, either."

II

"Teresa! Vieni qui!" Clara Tonelli called from the front steps of her neighbor's house where she sat eating roasted chestnuts. *"La strega!"* She cackled.

Teresa Piretti came to the door of her house in the Via Garibaldi and looked out, holding a broom of dried genestra twigs. She knew of whom Clara spoke. *"Dove?"*

Clara pointed toward the south end of town where some of the local farmers, *contadini,* were playing *boccie* in the street. *"Ecco."*

Today the girl was alone again. For the last three weeks, since the middle of August, she had made her weekly trips to the convent of Santa Cecilia accompanied by her sister, Livia.

" 'La Piccola Marchesa,' " Clara said and snorted, "she's *crazy!*"

Today, the girl seemed to be in a hurry. She walked with determination as she started along the road toward the darkening ridge of the Adele Ravine beyond the fields at the south end of town. "It's her parents who are crazy," Teresa said and looked across the valley where the sun was about to set behind the summit of Monte Grande, the largest of the hills west of Montefalco. It would be dark for sure today before the girl returned to town.

Clara gave a scornful clucking noise and dug into her black skirt for another chestnut. "She'll be caught by the curfew this time," she said, reading Teresa's mind. Last week, with the news of the American attack on Rimini, the Germans had imposed an after-dark curfew and a blackout on the town at night.

"Luisa Miceli's a fool to let Anna go to Santa Cecilia at this hour," said Teresa.

Clara shrugged. "The woman's a Berticelli."

Once, sometimes twice a week, Anna Miceli went to the convent of Santa Cecilia a mile south of Montefalco to earn a few lire sewing for the nuns. Admire the girl as she might for her courage, Teresa did not approve of the convent visits. Leaving town alone like that was not something she would permit her own daughter to do, not at a time like this, not with partisans in the hills around Montefalco and German soldiers swarming through the town. "The *tedeschi* will arrest her this time if she comes back after dark."

"Or worse, the Fascisti. The *carabinieri* would like nothing better than to arrest the little marchesa."

"It's her father's fault. He spoils her." Teresa left the stoop and went back inside to finish her sweeping. In Montefalco, Anna Miceli was called "La Piccola Marchesa" because her mother, Luisa Miceli, was the youngest daughter of the Marchese de Berticelli, once Montefalco's richest *padrone* before the Fascists confiscated his land. What small inheritance had been planned for Luisa she had lost when she married Angelo Miceli, a local dry-goods merchant. Angelo and Luisa had given birth to three children, a son, Piero, and two daughters, Anna and Livia. All three children had grown up to be independent and proud; but of all three, Anna was the proudest. She was also, by the grace of God, the prettiest girl in Montefalco. It did her little good, though, for her parents had come to grief with the Fascists. Their foolish monarchist loyalties had lost them their livelihood, and they now lived in poverty in the old *casa colonica* at the northern end of town. Anna, once the envy of all the Montefalco girls, no longer had the advantage of private education with the nuns, nor the enviable luxury of clothes imported from Bologna and Florence, nor the leisure of sewing fancy embroideries for the tourists who had once visited Montefalco's hot-water spas. Teresa reached the door again and swept the little pile of dust past Clara into the street. On the windy slope of her husband's recently harvested corn field, she caught sight of Anna's gray winter coat billowing in the wind. *"Chi va piano, va sano e lontano,"* she said darkly, quoting the famous old proverb, *"Ma chi va forte, va incontro alla morte."* Whoever goes slowly goes healthy and far; but whoever goes fast goes toward death.

Anna reached the crest of the Adele Ravine and stopped to draw a deep breath of cool bracing air. She had noticed the shortness of breath when she started up the steep grading above the chestnut grove. She had notice it once before, last Thursday when she came to meet Carlo. Perhaps this was a symptom of the *condizione*, as they called it. She drew her coat together and turned to look back toward Montefalco, cradled against the slope of the valley on the far side of the river. The western side of the valley was almost dark now. It was foolish to have left him the signal to meet her so late in the day. She had lied to her mother, saying she only wanted to buy thread in town and there was no need for Livia to accompany her.

With the deep blue evening shadow already creeping across the valley, it would be dark before she reached home. There would be questions, an argument, but she had no choice this time.

A mist was rising in the cradle of the valley, and she could scarcely make out the dark silhouette of the steel bridge across the Reno River, which Carlo would have to cross. When the Germans constructed the bridge to replace the old stone bridge the partisans had blown up, they had strung lights across the steel frame, but the lights were no longer lit at night because of the bombing raids in the last two weeks. Across the river, high up in the old town nestled in the hillside, she could barely see the cluster of buildings that marked the Piazza Nazionale where the Germans had their headquarters in the Municipio building. If Carlo had seen her pass through the piazza on her way from San Tommaso, he would know to go to the church and look for her signal. She had stayed in the church long enough to light the proper votive candle under the Sacred Heart, and when she passed through the piazza, the clock in the Municipio *campanile* had read four o'clock.

She took one more deep breath, then turned away toward the ravine. Perhaps he would come, perhaps not; they had sometimes missed each other's signal. But it was a gamble she had to take.

She started down the winding path into the ravine, careful to keep her coat free from the long acacia spikes. Last Thursday, the day after the Americans captured Lucca, she and Livia had come to the ravine, and Livia had waited for her at the top, near the road. She had worn her coat that afternoon and had torn it on one of the spikes. Her mother had questioned her about the tear, and Livia had kept quiet. It was her only coat now, and her mother had said there would be no more coats until the end of the war.

Just past the acacia trees the path narrowed as it zigzagged along the steep ragged face of the ravine. In the mountains, night came first to places like this. All through the summer she and Carlo had been careful to meet in the afternoons when there was plenty of light to see by. It would be dark when she reached the willows and pines along the riverbank. If he did not come, she would be forced to climb out alone in the dark, for there was only the one path, and the granite walls stretched all the way to the river.

She steadied herself against the slab-sided wall and remembered Carlo's warnings about this treacherous section of the path where the torrential rain last week, the first big autumn rain, had gashed the loose soil. It was not the little winding path that frightened her

—good God, she and her brother had played in the ravine as children!—it was the darkness at the bottom.

Piero's words from the night before came back to her: *The Americans and the South Africans will be here in a matter of three, maybe four days. And then, if the Germans are stupid enough to stay, we'll crush them like Sangiovese grapes!* Piero had sprung the news on them just before supper last night, when he came home briefly from the mountains where he had been hiding with the other partisans. He had stayed only long enough to eat, gather provisions from their parents' meager larder, and warn them about the approaching battle in the Reno Valley. In the last two weeks—only a week after Carlo had promised there would be no American breakthrough of the Gothic Line!—there had been rumors of terrible battles on the eastern side of the Italian peninsula. So far, here on the western side, the Allied advance from the south had been slow. Florence had already surrendered by the fourth of August, but Pisa and Lucca had lingered on in German hands. The Germans had now retreated into their bunker fortresses high in the mountains above the Tuscan plain. Until yesterday, when Piero came with the news that the Allies had attacked Pistoia to the south of Montefalco, no one had dreamed that the Americans would dare advance on the iron-clad German stronghold in the mountains. It would be only a matter of days, Piero had assured them, before the Americans reached Montefalco.

She felt a knot of panic tighten in her stomach as she rounded the next bend. She, her mother, Livia, and her grandmother had listened last night while Piero talked with Papa of the coming battle for Montefalco. They had talked of Piero's newly formed partisan band, the Stella Rossa, known sometimes as the Brigate Rosse, and Piero, who fancied himself a military strategist, had mocked the German battlements of the Gothic Line, saying the Germans had not read their own von Clausewitz on the subject of fixed lines of defense. The nuns had never mentioned this von Clausewitz in her literature classes. She had listened to her brother's boasts of certain victory with a growing feeling of terror, knowing that her brother was planning the death of her lover. Seeing that Livia was reading her thoughts, she had excused herself and gone to her room, and there, facedown on the bed, had spent the night awake, staring into her own darkness, trying to weigh the agonies about to descend on her family against those of her lover. The scale would not balance.

She stepped back against the cold stone face of the ravine and looked down into the claustrophobic gloom. Until only last week she had believed Carlo's promise that the line would hold. He had predicted months ago that the German Army and Mussolini's Fascists would stay on here in the north of Italy, and the Allies would keep the south. She had believed him because it meant they would not be separated by the war. Even so, she and Carlo were nothing more than expendable pawns in this uncertain chess game of war. She had steeled herself in the last week against the threat that the Allies would force Carlo to retreat now from Montefalco. *We'll crush them like Sangiovese grapes.* But she had not dreamed of the other absurd possibility: that Carlo and his fifty men would stay and fight against thousands! Stay, fight, and die.

Nor dreamed of this other frightening possibility. The sign had come last week. Her mother had once told her that the blood would sometimes come a little late, but not to worry; it would stop altogether only when she got married and was going to have a baby. But it *had* stopped, and she *wasn't* married, and she *couldn't*—unless she was prepared to have them both shot—marry a German soldier at this point in the war, least of all Lieutenant Karl Kruger, the commanding officer of the entire German garrison!

She started down into the darkness of the trees. If the blood stopped, though, how long did you have to wait to be sure? No one had ever told her that! And there was no one in Montefalco she could ask! Not her mother, not her sister, not her friends—for they would know at once her predicament from her question. They would know, too, that she had never been intimate with any local boy. She would be forced to name the man.

Either way now, if he stayed, fought, and died, or if he retreated until after the war, she was doomed. If her suspicions proved true, in a few months she would be huge with his child. And alone. He had promised their first child would come after marriage, when they went to live in Munich, where he was born.

Unable to move, rigid against the damp cliff wall, she began to cry. Everything—their lives, their divided loyalties, their irreconcilable responsibilities, the things they had done in the past and the things they had promised each other for the future—everything was so tangled now! As if God had twisted their lives together like the skein of a rope! In these last three months, they had made promises, only *hoping* they were telling each other the truth. There was *this* world they had made together here in the ravine, a beautiful *romanzo* world no larger than themselves; and there was that *other* one: Montefalco and beyond, and bigger than that, Italy, Germany, and the whole world now at war! Their little one would not fit into the big, the real one.

She opened her mouth and let go of the pain knotted inside her stomach. It came out in a loud cry that filled the ravine and reverberated back to her in echoes. She covered her mouth to silence it, startled by the rage bounding off the granite walls.

She crept down into the wedge-end darkness. Maybe her mother had meant several weeks; she had always discussed sex in vague generalities. But Carlo would know, Carlo had grown up in the big modern city of Munich.

III

At the center of the bridge Lieutenant Kruger looked back toward the sentries posted at the western end and quickened his pace. The light was fading, the sun no more than a fingernail of light above the summit of Monte Grande. Someone came toward him through the mist, pushing a bicycle. He recognized the uniform of Montefalco's middle-aged postman, Mario Brunetti. The *postino* gave him the usual reluctant salute and passed on. He returned the salute and quickened his pace to the eastern side of the bridge. At this rate, it would take another ten minutes to reach Anna in the Adele Ravine. He had tried to leave headquarters thirty minutes before, when he saw her pass through the Piazza Nazionale and turn down the Via Garibaldi on her way from San Tommaso. But a message had just arrived from General Lemelsen's headquarters, and it had taken minutes for Hans Reiger, his communications officer, to decode it. The message had changed everything. Yesterday, he had instructed Corporal Reiger to radio a request for permission to retreat north up the Reno Valley with the rest of the 362nd. In his judgment, with Pistoia lost to the Allies, the only logical thing to do was to regroup in the mountains north of Vergato. Outnumbered and outsupplied, it would be suicide for them to remain and defend Montefalco. But OKW had radioed back for them to remain in position—less than an hour ago! Additional supplies, three boxcars of mortars and munitions, were being shipped that night to Vergato, the last open railhead down the Reno Valley from Bologna, and it was up to him to organize a convoy to collect the supplies in the morning. He had ordered Reiger to acknowledge the reply, then quietly left headquarters, telling his adjutant, Sergeant Schreiber, that he wanted to walk for a while, collect his thoughts, and plan for the defense of Montefalco.

At the eastern end of the bridge he kept pace but edged to the far side, away from the two sentries. *"Guten Abend, Wecke!"* he called out to disarm the young private and his mate, Schutze. Given the recent partisan attacks, his soldiers were edgy.

"Guten Abend, Herr Oberleutnant!" Wecke called back through the mist.

"Alles in Ordnung?"

"Jawohl, Herr Oberleutnant! Alles in Ordnung!"

He smiled to himself at the shock he had caused in the two young privates. His afternoon walks had become a subject of gossip in the mess halls. His friend and adjutant, Schreiber, had repeated some of the gossip to him, saying a rumor had been started by the new quartermaster sergeant, Rudolf Oster, that he was carrying on a secret affair with one of the local girls. Schreiber had warned him to keep an eye on Oster, for the man had connections, he was convinced, with the Gestapo.

Beyond the bridge he crossed the double line of railway tracks and passed the old deserted wooden depot. No train had passed through Montefalco now for almost four months, not since the partisans began sabotaging the tracks and bridges between here and Vergato.

Ahead, where the street made an abrupt curve to follow the eastern slope of the valley through the newest part of town, he saw three women standing before the bakery owned by Giuseppe Vannini, one of the local Fascist bigwigs. They fell silent as he approached. He had forbidden his soldiers and the townspeople to socialize, an order the women of Montefalco welcomed. When he arrived in the town nine months ago to take command, the hatred of Germans was almost as deep as the hatred of Italian Fascists. His duty in Montefalco was to prevent partisan attacks from the mountains. A curious assignment, he had always thought: Germans protecting an Italian town from Italians. In his nine-month command, he had tried, at the same time, to administer an impartial civil justice to the local population. But it was too late to reverse feelings that had been boiling for two years in this population of divided loyalties. He greeted the women as he passed, *"Buona sera."*

". . . sera." The greeting in return was a reminder that if his soldiers were hated by the anti-Fascists of Montefalco, he was, as their commander, despised.

The Via Garibaldi, the only street on this side of town, was all but deserted. Through the window of the local *ammasso,* one of the two general stores owned and operated by the Fascists, he saw the storekeeper and his wife, the Albertinis. Like all the Fascists of Mussolini's new northern regime, they were living on borrowed time. Like most, they were greedy, exploitative, and filled with Fascist self-importance in their government-bestowed jobs and offices. When the end came, it would be the Vanninis and the Albertinis and the Comellinis who would fall from power, and the vengeance of their own fellow Tuscans would be swift and terrible.

The heavy transports pulling back from the area around Pistoia had left deep ruts in the main street. That day the sentries had counted twenty-two transports bound for the safety of the hills below Bologna.

Near the tobacco and wineshop at the southeast end of town, two enlisted men, Ehlert and Weidendorf, stood talking with their rifles crooked in their arms. Across the street a small group of local *contadini* were playing a noisy game of *boccie* against the wall of the wineshop. Both the soldiers and the *contadini* turned to watch him pass with looks of bewildered astonishment. He saluted the soldiers, and they returned the salute. Later, he knew, they would speculate why their commander had risked a walk into the hills at this hour of the day, alone. With studied calm, he tapped his finger against the visor of his cap and greeted the *contadini, "Buona sera."*

"Buona sera, Signore Comandante." The response was cautious.

He moved on, hooking his fingers leisurely into his holster belt, aware that they were all watching. The silence behind him was strained. It was, of course, absurd to be walking out in the open countryside at twilight. The hills around Montefalco were infested with partisans; they hid in the remote areas of the mountains during the day and came down at night to do their work.

He walked at a brisk, energetic-looking pace. Beyond the first field, in the deepening twilight, he caught sight of a movement on the road ahead: four men rounding the next bend. He unhooked his thumb from the belt and unsnapped his gun holster. Four homeward-bound *contadini* came toward him. They wore the familiar baggy work clothes and carried scythes over their shoulders. He let his hand rest on the butt of his pistol. All four men warily edged to the opposite ditch. He saw by the look in all four faces that the men were merely startled and confused by his presence on the road at that hour, and as they passed, the old man in the lead quickened his pace.

He smiled. They, too, would talk about the crazy German *comandante* that night at supper.

Ahead, the mist from the river was drifting up through the rotten stubble of a corn field, blanketing the road. He wanted to break into a run, but dared not until he reached the mist. On the breeze blowing up from the river he could smell the sweet woody perfume of the chestnut grove ahead. Last Thursday, the day after the news of Lucca reached Montefalco, Anna had brought a pocketful of fresh roasted chestnuts, the first chestnuts of autumn. She had promised there would be more to come as the crop ripened. Last Thursday he had promised to let her smoke a cigarette on her twentieth birthday, for she thought it would make her look modern and sophisticated. Even last Thursday he was still convinced the Green Line would hold, and he had assured Anna that a compromise peace would be struck, that he would stay in Montefalco until the war ended in the rest of Europe, and then return to Germany, borrow money from his father, and send for her. There would be only a brief separation, he had said, if any.

Seeing how the mist now sheltered him from view, he snapped the flap of his holster closed and began running.

He had promised her the scenario of a compromise peace because he had believed what his superiors at OKW had told him: the Green Line was invincible. He had grown *used* to believing! He had believed sixteen years before, back in 1928, when the Führer shouted to the people of Munich that Germany had been punished long enough under the Treaty of Versailles. That night, he had seen his father weep for the hope Hitler was offering Germany, for his father had come home ten years before from the Great War to eke out a living repairing bicycles, the only work the Fatherland could give him after the Great Defeat. That night, his mother had dared to cook sausages for them, for she, too, had tasted the Führer's hope. Five years later, when he was seventeen and the Führer came to power, he had heard the awesome victory speech on the radio from Berlin, and when the roar went up in the Sportsplatz, he knew that the whole nation had tasted the Führer's hope.

He left the road, leapt the ditch, and began running across the last pasture leading up to the ridge. The effort momentarily freed him from anger and frustration.

As a teen-ager, he had joined the Hitler Youth and felt proud for the first time to be German and part of the Führer's great new society. In the four and a half years he had served in the Wehrmacht, all through France and Norway, and then from Sicily to Montefalco, he had continued to believe, telling himself it *must* be; for this time, if they failed, Germany would vanish from the face of the earth forever, and there would be no future left at all for his father, his mother—anyone. Least of all for a defeated soldier.

He filled his lungs with cold air and started up the steep slope to the crest of the ridge, racing now.

I, Karl Gustav Kruger, swear by God this sacred oath, that I will render unconditional obedience . . . That afternoon on the parade ground of the *Offiziersschule* he and his class had pronounced the military vow: ". . . unconditional obedience to Adolf Hitler." Hitler had made promises, and everyone had believed. Believing Hitler, he, too, had made promises, vows: as a soldier and as a man, to Hitler and to Anna. If only the Gothic Line had held, he could have kept both.

His breath condensed, stabbing the air.

If he laid out the truth to her exactly as it was, without softening the edges with future consolations, surely she would understand and forgive him.

He reached the summit of the ridge and stopped to catch up with his pounding heart.

Thank God he had not jeopardized her with worse failures.

IV

From her resting place against the boulder Anna looked out across the river. Sometimes in summer the river shrank to a shallow lazy stream, but in autumn, swollen by the mountain rainwater, the Reno always became deep and treacherous. Her cousin had drowned in the Reno one autumn, fishing for trout. The mist from the river had deepened in the last half hour. If she waited much longer, it would be too dark to see her way out of the ravine. She left the boulder and started back into the grove of willows and pines.

June. That's when they first made love here: just there—under the pine trees on that thick bed of dried needles. They had met back in January, a brief cautious meeting in a shop where she bought bread when it could be bought. It had taken two months for the meetings to become regular weekly events here in the Adele Ravine, and not until April did they talk of anything more than a passing friendship. Afterward, they had behaved just like ordinary traditional Catholic *promessi*. They embraced, they kissed, but they went no further. But it was not their common religion that prevented them so much as their plans and promises for a proper future life together as husband and wife.

She stopped to breathe in the heavy sweetness of the pines. She had never wanted to be the wife of any local boy. Before the war, when there were *only* local boys, foreigners of every nationality, French, English, Scandinavian, German and Austrian, too, came to the mineral spas of Montefalco. She had always dreamed of meeting and falling in love with one of the handsome foreign men who passed through Montefalco. Then the war came, and foreigners who had been friends suddenly became enemies, and that puzzled her. *Nonna* Adelaida, her grandmother, had once said about people in war: *the passions of war are like the waters of the* torrente Rimaldi, *strong but shallow.*

In the dark tangle of vines she heard a sudden whirring sound. Startled, she drew back against a tree. It was there—hovering— more like a movement than a sound. She reached out impulsively to grab hold of another tree. Then the sound rose up into the leaves above. She followed it with her eyes. A cry formed in her throat, a curse leveled at Carlo, but she reached to her mouth to stifle it. Through a break in the leaves she saw a whirligig flutter of wings against the twilight. Then she knew. Piero had once brought a dead one into the house to frighten her. A bat. The memory of it came back with the flesh-crawling feeling of revulsion: black and pink, all bone and transparent skin and wet silken hair. Like something born in darkness, but only half born.

Overhead, the whirring flutter died away.

She held onto the tree. He would leave, return to the bigger, far richer world he had come from, and forget what he had done in Montefalco—*this.* She bent forward, felt the knot grip her stomach again, and began to weep.

He began running, knocking back the thorny raspberry runners, and reached for his pistol. The high, unbroken sound of a human voice, a woman's, echoed from the ravine walls. It came from the pine grove down by the river. "Anna!" he called out, heedless of the noise he made, and tore on through the underbrush. Near the mouth of the ravine he grabbed hold of a tree to break his momentum, and for a moment, in silence, they stared at each other in the darkness. His pistol dangled in his hand.

"You came," she said finally, stifling her sobs, amazed.

The way she stood slumped against the tree with her long dark hair matted crazily against her face frightened him. He moved forward and saw tears streaming down her terrified face. "Yes, I came. Of course, I came."

"I didn't know if you . . . I was scared you wouldn't."

He drew her close, mindless of the pistol in his hand, and closed his arms around her, tightly. He had held her countless times before, but she now seemed smaller than before. "I saw you in the piazza. I left as soon as I could." He sensed her need to be walled around, protected, and he circled her shoulders with his arms. For a while, neither of them spoke. The panic in her breathing began to ease, and she dropped her head against his chest. The rush of water over the nearby rocks and the buzz of crickets in the weeds made the silence seem restful. He kissed her hair. It smelled of perfume: the fragrance he had given her, a tiny bottle of black-market French perfume from Grasse.

"Karl?" she murmured.

He smiled to himself. She had always called him by the Italian form of his name. The German *Karl* made her uncomfortable. *Carlo* was her way of skirting the guilt of a collaborator. "What?" he asked.

She hesitated to answer.

"Was ist denn so wichtig, meine Kleine?" he asked with a gentle squeeze, "Hmm? What happened? What's so important?"

She drew back and looked up at his face. Under the cap's visor his eyes looked strained and tired. "I needed to see you. Something has happened."

"What? Tell me." He realized in all these months he had never seen her cry before. Tears made her big dark eyes even larger and magnified her fear.

"Carlo—" She pushed back the cap from his forehead, and the short dark forelock fell forward. His hair was drenched with sweat. "I don't—" She felt her determination waver. After all, she could be wrong.

"Tell me."

"I'm not sure. I'm not positive anything has happened, I don't know about such things." She ran her fingers across his forehead and felt beads of sweat where the brim had been. "I want to ask you something."

"Ask me what?" He saw a battle of fear and doubt in her eyes. He had never seen her in darkness, and her skin looked parchment white.

"I don't *know* about such things! I only *suspect!"*

He thought: she knows about the order to remain. But how? He had just received it. "What do you suspect?"

She moved her hand down the side of his face. He had not

shaved. It was unlike him not to shave, unless . . . *Crush them like
Sangiovese grapes.* She thought: if I tell him now about my *condizione,* he will think he *has* to stay. If he stays, and I'm wrong—but
even if I'm *not* wrong! In a twisted misery of confusion, she said,
"I'm not even *sure* yet! I could have waited, Carlo! I was frightened!"

"By what?" His mind raced ahead: if she knows about the order
to stay, then everyone in Montefalco knows! She learns about things
secondhand, when they're already common knowledge in the town.

"I don't know how to say it! There was only—" The flash of terror she saw in his eyes silenced her. If Piero is right about the Allied
advance, she thought, then the Germans will have to choose between
going and staying. That explains all this exhaustion, terror, and
doubt in his face.

"*Um Gottes Willen,* Anna! Tell me!"

And now, not even sure of my own fears, I'm about to double his!
She wondered suddenly if she was playing tricks on herself, if she
was lying to herself, if she was using the blood thing just to hold him
back. The logic of it coiled like a fist in her mind: even if I *am* pregnant, if he stays, he will fight and die! She stepped back. "Yesterday
—" She reached out in her mind for some plausible lie for calling
him here.

"Yesterday what?"

"Two days ago—two days ago, I was at home. We were at home.
My family. My father and mother, my grandmother, my—" She
caught herself, remembering Carlo and the Germans knew nothing
of Piero. He had hidden in the barn under the hay when they came.
"My family was at home, and some SS men came to the house. They
came in and questioned my father and mother and grandmother."

"Go on," he said, alarmed on the one hand, relieved on the other.
Intelligence officers from the XVI SS Panzer Grenadier Division stationed north of Vergato had been combing the Reno Valley in
search of partisans and their collaborators. The XVI SS Panzers had
carried out a reprisal execution of civilians near Vergato two weeks
before.

"The SS threatened my family."

"You're sure they were SS?"

"I know the uniform. They wanted to know about the partisans around Montefalco." She recounted how the four SS men had
drilled her father and threatened him with deportation to Germany if
he did not give information about the hiding place of Il Lupo's Red
Brigade. "They vowed there would be a *rastrellamento* in Mon-

tefalco if the partisans attacked here again," she said, thinking of Piero's stories of Italian women who had been shot by partisans for sleeping with German soldiers. She saw by the look in his face that she had succeeded with her clumsy deception.

"The SS threatens everyone, Anna. But they will do nothing to your family. Your family isn't involved with the partisans."

She tried to smile gratefully. The deceptions forced upon them by the war were like contagious diseases, infecting everything and everyone. "I was frightened," she said, "I had to see you. They threatened to come back." She could be wrong, after all, about the child. In either case, it would be a long time before the truth made a difference for either of them. But the danger for Carlo, if he stayed in Montefalco, was immediate.

She looked like a defenseless child. He took hold of her shoulders. "Listen to me, Anna. In the future, tell them what they want to know. Don't argue with them. Those men—the SS—they're capable of anything. You understand?"

"Yes."

The SS, he thought, are indifferent to morality and the rules of war. He had often seen them coming and going, but he had never seen them in action. "They can't carry out a *rastrellamento* here without the Wehrmacht's authorizing it. Do you understand?"

"Yes."

The presence of the SS and Gestapo in German life had always confounded him. Though he had seen nothing, the rumors that were circulating in the army confounded him. He sometimes wondered if a small portion of Germany had gone berserk. He went on, "I'm a Wehrmacht soldier, an ordinary soldier. I take my orders from the Army High Command. The SS is different. They take orders from someone entirely different." He heard the shameful excuse in his own voice. "I have no authority over the SS, save where my own military orders are concerned. Montefalco is under my authority, not theirs."

"I'm so frightened," she said, but meant something else, and her words only grazed the surface of her real fears.

"Don't be, my love." Her body trembled in his hands, and he drew her against him. "Don't be frightened. It will all be over soon, it will all work out for us." He realized, suddenly, he could not bring himself to tell her what he had come to say. He would tell her some now, the rest tomorrow. She was too vulnerable at this moment. "I promise you, it will all end well for you and me. Trust me," he added, lamely, searching for a phrase in which to couch his partial announcement of retreat.

"End?"

"I also have something to say. I came to tell you something, too."

She remained motionless in his arms, knowing already what he would say, dreading it. "What, Carlo?"

"The Americans are going to try to break the line here in the west. Above Pistoia."

"I see." She saw a winepress and the mauled mush of trampled Sangiovese grapes inside.

"I didn't think they'd try here, not after Rimini and Coriano."

"Will they come here—to the Reno, to Montefalco?"

"There are only three ways to reach Bologna. Through the Porretta Pass here and the Futa and Giogo passes to the east."

"What if they choose Porretta?"

"They'll bombard the pass and then move on to Spedaletto."

"And then to Montefalco."

"Yes."

"You have only fifty men." She looked up at his face above her. "They have hundreds! Thousands!" The wine crushed from the Sangiovese grapes had always tasted bitter to her. "You must leave Montefalco, Carlo," she said, grasping his neck.

"Anna—"

"It's suicide to stay here! The Americans, the partisans—they will kill you all!"

He nodded. "I know."

"Please! Please, Carlo! I don't *want* you to stay now! Everything has changed now! Believe me, I *understand!*"

He held onto her, wanting suddenly to cry for the bitterness of this small—small, at least, as far as the generals and the field marshals were concerned—this unimportant human defeat.

She cupped his face in her hands and read the silent admission in his eyes. "It won't be for long," she said, trying to imagine how long the loss of him would be—long enough for a child to be born?

"No." His voice broke on the single word . . . *and will be ready as a brave soldier to risk my life at any time for this oath*. He had promised her what he was not free to give: himself. He had given that to the Führer—to the war. The war took everything. He said, shakily, "I love you," and drew back the long fine dark hair matted across her face, letting it run through his fingers.

In the darkness, the face in her hands was like a small frightened boy's. His lips parted, and she read his thought, for the language was now in her blood. She pulled his face down to hers and covered his lips with her mouth, letting go of the make-believe child within her. He pulled her up, making small wounded sounds in his throat. She wanted suddenly to lie down with him here in the weeds and let her body speak for her, but she heard a low sound rise to his throat —a wordless avowal of defeat.

A flash of faint light glittered down through the trees: the heat of desire, he imagined, reflected in the eye.

She gripped the short scruff of his hair, relishing this new animal freedom of the blood. It came again, a faint shimmer of soft light through the foliage of the trees.

They drew apart, startled, and looked up, waiting. It came a third time, a distant flash of pale orange light in the sky above the eastern end of the ravine. "Anna," he said and swallowed.

"Rain again," she said.

A fourth light shimmered up into the cloudless evening sky, a strange red color this time. "No. Not rain." He pulled her close to him, and they waited again.

Even before it exploded again far off to the east above the mountains, she knew it was not lightning. "Carlo," she said.

"We have to go back. Immediately."

She looked down helplessly at the dry weeds around them. *"Nient' è giusto,"* she said, absently lapsing into her mountain dialect. She let him begin guiding her through the darkness. The soundless explosion lit the trees around them. "Nothing is just," she repeated.

CHAPTER 2

I

At the junction of the Via Garibaldi and the Piazza Nazionale, Kruger turned to look back. From here, high in the old town, he could see the entire eastern horizon. The far-off explosions were coming faster now, shimmering flashes of deep orange light. The summits of Monticelli and Monte Altuzzo were silhouetted against the pulsing glow of lingering fires. Estimating the line of fire against the horizon, he judged that the air strike and the artillery fire had hit the mountains just south of the Futa and the Giogo passes. The Americans would be ten, perhaps twelve, kilometers north of Florence by now.

He drew in a deep breath, stunned by the thought of it. So the Americans had made their move, with their major thrust not against the Reno Valley flank, but—thank God—against the center, Route 65, the main road running north from Florence to Bologna. Against the biggest fortress in their whole Green Line. The Americans, at least, had nerve.

A bright prolonged shimmer of light illuminated the narrow Via Garibaldi below from the piazza down to the bridge. For an instant, he saw a single figure in the deserted street: Anna. She had crossed the bridge. So far, she had not been stopped for violation of the curfew. Twenty minutes ago, when they reached the crest of the Adele Ravine, he had known at once that it was an air strike they were seeing far off in the east in the vicinity of the passes. They had run most of the way back, taking the path by the river to avoid encountering his soldiers on the road. He had left her on the path just at the edge of town, holding her for one brief moment before they took their separate ways, she along the river, he on the Garibaldi as he had come. There had been no time to tell her how to cross the bridge without alarming the sentries, no time to warn her where she might encounter soldiers or police in the streets. Again, there was another but fainter explosion of light. She had turned into the road leading north out of town, heading toward her home.

He turned toward the Municipio building at the far side of the piazza. By the *campanile* clock it was 5:50. He should have been at his desk thirty minutes ago. He hurried across the cobblestones, then stopped abruptly, hearing footsteps from the direction of the old Palazzo Berticelli where Montefalco's Banco Commerciale had its offices. In a reflection of firelight he saw some eight or ten men turn from the southeast corner of the square and hurry along the facade of the bank building. The raspy voice of Aldo Peschi, the Fascist chief of police, called through the darkness, "Spread out! Clear the streets! Arrest anyone you find!" In the garble of voices he recognized those of Gino Alberti and Franco Milli, two of Peschi's *carabinieri*. The group separated and dispersed across the square, four of the men down the Garibaldi where Anna had been. He realized he was powerless to stop them. He cursed to himself and moved on toward the Municipio. The place in front of the building reserved for his staff car was empty. Schreiber, his adjutant, had undoubtedly sent men to look for him.

"Halt!" One of the two guards stationed at the Municipio door stepped forward with his rifle aimed.

"At ease, Beuchler," Kruger called to the young private.

"Ah." Beuchler lowered the gun. "Herr Oberleutnant." He snapped to attention as Kruger approached. "Heil Hitler."

"Heil Hitler." Kruger hurried up the steps. "It's a good forty kilometers from here, Beuchler," he said, seeing the young man's look of terror.

"*Ja, Herr Oberleutnant.* A good forty." The tension in the young private's face was like a burning fuse.

Kruger thought of the undercurrent of mutiny he had sensed in his men of late as he pushed open the door into the reception area of his command headquarters.

"There's a war in progress, Corporal!" Rudolf Oster, the quartermaster sergeant, was shouting. "There's no excuse for Kruger to . . . !" He stood facing Corporal Reiger, the communications officer, with his bony head thrust forward. The two men turned to see him at the door.

"Herr Oberleutnant." Young Reiger snapped to attention.

Caught short, the prim bespectacled Oster stiffened behind the adjutant's desk and gave a silent salute.

"At ease, gentlemen." Kruger closed the door. The big, sparsely furnished room was deserted except for the two officers.

Oster said, "We've been looking for you, Herr Oberleutnant."

Kruger ambled toward Schreiber's desk, where Oster stood. The sergeant eyed him suspiciously. Punctilious to a fault, down to the regulation cut of his prematurely receding black hairline, a Berlin civil servant before the Wehrmacht gave him a larger destiny, Oster carried out his duties of dispensing quarters, clothing, food, fuel, and transportation with the efficient precision of a German factory machine. He had joined their little staff four months ago, the middle of May, transferred from the eastern front with a promotion in rank that placed him third in command here in Montefalco. "I took a walk, Sergeant," he challenged. "Obviously, the Allies have a poor sense of timing."

Oster's mouth curled with a slight hint of contempt. "In your absence, Lieutenant, the enemy opened an attack on the Futa and the Giogo passes. We've received three reports confirming the fact. A commander who leaves his post—"

Kruger cut him short. "Give me the reports, Reiger." Of the six officers on the staff, Oster was the only one who still, this late in the war, quoted Hitler's and Goebbels' war propaganda. He had disliked and distrusted Oster from the start.

Reiger offered the three handwritten pages. "One from the Porretta Pass, one from Spedaletto, and the third from Vergato, sir." He stepped back, glancing nervously toward Oster. In his mid-twenties, a prototype of the Führer's blond ideal, Reiger had the look of a Rhenish farm boy and the self-effacing shyness of a newly enlisted cadet, though he had served in the Wehrmacht for three years. His timidity, Schreiber had said, was a cloak he wore over a deeper cowardice. "Porretta reports infantry movements south of the pass, sir," he ventured.

Kruger glanced through the pages. "And while we're occupied in the Futa and the Giogo, they attack through the Reno, right? The old story, divide and conquer. Where's Schreiber?"

"He left ten minutes ago in your staff car to look for you, Herr Oberleutnant," Oster replied.

Kruger started toward his office. "When he gets back, send him in. Inform Weiss and Haldner there will be a staff meeting at"—he checked the reception-room clock—"at six-fifteen. We'll chose an officer to head the convoy to Vergato in the morning."

"Speaking of Vergato, Herr Oberleutnant," said Oster, "I have taken the liberty in your absence of requisitioning three transports for the mission. I would recommend a single officer and five enlisted men for the operation." He stepped from behind Schreiber's desk, where he had no business to be.

"You seem to have a knack, Oster, for reading my mind," said Kruger, turning. He had already informed Schreiber that six volunteers would risk the mission.

"I try to be provident in my job, Lieutenant."

"By the way, sir," Reiger interjected, "Vergato has reported partisan movements in the mountains north of here."

He saw the look of fear in Reiger's face and recalled the boy's announcement two days before in the officers' mess hall that his wife had given birth to their first child, a son, the week before. They had celebrated the event with a bottle of cheap Italian brandy, and in his drunken exhilaration, Reiger had confessed that his only goal now was to come out of the war alive and return home to see his son. Kruger moved on into his office, thoughtfully weighing the options for Reiger. He called back, "I assume, Corporal, that your messages to Vergato were sent in code."

"Yes, sir. Of course." Reiger hurried to the door.

He thought, if Reiger is occupied with communication business when the selection of an officer to lead the convoy is made, he will avoid the dangers of that thankless responsibility, and the others will avoid the dangers of his cowardice. He motioned Reiger into the room. "While we're waiting for Schreiber, Corporal, I have a job for you." He continued to his desk. "Come in, please." He turned on his desk lamp and searched among his papers for the coded copy of the order he had received that afternoon from Lemelsen's headquarters.

"Yes, sir?"

"I want you to decode this message from Lemelsen again."

"Again, sir?"

"Yes, Corporal. Again. I want an accurate wording of it this time."

Reiger took the page, puzzled. "Yes, sir."

"I want you to spend whatever time you need to get a very accurate translation. I should think that will take you at least an hour, no?"

"But you called a staff meeting, sir."

"Never mind the meeting. I need an accurate wording of that order."

Reiger, he saw, read his meaning. The young man's blond boyish face registered shock and relief, than went red with embarrassment. At least the cowardice was no secret to him. "Yes, Herr Oberleutnant."

Beyond, through the open door, Oster stood listening to their exchange.

"In the future, Corporal," Kruger added for Oster's sake, "you must be more careful in the wording of official messages."

"Jawohl, Herr Oberleutnant."

The gratitude he saw in the pale Aryan blue eyes brought a guarded smile to Kruger's mouth. "That's all, Corporal."

Reiger saluted, crisply. "Heil Hitler."

"Heil Hitler." When the door closed behind Reiger, Kruger sat down at his desk and rested his head on his arms, grateful for these few brief moments of quiet before the storm.

II

Anna caught sight of a movement at the far end of the clearing between the path and the barn: a dark shape moving across the field in the direction of the house. "Gianni," she said with relief, recognizing her father's mule racing toward the safety of the trees at the top of the hill. Even Gianni—even the animals know, she thought. Her parents' big *casa colonica* came into view behind the grove of oak and pine trees. A quarter moon had risen over the hills behind the house, illuminating its dark stone facade. The house stood at the butt end of the slope, overlooking the surrounding pasture, which had grown to seed with the wartime slaughter of the sheep. With the blackout curtains drawn, the house looked deserted, but she knew they were waiting for her in the parlor, her mother, father, sister, grandmother, and perhaps, if he had come back again, Piero. She raced up the hill and rounded the edge of the grove. A thread of smoke trailed from the chimney. Reflected against the gray stones of the house, another orange burst of light shimmered across the sky. She thought of the towns that lay beyond the mountains to the east, Vicchio and Dicomano, and perhaps even Firenzuola, where she had distant cousins: it was terrifying to imagine those familiar towns in flames.

At the heavy wooden front door she stopped to catch her breath, dreading what she knew awaited her on the other side. Strange, she thought, how quickly things had changed for her and Carlo after the restful lull of summer—all within a few short hours! She heard her mother's high-pitched voice in the parlor. "If you won't go out and look, Angelo, *I will!*"

Composing herself, she raised the latch and let herself into the darkened foyer. Her mother had just dropped a log into the fireplace and turned to look back, wide-eyed. They were all there, except for Piero: her father in his stuffed armchair by the fireplace, *Nonna* Adelaida in her cane-backed chair near the blazing *gassometro* carbide lamp, Livia near the mantelpiece with her back to the meager fire. "Mamma?" she said.

Her mother came toward her with her fierce deep-set green eyes blazing with rage and, at the same time, looking relieved. At thirty-nine her mother appeared older than her years. Her homely face, crowned with dark hair streaked with premature gray, had already succumbed to wrinkles. "Where have you been, young lady?" she demanded, throttling her rage.

"At the convent." Anna set her basket on the foyer floor. "I bought the thread, then I remembered Sister Teresa wanted me to collect some shirts to mend." She had worked out her alibi on the way home after she left Carlo at the river. "There was no point in my coming all the way back to get Livia," she added, "it was quicker for me to go alone." The alibi, she knew, was her weakest yet.

"Have you lost your mind? It's after dark, there's a curfew! And the Americans have started bombing!"

"The bombs are a long way off, Mamma." She removed her coat and hung it on the hook in the foyer wall.

"You could have been *shot* walking the roads at night!"

"I wasn't shot. I'm perfectly safe."

"*Grazi' a Dio,*" murmured her father.

Nonna Adelaida followed up, muttering under her breath. Livia had escaped by turning to face the fire.

"The nuns let you walk home alone after dark?" her mother challenged.

"I left the convent before dark. When the bombing started, I hid until I knew it was safe to go on." She realized she had ventured out on thin ice. "Anyway, I didn't have to walk home alone," she added recklessly. "Father Alessandro gave me a ride in his automobile."

"I don't believe you."

"There's no point in arguing, Luisa," said her father from his armchair. "The girl's home, and that's what's important." He rubbed his thick black moustache and rolled his small dark eyes. Though her mother's age, he nonetheless looked younger and prided himself on his moustache and thick wavy black hair. Piero had inherited his father's good looks.

Her mother came into the foyer, where she stood. "There's mud on your coat." She pointed. "Where did you get mud on your coat?"

"Luisa," her father pleaded.

"Be quiet, Angelo!" The Berticelli temper came boiling up. "I want to know what's going on, young lady!"

"I slipped in the mud coming up the path." She started past her mother into the parlor.

"The mud on your shoe—on your coat—is dry." Her mother caught hold of her arm.

"The girl is hungry, Luisa," said her father, "let her go eat."

"She lying! She hasn't been to the convent!"

"If you don't believe me, then ask the sisters. Look in my basket. There are shirts in my basket." She remembered the table cloth as well, and quickly moved on.

"I left a plate of pasta on the stove for you," said Livia, shooting a warning look from the fireplace, "and there's bread in the bin, if you want it." The warning turned to disgust as she lowered the flame on *Nonna's* carbide lamp. Anna recognized the dangerous look. Pushed to the limit, her sister had a temper more violent than her mother's. It was born, she was convinced, out of her lifelong repression of feeling. Like her mother, Livia suffered the agonies of the plain. She resembled her mother as she had been at eighteen, the same hollow-socketed eyes, the same unruly mouse-colored hair. It was she who had made herself into the "little sister," loving the vicarious and safe pleasures of the dangerous secrets she begged her to share.

There was a wry chuckle from *Nonna* Adelaida as she passed by on her way to the kitchen, and another murmured cynical proverb.

"Scarpe grosse, cervello fino." Thick shoes, thin mind. She had worn her old shoes with the thick convent-school soles that afternoon. Her grandmother raised her small crafty dark eyes, her son's eyes, and winked naughtily as she passed. Though only in her mid-fifties, *Nonna,* a widow for the last eight years, had allowed her son to turn her into a little old lady, dominating the family with her sage advice.

Her mother caught up and blocked her way into the kitchen. "I want the truth, young lady. You've been visiting the convent now for seven months. I want to know where *else* you've been."

"Nowhere!"

"This is no time for a fight, Luisa!" Her father got to his feet with an effort to sound resolute. "We may be *bombed* before the night is out!"

"The devil take the bombs! You have made excuses for this girl since she was a child! Look at her! Can't you see she's *lying?*"

"I'm not lying!" Anna exclaimed, trapped into another lie. She turned back to the staircase leading to the second floor, feeling her heart pound in her breast.

Again, her mother blocked her retreat. "You have been seeing some *man,* haven't you?!"

Anna swung away, stunned. She saw Livia cover her face. "Seeing a *man!*" The amazement in her voice was not convincing, she knew. *"Who,* Mamma?" she went on, masking fear with defiance. "If I've been seeing a man, then tell me *who!* There *are no men* my age in Montefalco! They have either joined the army, been sent off to German work camps, or they've gone off to join Piero in the mountains!"

"They come down from the mountains, too," said *Nonna* Adelaida *sotto voce,* chuckling.

"There are also Fascisti," added her mother, venomously.

Her face felt suddenly hot. "'Fascisti? Do you think I would go with a Fascist? I hate the Fascists! They are a million times worse than the *Germans!*"

Her mother circled her. "There are only two kinds of men who dare go out at night in these parts, young lady," she threatened, "Germans and partisans. You've been seeing one of Piero's friends, one of the Brigate Rosse, haven't you?"

The accusation, absurd as it was, gave her a curious feeling of relief. "No, Mamma." She let a note of admission creep into her voice. "I haven't been seeing one of Piero's friends."

"You know what the Germans will do to you if you are found

with a partisan, don't you? You will be shot. If Piero is caught, he will be shot. The Germans will shoot us all."

"Piero is the only partisan I know," she said with conviction.

"For your sake and ours, I hope you're telling the truth. But after tonight, you will remain at home. There will be no more visits to the convent, and no more visits to town alone. Now go up to your room and change your clothes."

Relieved by the strange left-handed reprieve, Anna climbed the stairs to the second floor. A kerosene lamp burned in the hallway with the wick turned low to save fuel. On the wall above the lamp hung four framed holy pictures: Santa Lucia lying on her cold marble tomb, headless from martyrdom, the patron saint of Montefalco; San Francisco with his arms outstretched toward his heaven of birds, his face radiantly innocent; San Cristoforo, waist-deep in a turbulent river with the Christ Child on his shoulder; and a reproduction of a Cellini Madonna from Florence. In the wavering lamplight the saints stared at her, knowingly, accusingly. She took the lamp and hurried to her bedroom.

The room was as she had left it that afternoon, with the bed-clothes still unmade. She closed the door and set the lamp on the bureau. The room was bitterly cold. Its window looked eastward across the Reno Valley, and far off in the direction of Monticelli and Monte Altuzzo the sky glowed a deep fiery orange rising to red. She pressed her nose against the cold glass pane, mesmerized by the awesome spectacle. Until now, she had pretended to herself that her love of Carlo and his for her was secret and apart from the war and therefore privileged. But that was foolish. Like everyone else they would be swept away, as had all the animals and crops in the torrential floods last winter. Tomorrow—though it was true, he had not actually *said* tomorrow, but she knew—tomorrow he would retreat with his soldiers. But he *had* to retreat: the other alternative was unthinkable. Everything seemed so hopelessly tangled and confused!

She covered her face and began to weep, uncontrollably. They had both fallen, it seemed, into a dark bottomless hole.

III

By the clock in the *campanile* it was 1:30 A.M. when Kruger left headquarters in the Municipio. Except for two soldiers on duty at the door of their German headquarters, the piazza was deserted. In the three hours left before the convoy set out for Vergato, there was nothing more he could do. He drew up the collar of his coat and walked briskly toward the Via Benedetto at the northwest corner of the square. It was but a short walk to his officers' quarters in the Hotel Montecatini.

At the staff meeting in his office they had drawn lots to see who would lead the convoy to Vergato. Neither he, of course, nor Reiger, who remained occupied in his radio room, had participated in the lottery. To his secret disappointment, Schreiber, his friend, had drawn the unlucky straw. He would have preferred to see Oster or Oster's henchman, the parasitic Corporal Haldner, draw the lot, but this war no longer favored the innocent or the just.

The fact is, Herr Oberleutnant, we've lost this war. Schreiber's words rang in his ears. After the others had gone, Schreiber had stayed on to discuss plans for the convoy. They had talked at length of the shrinking German map of western Europe. Schreiber, in his mid-twenties, had already spent four years on the eastern front in Poland and in Russia. Tonight he had told another story of what he had seen on that terrible front: a grim tale of *Einsatzgruppen,* as they were called, and the murder of innocent civilians by the thousands, millions he had said. It was hard even now to believe that the Wehrmacht could have allied itself with criminals.

At the corner of the square where the Via Benedetto intersected with the little Via Santa Lucia, Kruger drew up. Suddenly, from nowhere, a sentence came to him: *All the lights in Europe have gone out.* He felt a sudden sinking sensation. Where the words had come from, he could not remember. Perhaps a speech he had read somewhere.

On his left, the Via Santa Lucia ran west up the slope of the hill, into the old town. Rest, he realized, was not what he really wanted. He started up the steep narrow Via Santa Lucia. There was almost no light at all between the two- and three-story buildings lining the street, but he knew every foot of the cobblestoned way, having taken it a hundred times in the last seven months to the church of San Tommaso to leave or find the signals for a meeting with Anna. He moved quickly but quietly, for there were soldiers and Fascist *carabinieri* on patrol duty; both had orders to shoot anyone caught in violation of the curfew, and both were edgy and depressed. Since the attack and breakthrough at Rimini, the morale had been low. What hope the men had entertained for the battle of Italy had been lost with the Allied breach of the Gothic Line.

Kruger caught sight of the small Fabbiani bakery. Signore and Signora Fabbiani would be upstairs on the second floor, asleep. In the months he had spent in Montefalco, he had often dropped into the shop, for Signora Fabbiani made the best *mistocca* in Montefalco when she could get sugar. It was in the Fabbiani bakery that he had first spoken to Anna back in January, the afternoon he went in for a *mistocca* and found her arguing with the signora about the sudden rise in the price of bread. "It's unfair! You have no right to raise the price!" Anna had shouted. "The price of flour has not gone up since last week! You raised the price because the Fascists permit you to make an unjust profit!"

He remembered how she had turned to see him at the door behind her and paled at the sight of his Wehrmacht uniform. He remembered, too, the feeling that had come over him at the sight of her angelic Tuscan face, like that of a Botticelli *giovanezza*, half saint, half wild animal, arrested as it was in an explosion of anger and outrage. He remembered feeling that he had been suddenly touched in a place where no human being before had ever reached: at the soft center between body and soul, and the feeling had left him irrevocably changed.

Kruger passed the bakery and began the zigzag turns through the oldest section of Montefalco.

His words to the Fascist baker and his wife came back to him: "You will return to the prices of last week. It will not be said of the German Army, signore, that we collaborated in profiteering during our occupation of this town." Signore Fabbiani had stared at him in utter astonishment. That afternoon, for the first time, he had used his authority to intervene between the Fascists and the local townspeople. In the months that followed, he had intervened in other disputes, and in the process had made enemies in the local Fascist government. In retrospect, Anna had been the one to awaken him to the plight of the people of Montefalco. Before Anna, he had remained aloof to local squabbles. In truth, the more he came to care for Anna as a woman, the more he came to see her sufferings mirrored in the faces of her fellow townspeople. It was Anna who had brought that curious change in him. In fact, it was Anna who had made him first question the justice of this war.

The Via Santa Lucia abruptly narrowed at the intersection with the Via Migliori. Here the street was less than three meters wide and smelled of garbage and stagnant rainwater. Above, in one of the darkened ancient two-story houses, women were arguing. He leaned against the wall of a building to get his breath. Perspiring, he opened the flaps of his coat, then began the last steep climb toward the Piazza San Tommaso. Suddenly, from an intersecting alleyway, he heard a low, soft chuckle. Startled, he drew back into the darkness. There were footsteps approaching, the heavy thump of boots, and then he heard the low muttering of a man's voice. Four houses back he saw a recessed doorway and hurried toward the portal. The enclosure was scarcely large enough for one person. He drew back against the wall. The voices and footsteps came closer. He heard a crisp German accent as two soldiers came out of the alley and stood in the center of the Via Santa Lucia with rifles crooked in their arms.

"Which way now?" The voice was that of Private Stofel.

"Take your pick. It doesn't much matter, we've covered these bloody alleys four times." Private Appel. His voice was tired and apathetic.

"This way." Stofel turned down the Via Santa Lucia. Kruger stiffened. The two soldiers ambled by slowly.

If they saw him lurking in the shadows of the portal, they would shoot. They would have every right to shoot. He himself had given the order.

"Wait up." Stofel stopped a few meters from the portal. "I need a cigarette."

"It's against rules."

"Screw the rules." Stofel dug in his pocket and brought out a pack of cigarettes. He struck a match, cradling his rifle in his arm.

"Put that match out," said Appel. "You know there's no fire allowed at night."

"Who's gonna see?" Stofel lit the cigarette. "You think the Americans can see a fuckin' match all the way from Pistoia?" He laughed and inhaled. The cigarette made a small orange glow in the darkness.

"You know the rules, Kurt."

"Rules," Stofel sneered. "You sound like Kruger. Kruger would shoot his mother if it was in the rule book." He laughed softly, adjusted his rifle in his arm, and joined his companion, moving off down the street.

"Look at that sky," Appel said. "I'll give them two days. In two days, the Americans will be Montefalco. In two days, we'll be dead."

"You're talking crazy, Stofel. Kruger's not going to force us to defend this town. He may be a stickler for rules, but he's no fool."

Kruger listened to the dull thud of their boots diminish down the street, bewildered by their easy opinion of him. But Stofel and Appel were both too young to know what it had been like after the

Great War—or to understand the catastrophe awaiting Germany if they now weakened on a single rule. *Kruger would shoot his mother if it was in the rule book.* The sneering words cut like a knife. Elizabeth: he had seen his mother only once in the last four and a half years. For two brief days between *Offiziersschule* and his first assignment in Holland. She had aged terribly in his absence. The war and his involvement in it had brought back memories of his father's disaster.

Kruger left the portal and hurried toward the summit of the hill where the street was lit by the pale red glow of the distant fires. He looked back and saw pockets of concentrated fire: the towns of Prato, Borgo San Lorenzo, San Pietro, Scarperia. Defense line by defense line, all the way up Italy, he had seen what the Allies had done to towns with artillery and bombs. Because of his decision to obey that night, they would now do it to Montefalco, too. Anna's town. The picture he had kept at bay these last few hours broke in his mind like an exploding grenade: Anna burning.

As officers of the German Wehrmacht, gentlemen, you are committed to the Principle of Leadership, Major Stahmer had said that afternoon when he addressed the cadets at the officers' academy. *Authority descends from above downward and responsibility from below upward. As soldiers of the Reich, that is your guiding principle.*

He had vowed obedience to it with his life.

The Via Santa Lucia opened into the Piazza San Tommaso fronting the ancient Romanesque church with its tall square belfry tower. The piazza, surrounded by two- and three-story houses, was deserted. He walked toward the massive facade of the church. In the darkness of the blackout, lit only by the eerie red glow from the horizon, the church looked gloomy and forbidding. The big wooden doors were closed. In the center of the piazza a small piece of discarded paper, a wrapper of some kind, fluttered toward him across the cobblestones, caught up suddenly by the gust of cold wind over the roofs. He felt curiously isolated in the expanse of the square. Isolated and somehow foolish. He should not have taken exception to his own curfew order. He did not have that right.

All the lights in Europe have gone out. Again, for no reason, the words came back.

He moved on and entered the church. The big door swung closed behind him. Except for the faint red glow of the sanctuary light, the church was dark. In the profound silence he heard the sound of his own breathing. Until tonight, he had visited the church only to leave signals for Anna and had felt nothing more than a childhood nostalgia for the reverence of ancient statues, the altar, and the tabernacle. Here and there along the walls, the gilt of a carved station of the cross glinted in the flickering red candlelight. He waited until his eyes adjusted to the darkness, making sure he was alone in the church, then walked up the central aisle toward the sanctuary.

As a child he had accompanied his mother at night to the famous Frauenkirche in Munich's Kaufingerstrasse for Benediction services. The poverty after the Great War had deepened his mother's religious devotion and she had survived those years on the strength of her belief in God. As a child he had preferred the comfort of his mother's faith in God's future Providence to his father's hopeless cynicism. Walter, his mother had once said, had been raised a Catholic but had lost his faith in the war. She had always assured him in childhood that everything would come right again. *God works in mysterious ways,* she had said. She had told him that God held him on a rope. She had explained free will, good and evil, Providence, man's war and man's peace, his father's despair, by telling him how God would let loose of the rope for a while, let go of Papa for a while, then pull the rope back in. In the end, God would always pull the rope back in, she had said. He would never let go of him or Papa or Germany.

In the first pew, a few steps from the sanctuary rail, he sat down and looked at the bank of votive lights at the foot of the Sacred Heart statue. The candle Anna had lit at four that afternoon had gone out. Four other candles burned in the rack.

He turned toward the carved gilded tabernacle on the altar, suddenly remembered he still wore his officer's cap, and removed it. His eye rested on the tiny glint of metal on the brim of the cap: the little *Hakenkreuz* sewn to the center of the brim above the bill.

The fact is, Karl, we have lost this war.

His mother's Mysterious Ways of God had given them a savior in the person of Adolf Hitler. Hitler had made it possible for his father to feed them again, Hitler had made his father feel proud again. He had seen his mother's prayers to heaven answered here on earth. He had stopped accompanying his mother to church and had followed his father to the Munich meetings of the new Socialist Party. He had turned his childhood zeal for his mother's heavenly kingdom into zeal for the tangible and immediate fruits of his father's and Hitler's earthly kingdom. Hitler had promised *Lebensraum,* room for them to live with dignity.

As a teen-ager he had worn Hitler's *Hakenkreuz* pinned to the armband of his Hitler Youth shirt, proudly.

We have lost this war.

Hitler had promised—had vowed—victory.

Hitler: the Mysterious Ways of God.

Sometimes, his mother had said, *it will seem that God has let go of the rope. But we must have faith. God will never let go of you or Papa or Germany.*

Kruger leaned forward in the pew and rested his elbows on the wooden bench. At the corner of the sanctuary the candle signifying God's presence in the church flickered, guttering in a draft. But it would not go out as long as the Sacrament was present. It had burned here in San Tommaso for centuries.

"I swear by God this sacred oath," he said silently, "that I will render unconditional obedience to Adolf Hitler, the Führer of the German Reich and people, Supreme Commander of the Armed Forces, and will be ready as a brave soldier to risk my life at any time for this oath."

He looked toward the tabernacle.

If he gave up now, if he broke his oath now with the enemy moving on their lines, there would be no hope for Germany. This time, if defeat came, there would be no world left for him or Papa or Germany.

Suddenly, for the first time in years, Kruger inched forward and brought himself to a kneeling position in the pew. He covered his face.

He had once believed that all power and all Providence rested in the tiny wafer inside the tabernacle.

God had given them Hitler, had let out a little rope on earth in the person of Adolf Hitler. All that was needed now was a little faith. God would not let go of the rope altogether.

All power and all Providence: if not finally in the Führer, perhaps there. In the little wafer. Maybe at this last hour it was worth the chance.

Silently, scarcely moving his lips, he prayed for Germany, that she might not be swallowed up in another monstrous catastrophe; he prayed for his mother and father, for whom he could not bear to imagine another long period of suffering; he prayed for his soldiers, the men for whom he was responsible and whose lives he had that night wagered; he prayed for Anna, the one person in the world that he loved above all others, the woman who had touched him at the center of both body and soul, the woman he had promised so much to and to whom he had delivered so little. And he prayed finally for himself, for the light to see what was right and good and just and the faith to follow it to the end.

CHAPTER 3

I

"I need both loaves. I may not be back for a week or more." Piero Miceli reached for the second loaf of homemade bread on his mother's kitchen table.

"No! *One!* Only one!" Luisa Miceli shouted from the tin sink where she was washing the breakfast dishes. "I am not feeding your entire Brigate Rosse!"

Piero glanced at his father seated at the table and smiled. It was a game he and his mother had been playing for the last seven months, since his desertion from the Italian Army when he joined Il Lupo's Stella Rossa partisan brigade. Once every ten days or two weeks, he would make his way down from the mountains to collect food and clothes for himself and his fellow partisans. He would usually appear and leave on the same night, though this time he had decided to sleep the night in his old bed and leave early in the morning. As usual, the attack on his mother's larder had brought down an avalanche of protests, but he knew that it was only to demonstrate her disapproval of the partisan life that she went through the motions of denial. Piero took the loaf from the table and started to place it in the knapsack with the two bottles of his father's *negrettino* wine, the wedge of cheese, and the bag of chestnuts Livia had picked for him that morning.

"No!" Luisa let the plate she was washing fall back into the water. "It is enough! You will take no more food from this house for that band of murderers!" She grabbed the loaf from Piero's knapsack. Her son's dark-bearded ruddy face looked more like an innocent child's than a twenty-year-old *ribelle*.

"Mamma," Piero chided.

"We have no food! What are we to do, starve ourselves so that Il Lupo can go to sleep at night on a full stomach?"

"Give the boy his loaf." Angelo took the loaf and tossed it to Piero. "It is the least we can do for the only brave men left in Italy."

From the cupboard where she was helping Livia to fold linen Anna caught Piero's eye and smiled. The terrible bombings last night had stretched everyone's nerves to the breaking point.

"The Americans will be here in a few days, Piero." *Nonna* Adelaida looked up from the raw egg she was tapping with her spoon. "Il Lupo should let the Americans fight this war now."

"*Nonna* is right," Luisa said. "In a few days you can come down from that detestable mountain. The Americans will drive the Germans out of Montefalco."

"Maybe." Piero stuffed the loaf of bread into his knapsack.

"Maybe? What can these stupid Germans do about it? What can fifty soldiers do about an *army* of Americans?"

"If the Americans take Montefalco, the Germans will only move farther north." Piero tied the string on his knapsack. "The Americans are only shifting the German line of defense, not breaking it."

"He's right," Angelo added. "And if they don't move fast, they won't break the line for a whole winter. The autumn rains will see to that."

"When the rains start," Piero went on, "the road to Vergato will be impassable. The Americans won't have a chance once the rains start."

"Vergato is not your home!" Luisa exclaimed. "Montefalco is your home! Why should you die for those people in Vergato?"

"Listen to your mother for once, Piero," *Nonna* Adelaida said. "If Il Lupo wants to fight Germans all the way to the Alps, let him. You should think of your family and come home."

Anna glanced at Livia, gave her younger sister a knowing look, and said in an offhand voice, "Yesterday, Signore Bosca was talking with the *maresciallo* when I went into his tailor shop. The *maresciallo* told Signore Bosca that the Germans were going to retreat from Montefalco. Soon. Perhaps even today."

"It isn't true," said Piero.

"The Fascist chief of police ought to know." Anna gave Livia a faint smile.

"Since when have the Fascists started telling the truth?" Piero dismissed his sister with a gesture. "You women believe *all* the gossip you hear."

"It isn't gossip! It's a fact! The Germans are leaving Montefalco!"

"Not until they've fought the Americans for it."

"How do you know? You come down from the mountains only long enough to take food!"

Piero went to the corner, where he had propped his rifle. "I know what I know. If you're so informed about the Germans, you should join the Stella Rossa. You could run our intelligence operation."

"If you don't believe me, just wait and see."

"Be quiet, Anna." Angelo glanced back over his shoulder. "Your brother knows what he knows." He gave his son a nod, signifying it was time for him to go.

"So do I! I know what I know, too!"

Livia held her breath and nudged Anna's leg with her foot.

"How do you know?" Piero smiled disdainfully. He had argued with his little sister like this for years.

"People talk. I have ears. If you don't believe me, go back up to your mountains and wait."

Annoyed by her idiotic persistence, Piero blurted out, "If you're so sure they're pulling out, then why did they send three trucks to Vergato this morning to collect supplies?"

Anna stared at him dumbly. "What do you mean, three trucks to Vergato?"

"Yesterday we got word from Vergato that a shipment of military supplies had arrived. That's why I came last night, to watch the road leading out of Montefalco. This morning, before dawn, a German convoy left town. They've gone up to Vergato to move the supplies down to Montefalco."

"Santa Maria," Luisa muttered and crossed herself.

Piero hoisted his rifle onto his back.

"I don't believe you." Anna's voice trembled.

"Then wait and see." Piero grabbed his knapsack from the chair.

Nonna Adelaida sat back with her vivid blue eyes fixed on the cracked egg before her on the table. "You will curse yourself, young man, if you bring a *rastrellamento* to Montefalco."

"Papa!" Anna started toward her brother. "Stop him! Don't you see what he's doing?"

"Anna!" Livia cautioned.

"You're planning to ambush those soldiers, aren't you?" Anna persisted. Piero went to the door. She yelled after him, "If you leave the Germans alone, they will leave!"

"If they don't have guns and ammunition to fight, they will leave."

"And if you kill them, they will kill us! You have no right!"

"Anna! Be quiet!" Angelo commanded.

"I've got to leave."

Anna took hold of his arm. "Piero," she implored, "you don't know what you're doing. Let the Germans have their guns, what difference does it make? They have lost anyway."

"She's right." Luisa came forward. "You should leave well enough alone."

Piero pulled free. *"Women!* You know nothing of war. If the Germans get these guns and munitions, there will be a battle for Montefalco. There will be nothing left of it when the Americans finish."

"No! Lieutenant Kruger will not let that happen, he . . . !" Anna caught sight of the shocked expression on Livia's face across the room.

"He what?"

"Kruger is not like the others."

"Kruger is a Nazi just like the rest. I hope the bastard is with them in the convoy. We need a good hostage."

"That's enough." Angelo rose from his chair. "Take the food, son, and go. The sun is already over the mountains."

"Papa!" Anna cried.

Luisa moved toward Piero at the door with his sack of food in one arm, his rifle crooked in the other. "Two weeks ago the SS shot twenty-four innocent people for the murder of one German soldier. Four of them were children."

"I must do what I must do."

Anna watched the door close behind her brother. *"Alla faccia tua!"* she yelled after him, then ran to the door leading into the front of the house.

"Anna, wait!" Livia called.

In her bedroom upstairs Anna slammed the door. Her mind was racing. If Karl was with the men, he would die before the day was out. If Il Lupo and his men failed, then Piero would die. She was trapped. She could do nothing to help either. She gripped the wooden bedpost. Behind her the door opened.

"Anna," Livia said in a soft voice.

"They will kill him." Anna stared blankly at the crocheted coverlet on her bed.

"Don't say that. You don't know that."

"Either Piero will kill Carlo, or Carlo will kill Piero. They know nothing of each other."

"Listen to me! You don't know if Kruger is with them. You don't know that."

"I am to blame."

"You? Don't be stupid."

"He would have left before this if he had not loved me."

"That's not true. He's a soldier. He does what he is ordered to do."

Anna pulled free. "I must know. I must find out if he's with them."

"How? It's impossible!"

"I will go to Montefalco. I will go to the Piazza Nazionale, to the Municipio. We will go together. You will tell Mamma you have something to buy for the kitchen."

"I cannot *lie,* Anna."

"I can. I will find an excuse for you."

"You have lied enough!"

"Help me! Please! Help me!"

Livia embraced her sister. For the first time in her life, she felt a dizzying sense of power, as if she had suddenly crossed over into the responsibilities of womanhood. She said, "I will do what I can."

II

Kruger went on pacing the length of his office. The ancient floorboards creaked under his boots. "Vergato says they didn't leave until ten?" he asked.

"Yes, Lieutenant. A little after ten," Reiger replied.

Kruger stopped at the window behind his desk overlooking the Via Santa Lucia. The facade of the opposite building was bathed in sunlight. There had been no rain to delay the convoy. If he was right, the convoy would not reach Montefalco now until afternoon.

Through the open door behind Reiger, Oster began shouting again at the young Italian his men had arrested an hour before and brought to the Municipio for questioning.

Kruger turned from the window. "Bring reports to me at once, Corporal, and don't bother typing them after this. We haven't got time for secretarial work."

"Sergeant Oster ordered me to type them, sir."

Oster, next in rank after Schreiber, had been quick to point out his right to replace Schreiber as adjutant during the sergeant's absence. "I'm in charge here, Corporal," Kruger said.

Reiger saluted. As pro-tem adjutant, Oster had obviously succeeded in intimidating the shy young corporal. Kruger followed Reiger into the reception area. Surrounded by Oster and two armed soldiers, Privates Gosinger and Deutsch, the young Italian prisoner sat hunched in a chair at the far end of the room. For the last thirty minutes Kruger had listened from his office to Oster's strident voice hammering at the prisoner. The boy was not more than eighteen or nineteen. He wore dirty baggy trousers and a filthy white dress shirt, clothes undoubtedly given him by one of the local farmers to replace his Italian uniform. He had claimed to be a deserter from the Monte Rosa Division of Graziani's army. Reiger hurried on through the reception room toward his office. The sunlight from the Piazza Nazionale flooded the room, throwing the prisoner's face into shadow where he sat with his back to the window. "Who is this man?" Kruger asked.

"He says his name is Machiavelli!" Oster laughed mockingly. "A private in the Italian army named *Machiavelli?*"

Taking Oster's cue, the two soldiers chuckled.

"That will do, gentlemen," Kruger warned. Gosinger and Deutsch looked at each other warily. Clearly, Oster was already brokering in influence. "Your name?" Kruger asked in Italian.

"Machiavelli." The young man's face was that of an adolescent, the beard nothing more than a patch of reluctant splotches. His eyes —big, dark, and brown like Anna's—were exhausted and terrified. "Lucio Machiavelli. Private Machiavelli, Monte Rosa Division, I.D. 657843."

"Are you a deserter, Lucio?" Kruger asked mildly.

"Yes, sir."

"Where did you leave your division?"

"Near Tavoletto. I—" He clutched his hands together, anguished. "I did not want to die fighting for Il Duce. The war here is lost."

Kruger quoted words he had said since his days at officer school: "A war is lost when its soldiers lose the will to fight."

The boy looked up, puzzled. "I do not want to fight anymore. I want to go home and work on my father's farm. Il Duce—" Again, he hesitated. "Il Duce has betrayed Italy. If I am to die, it will not be for Il Duce's Italy. There are better things to die for."

Oster, who did not speak Italian, interrupted, "The man's a partisan. Haldner questioned him in Italian, and he talks of the Duce like a partisan."

"You had Haldner question him?" Kruger observed fresh bruises on the man's cheekbones.

"Haldner says the man's a Bolognese, a mountain peasant."

Kruger looked down at young Machiavelli. "You realize, don't you, that in the end the law is the same for both deserters and partisans?"

"Yes, sir. I know."

"The only difference is who will be your executioner."

"I have told you the truth." The boy raised his eyes, fixing Kruger with a look of penetrating concentration. "I am a deserter. I wish I were a partisan. I would rather be shot by Germans than shot by Italians in the name of that fat clown Mussolini."

Oster stiffened at the sound of Mussolini's name.

"I see." Kruger moved toward the window behind the boy. He was right. There were better things to die for than this failing *opera buffa* of Mussolini's Italy.

"There are better things for you to die for, too, signore," added the boy, reading his mind.

"I do not intend to die for Mussolini, soldier," said Kruger, gazing through the window into the sunlit Piazza Nazionale.

"I don't mean Mussolini, signore. I mean his friend, Signore Hitler. He has misled your people just like Il Duce has misled us. Your Führer has lost his war, too."

Oster started threateningly toward the boy.

"Oster!" Kruger turned to see rage flash across the prim face. "Your Gestapo technique, Sergeant, is out of place in the Wehrmacht." Oster stepped back. A thin sour smile played around his mouth. Kruger recalled Schreiber's warning soon after Oster had arrived in Montefalco: that the Gestapo and the *Sicherheitsdienst* had quietly infiltrated every branch of the regular armed forces. "For the time being, I want this man held in custody here in Montefalco. If he's a partisan, he may want to talk to us." He saw the intention of his delaying tactic register in Oster's mind, for if he turned the soldier over to the Italian Fascist authorities, they would shoot him at once. Behind Oster's smile, the order registered in the neat civil servant's memory like a piece of incriminating evidence on a dossier. "Take the man and hold him in the guard house until I have time to personally question him."

"*Andiamo,*" Oster ordered, improvising in Italian. He had never condescended to learn Il Duce's language. "*Schnell!*"

Kruger turned back to the window. Across the square in the deep shadow of the Palazzo Berticelli two young women stood apart from the passing crowd. The one with her back toward the Municipio wore her hair tied back like a schoolgirl's with a long green ribbon, a familiar trademark of Anna's prewar vanity. With a rush of hopeful relief, he followed Oster and his prisoner out into the piazza.

III

Livia took hold of Anna's arm. "There! You see?"

Anna watched Karl leave the front door of the Municipio and turn across the piazza toward the Via Benedetto.

"What are you going to do?"

"Follow him. Stay here. Go into the bank, pretend you're doing something for Papa." She saw Karl look back in her direction as he continued on into the Via Benedetto.

"You're a fool," Livia called after her as she started across the square.

Kruger glanced back again as he passed the shops lining the cobblestoned Via Benedetto and saw Anna thirty meters behind him. Catty-corner to the Hotel Montecatini he reached the government-run Comellini *ammasso.* Most of the other shops were closed that morning, following the bombings last night. If they were to meet, it would have to be swift and appear accidental. The proprietors of the *ammasso,* the Comellinis, were both Fascists. The elderly signora who ran the store was hard of hearing. She sometimes did little favors for the German officers, like darn their socks or knit a pair of gloves. At the entrance Kruger stopped to pull a button from the sleeve of his uniform.

Ersilia Comellini was behind her counter, arranging packages of wartime cigarettes, when the bell sounded over the door. The bell, a large school bell, had been attached to the door to protect the shop from the neighborhood boys who came in and stole things when she wasn't looking.

"*Buon giorno, signora.*" Kruger made his way toward the rear of the store. The woman's wrinkled face, framed by tufts of white hair protruding from under the black kerchief, was a furnace of nervous energy. Greed, he had often thought.

"*Signore Comandante!*" she shouted up as if from a deep well, wheezing the while.

Behind Kruger the bell sounded and he saw Anna reflected in a plate-glass cabinet. "A pack of cigarettes, signora," he said. "Coronas."

Anna busied herself at a rack displaying canned goods, things no one in Montefalco could afford.

"Matches, Signore Comandante?" Ersilia Comellini inquired.

"Yes. Matches, too."

"And what else, signore?"

"This button. I've lost a button from the sleeve of my uniform."

"Ah!" The old woman's face brightened. "You German boys are no different than Italian boys without your mammas! Take off the jacket, signore!"

He handed the jacket across the counter with the button. "Here. This sleeve."

Signora Comellini saw Anna standing behind him, fingering a small tin of dry biscuits. "You have money for biscuits, young lady?" she shouted.

"No!" Anna replaced the painted can. "Needles. I want to buy needles, signora."

"You'll have to wait until I sew the *comandante's* button!" Signora Comellini yelled up from her well of deafness.

"Take your time, signora!" Kruger shouted back. He waited until the old lady had vanished through the door into the rear of the shop, then turned to Anna. "Last night I should have told you the truth. We're not leaving."

"Why?"

"We were ordered to stay."

"Fifty men against a whole army?" Pushed by anger into sarcasm, she added, "If Hitler told you to jump off the Reno bridge, would you do it?"

"*Anna.*"

"What does he expect you to do with fifty men? You can't win! You will all be *killed!*"

He knew before he spoke that it was only a remote possibility. "I've asked for reinforcements; they'll send what they can."

"And then what?" She tried a different tack: "You'll make the Americans *fight* for Montefalco! They'll send airplanes, they'll bomb us like they bombed San Lorenzo last night—" She realized she had said more than she should know. Piero had told her of San Lorenzo. "They'll bomb Montefalco, they'll kill everyone in Montefalco, and for what?" She saw that he had paled. "If you stay here, we will *all* die!"

He said, mutely, "I cannot give an order to retreat without permission from the *Oberkommando der Wehrmacht.*" The use of the full German name seemed to give credibility to his words, easing his shame.

"Which is more important, Carlo, dying for Hitler or living for me?"

"Leave Hitler out of this."

"How can I?"

He sighed. "I have a duty, a responsibility as a soldier. If every soldier did what his heart told him to do, then—" He ran aground before he finished, thinking of the war as a whole.

"You're a Catholic, Carlo. What about your conscience?"

"Gianni! *Vieni!*" Signora Comellini shouted to her husband in the back of the store. Kruger said, quickly, "Listen to me. I want you to leave Montefalco. I want you to take your parents, your sister, and go to one of the villages in the mountains. Lizzano or Gaggio-Montano. Tell your parents to stay there until the fighting is over."

"I have a grandmother at home. How do we take *her* to the mountains?"

"You said your father has a mule."

"Gianni!" Ersilia yelled again. "Bring me my scissors!"

Anna laughed. "Gianni, Papa's mule, is even older than Gianni Comellini. He couldn't get as far as Granaglione."

"Then I will supply transportation."

Anna shook her head. "Papa won't go. I know him."

"He must." He hesitated, weighing discretion against the imminent danger. "Tell him that I said—" He realized that his impulse to tell Anna of the convoy was rash. "Tell him you heard the Germans were getting fresh supplies. Mortars, heavy guns, a whole shipment of artillery and munitions. The fighting in the valley around Montefalco will be heavy."

Anna stared at the floor. Her heart pounded and she could feel the blood in her face. She said, breathlessly. "That's impossible. The train tracks, the road . . . the partisans will—" She left off as a steel door slammed closed on her thought.

"By the time the partisans know, it will be too late."

She tried to phrase her words carefully, knowing she was now bartering her brother's life. "The partisans know everything that happens in the Reno Valley."

"That's a chance we had to take."

"You must stop your men. Before it's too late." Tears broke in her eyes, but no feeling came with them.

"Too late for what?"

"The partisans always know! They know everything you do here! They will kill your men, I know they will!"

"Listen to me!" He gripped her shoulders. "Stop worrying about what doesn't concern you. Take your family and leave Montefalco. When it's over, I'll find you."

The room around her seemed to go flat and colorless. "You will *die*. You, your soldiers, everyone. For nothing. Is that what you want?"

"No. I don't want to die. I love you, you know that. But I cannot change what—" He left off as Signora Comellini shouted to her husband. "Listen to me. Go to Tommaso at four o'clock. I will come to the church. I will explain everything."

She shook her head, knowing what she knew would happen in the meantime. She began to cry openly. "You will die if you stay here."

"I have no choice, Anna."

She pushed back, holding him at arm's length. Suddenly at the end of her options, she said, "If you won't go for my sake, if you won't go for *our* sake, then maybe it's time you knew there is someone else!"

"If I could go, I would! For you, for your sake!"

"You don't understand. Last night, when you came to the ravine—"

"Ah! *Ecco!*" Signora Comellini came through the door from the back of the shop. "Signore Comandante! Look!"

Anna drew away as Karl turned toward the counter, flustered. "Yes, signora. I see. Good."

The old lady held up the jacket, displayed the sleeve, and rattled on about the price of buttons and thread. "At four," Anna murmured, "San Tommaso. I have something to tell you, Karl." She started toward the door.

"Signorina Miceli!" Ersilia called out after her. "Your needles!"

"I've changed my mind. I don't want needles, thank you." The bell clanged above her head. She brushed her hand across both cheeks to remove the evidence of her crying and turned down the Via Benedetto toward the piazza. It was Friday. There would be confession in the church from three to five. Her mother would not object to Livia and her making a Friday confession. There would be a crowd of women at San Tommaso, but there were dark corners in the back of the church where they could talk. Where she could tell Carlo that he had given her a child, and if he died there would be no father.

Kruger stepped out into the street and closed the door behind him. He looked at his watch: 11:05. Two soldiers patrolling the Via Benedetto saluted as he passed. He returned the salute halfheartedly, only vaguely aware of the people around him. He knew most of them by sight, but only a few by name. *They'll send airplanes, they'll bomb us like they bombed San Lorenzo last night. . . . If you stay here, we will all die.* Even if he wanted to order a retreat, it was now too late. With or without him, the die had already been cast.

He looked for a pocket to put the cigarettes and matches in. He didn't smoke cigarettes. He saw two boys, perhaps fourteen or fifteen years old, approaching, scrutinizing him warily. They were the "street brats" Signora Comellini had denounced a few weeks ago to the Fascist *carabinieri* for stealing foodstuffs from her store, boys whose fathers had gone off to fight for Mussolini's Italy. The taller, older one whispered to his curly-headed companion, trying to appear unafraid of the Nazi commandant. Once, Kruger remembered, as a kid, when his parents had nothing left at home to eat and his father was jobless, he had stolen a chicken from a local meat market in the Neuhauserstrasse.

He slowed his pace and edged toward the boys.

He had carried the chicken home stuffed in his trousers. When his mother asked where he had acquired the bird, he had lied, saying it was a gift from a generous neighbor, a transparent lie, but his mother kept the chicken, said nothing, and cooked it that night for dinner.

The taller boy, showing his defiant courage, reached into his shirt pocket and took out the smashed butt end of an old cigarette. He put it in his mouth and fixed Kruger, challengingly. Oftentimes, some of the soldiers gave the boys of Montefalco the butts of their finished cigarettes. He had seen Schreiber do it.

As Kruger ambled toward the boys, they straightened themselves against the wall. The taller one had large dark eyes that widened with fear and implacable hatred. The smaller boy began edging toward the alley leading off the street. The tall boy's eyes fixed on the package of cigarettes in his hand.

Kruger smiled. "Here." He tossed the pack of cigarettes and the box of matches. Startled but instantly alert, the boy caught both. He looked up, saw Kruger nod with approval at his agile speed, and returned the acknowledgment with a cautious smile.

CHAPTER 4

I

Once more, the church door opened, throwing a shaft of soft afternoon sunlight down the dark nave. From the pew where she knelt with her mother and sister, Anna looked back. The short plump figure of Signora Zagoni shuffled across the rear of the church.

"Anna." Her mother reprimanded her with a nudge.

She turned back to face the sanctuary. The draft from the opened door stirred the flame of the sanctuary lamp near the altar. Each time someone had come in, she had turned to look, but so far only women had appeared. Carlo had said four o'clock. It was now four-thirty. Signora Mengoli emerged from the carved wooden confessional box, rattling the metal rungs of the heavy drape. Livia quickly got up and took Elvira's place, pulling the drape closed behind her. Her mother's turn would come next.

Anna quickly ran through the list of sins she had prepared: three lies in the last two weeks, two losses of temper, two acts of disobedience, and two falls into vanity. No. Better three falls into vanity. She would confess her venial sins to Don Alessandro, but not the mortal sins; for if she confessed the mortal ones, the eight sins of fornication (the word sounded hideous), the twelve sacrilegious Communions (they had piled up in her soul like immovable stones), and the eleven sacrilegious confessions (those made her look obdurate, like she was gambling with God), he would ask questions and know that she had been mocking God all along. After that first time with Karl she had examined her conscience as the nuns had taught her to do, and all the conditions for mortal sin had been there: sufficient reflection (she had known what she was doing), grievous matter (fornication was at the top of the list of mortal sins), and full consent of the will (she had wanted to do it with all her heart). Worse, she had known from the beginning that she would go on sinning, and it was pointless to promise God or Don Alessandro that she would not.

Besides, if she now confessed her mortal sins, she would have to tell the priest she might be pregnant. And then he would tell her she would have to marry the man who had made her pregnant. The Church was strict about that!

Again, from the rear of the church came the squeak of the door opening. She turned impulsively and saw a man framed for an instant in the bright light.

"*Anna!*" Her mother pinched her arm.

She turned back toward the altar. She could hear the tap of boot heels on the stone floor at the rear of the church, moving toward the far side of the nave. Livia emerged from the confessional, rattling the metal rungs, and waited at the end of the pew for her mother to pass.

"He's here," Anna whispered to Livia when she knelt down beside her.

"You can't," Livia whispered, "not now."

"Tell Mamma I felt faint. I went outside for air." Anna rose, forcing Livia to let her pass, and turned down the aisle. She saw him kneeling in the far corner, partly hidden behind one of the big stone pillars. Saw, at least, his dark head and the faint glint of his uniform insignias.

Crossing the rear of the church, she thought, I will tell him outright . . . no preface, no explanations. Outright.

She did not think to genuflect before the tabernacle as she crossed the center aisle.

If he will not leave Montefalco for me, if not for me, then for his own child. He had talked countless times about the son that he wanted. There were other responsibilities now besides the war and soldiering.

He knelt at the end of the pew, his head cradled in his hands, praying. She tiptoed, cautiously, and stopped just this side of the pillar. In the shadows she could see only his back. "Carlo," she whispered.

Startled, he raised his head and quickly turned: with not Karl's but a stranger's face, lean, hollow-eyed, and frightened. *"Ja?"*

"I . . ." She stepped back into the aisle. "I'm sorry, I thought you were . . ."

The young soldier whispered in German to her.

She kept moving backward. "I'm sorry," she said hoarsely, "I've made a mistake. It's nothing . . ." With that, covering her mouth to muffle the cry threatening to break from her throat, she hurried, unaware at first that she was running, toward the far side of the church, oblivious of the noise her feet made, heedless where she was until she saw the confessional curtain slide back with a loud rattle and her mother step out into the aisle.

Anna slowed, trying to suppress the sound of her breathing, and continued toward the dark empty confessional booth. From the pew her mother stared at her with surprise. There were whispers from the kneeling women. Inside the confessional box she pulled the curtain closed and leaned against the wall, grateful for the darkness.

It was he who had said four o'clock in the church! He knew she had something important to tell him! The thought came to her for the first time: he has been lying to me all these months. I have been used.

She began to cry for the misery of her helpless dilemma. She tried to stifle the sound, but it came up, a wavering whimper, and stuck in her throat, magnified in the boxed enclosure. The priest heard her behind his grille; there was a rustling noise.

"Please kneel," he murmured. Her feet and shins, she saw, were plainly visible in the space beneath the curtain. She knelt. Behind the thin purple cloth Don Alessandro leaned toward the grille, alert to the sound of her rapid breath. "Take your time," he said patiently, "there's no hurry."

But there is, she thought. Everyone, her mother and her sister, everyone is watching! "Bless me, Father," she forced the words out, "for I have sinned."

She closed her eyes and took a deep breath. "My last confession was one week ago." She began confessing the list of venial sins she had prepared for him, but absently, for her thoughts had raced off into the real world: she had heard stories of other girls and German soldiers, but she had never dreamed that Karl was that kind of man. She pictured him in the Adele Ravine and recalled the promises he had made, the prospects he had laid out for the future. How could he have not meant what he said? He had joked about the troubles they would face in life. People who trick and deceive don't joke about their failures and shortcomings, not men at least! At least she knew *that* much about human nature!

". . . and I told two lies," she said, reaching the end. She opened her eyes. The priest had not moved, except to rest his forehead against the tips of his fingers, which made him look somehow doubtful.

"Is there anything else, my child?"

Hatred, she thought. Is this what they mean by hatred? The end of love and the beginning of hatred? In the *romanzo* she had read the man had run away with another woman, and the woman had closed herself up in the *castello* to spend her nights wandering atop the *parapetti merlati,* weeping bitterly for the lost lover; but the woman had triumphed in the end, when the other woman poisoned her lover. The author had described the woman's hatred.

"Speak up, my child, have you anything else?"

Revenge, she thought, but she could not confess a sin before she committed it. She said, suddenly realizing that Carlo's rejection had freed her from future sin with him, "Yes, Father."

Don Alessandro leaned closer. "I can't hear you, my child."

She pressed her face to the curtain over the grille. "I have . . . I have been seeing a man."

"Do you mean you've had sexual relations with the man?" he asked without hesitation or any sign of shock.

"Yes, Father."

"How many times?"

The number somehow seemed inconsequential. She pictured Karl's face, and with the image came the realization that the choice of future sin with him was really his, not hers, and she would have gone on committing fornication with him for the rest of the war, if he had wanted. Her confession was meaningless. "Eight," she said, almost defiantly.

Alessandro considered the number. "Are you married?"

"No, Father."

"Is he?"

"No, Father." Adultery was a different sin from fornication.

"Are you aware that fornication is a grave mortal sin?"

"Yes, Father."

"How long have you been having relations with this man?" His voice was weighted now.

"Several months, Father." *This man:* the expression sounded loveless and dismissive.

"And have you confessed in that time?"

He knew, of course, that she had; he had heard the confessions himself and knew the sound of her voice and who she was: the curtain between them was a mere pretense. "Yes, Father." She didn't wait for him to ask how many times she had made sacrilegious confessions. "Eleven times," she said. The number, spoken, sounded enormous.

"But you did not confess your impurity?"

"No, Father."

"Were you afraid to confess?"

"Yes, Father." She knew, though, that she lied even now, for it was not fear that had prevented her, but obduracy.

"Are you sorry for your sins?"

"Yes, Father." Again, she lied: sorry, yes, for the sins, but glad— wonderfully glad—for the loving deed.

"Have you received Communion during that time?" The question brought her back abruptly.

"Yes, Father. Twelve times." He knew that, too. He had himself given her the Sacrament.

He sighed heavily, lifting his head. "My child, you must reflect on the gravity of these sins. You have been living in a state of mortal sin now for months. In these times, you cannot overlook the dangers we live in. If something should happen—a battle here in Montefalco, for instance—and you are killed without an opportunity to repent, you risk eternal damnation. Do you realize that?"

She had thought of it often, especially at night when she was alone in bed, the game she was playing with God, but the risks for the prize had seemed worth taking. "Yes, Father."

"The sins you have confessed are forgivable, sanctifying grace can be restored to you, but what is lost forever now is your virginity. Worse than impurity, though, is the sin of sacrilege—your mockery of God's mercy in confessing to Him without repentance. Receiving His body and blood in a state of mortal sin. In doing so, you crucify your Savior all over again. Do you understand what I'm saying?"

"Yes, Father."

Someone waiting to confess coughed and cleared her throat.

"In the future, my child, you must resolve never to see this man again. The only way you can continue your relationship with him is to sanctify it with the sacrament of matrimony. Does he live here in Montefalco?"

"Yes, Father." Her face felt suddenly hot.

"If he is an honorable man, he will ask your hand in marriage. Think also of this—if you should become pregnant with his child, your life will be a misery. Montefalco is a small town. Your sin would become known to everyone, and you would cause grave scandal if you were not married. And the child—" he added. He was talking, she realized, of her present horror as if it belonged far off in the future. "—think of the future of a child born out of wedlock. Your child would carry the burden of your sin for the rest of its life. Have you thought of that?"

She dropped her forehead against the grille. "Yes, Father." The tears began again, falling on her folded hands. Either way, she thought—whether he stays and dies fighting, or leaves and lives and forgets me and what he has done to me—either way, I am destroyed. I am damned.

For a moment she wondered if the child itself was a sin to be confessed like the other mortal sins. Would it be born damned?

Don Alessandro gave a sigh of fateful resignation. "For your penance you will recite the rosary before the statue of Our Blessed Virgin. When you do, think how passing the joys and pleasures of human love are compared to the eternal love of God, or to the unimaginable horrors of eternal damnation. Now say the Act of Contrition while I give you absolution." He adjusted the purple confessional stole on his shoulders and began the Latin prayer.

"Oh my God . . . I'm heartily sorry . . . for having offended Thee . . ." The prayer came in fragments between muffled sobs. She said the words mechanically, knowing that she wept not for the offense of her sins but for the unimaginable horror already before her: Karl's death here in Montefalco, if he did as she had intended to ask; or his permanent separation, if he left. She wept for the child —their child—she dreaded was already there. And worse than all, she wept to think Karl might vanish now, leaving her to wonder if he had really loved her at all.

II

"They are four hours late, Corporal!" Kruger shouted, slamming the desk drawer closed.

"Vergato insists Blackbird left the railhead at half past ten this morning, Herr Oberleutnant," Corporal Reiger repeated his statement, looking for support from Sergeant Haldner, who stood scanning the map of the Bolognese Apennines pinned to the wall. Blackbird was the code name given to the convoy of three trucks.

"We've sent out a search party from here, Lieutenant," Haldner said. "If there's been trouble, we should hear within the hour." He tapped the map with a finger. "Our last report puts Il Lupo here, between Monte Belvedere and Gaggio-Montano." Head of partisan reconnaissance, Haldner had made daily forays into the mountains to observe the movements of the Red Star Brigade.

"Our concern, Sergeant, is not where the partisans have camped, but what they have done to our convoy," said Kruger, exasperated. "Reiger, I want you to send another message to the Sixteenth SS Panzers in Vergato. Request the commanding officer to send a reconnaissance patrol south as far as Porretta Terme. Ask him to verify the fact that Blackbird has safely cleared his zone. Request an immediate reply."

"*Jawohl, Herr Oberleutnant.*" Reiger started out of the office.

"And, Corporal—"

"Sir?"

"The messages between here and Montefalco were sent coded, were they not?"

"Of course, sir."

"Then ask the Panzer commander to check his communications staff for a security leak. Send the message marked 'Urgent' and 'Most Secret.'"

Reiger saluted and hurried from the room.

Kruger joined Haldner at the map. He pointed. "If there's been an attack, it would likely have occurred here, between Monte Stanco on the east and Castelnuovo on the west. The road here is exposed to the hills on both sides."

Haldner nodded. "Il Lupo watches rail shipments to and from Vergato. The shipment from Vergato to Montefalco should have been made, as I said to Schreiber, at night."

"There wasn't time, Haldner. We have less than thirty-six hours to get ready for the Americans."

In the outer office a door slammed. A moment later Corporal Weiss, the young officer who had led Haldner's reconnaissance patrol, stood at Kruger's open door. "Oberleutnant Kruger," he said. Under the steel helmet his sunburned Teutonic face was an open map of panic and fear.

"Blackbird," Kruger said, "have you found them?"

The pale blue eyes wavered. "Foertsch, Lieutenant. We found only Private Foertsch."

"The others?"

"Ambushed, Herr Oberleutnant. They were attacked by partisans. We found Foertsch on the road south of Porretta Terme."

"Where is he?"

"Outside, in the van, sir. He's been wounded."

Kruger pushed past the corporal into the reception area. "Come with me, both of you." He threw open the front door and stepped out under the archway overlooking the Piazza Nazionale. Parked at the entrance were two armored reconnaissance vans. A group of soldiers, Sergeant Oster among them, stood in a circle between the vans, observing a man lying on a stretcher placed on the cobblestones. As Kruger made his way down the steps, the soldiers parted for him to pass. Private Foertsch looked up from his stretcher, an expression of mute anguish on his round monkish face. "Only one man?" Kruger asked, not directing the question to any single soldier.

"One." Oster throttled his fury. "Only one, Herr Oberleutnant."

Kruger knelt down on one knee next to Foertsch. The man's face was smeared with dried gray mud. Slashed from the thigh to the ankle, his uniform trouser leg was saturated with blood. "You'll be all right," Kruger said quietly, "just lie still."

"The convoy, sir—"

In the private's glazed eyes he saw the pinpoint reflection of his own defeated rage. "Partisans?" he asked.

Foertsch nodded. "On the road. There was nothing I could do.

They were dead, sir. They were dead . . . or dying. I couldn't help."
He made a futile gesture with the hand slung across his chest.

"How many partisans?"

"I don't know. A hundred. They were all around. On the cliffs,
behind the rocks. They surprised us."

"Where?"

"South of Vergato. Near Castelnuovo. Where the valley narrows."
He lifted his head, staring vacantly at the soft ocher-colored cloud-
less sky. "We came around a bend in the road. I was with Fanger.
In the last truck. The others were hit. The first . . . with Schreiber
and Stofel . . . in the ditch." Kruger lowered his eyes to conceal the
stabbing pain in his gut. "Ritter and Felsch . . . were in the road.
Dead." A look of amazement flooded Foertsch's face. "Ritter . . .
his rifle was strapped to his back. . . . We were in the ditch . . .
Fanger and me—" He appeared to galvanize himself. "They shot
Fanger in the cab of our truck! We were in the ditch! I went down
in the river! Schreiber was yelling—screaming! He was hit, but he
was alive! I stayed in the river!" Foertsch's head fell back on the
stretcher. "There was nothing—Lieutenant, there was nothing I
could do." A soft rush of air came from his mouth. Foertsch closed
his eyes and began to cry like a child.

Kruger stood up. "Get this man to the medics." From behind the
Municipio the sun had traced a long jagged shadow across the
length of the piazza where small groups of locals stood watching
anxiously. "Oster!" He pushed through the soldiers toward the
Municipio entrance.

Oster was behind him in the next instant. "Herr Oberleutnant."

"I want the sentries doubled on the road leading in and out of
town. I want every available man on patrol tonight."

"Jawohl, Herr Oberleutnant!"

"The rest of you—!" He turned on the steps. "Return to the compound, get something to eat, and . . . get ready to move out!"

On the way through the reception area to his office, Kruger realized he had been premature in his announcement of retreat. The ultimate orders had to come from OKW: but what choice was left to
OKW? He turned to Oster, following him. "Get Reiger in here. On
the double."

Oster scurried off toward the radio room.

At his desk Kruger began jotting facts, his reasons for a retreat:
the Allied advance, the loss of supplies, the convoy . . .

Schreiber was yelling—screaming! He was hit, but he was alive!

He threw the pen furiously against the wall and its black ink splattered across the white plaster.

Schreiber had planned to finish the university and teach school after the war. Others—Oster, Haldner—the rabid fanatics who still believed in victory—should have drawn the straw!

I swear by God this sacred oath, that I will render unconditional obedience to Adolf Hitler. . . . Hitler, Kesselring, Lemelsen: the authority and the power descended from above, no different in kind from—and the thought of it bewildered him—last night's brush with God's Providence, and just as merciless when seen from below—from this human misery.

He looked up at the clock: 5:11. Anna. She would have waited for him in the church, but would have gone by now. There was so much to say and so little time.

Oster, followed by Reiger, came through the door. "The swine—the Americans—they've attacked the Porretta Pass! They've broken through!" He held up the paper he carried.

"I just received word from Spedaletto, sir," Reiger said.

"Did you think it would hold?" Kruger asked, amazed.

Reiger replied with a shake of the head. Oster set the paper before Kruger on the desk. "Spedaletto requests a report on the state of our defenses."

Kruger pushed the paper away. "Take down the following message to General Lemelsen, Reiger. 'Urgent' and 'Most Secret.' Convoy Blackbird ambushed by partisans. Trucks and supplies captured. Six men shot. Impossible now to defend Montefalco. Request immediate—repeat—*immediate*—permission to withdraw and regroup north of Vergato. Heil Hitler. Kruger. Group commander. Montefalco. Code the message and send it at once."

Reiger saluted and left the room.

Oster had turned toward the splattered ink on the wall. "Captain Kleisner in Spedaletto requested an immediate situation report, Herr Oberleutnant," he said, watching the ink trickle down the plaster.

"He'll have to wait till Lemelsen issues an order for retreat."

"I think Lemelsen will refuse, Herr Oberleutnant."

"What you think or *don't* think is irrelevant. For the time being, you will take your orders directly from me. Is that clear?"

"Of course, Herr Oberleutnant." The repetitious use of his title reminded Kruger of the civil servant behind the Wehrmacht officer's uniform.

"Tell Haldner I want all reconnaissance vehicles checked and refueled before sundown. Weiss will take over your quartermaster duties. Tell him I want a complete rundown on supplies. Do it now, Sergeant."

"*Jawohl, Herr Oberleutnant.*" Oster saluted, scarcely concealing his disgust, and withdrew.

Kruger switched off his lamp and turned to the window overlooking the Via Santa Lucia. The sun had settled behind the ridge, throwing the narrow lane into shadow. Several people hurried by. By now word would have begun to spread about the partisan massacre of his soldiers. Word traveled fast in Montefalco. He leaned his forehead against the window. Schreiber. In all the months he had been in Montefalco, Schreiber alone had become a friend. There would now be the usual curt message to his family in Frankfurt announcing their son's death. A phrase or two of praise for Schreiber's sacrifice to the Fatherland. The irony was, Schreiber had lost faith in the Fatherland months ago, when he left the eastern front.

In the corner of his eye Kruger caught sight of three figures hurrying down the street. The curfew would be in effect in a half hour. Three women, he saw, two in long peasant dresses, the third in a dark short-skirted dress with a black kerchief covering her head. He stepped back from the window, recognizing the woman's graceful movement. A few meters from his building she slowed to let the others run ahead. Anna's gaze, he saw, was directed toward the window, but she could not see him in the darkness.

"Anna!" the older woman called back, "*Vieni! Il coprifuoco!*" The curfew. Anna had taught him that word herself.

She reached the window and looked up with no expression at all in her face.

He murmured, "Anna."

She passed by.

CHAPTER 5

I

Anna felt herself rise suddenly to a surface where there was a faint but familiar light, a face she recognized, and a smell she remembered: kerosene.

"You were dreaming," said Livia, close to her on the bed. The bedclothes around her legs, the feather pillow under her arm, her sister: they brought with them a feeling of safety and warmth, though the room was bitterly cold. "Mamma sent me. You have to get up. Something's happened." In the light of the lamp she had carried in from the hall Livia's eyes looked huge with fear.

"Happened? What?" Anna thought first of Karl, then of Piero, then remembered the news Dr. Fillipeti, their neighbor, had brought to them after supper that night.

"Piero is here. He came a while ago. He's . . . he's downstairs with Mamma and Papa and *Nonna*."

"He's here?" Anna knelt up. Livia had been crying, she saw.

"Get up, Anna. Something terrible has happened. Piero—he was with them—they killed the German soldiers. He came back to warn us."

Anna left the bed and followed Livia through the dark hallway to the staircase. Passing the holy pictures on the wall, she murmured a prayer. Her parents were downstairs arguing. She thought, Piero has committed murder! And the thought of it astonished her.

"You're a fool!" her mother shouted to Piero as they reached the foot of the staircase. "You know where this will lead, don't you!"

A fire had been lit and the wavering light played over Piero's contorted face. He was stretched out on the divan close to the fire. Her father and *Nonna* Adelaida were bent over his right leg.

"It had to be done," Piero muttered, "we had no choice." The logs in the fireplace gave a loud snap. Anna saw that his trouser leg had been torn back and the fabric was soaked with dried blood. A wide gash ran across the white skin of his thigh, just above the knee.

"Piero," she said, knelt down at his shoulder, and grasped his hand. He smiled at her. His face was dirty.

"Where did it happen, son?" asked her father, tearing a piece of white cotton into strips. Anna saw that he was making bandages from the old tablecloth she had taken to the Adele Ravine two days before.

"South of Vergato. Near Castelnuovo. Where the road runs under the hillside by the river."

Someone had washed the tablecloth. She had left it in the kitchen clothes hamper, filthy with mud from her lovemaking.

"How many?" asked her father.

"Six, I think. There wasn't time to count."

Her mother stood at the head of the divan. "Two Germans were killed in Fulvio. In Fulvio the Germans shot men, women, and children. Did you think of *that* when you shot Kruger's soldiers?"

"Yes, Mamma. We thought of that." He winced. "But if the Germans got hold of those guns—they'd be forced to stay. They'd fight the Americans for Montefalco. The Americans would blast Montefalco off the map. This way—" He winced again. "This way, they'll have to pull back."

"There will be a *rastrellamento!* They will kill us all!"

"They don't have time for reprisals, Mamma."

Nonna Adelaida murmured something *sotto voce* to herself.

Anna said, looking from Piero to her mother, "There will be no reprisal. Kruger wouldn't do that, he's not like the others." She saw Livia turn with a look of mute horror.

"You don't know what you're talking about, child," *Nonna* Adelaida said, folding a bandage strip over the wound, "you live in a world of childish dreams. The man's a *tedesco*—a German like all the rest. He will do what he is told to do."

Her father tore another strip from the tablecloth. "You shouldn't have come here, son. They'll search every house in the valley."

"I didn't come to stay, Papa. I came to tell you to leave. Il Lupo says you must leave tonight. I will take you up into the hills. You'll be safe there until the Americans arrive." He went on, oblivious of the looks around him. "Eight men came down with me tonight. They're going to every farmhouse in the valley, they've sent word into the village. Before morning, everyone will be safe in the mountains. Pack a few things, only as much as you can carry uphill. *Nonna* Adelaida can ride on Gianni, he can make it as far as we have to go." Seeing their mute faces, he sat up. "What's wrong?"

"Piero," Anna gasped.

"We can't leave, son," said her father.

"What do you mean, you can't leave? It's only four kilometers!"

"The *carabinieri* came this morning and took Gianni. I didn't have the money for our taxes."

Nonna Adelaida got to her feet. "The rest of you will go. I am an old woman. I cannot make the climb. They will not harm an old woman. I will stay."

"If we are gone when they come, Mamma," said Angelo to his mother, "they will know. They will kill you."

Luisa said quietly, "We will stay."

"Nothing will happen! I know it!" Anna looked at Livia, appealing for help. "The Germans will leave Montefalco!"

Livia said, "I hope for your sake they do."

"We have no place to hide you, Piero," Luisa said. "If they find you here in the morning, they will kill everyone. You must go. Tonight."

"His leg, Mamma!" Anna pleaded.

"It's nothing." Piero swung the bandaged leg from the divan. "I came down," he said, affectionately mussing his sister's hair, "I can go back up. Get me a clean pair of trousers, we'll burn these in the fireplace."

"I'll get food for you." Luisa started toward the kitchen. As Piero gingerly got to his feet, a soft boom rolled suddenly through the house. Anna grabbed her brother's hand. For a moment, no one moved.

"Thunder," Piero said and chuckled.

Anna stood up and glanced from Piero to her mother. "There will be floods in the mountains, he can't go up Gaggio-Montano in the rain! All the *torrenti* will be flooded!"

"Nonsense." Piero hobbled toward the kitchen door. "Get me *Nonna's* walking stick."

"Look at him, Mamma!" Anna exclaimed.

"They are both right," said *Nonna* Adelaida, "he can neither stay nor go." She looked back at Anna, meaningfully.

A second deep boom rolled across the valley. *Le passioni della guerra sono come l'acqua del torrente Rimaldi, forte ma bassa.* Anna recalled *Nonna's* sage observation: the passions of war are like the waters of the *torrente* Rimaldi. . . . She said, brushing her doubt away like a spider's web, "They won't come before morning, Papa. The storm will pass. He can leave in the morning—before dawn."

"You're right." Angelo handed Anna the shredded remains of the tablecloth.

"Don't be a fool, Angelo!" Luisa protested.

"It's eleven-thirty." Angelo turned to his son. "You will leave, son, at four-thirty, before dawn."

Livia looked at Anna. "God have mercy on us."

II

The rain slashed at Kruger's face as he hurried down the Via Benedetto from the Hotel Montecatini toward the Piazza Nazionale and the Municipio. A little after midnight the rain had swept down the valley from the north. At 9:30 a report had come in from Spedaletto that the Americans had advanced through the Porretta Pass and reached the German defense line south of Spedaletto. This time the rain had proved a blessing, for the Americans were now bogged in mud.

The wind blowing up the hillside through the old town drove the rain in sheets across the dark open space of the piazza. Except for sentries, the square was empty.

He had gone to the Montecatini to eat and shave, and had been absent from headquarters now for forty minutes. The clock on the *campanile* read 1:20. If permission to withdraw had come in his absence, there would be only four and a half hours before dawn to put the wheels in motion. Far up in the valley another bolt of lightning zigzagged through the sky and splintered, illuminating the two soldiers on either side of the Municipio door, Privates Roepke and Hausner, who had been on duty since 6:00 that evening. Under the portico Kruger shook the rain from his leather coat. "It's a hell of a night, men. You should be glad you're on duty here and not out on the road."

"Yes, sir," Roepke said, opening the door for him. A wedge of light fell across the young soldier's featureless young face.

"How old are you, Roepke?" Kruger asked.

The question startled the boy. "Nineteen, sir." A curious odor swept past Kruger's face on the soldier's breath. The sharp sour-sweet odor of schnapps. It was unmistakable. "When did you come on duty, Roepke?" he asked.

"At six-thirty, Herr Oberleutnant." The boy perceived his scrutinizing stare. The eyes—the strained lids, the dark blotches—betrayed the reek of terror.

Kruger said, looking directly at Roepke, "Tell me, Private Hausner, what kind of soldier is Roepke here?"

"Sir?"

"I asked you what kind of soldier Private Roepke is."

"He . . . he's pretty good, Herr Oberleutnant."

"In your opinion, Private Roepke, what is a good soldier?"

Roepke swallowed. "One who does his duty, Herr Oberleutnant."

Kruger saw sweat on the boy's face under the rim of his helmet. "A good soldier, Roepke, is a man driven by belief and faith. This morning, Sergeant Schreiber's men gave their lives for the Fatherland. Their duty was to bring a cargo of munitions from Vergato. They failed in that mission, but they succeeded as soldiers. It was faith and belief that drove them, not merely duty. Do you understand, Private Roepke?"

"Jawohl, Herr Oberleutnant."

Kruger realized that both young men were too young to have lived without hope for any length of time. "You will—both of you—report to me when your guard duty here is finished."

"Herr Oberleutnant." Roepke snapped to attention. Hausner followed suit.

Kruger went into the reception room and closed the door behind him. Seated at his desk, Oster stood up at once, saluting. *Authority descends from above downward and responsibility from below upward:* the words moved through Kruger's mind like a reflex. "At ease, Sergeant." Kruger removed his topcoat.

"We received a reply, Herr Oberleutnant."

"Six hours late, I might add." Kruger threw his coat on a chair and moved angrily toward the sergeant's desk. Where, he thought, had the men found schnapps? How many drank on duty? "Where is it?" he asked.

"On your desk, Herr Oberleutnant."

Continuing into his office, still distracted by the ominous symptoms he had just observed, Kruger thought, if they've lost the will to fight—if they mutiny now, at the brink of retreat—there will be no turning them back. *Responsibility from the bottom, authority from the top.* They might be responsible for their own disobedience, but he would be responsible for their defeat. Oster followed him into the darkened office. The message lying on his desk had been typed. He hesitated to pick up the page or to turn on the desk lamp. "Lemelsen sent the reply?" he asked.

"No, Herr Oberleutnant. Herr General Lemelsen passed your request on to Oberkommando Headquarters."

OKW was Kesselring's headquarters. "I see." With a feeling of dread, Kruger switched on the lamp. The reply had come from the Supreme Commander of all German forces in Italy. He circled the desk and lifted the paper. *To the Commander, Company Y, XIV Army Infantry, Group Field Headquarters, Montefalco. Most secret.*

Oster's black polished boots came to rest next to the desk.

Kruger found it difficult to focus his vision on the words: *Your request to General Lemelsen, Commander XIV Army, for permission to withdraw from your position in Montefalco has been transmitted to OKW, Group C, for consideration. Due to enemy attack on the Porretta Pass, your position in Montefalco is deemed essential to the security of troops north of Montefalco. Despite limited supplies and personnel you are hereby ordered to hold your position and prepare defenses.*

Kruger looked up from the page and saw on Oster's face the hint of a smile. He looked down again, quickly.

Regarding your report of the murder of German soldiers by Italian partisans. In obedience to the Führer's order of April 10 and my own directive of June 17, you are to take measures to prevent future attacks. Unless the partisans responsible for the murder of German soldiers are apprehended within eight hours of your receiving this order, you will carry out a military reprisal execution of ten Italian male civilians for every soldier shot. The fight against the partisans must be carried on with all means at our disposal and with the utmost severity. Heil Hitler. Field Marshal Albert Kesselring.

Kesselring. The Supreme Commander of all German forces in Italy. He remembered the June 17 order which had been issued to all commanding officers: *The fight against the partisans must be carried on with all means at our disposal.* Kesselring had even quoted himself. And on June 20 a second order had come, ordering all commanders to punish acts of partisan violence immediately and to send details of the countermeasures taken. Eight hours! There was no way word would reach the partisans to surrender in eight hours! And ten to one: Hitler himself had ordered that ratio.

A sudden deafening clap of thunder nearby brought Kruger back to himself. Oster moved close to the desk, scrutinizing him with quizzical impatience. "It is now one-fourteen, Lieutenant. If we are to carry out the order by, say, nine-thirty, we must get moving."

"Nine-thirty?"

"Eight hours, Herr Oberleutnant."

"A notice has to be posted in public, Sergeant!" Kruger said, appalled by the man's monstrous efficiency. "This is the middle of the bloody *night!*"

"The field marshal was explicit. He will expect a detailed report on your—on our performance."

Kruger looked away at the clock and saw the long hand click forward one minute. He reread the name again, Kesselring, and felt a huge leaden weight sink inside him. "The report is my responsibility, Oster, not yours."

"Of course, Lieutenant."

He thought again of Schreiber's warning about Gestapo infiltration into the Wehrmacht and reread the reprisal order, searching the words for a means to delay. The Americans would reach Montefalco within twenty-four to thirty hours if the rains abated.

Oster read his mind. He said, "If you intend to appeal the order, Herr Oberleutnant, any countermand will have to come from Berlin. Knowing the Führer's mind regarding partisans, I doubt there will be any alteration. You will only succeed in infuriating the field marshal."

Kesselring, Keitel, and the Führer. There were only two superiors above Kesselring, and neither man would alter Kesselring's order. "If I want your advice, Oster, I'll ask for it." Kruger walked slowly toward the far end of the room. Another clap of thunder struck, this time from the western side of the valley. Overnight, the rain would pass. At this point the only purpose of the reprisal was to prevent future partisan attacks, but with the Americans on their doorstep there was little danger now of attacks. It could be argued, there was no *military* purpose for a civilian reprisal. Kruger turned back to his desk. "Get Reiger in here. I want to send a radio message."

"To Berlin, Herr Oberleutnant?" Oster's eyebrows shot up in amazement.

"Never mind to whom!" Kruger exploded. *"Get Reiger!"*

Oster went out, closing the door behind him.

Kruger sat down. *Authority from the top down, responsibility from the bottom up:* the phrase resounded like a voice on a damaged phonograph record. He thought of Anna, watching a small yellow moth flutter in circles around the bulb of his desk lamp. Outside another clap of thunder exploded.

The moth threw itself against the bulb, trying frantically to reach the light.

A pain crept up the back of his neck and spread across his head. Ten to one. At least Kesselring had said ten male civilians and not civilians in general. Eight hours? Impossible. He tried to recall from the Geneva Convention International Rules of War the conditions laid down for a military reprisal: a distinction had been made between a reprisal for prevention of future partisan attacks and a reprisal for punishment of past attacks, but he could not remember the difference. Surely Kesselring had consulted the Rules of War!

The moth's body made frantic little tapping noises against the light bulb. The dumb little creature did not know that the light was only an illusion of warmth. It would go on beating itself against the bulb until it fell dead.

He shaded his eyes with his hands, trying to word in his mind the message he would send. Worded properly, it could justify his delay in carrying out the order.

At the pit of his stomach he felt a movement of nausea.

Ten to one.

Funny, he thought, if I execute men in Montefalco, I will not know but a handful by name.

The moth began hurling its body fiercely against the bulb.

Anna: he pictured himself alone with her in the Adele Ravine. Together, they seemed to belong to some other place and time.

The sound went on: rat tat tat. On an impulse, he grabbed the tiny creature in his fist and squeezed. Then realized he could have merely turned out the lamp to end its futile struggle.

There was a rap and the door opened. Oster, followed by Reiger carrying a notepad, came in. "You wish to send a message, Herr Oberleutnant?" asked Reiger. He glanced nervously at Oster.

Kruger dropped the moth on the floor beside his desk. "Send the following message 'Most Urgent' and 'Top Secret' to Field Marshal Kesselring at OKW headquarters." Oster turned toward the wall where the splattered black ink had dried. "Request clarification of your order for a military reprisal. Given our military situation with an enemy attack expected within hours, no future partisan attacks are possible. I respectfully submit that conditions no longer warrant a preventive military reprisal against civilians under the Geneva Rules of War. I await your reply before acting on your earlier order. Sign the order as usual in my name, code it, and send it at once."

Reiger gave a quick salute and withdrew.

"Perhaps, Herr Oberleutnant, while we are waiting for the field marshal's reply, I should compose a public notice stating the field marshal's demands."

"You may *compose* whatever you wish, Sergeant. But you will post nothing without my orders. You may go."

"Heil Hitler."

"Heil Hitler."

Kruger opened his desk drawer and rummaged for the office copy of the Geneva Rules of War. Schreiber had been the last to consult it. There was another rap on the door. "Come in!" he shouted, annoyed.

Oster reappeared. "There are two men outside, Herr Oberleutnant, waiting to see you."

"What men?"

"Privates Roepke and Hausner. They say you ordered them to report to you when they finished guard duty."

Kruger closed his desk drawer. *A good soldier, Roepke, is a man driven by belief and faith.* "Tell them to come in, Sergeant," he said, recalling the smell of mutiny and schnapps.

CHAPTER 6

I

"Anna!" Luisa called from the kitchen.

"Coming!" Anna left off sweeping Piero's mud tracks from the floor and hurried into the kitchen. After her father and Piero set off together before sunrise, they had busied themselves with housework. At breakfast her father had announced that he would take a basket of figs to the Riselli market in town and earn a few lire from their sale. Luisa had protested, but her father had dismissed her fears, saying the figs would be too ripe to sell if he waited another day.

"I want you and Livia to take the cauldron and empty it in the garden," her mother said at the sink. She looked anxious and her hair hung about her face in loose sweaty strands.

Anna propped her broom against the wall and joined Livia at the stove where the cauldron of steaming wash water sat. Livia gave her a fearful look.

"It took some scrubbing, but the stain came out," said *Nonna* Adelaida. She held Piero's dripping white shirt. She had spent over an hour washing the bloodstains from the shirt. Luisa had wanted to burn it, saying the Germans might discover the evidence, but Adelaida's thrift had prevailed.

"You'll need this." Livia handed Anna a dishcloth. They lifted the hot cast-iron pot from the stove and carried it through the back door into the garden. A billowing vapor of steam rose from the water in the cool morning air as they hurried toward the little gulley beside the tool shed where they always dumped the dirty wash water. Anna looked down into the pot, knowing that the rose tint in the soapy water was her brother's blood.

"Something's wrong," Livia said, "I can feel it. There's something in the air. It's too quiet."

"You're imagining things."

"Am I? Father Alessandro didn't ring the bell for the six o'clock Mass this morning. He never fails to ring the bell."

"How do you know he didn't? You can't always hear the bell from here."

"Mamma said the bell never rang."

They set the cauldron down and tilted it forward to let the murky water flow out. "That doesn't mean anything," Anna said. "Maybe Father Alessandro was sick this morning and canceled Mass." She tried to remember when Father Alessandro had failed to say morning Mass, but could not recall a single occasion.

"We'll know soon enough." Livia grabbed hold of the handle and they started back to the house.

"Nothing's going to happen!" Anna blurted out, unable to suffer Livia's accusing silence. "He's not that kind of man! Carlo isn't that kind of German! I know him!"

"For your sake, for the sake of the baby you're carrying, I hope you're right." She stopped abruptly and turned toward the field separating the house from the barn.

Anna drew up. "What's wrong?"

Livia had been the first to hear the sound coming from the direction of the field, the first to see the figure hurrying toward them across the muddy furrowed ground.

"Luisa!" Carmella Filipetti called hysterically to them across the field.

"Holy Mother of God," Livia said under her breath, watching the young wife of Duccio Filipetti, the local doctor, stumble toward them.

"Anna! Livia!" Carmella reached the edge of the field, jumped the last furrow, and began running toward them. "Help me! Oh God, help me!"

Livia let go of her side of the cauldron and it fell to the ground. Carmella's face was streaked with mud and tears, and her long black hair had fallen wildly about her face and shoulders. Absently, Anna let go of the cauldron handle, thinking of her father with his figs at the Risellis' market in town.

"They've arrested Duccio!" Carmella grabbed hold of Livia. "They've taken him away!"

"Who arrested him?" Anna asked, numbly. The question sounded idiotic.

"The Germans! Six of them! They took Duccio away!"

The back door to the house flew open with a bang. "Carmella!" Luisa cried. She hurried toward them, followed by *Nonna* Adelaida.

"Mamma!" Livia called. "The Germans! They arrested Dr. Filipetti!"

The SS, Anna thought, grasping desperately for one grim thread of salvation for Karl.

"He's innocent!" Carmella wailed. "He's done nothing!"

"Where did they take him, Carmella?" Luisa pressed.

"Into town—to German headquarters!" The young woman sank against Livia.

Anna wanted to tell Carmella that the doctor was safe, but the words locked in her throat. Listening to the women, she felt strangely detached. Livia leveled a horrified look of accusation at her.

"They put him into a truck," Carmella was saying, "with others! He was not alone! I saw Signore Cavallero and Marco Vianelli! It's a *rastrellamento,* I know it is!"

Luisa drew back. "Papa! Oh dear Mother of God!"

Nonna Adelaida broke in, "Carmella, how long ago did the Germans leave your farm?"

"Minutes ago! I came to warn you and Angelo!"

"He has gone to town," Luisa said. She looked frantically from Livia to Anna. *"Nonna* will stay with Carmella, we will go to town. Quick." She started off.

"It's no use, Livia!" Carmella shrieked.

Livia hurriedly freed herself, leaving the weeping woman in the arms of her grandmother. Anna said, "You're wrong! It's not possible!" She stood mesmerized, watching Livia and her mother run down the hill through the trees alongside the house.

"Anna!" Luisa shouted back to her.

It seemed as if she was rooted to the ground.

Livia called fiercely, "For God's sake, run!"

Anna obeyed. Ahead, Luisa slipped in the mud and cursed. The sound of a curse coming from her mother awakened Anna: she had never heard her mother take God's name in vain. "Karl," she said to herself.

Luisa and Livia broke through the trees and reached the pasture. The mist swirled around them. "Hurry!" Livia yelled back.

Anna let go of the dishcloth and broke through the trees into the pasture, following the paths her mother and sister had trampled through the slippery grass. The mist billowed in her passage.

Her mind seemed detached from her body. The grass smelled sweet in the cold damp air.

Suddenly, she felt a sharp pain in the lower part of her stomach. Breakfast, she thought. The cold *gnocchi* she had eaten. Then the other thing. The life she carried in her belly, half hers and half Karl's. "Oh, God, no—please." Her eyes brimmed. What if—and the thought of it amazed her—what if I should lose the thing: here, at this very minute, *now?* Livia had said that it happens all the time to women during the war. She had said those words yesterday to comfort her. Things like this don't happen, she thought, not even in *romanzi*. The pain struck again. Would it be a blessing or a punishment? Could God do both things at the same time, bless and punish?

She wanted to scream. Her mother would think her scream was for Papa, but it wasn't: it was for herself.

Luisa and Livia waited at the foot of the hill by the roadside. "Hurry," her mother said, starting off down the road, "there's no time to lose."

"I warned you, didn't I?" Livia exclaimed savagely.

Anna followed, keeping pace, and looked back up the road, hoping for a truck to give them a ride. There was nothing. They had once had an automobile before Mussolini had ruined her father. The war had taken everything.

Yesterday, at the Comellini *ammasso*, Karl had offered to provide them with transportation into the mountains. Could he have known even *then?*

In the distance, washed with bright yellow sunlight, Montefalco's rooftops came into view, clustered against the hillside. High on the hill above everything stood the bell tower of San Tommaso, serene and immutable.

The war had taken everything, perhaps even God.

II

"Nothing, Corporal?" Kruger asked, looking through the reception window at a group of women gathered in the piazza near the bank building.

"Nothing, Lieutenant," Reiger replied. "I've radioed Vergato. They've seen no partisan movement in the hills. Nothing."

Kruger thought, no one could have missed seeing the notice they posted just before dawn at all the major intersections and on all the major buildings of Montefalco. It had read in both German and Italian: *Attention! In response to the murder of German soldiers by Italian partisans we are forced to take military action. Hostages have been arrested from the civilian population of Montefalco in accordance with the Geneva Rules of War. Unless those responsible for the murders surrender themselves by 10:00 A.M., September 14, the hostages will be executed in public military reprisal. Karl Kruger, Commander, Montefalco.*

Kruger looked at the reception-room clock: 8:55. An hour and thirty-five minutes remained. Six hours had passed since they received Kesselring's reply for clarification of the reprisal order. The argument for rescinding the order had proved useless. Kesselring, more angered than before, had reordered the execution, and this time he had allowed only six hours for the partisans to respond. Hostages, ten for every single soldier shot, were to be arrested at once. Oster had wanted to make no distinction between men, women, and children, but relying on Kesselring's first message, he had ordered the arrest of adult males only.

The command truck carrying Oster and four armed soldiers turned into the piazza from the Via della Republica at the far southeast corner. "When Oster gets here, tell him to come to my office," Kruger said to Reiger.

"Yes, sir."

The women who had gathered in front of the post office where the notice had been posted scattered toward the Via Garibaldi as Oster's command car passed. As yet Anna had not been seen in town this morning, though he was certain she would know by now of his posted threat and the arrest of the local men.

Leaving the window, he returned to his office and reread the most recent message from Spedaletto. Last night's rainstorm had slowed, not stopped, the American advance, and the town was now under heavy fire. Kleisner would hold on, the message said, as long as possible, then pull back and regroup north of Montefalco, blowing up the bridges across the Reno in his wake. Having the larger share of men and equipment, Kleisner would depend upon Montefalco for rearguard support in his retreat. The implication was, of course, that his garrison in Montefalco would be sacrificed.

He had warned Anna yesterday to remove her family from the fighting zone. The Miceli farm, a little over a half kilometer to the north of Montefalco, would, by tomorrow, be under direct enemy fire.

"Anna," he whispered her name to himself, picturing her face to face with the threatening notice of execution: her shock and horror at seeing his name printed at the bottom.

Out in the reception room, the front door of headquarters burst open. Oster barked an order to one of his subordinates.

Kruger looked at the framed photo of Hitler on the wall above his desk. *I, Karl Gustav Kruger, swear by God this sacred oath, that I will render unconditional obedience to Adolf Hitler.* How could Anna possibly understand? He thought again of his parents in Munich for whom the Thousand Year Reich was nothing more than the dignity of a living wage, a comfortable home, and a Sunday walk in the Englischer Garten to watch the rowers boating on the Kleinhesseloher See.

How could he explain to Anna the overriding faith of a German soldier in his Fatherland? He had long ago sacrificed his personal life to the larger higher imperative. *Unconditional:* the word was absolute. And was faith really faith if you could reason your way to the end?

"Herr Oberleutnant Kruger," Oster announced at the door with a snappy click of his heels.

Kruger asked, with his back to the door, "I take it you've completed the arrests, Sergeant?"

"No, Lieutenant, we have not."

When he looked around, Kruger saw that Oster had fitted himself out in the full-dress uniform of a Wehrmacht sergeant, his Iron Cross First Class and all. The knee-high boots had been polished. He looked ready for a parade. "What do you mean?" asked Kruger, irked.

"Either we take women and males under eighteen from within the town, Lieutenant," Oster said, removing his gloves, "or you will have to alter your restriction of a half-kilometer radius. So far, we have found only fifty-five males between the ages of eighteen and forty-five."

At four-thirty that morning Kruger had signed the order of arrest in the presence of Oster and Reiger with the stipulation that the search for hostages extend no farther than a half-kilometer radius of the village. Anna's family farm, he had calculated, was just beyond a half kilometer from the center of town. "The half-kilometer limit will stand, Sergeant."

"We have a ten-to-one quota to fill, Lieutenant," Oster said, smoothing his gloves. "I've already ordered the arrest of five women."

"No! You will not take women!" Kruger shouted, his temper shortened with exhaustion. "You will restrict yourself to men between eighteen and forty-five!"

The color rose in Oster's face. "Perhaps, Lieutenant, you have specific reasons for limiting us to a half kilometer?"

"We are not free to take hostages indiscriminately."

Oster considered the statement, then said without venturing eye contact, "According to this map, Lieutenant"—he turned to the wall —"a half kilometer south of town would exclude the Adele Ravine, the Convent of Santa Cecilia, et cetera. A half kilometer north of town falls just short of the first farms on that side of town. Am I wrong?"

Kruger recalled Oster's relentless curiosity about his afternoon walks. For the moment, he felt utterly powerless. "So? What of it?"

"I merely ask because Field Marshal Kesselring will expect a full account of why we failed to carry out his orders to the letter. He specifically stated ten to one." Oster's smile was an open threat.

Trapped between anger and guilt, thinking of his own order regarding associations between soldiers and villagers, Kruger reached into the papers on his desk and rummaged for Kesselring's final order. He turned to conceal the flush rising in his face, and scanned the message until he came to the words: . . . *ten civilians for every soldier shot.* In the predawn collapse of his hopes when the reply came through, he had signed the order and turned over its execution entirely to Oster. He had said nothing about quotas. The word *shot* glared up at him from the page. He said, "Get Corporal Reiger, Sergeant, tell him to bring with him a copy of the Führer's September 1941 order regarding partisan military reprisals."

"There is no mention of *radii* in that order, Lieutenant."

Kruger exploded. "Do as I order, little man!"

Waiting for their return, Kruger rummaged in his desk for the copy he had kept of Kesselring's June 17 and June 20 orders. He found them in the strongbox at the rear of the drawer. He reread the orders and saw no distinction between soldiers shot and soldiers killed.

"You wish to see me, Herr Oberleutnant?" Reiger came in, followed by Oster.

"Close the door, Sergeant."

Reiger brought the typed copy of Hitler's reprisal order to the desk where Kruger sat. "You asked for this Führer order, Lieutenant?"

Kruger reread the order. Its meaning was quite clear. He said to Reiger, "You will take notes, Corporal, of what I'm going to say."

"Yes, sir." Reiger glanced questioningly at Oster and opened his notepad. He looked frightened.

Kruger directed his words to Oster, who stood with his hands behind his back and an expression of repressed fury in his face. "Following the reprisal execution, Sergeant Oster will send the following report to Field Marshal Kesselring at OKW headquarters. He will state in his report that the execution was carried out in exact obedience to the Führer's explicit orders regarding the military reprisal execution of civilians." Oster, he saw, had already divined his intention: the lids of his colorless gray eyes, magnified by the lenses of his glasses, widened. Kruger went on, "State the following facts, Corporal Reiger. On September 13, 1944, six Wehrmacht soldiers were shot by Italian partisans while carrying out a transport mission between the Italian towns of Vergato and Montefalco. On the morning of September 14, 1944, in obedience to orders from the Supreme Commander of German forces in Italy, in compliance with the directives of the Führer, ten Italian civilians of the town of Montefalco were executed for each soldier known to have died. The sixth soldier was wounded and survived. Consequently, following the Führer's command, we have executed fifty Italian male civilians. Sign the order in my name, Corporal, and send it after we have completed the execution."

"*Jawohl, Herr Oberleutnant.*" Reiger looked at him with relief and knowing complicity.

"The field marshal's order, Herr Oberleutnant," Oster said in a toneless voice, "states ten civilians for every soldier shot."

"*Shot,* I'm afraid, is an ambiguous word, Sergeant. As the field marshal is himself subject to the Führer's will, I am free to interpret the word according to Herr Hitler's express orders. We will therefore limit ourselves to *fifty* male civilians, is that clear, Sergeant?"

"Perfectly clear, Herr Oberleutnant."

Kruger fixed Oster with a point-blank unblinking stare. He smiled. "You will therefore *release* five of the men you've arrested, Sergeant. And you will cancel the order to arrest five women."

Oster murmured something under his breath.

"What did you say, Sergeant?"

"Nothing, Herr Oberleutnant. Nothing."

"You may both go."

For a moment, after the door closed behind them, Kruger sat staring at the big hand on the clock across the room, waiting for it to jump forward from 9:14 to 9:15. He could not now, of course, go back.

III

Anna kept pace with her mother and sister. Except for the German soldiers and Fascist *carabinieri* patrolling the Piazza Nazionale, the square was deserted. On the wall of the post office she saw another copy of the notice. By now she knew the wording of it by heart; it had been posted at every major street corner of the town. At the bottom, barely visible, was the signature, *Karl Kruger.* She looked away, still refusing to believe what she saw. In their long zigzag passage through the town looking for her father, the reports had been the same: German soldiers had come in trucks a little after dawn and arrested men between eighteen and forty-five. They had taken them away to the military compound on the southwest side of town. No one, though, could remember seeing Angelo Miceli in the covered trucks.

Her mother turned into the Via San Vitale. Hope was running out. They had visited all the obvious places. Livia said to Anna under her breath, "She's wasting her breath. Papa never plays cards with Leonardo Turatti in the morning, she knows that."

Luisa reached the big oak door fronting the Turatti house and rapped the big iron knocker. "Leonardo!" she yelled up, "Bianca! *C'è Luisa!*" The blue shutters on all three upper floors of the house were closed. Luisa rapped again.

"Mamma," Anna said, "it's no use. There's no one home."

"There must be! The Turattis never leave home! Bianca's an invalid! She can't leave!"

Anna took hold of her mother. "He's not here! There's only one place left to look!"

"Where?" Luisa swung around, hope flooding her hysterical face.

"We must go to the German camp."

Livia broke in. "We can't go there! It's forbidden! We'll be *shot* if we go there!"

"It's our only hope. I will ask to see Lieutenant Kruger." Livia read the meaning in her look. "Come, Mamma." She pulled her mother up the street.

They turned south on the Via Firenze. From here to the German camp was a ten-minute walk. If Karl himself was not in the camp, she would demand that a message be sent to him: a message, she would say, from Anna Miceli. She would even say she was a personal friend of the commandant.

Ahead, the sunlit Via Firenze was deserted, with the metal blinds drawn on its ground-floor shops.

Anna looked up into the cloudless autumn sky. She thought, Karl doesn't know Papa, has never seen him, I made sure of that. The sun, two inches from its autumn meridian, stared down at her with light but no warmth, like a big jaundiced eye. The stinging liquid in her eyes was not sweat, she realized, but tears. She tried as she ran to think of a prayer: *Our Father,* she said to herself, *Who art in heaven* . . . She remembered her confession yesterday and the damning hoard of mortal sins heaped on her soul. But I have made my choice, she thought. Karl before God—months ago. To pray now is monstrous—like stealing back to a rejected friend to ask favors. Like (and the idea horrified her) the woman in the *romanzo* who betrayed her lover and was, in turn, betrayed—who killed herself in the end.

Then if not a prayer, she thought in a sudden misery of panic, perhaps a bribe.

"For God's sake, Anna," Livia yelled at her, "try to keep up with us!"

She had fallen behind. Hurrying to catch up, she said silently, Dear God, if someone must die, then let it be me. Not Papa. Papa is innocent of everything.

Ahead, where the houses abutted the hillside, last night's downpour had flooded the street with gray ooze. Garbage from the houses had been dragged into the street with the mud. A huge black bird, a *corvo,* rose up from the garbage, flapping its immense wings.

"Santa Maria." Luisa crossed herself and grabbed hold of Livia's arm. Though Catholic, she kept room in her Tuscan imagination and memory for signs and omens.

Livia was the first to hear it: the low sound of an engine climbing the hill from the Rimaldi Ravine at the end of the street. "Mamma!" She drew her mother to a halt.

Anna said, knowing her question was meaningless, "What is it?"

No one bothered to answer.

The air ran out of Livia's mouth as she pointed to an armored German car rising over the crest of the hill. And behind the car, groaning from the pull, a huge transport with its cargo space draped with camouflage tarpaulin.

"Hail Mary, full of grace . . ." Luisa began reciting the prayer breathlessly.

Behind the armored staff car, three transports came into view with rifles pointing from their sides like the bristling quills of a *porcospino.*

Luisa's unfinished prayer gave way to a long agonized moan. She covered her face.

"No, Mamma—!" Anna cried. "Don't! Please don't!" She meant not the pain Luisa had let go of, but the hope she herself had lost. Until now, she had kept her scale of belief in Karl balanced. The sound of hope falling away in her mother's voice tipped the scale down: she had, she realized, beguiled herself all these months.

Four Germans sat in the approaching armored car. Through the dirty windshield Anna saw a familiar face riding in the passenger seat: one of Karl's officers. The lenses of his gold-framed spectacles caught the sunlight. The man's cold gray eyes widened with surprise. He stared at Anna with a look of recognition. A chill ran through her body. As the car passed he smiled to himself with a faint but unmistakable hint of triumph.

She thought of San Tommaso, the Adele Ravine, Karl, and herself —the secrets they had kept—and wondered at the appalling limits of Karl's betrayal.

The first transport passed by.

"Angelo!" her mother cried, reaching out.

Anna pulled her back against the wall. In the open backside under the tarpaulin mute faces stared out at them. She knew them all: Gianni Bosco, their local tailor; Matteo Bruzzno, the blacksmith; Emilio Cassla, the *contadino.*

"*Mostri!*" Livia flattened herself against the wall, terrified.

The last of Anna's hope and belief fell away, and rising in their place she saw, for the first time, despair.

The second transport passed by. The soldiers looked down at them with utter indifference.

Anna held her mother fast against the wall. She recognized more hopeless faces peering out. Carmella's husband, Dr. Filipetti. Behind him, far back in the truck (the shock struck her like a stone) the familiar carefully trimmed full black moustache.

"Angelo!" her mother shrieked and lunged forward.

Anna pulled her back out of the path of the third transport.

"*Mal faccia tua!*" Livia screamed.

The third and last transport lumbered by with the faces of friends huddled together in the darkness.

Standing in the center of the street, Luisa began to weep uncontrollably, holding onto both daughters.

"He was with them!" Livia exclaimed. "She saw him!" There was savage accusation in her voice and eyes.

Numbly, Anna said, "They're taking him to the Piazza Nazionale. I will go to Kruger. I will stop him."

Livia embraced her mother protectively. "We'll go to the piazza, Mamma, to the Municipio. Anna will talk to Kruger. She's the only one now who can save Papa."

CHAPTER 7

I

Sergeant Haldner began loading his pistol, spinning the barrel with each bullet. Kruger reached the end of the reception room and turned back, pacing. Outside, a motorcade of trucks rumbled into the piazza with their motors sputtering from ersatz wartime petrol.

Twenty-one minutes left, Kruger thought, and looked out again at the crowd of women ranked along the north and south sides of the square behind the cordon of soldiers. "How many men have you detailed to the square, Haldner?" he asked.

Haldner, in command of the troops on guard duty around the town, said, "Twenty-two, Lieutenant. The rest are posted on the south and north ends of town. Reiger's in touch with those men by radio. If there's any partisan response, they'll let him know." He spun the barrel of his gun and chuckled.

Kruger went on pacing. It would have taken the partisans hours to learn of the notice of hostages and get word down from the mountains, one way or the other. Kesselring's six hours was absurd. They needed the original eight in the first order.

Reiger came in from the radio room. "Lieutenant Kruger!" he called.

"They've replied?"

"No, sir. Kleisner has just radioed a bombing raid over the valley around Spedaletto. They've had heavy casualties."

"Kleisner's a fool! He should have pulled out hours ago!"

Haldner looked at him with quizzical disapproval.

Kruger began pacing again. "What are we using for the execution?"

"Two machine guns. Weiss is keeping them out of sight in a truck parked off the square until Oster gets everything arranged. He thought it better that way."

Kruger nodded and turned away, ashamed of himself. He had delegated preparations for the execution to Oster, who had in turn delegated his subordinates with the macabre tasks of equipment, personnel, and transport. *Authority from the top down, responsibility from the bottom up.* The Führer principle had little comfort, though, in these last six hours. In the end, the actual order of execution would be his, not Oster's, to give.

Somewhere out in the square a woman cried out, "Paulo!" The cry unleashed a wail in the crowd.

Kruger went to the window. In the last fifteen minutes the women of Montefalco had streamed into the Piazza Nazionale. There were now some hundred or so packed against the walls of the Fascist headquarters and the Banco Commerciale, held back by armed soldiers posted at close intervals. The three covered transports holding the hostages were drawn up near the post office in the northeast corner facing the Via Garibaldi, guarded by armed soldiers. Oster, accompanied by Weiss, had just left the transports and was walking briskly toward the Municipio, imperiously scanning the terrified crowd of women on both sides of the piazza. Kruger searched the crowd of dark-haired, dark-eyed faces for Anna's. She wasn't there.

He left the window as Oster and Weiss reached the steps leading to the Municipio and began counting the seconds, wondering if God would do what he himself could not, wishing he still believed in the absurdity of miracles as he had once believed.

Oster left the door for Weiss to close behind him. He lifted his arm like an arrow. *"Heil Hitler."* The spirit of power was upon him.

"Alles in Ordnung?" Kruger asked, making no effort to hide his contempt for the civil servant turned executioner.

"Alles in Ordnung." Said in his best Berlinese, the reply was intended as a challenge. "You will, of course, as senior officer, represent the Reich, Herr Oberleutnant."

Kruger turned away and adjusted the ribbon of his Iron Cross First Class on the buttonhole of his tunic.

"It's time, Lieutenant," said Oster.

Kruger thought back to that day in September 1932 when he sat by his parents' radio listening to Adolf Wagner, the gauleiter of Bavaria, address the crowd who had assembled to celebrate Germany's landslide vote granting Hitler absolute power: *The German form of life is definitely determined for the next thousand years. The Age of Nerves of the nineteenth century has found its close with us! There will be no other revolution in Germany for the next one thousand years!*

He had taken pains to memorize the gauleiter's words.

II

"Let me pass." Anna pushed her way through the crowd at the corner of the Via Firenze. The women stood four-deep along this side of the square, held back by armed German soldiers. "Let me through! Please!" She squeezed between Signora Spisani, the young wife of Montefalco's only attorney, and Signora Auriti, the wife of a local *contadino*. Their faces were turned toward the post office, where the Germans had started unloading the hostages.

Anna scanned the square, searching among the soldiers for Kruger. He had not appeared. To reach Karl she would have to pass through the soldiers ranged along the facade of the Municipio. "Let me through!" she exclaimed to three women huddled over Signora Vianelli, who had sunk to the pavement sobbing. Anna caught sight of her father in front of the post office, lowering himself slowly from the rear of a truck. He raised one hand to shield his face from the glaring sunlight and looked around at the soldiers and crowd with bewildered shock. A soldier at the rear of the truck forcibly pulled him to the pavement. As his feet struck the cobblestones, he stumbled forward and fell against another man, Luigi Tattoni, who caught and held him.

"Papa!" Anna cried out. Startled, her father turned to search for her in the crowd. "No!" She lunged through the women toward the open square. "Papa!"

"Anna!" Behind her, around her, hands came out and pulled her back into the crowd. "You cannot help!" The voices of the women holding her rose in a shrill babble of protests. "They will kill us all!"

High up in the *campanile* over the Municipio, the big hand of the clock touched the six. It was 10:30, exactly. A small open truck appeared from the Via Santa Lucia, turned into the square, and started slowly toward the post office. It carried six German soldiers and, Anna saw to her horror, two machine guns poised on tripods. A murmur rolled through the piazza. The line of soldiers extended to the corner of the Municipio building, preventing the crowd from reaching Karl's German headquarters. Anna started forward again, squeezing between the closely packed bodies. "Please let me through!" She thrust her arms between two women and found herself suddenly in the open space between the crowd and the line of German soldiers.

A wave of frightened protests swept through the crowd behind her.

Defiantly, Anna stepped forward. The soldiers standing between her and the Municipio raised their rifles and aimed point-blank at her breast. Under their helmets, behind the stoical menacing sun-burned Teutonic faces, she saw fear ignite in their eyes. "Halt!" the young soldier directly in front of her commanded.

Anna said in a clear resolute voice, "I want to see the commandant!" By the vacant look in their faces she realized they did not understand Italian.

"*Zurück!*" The young soldier thrust his rifle at her. "*Zurück! Oder ich schiesse!*" His finger played nervously on the trigger.

"*Ich wollen den Kommandant—*" She tried to remember the words in German for *speak* and *see*.

"*Zurück!*" The German waved his rifle at her. "*Zurück!*"

"Anna! Come back!" One of the women grabbed hold of her arm and pulled her backward.

"I must get to Kruger!" she yelled. "I must talk to Kruger!" She fought savagely to free her arms, but the women held firm.

"You don't understand!" Her words were drowned by the shrill cacophony of a dozen female voices. The crowd closed around her. "I can stop him! You don't understand!" She left off as the Municipio door swung open. Karl stepped out onto the entranceway between the colonnades and two soldiers. He let his gaze sweep slowly over the piazza. At once, a hush came over the crowd. As he started down the steps, the metal insignias on his gray officer's uniform glinted in the sunlight like bits of ice. She held her breath, raised her hand in a silent gesture of appeal, and watched him move toward the soldiers unloading two machine guns from the truck. He looked neither to the left nor to the right. The stiff aloof carriage of his body, the glint of sunlight from his black polished boots, and the upward tilt of his chin sent a chill through her body. "Karl—" she muttered, swallowing the word in a dry throat. Her father had been herded with the other hostages (dozens, it seemed) against the post-office wall. He raised his hands to appeal to the Germans, then slumped forward helplessly.

"Anna!" Her mother's desperate voice called from behind. With Livia, she pushed through the crowd and reached Anna. "Papa! Where is he?"

Anna gestured toward the post office. "There's nothing to be done, Mamma."

Kruger reached the soldiers at the truck and indicated where they should place the guns. "Carlo," she whispered, astonished by the equanimity of his hand.

Beyond, clustered in the motley clothes they had been arrested in, the men of Montefalco—she knew them all, except for one— shuffled toward the wall of the post office: her father, Matteo Fracci, Leonardo Turatti, and behind Leonardo—

The sight of Piero's face stopped her heart. "Oh God," she said.

"Piero!" her mother screamed with simultaneous recognition.

Unshaven, exhausted, Piero looked around to find his mother in the crowd.

Before Anna, the vision of everything—the square, Karl, her father and brother—went suddenly flat like a cheap photograph. She felt her mother's hands clutch at her body, frantically. She belonged, it seemed, to a strangely separate world.

Like something rolling up from under the earth, a murmur undulated across the square.

"Oh, Carlo," she said, then saw, scrawled across her mother's face, the twisted wreckage of a question.

III

The soldiers were having trouble stationing the tripod legs of the gun mountings on the uneven cobblestones. Kruger stared at the short midday shadow of his body on the cobblestones, unable to look at the crowd, knowing that if he looked he would certainly find Anna among the women.

"Move! Get back!" Oster barked, striding back and forth in front of the post office, directing the hostages toward the wall of the building. "*Schnell!* Back! Move!" His commands were echoed by the soldiers assisting him. The sound of the female voices around the square, punctuated by female sobs, sickened Kruger. The murmur suddenly took on an ugly, menacing sound which, he knew, was the collective voice of accusation and frustrated rage. He thought he heard Anna's voice over the murmur from the southwest side of the piazza, behind him.

Like a contagious disease, the wail spread across the piazza and mingled with the frantic garble of voices trying to restrain and comfort. Pressed back against the white wall of the post office, the hostages stared helplessly at their women and at the soldiers mounting the machine guns. On their fifty faces Kruger saw a jigsaw of feelings: terror, hopelessness, resignation, incredulousness, confusion, and in two or three a defiant challenge. As his gaze swept over the faces, he saw some he knew by name: Bosco, the tailor; Vaninni, a *contadino.* He knew none of them well. He could safely call them all strangers. In retrospect he was grateful for the distance he had kept from the people of Montefalco. The men facing him were as he had ordered: between the ages of eighteen and forty-five, the age of partisans. Some were probably partisans, most only innocent villagers. *The German form of life is definitely determined for the next thousand years!* Gauleiter Wagner's voice had sounded triumphant over the loudspeaker in the Luitpold Hall that afternoon. *The Age of Nerves of the nineteenth century has found its close with us!* Could this—fifty pathetic Italian villagers—be what he had meant?

The fifteen soldiers guarding the hostages raised their rifles threateningly. Some of the hostages, the older ones, held onto the men next to them. One frightened man began to weep uncontrollably, like a small boy. Oster, Weiss, and Haldner came toward him across the square. The time had come. He looked again at his watch: 10:32. He was sure that more than four minutes had passed since he had arrived. A bizarre thought came to him: his watch, the clock in the *campanile,* all the clocks in the world, had run down—time for the entire Thousand Year German Reich had stopped.

Nearby, a soldier pulled a long machine-gun bullet belt from a wooden box and the shiny metal bullets rattled against the cobblestones like strands of falling glass beads. The soldiers chuckled as he fixed the belt in the machine gun.

Kruger turned his gaze to the flags hanging from their masts above the post-office door: the bright flag of Mussolini's new Republic on the left, and the flag of the National Socialist Reich on the right. Except for the approaching sound of the officers' boots, the piazza was now silent. He had insisted with Oster that a short speech of explanation was necessary. He lowered his eyes, trying to recall the words of his short speech.

Oster cleared his throat. "Herr Oberleutnant, we are ready." The polite formality of the statement, as if announcing the commencement of a Wehrmacht military banquet, was like an icy hand on Kruger's neck. A serene expression of triumph rested on the adjutant's face. "If you care to speak to these people," Oster said with a condescending gesture of the hand, "now, I believe, is the time."

People of Montefalco: the words of his speech came back.

If nothing else, Kruger thought, if I cannot relieve myself of this inevitable duty, I can at least postpone it. As he opened his mouth to speak, the rope of silence unraveled and snapped. From the southwest corner of the square a woman cried out: a wordless cry that ricocheted across the square. Instantly, triggered by the cry, a roar went up and rolled across the piazza like a brush fire, igniting again along the Fascist headquarters. Behind the cordon of soldiers at the post office, the prisoners began to move hopefully.

"Carlo!" Someone, he was sure, shouted his name over the shrill voices of the women.

As Oster raised his arm to give an order to the soldiers lining the square, Kruger realized that his choice had been made long before this moment—before he came to Italy, before Montefalco, before he ever met and fell in love with Anna Miceli—had, in fact, been made in Germany when he stood that afternoon in Munich's open stadium and heard Hitler offer hope to millions of disillusioned Germans.

The soldiers raised their rifles toward the crowd, waiting for Oster's order to fire. A tense hush once again fell over the crowd.

Kruger realized that if he did not act, and act soon, the women would reach their breaking point, and there would be a massacre instead of a military reprisal. Weighed on the scale of the Third Reich, against the good of his country and his duty as a soldier, his own personal beliefs had never, he realized, since that afternoon in 1933, mattered. He turned to Oster. "I have nothing to say." Even those few words were difficult to pronounce in a dry mouth. "Proceed."

IV

The officer Karl had spoken to barked an order to the soldiers with the machine guns. He was the same officer, Anna realized, who had stared at her so knowingly in the Via Firenze.

Piero had worked his way through the cramped bodies and now stood next to their father, just behind Marco Vianelli, Pietro Faggioni, and Duccio Morera. Her father was shorter than the other men; only his head showed above their shoulders. His eyes looked enormous. She had never seen terror in her father's face. Piero said something and kissed him on the forehead. Anna gripped her mother, who had seen what Piero had done and had shuddered. Piero, a head taller than those around him, stared at Karl with a defiant look of pride and scorn. *We will crush them like Sangiovese grapes.* The son of a failed shopkeeper, her brother had dreamed of rising above his Miceli mediocrity on the shoulders of a glorious Italian victory. And now, if not that, at least with dignity, he was trying to claim his pride in one brief moment of heroic martyrdom. From among the living, though, his defiance and pride looked like nothing more than a gesture in a meaningless dumb show. Anna wanted suddenly to curse him for his wasted investment in the war.

In the dead silence of the piazza there was only the clack of the bullet belts slapping the pavement. For one moment Anna wondered if they were all not watching some kind of theatrical performance like the carnival shows at Eastertime. Except for the soldiers with the jammed machine gun, no one in the piazza moved.

Anna felt her mother's body sink down beside her. With Livia's help, they drew her up. Her mother's gaze, she saw, was fixed vacantly on the woman in front of them. Her head rocked back and forth on her shoulders like the head of a doll. From her open mouth a trickle of saliva ran down the side of her jaw. "Mamma," Anna murmured, trying to comfort, cursing Karl at the same time for the cruelty of his delay.

"*Schnell!*" the officer pacing between Karl and the soldiers shrieked. The echo of the German word sounded hideous. Karl hooked his thumbs into his holster belt and looked down at the ground. He had always done that when he felt embarrassed. Anna gazed at him, searching for a single word to embrace the whole of her feelings at that moment, but there was none.

Then she saw the officer nod. Karl returned the nod. The gesture seemed too small for what he, her lover, had chosen to do: murder her father and her brother.

"*Anlegen!*" the officer shouted. The soldiers at the guns held themselves motionless, waiting. Behind Pietro Faggioni, her father made the sign of the cross. The thought of God's mercy, at that moment, appalled Anna. Piero drew her father's head against his chest and covered his face with his hand. Their movements, the sight of the two of them locked together in this final pathetic embrace, flooded her with sudden unspeakable grief.

"*Fertig!*" This time the officer's voice was an octave higher, a savage scream of fanatical hatred. Awakened by the shout, her mother rose up and gripped both Livia and Anna by the arm. Piero buried his father's face against his shoulder and stared fixedly at his executioners. Around them, like people posed for a snapshot, the men stood frozen.

"*Feuer!*" the voice shrieked.

The sound that filled the piazza was like a rattling stone slide down the face of Monte di Granaglione. The men in front were the first to move: a body hurtled backward against the others, an arm was thrown out and up, another body twirled around like a top, still another doubled over like a limp doll—it was happening, she knew, in the space of a short moment, but it seemed like an eternity. Brilliant vermilion patches spread across the shirts and trousers of the men as they spun and fell to the pavement. The guns swung back and forth, spitting short yellow tongues of fire. The mechanical racket was deafening.

As the men in front fell, those behind were caught up in the spray and were, in turn, hurtled backward. Anna saw Piero let go of her father, and his head, thrown back by the impact, twisted impossibly on his shoulders. His mouth had the look of a wide rip as his teeth caught the sunlight. Then his arms seemed to leave his body and fly backward, as if he had been caught in a violent wind. His white shirt was peppered, then suddenly drenched, with blood. He fell backward, spinning, against her father, who at that moment turned his face toward the machine guns and, before the surprise could form in his face, doubled over, striking his stomach with both hands. The bullets went on as she watched the last men along the wall dance crazily like puppets in a traveling carnival, then fall to the pavement.

The silence that followed was itself deafening. A faint vapor of smoke hung motionless in the air. In the center of the square, like a statue carved from granite, Karl stood erect.

A single pigeon glided to rest on the terra-cotta roof of the post office. Below, from the mass of torn bodies, there was a soft sound, then a faint movement. An arm moved. A groan filled the space of the piazza. Then another. Slowly, a dark head moved. Anna saw her father's face rise up, then fall down. Nausea flooded her stomach. She thought of the monstrous life she carried and, for one moment, imagined that it would come out if she now vomited.

Karl started toward the men on the pavement. The officer who had given the orders joined him. They moved side by side, walking stiffly like soldiers in a drill exercise. A few paces from the dead, Karl stopped, said something to the officer, then reached to his belt and unsnapped the flap on his holster.

V

"It is not, as you see, the most efficient method," Oster muttered. "Some insist on special treatment. Two, it looks like. One near the wall." He pointed. "And one behind the fat one in the blue trousers."

Kruger raised his holster flap but said nothing. The man next to the wall clutched his belly and groaned like an animal. The other man, a middle-aged *contadino* with a carefully trimmed black moustache, tried to lift his head but the effort was useless.

As if awakening from sleep, the crowd moved.

"I would do it myself, Herr Oberleutnant," Oster said, "but duty requires the commanding officer—"

"I know what duty requires, Sergeant." Kruger cut him short, drawing the pistol from the holster.

"Otherwise, the soldiers will think you are a coward," Oster added venomously.

Kruger forced himself to walk around the perimeter of the bodies toward the man clutching his belly. I will do my duty quickly, he thought, I will use one bullet for each of the two men. I will end their pain, finish what I have started. Then it will be over. The dead do not suffer afterward. Only the living.

The crowd had again stopped moving: the hush was deafening. A hundred pairs of eyes watched and recorded. Anna, too, watched and recorded.

Kruger carefully stepped into the small space between two bodies. Blood was everywhere. His boot made a print on the pavement where he placed it in the sticky ooze between an arm and a twisted leg. A curious heat rose up from the motionless flesh around him. Some of the faces stared at him with blank but comprehending looks of surprise. Those whose eyes were open seemed to know something beyond human imagining, as if at the moment of death they had been granted the gift of seeing, as no living person could see, into the vast heart of this human darkness.

He reached the man lying against the wall and looked down into his dark Italian eyes, recognizing the face: the man who had been arrested yesterday, the man who had said he did not want to die for the Duce. Kruger realized that he himself had passed the death sentence by stating the man might be a partisan.

He released the safety catch and pointed the barrel at the man's face. The impulse was to fire at once and obliterate the look of recognition in the man's eyes, but something prevented him: an expression forming in the dark handsome young face. Not the expression he had expected, a look of judgment and accusation, but something else, something he could not at once identify. The man made a soft broken sound that was both a plea and a cry of pain. Blood spilled from his mouth and ran down his chin. He looked up, waiting.

"Go to God, my friend," Kruger whispered and then fired point-blank into the man's forehead. The head jerked once and then was still. The bullet had made a clean red hole in the smooth olive skin. As the report echoed across the square, there was the sudden flutter of wings from the startled doves on the roof of the post office. Under the man's head the blood flowed out in a widening vermilion pool. The eyes were frozen in the expression of the man's last living thought: a look Kruger now deciphered as sorrow. And the sorrow, he could tell, was not sorrow for the victim but for the executioner. Carefully, trying not to desecrate the twisted human wreckage with his boots, he began making his way toward the other dying man.

VI

As Karl stepped between the bodies his movements were like those of a man crossing a mountain *torrente* on small stepping-stones: cautious and self-absorbed. His pistol glinted in the sunlight.

"Angelo." Her mother's head rolled forward and then fell backward like that of a person fighting sleep. It seemed an eternity had passed since the machine guns had stopped.

Karl stepped over the bodies of Gianni Cavallero and Marco Vianelli. Though Anna had known both men all her life, they looked different in death, like grotesque wax caricatures of themselves.

Livia covered her mother's face. Luisa resisted, then gave in, and let Livia draw her head into the cradle of her neck.

As Karl reached her father, the sound of the breathing all around them stopped altogether. This time, her father's entire profile rose up, and beneath the black moustache his mouth fell open, gaping with terror at the man above him. Karl's arm swung out from his body, aiming the pistol. From all around, hands came out from the crowd to touch and hold Anna, Livia, and their mother in silent gestures of commiseration.

Anna felt a sudden excruciating spasm, like the stab of a knife, pass through her from behind. *Carlo:* as the pain went through her body, his name went through her mind, dragging with it in its wake all the air from her lungs.

For one instant, Karl stared down at her father and her father stared up at her lover—both with staggering ignorance.

Then he did it again: pulled the trigger. Her father's head vanished behind her brother's shoulder. The report of the pistol, a quick, efficient snapping sound, ran back and forth between the buildings.

The spasm in Anna's belly spiraled upward, a spinning whirligig knife that shredded everything in its passage. In the vacuum of silence she bent forward and made a low, unbroken keening sound, trying futilely to empty herself of the pain.

CHAPTER 8

I

The bulb in his desk lamp flickered again. *"Scheisse."* Kruger lay his pen on the topographic map spread out on his desk and wriggled the lamp's gooosenecked head. The bulb flickered again, then dimmed to a faint pulsing glow. Damn! he thought. Hours of work to do, and now a bloody burned-out bulb!

"Oster!" he shouted.

There was no response from the outer office.

He got up and went to the door. Damn you, Oster, he thought.

The reception room was deserted. Then he remembered. He had detailed Oster, Weiss, and Haldner to secure the town and begin distribution of supplies and munitions for the anticipated Allied attack at dawn. He and Reiger were the only ones left at headquarters. Faint sounds of Reiger's wireless came from the rear of the building.

He wondered where Oster kept the light bulbs. Never mind. He'd take the bulb from Oster's lamp. He went to the desk and turned on the lamp to check the bulb. Like his own, it flickered and then dimmed to a pulsing glow. He stepped back, stunned.

It was not the bulbs but the generators.

"Damn!" he cursed aloud, thinking of the long night of preparations ahead of them for the attack at dawn. The generators were either breaking down or running out of fuel. Without electricity, the town would be thrown back into the Middle Ages! An indefensible pile of stones! The generators were Weiss' responsibility. If Kleisner and his unit passed through at midnight, the Americans would reach Montefalco by dawn, even if Kleisner blew up the bridges between in his wake. Without electricity, they would never organize their defenses in time.

Kruger left the lamp burning, returned to his office, and closed the door. I must get ahold of myself, he thought, realizing his nerves were at the breaking point. He had been walking a tightrope now for the last ten hours, since he left the square after the execution. He went to his desk, turned off the lamp, and threw back the blackout curtain over the window. Reflected from the stucco wall of the opposite building were the lights from the distant artillery fire to the south, the last of Kleisner's defense of Spedaletto. Shortly after six, Kleisner had radioed to say that Lemelsen had ordered him to pull back. He would pass through Montefalco sometime before midnight.

Kruger's gaze rested on the street sign set in the wall of the opposite building at the corner of the Via Santa Lucia. Between the execution and dusk someone had splashed paint over the last letters of the street sign Piazza Nazionale. In mocking defiance it now read, Piazza Nazi.

The gesture should have outraged him, but he felt only shame. He closed his eyes, leaned his head against the glass pane, and let the thought he had kept at bay all these hours flood his mind: she was there. Anna was there. She saw me give the order to execute fifty innocent men, her friends. Between now and the battle for Montefalco, there will be no chance to see her, to explain, to ask forgiveness.

Explain?

He lifted his forehead from the glass and let the thought he had kept at bay unwind to its inevitable conclusion: *authority from the top down, responsibility from the bottom up.* To explain would mean taking her back to his own childhood Germany, to Munich between the wars. She had known the man, but had never seen the boy. Only God had seen both. Perhaps only God Himself could see the human light at the far end of this human darkness.

"Lieutenant Kruger?" Reiger's voice came from the darkness behind him.

Kruger opened his eyes and swung around, startled. The corporal stood just inside the door, framed in a wedge of faint light from the reception room, holding a sheet of paper. "Close the door, Corporal." He pointed. "The light."

Reiger closed the door, leaving them momentarily in darkness. Kruger dropped the blackout curtain over the window and felt his way to the lamp on his desk. When he turned it on, Reiger was halfway across the office. "This came over the radio, sir," he said, stopping shy of the desk.

"Kleisner again?"

"No, sir."

Kruger saw dismay in the pale blue eyes. "Kesselring?"

"No, sir. Major Grunig, the field marshal's chief of staff." Reiger's youthful face colored with apology.

Kruger sat down. "Give it to me, Corporal."

Reiger approached and handed the paper.

The light was too dim to read the handwritten script. "I'm afraid you'll have to tell me yourself, Corporal. Our generators have broken down."

"The general, sir—the general orders us to join Kleisner and pull back to a defensible position north of Vergato. He says we are to take what supplies we can move by available transport and destroy the rest." Reiger read the look in his face. "I'm sorry, sir. I mean, the reprisal and all." He made a small futile gesture.

"Go on, Corporal."

"We are to destroy the bridge over the Reno and burn all the official public buildings here. We will join the Panzer XVI and hold the Reno Valley in the north."

"Retreat?"

"Yes, sir."

Kruger dropped back in his chair and in the wake of his amazement giggled idiotically. "He's crazy!" He laughed again. "A reprisal —then retreat? Kill fifty civilians to show the partisans we mean business, then *retreat?*" He sat forward. "For God's sake, man, we're not—!" He stopped, hearing mutiny in his words, wondering in the same breath if the word he had started to say, *monsters,* was not, in fact, an apt description. "No mention of the reprisal?" he asked.

"No, sir."

"I see." He saw, in retrospect, that Kesselring's order had been for punishment and revenge.

Reiger seemed to read the expression in his face. "I'm sorry, sir."

Kruger said, "Revenge is the last act of a coward before defeat, Corporal."

"Yes, sir." He cleared his throat. "Then what will you do now?"

"What will I do?"

"Yes, sir. I mean, about the order."

"You mean, what will *we* do. There's no single *I* in the German Army, Corporal. We will do what we've been ordered to do. I will do what Kesselring orders, you will do what I order, and so on down the line—to the last private in the lowest outfit in the army. Inform Sergeant Oster of the order to retreat. Tell him I said to begin preparations at once. We will surrender Montefalco to the Americans and join Kleisner. It's just as well, too. We've outstayed our welcome in Montefalco."

"I take it, sir, you don't want to read the particulars of the order?"

"Later. Give the paper to Oster. Tell him I said to follow Kesselring's—Grunig's—orders." He thought, the machinery of this war will move with or without me.

"Yes, sir."

"You may go, Corporal."

When the door closed, Kruger turned out the light, rose, and drew back the blackout curtain.

Anna: the name struck his mind like a dart. For an instant he started to think of ways to reach her before the time came to depart, then saw the absurdity of his hope.

Across the street, on the second floor of the opposite building, a cat crept gingerly along the ledge of a window. It paused, looked across the street, and seemed to observe him watching.

Among living men, he was surely one of the greatest of fools.

In the darkness two small eyes caught the red inflection of the Spedaletto artillery fire and glowed for a moment like two small embers—malevolent and knowing.

II

"Anna," Livia said at the open bedroom door, "you must come down. Mamma wants you there." From the hallway came the murmur of voices in the downstairs part of the house. Livia's kerosene lamp cast a soft yellow light across the bed where Anna sat with her back to the door.

"Who is there?" Anna asked.

"Carmella Filipetti, Angela Guardini, the Venanzi brothers, the Cimonis and their children, Mamma, *Nonna* Adelaida, and myself."

"Papa and Piero?"

"Yes. Signore Cimoni and the Venanzi brothers brought Papa and Piero in a little while ago. Piero looks very handsome in his black suit. Papa, too. It isn't as bad as you thought it would be. They both look very peaceful."

"Mamma shouldn't have to see them. They should have closed the coffins."

"Mamma wants to see. It's better this way."

After a moment, Anna asked anxiously, "The coffins—what did they find for coffins?"

"The Venanzis made them. They're simple, but they're sturdy. Carlo—" She caught herself before the name was out. "Signore Venanzi," she went on, "is a good carpenter." She came forward into the room. "Anna! You cannot stay here in your room!"

"Father Alessandro hasn't come. We can't begin without Father Alessandro."

"He will come. He has other houses to visit first."

"Blow out the light," Anna said. Through the window she saw the pulsing glow of the American and German guns beyond the distant mountains. "They'll be here tomorrow," she said absently, "or if not tomorrow, the day after."

"Anna!" Livia blew out her lamp, then lowered her voice so she could not be heard downstairs. "You have been sitting here in the dark for the last two hours. People are beginning to ask questions. Mamma says if you don't come down, she will send Carmella up to talk to you."

It was entirely dark now in the room.

She had come to her room before sundown and had sat on the bed, trying to comprehend what had happened since that morning. Nothing seemed real to her. It was as though she had dreamed the entire day: these things did not happen in the real world, she had never even read such things in her *romanzi*. For the last two hours (she had thought twenty had passed) her only feeling had been a kind of dull throbbing ache which she could not call pain, for it had no sharp center. Grief, loss, horror, rage—those feelings had flowed up at the thought of her father and her brother; but then came Carlo's face, always his face kept coming back to her, and then she would feel a different kind of loss which pulled at her body as well as her heart, a profound confusion, a disbelief that left her with a feeling of vertigo (like standing on the edge of the cliff above the Adele Ravine), self-reproach, and, what most astonished her, an insane urge to shriek with laughter when the thought came to her that she had now fallen into a well of hatred as deep as the well of love she had once drunk from. "Only two hours?" she asked.

"Yes. Two hours." Livia came toward her around the bed.

They and the other women had gathered up the bodies in the square after the Germans had left. The bodies of her father and brother were washed and dressed in their best clothes. Both were given white shirts and black ties. Their skin had been bluish gray in the hot afternoon sunlight. The blood on their bodies, especially the blood on her father's forehead, had dried to a deep reddish brown. Before the women began their work, they had led Luisa to her room, leaving Livia to watch over her while they performed their duties with the dead. It had been a strange mortuary, the garden. And the women were strange morticians. She remembered it now only as something she had dreamed.

"If you do not come down now and pray with the family, Mamma will send Don Alessandro to talk with you," Livia said.

"Let him come. It will be months before he will see anything." At
the far end of the bed, Livia gaped at her, shocked. "It was a good
five months before Cousin Marcella's baby showed," Anna went on,
letting the sharp edge of her confusion rise to the surface in the form
of sarcastic anger. "If the Germans leave us soon enough, and the
Americans come, maybe we can pretend it's an American's baby.
That would suit everyone much better, don't you think?"

"*Anna.*"

"By then, the Americans will also have come and gone. Piero said
that Italy was full of American babies. People won't mind so much
if it's an American's baby, the Americans are our liberators."

"What are you saying?"

"I'm saying there are facts to face."

"You don't know for sure. You're talking nonsense."

"I do know. *He* doesn't know yet, but I do." She sat forward and
said venomously, "I'm going to have a Nazi baby, Livia."

Livia took a step forward in the darkness. "You don't know that."

"I knew when we had sex that it was the right time to have a
baby. Not only that, I have stopped bleeding." The word on her
mouth brought back to mind the image of her father and Piero in
the garden that afternoon, and the vermilion stains. "I lied to you,
Livia. The truth is I wanted him to give me a baby." Her voice scattered through the room. "I wanted to make sure he did not leave
and forget me after the war, I wanted to be sure he would marry
me."

"Stop this talk!" Livia took hold of her shoulders. "There is nothing we can do! Not tonight! You must think about Mamma, not
yourself! You must come downstairs. Papa and Piero are here!"

"I know they're here." Anna looked up into her sister's wraithlike
features. Tears came up and flooded her eyes. "I *can't* come down. I
don't want to see them again. I don't want to look at Papa and Piero
like this. Don't you understand?"

The grip on her shoulders relaxed. "Oh, Anna." Livia moved
closer, sat on the bed, and pulled her gently into her arms.

"They know now. Papa and Piero are in heaven and they know
now." She buried her face against Livia's breast and began to weep
softly.

"You didn't mean to do wrong. They know you didn't mean any
harm."

"But they are dead." She drew back. "And the dead know everything. They know I loved Karl. They know he loved me. They know

I could have stopped him. I could have made him leave Montefalco."

"That isn't true."

"He loves me. I know he does. He would not have killed Papa and Piero if he had known who they were, I know that."

"You're wrong. He killed fifty men, Anna. He's a German soldier. He does what they order him to do."

Anna tried to reach out in her mind to the outer boundaries of the truth. She said quietly, "No human being is that evil."

"He has done what he has done." Livia left the bed. "He is what he is. And you will now have to live with that."

Absently, Anna drew in breath and held it.

"Now you must think of Mamma. Get up, wash your face, come downstairs, and try to pray."

III

Socks, underwear, and handkerchiefs: Kruger hurriedly dropped the three small stacks of clothes into the duffel bag on the bed. There remained now only a few toilet articles, his second pair of boots, and the two uniforms in the closet. The rest—he looked around the bedroom of his third-floor suite in the Hotel Montecatini—the rest will have to stay: the little oil painting of the Madonna and Child he had bought in Sicily for a few packs of French cigarettes, the cheap souvenir trattoria plate from Frascati, the silver spoon from Siena— the things he had collected for the last year as they retreated, battle by battle, up the boot of Italy.

He wiped his face with the damp hotel towel. He had been sweating ever since he arrived a half hour ago to gather his things, but the room was cold. He dropped the towel on the bed and turned to the big Victorian bureau to close the drawers he had left open.

Again, it came over him: a leaden feeling of exhaustion. This time, he felt suddenly dizzy. He reached out to grip the edge of the bureau. His vision had blurred. He thought first of disease: the specter diseases of war, typhus and dysentery . . . but there was no fever, no nausea. He tried but could not lift his head.

What's happening to me? he thought.

The feeling had first come over him two hours ago in his office when Reiger brought the order of retreat: of something huge falling away inside him, and afterward a sense of silence and emptiness.

Something moved at his feet where the rug should have been. The light was bad in the room. The generators were failing. There were ugly stylized flowers in the oriental rug, he recalled. Flowers and leaves coiled around each other.

Typhus, dysentery . . . and in recent days, he had heard, madness. Schreiber had talked of madness in eastern Europe.

It's only in my mind, he thought: this thing, this weight is in my mind—pulling me down. And I will let go of it.

With a simple act of will, of recognition and will, he let his mind go free. "Anna." He said her name without thinking, staring at the things moving at his feet: not flowers and leaves, but a coiling repetition of—and the sight of it stunned him—of human bodies moving together in a slow dance of violent death. Across the whirling pattern he saw the shadow of his own body.

He tried but could not lift himself from the nightmare. It had been there in his mind, he realized, the whole day, held back by the machinery of sheer willpower.

The coiling movement at his feet suddenly stopped. At the center of the arrested dance he saw two naked bodies locked together in an embrace. They looked very small and insignificant lying between the violently dead. They receded, growing smaller, falling away into the darker background. A feeling of loss flooded through him like water spilling into a huge hole, running out.

I am not mad, he thought. I am now, by choice and responsibility, among the damned.

It was not only Anna that he had lost, but God as well. He let go of the bureau and fell forward. His head struck the bureau, but he felt no pain: his body belonged to another. Jackknifed upright, head bang-up against a drawer, kneeling like a discarded child's puppet, he lay where he had fallen, damned and absurd.

I could have stopped everything, he thought, done the other thing. "Anna," he said. With her name came the knowledge of what he had seen fall away into nothingness: his right, his claim now to any love, human or divine.

For a long while (he neither knew nor cared how long) he lay slumped against the bureau, for a kind of peace like death had come with the knowledge.

Then a sound came from beyond his place of peace. A low humming noise. It grew louder, more distinct. He opened his eyes and looked at the carved foot of a lion on the leg of the bureau. The sound came from outside in the street, a truck motor in the Via Benedetto, then voices—German voices—and an exchange of shouts.

Transports. A first, then a second, passed, heading in the direction of the Piazza Nazionale.

Kruger lifted himself from the floor. At the foot of the bed he wiped the sweat from his face again with the wet hotel towel. Oster had taken charge of the preparations for their retreat.

With or without me, he thought, it will all go on quite smoothly.

He dropped the towel on the floor. Beside the bed pillow he saw his pistol belt and holster. The machinery of this war had been set in motion long ago, before Hitler came to power, before any of his soldiers, before he himself, had been born: perhaps even before his father's defeat in the Great War.

He lifted the pistol holster and belt. And so it will grind on. Like huge engines in the bottom of a great ship, it will grind on—far down in that hellish darkness at the bottom, out of the passengers' sight. The Führer, Keitel, Kesselring, Lemelsen—all the way down —myself: we are all merely passengers in this war. On this voyage we are all dispensable passengers on a huge ship moving through dark rolling waters, like the *Lusitania* on its last voyage.

Mechanically, Kruger opened the flap of his pistol holster and drew out the Walther P38. The smell of burned powder was still fresh in the muzzle from that morning. Two bullets were missing.

Absently, without any fear or thought of remorse, he studied the gun: it was well-made, he had carried it since he left *Offiziersschule*. It was German.

He thought, which way? Through the mouth or through the temple, then realized that it really did not matter. Pain at this point was a childish concern. Compared to the pain he had seen that morning, this pain would be a pleasure. Compared to the lifetime of pain waiting for him, this would be an insignificant instant.

Through the mouth, then, he said silently, turning the pistol to his face. The wrist maneuver was, of course, awkward. He steadied his arm and formed his lips into the shape of a kiss. The tip of the pistol muzzle tasted bitter. He thought of the sweetness of Anna's mouth that last time in the ravine. The bitterness of that sweet remembrance would be left behind—and for good—when he fell away into that dark peaceful nothingness.

His gaze rested for a moment on the leather-bound triptych of photographs. One was of his parents taken on their wedding day in front of their parish church. They grinned up at him, Walter in his dark, ill-fitting suit, stiff white collar, and black cravat; Elizabeth in her sister's ankle-length white lace wedding dress and waist-length veil. She clutched a bouquet of spring flowers. He felt foolish with the pistol barrel in his mouth, with their eyes frozen on him in looks of innocent expectation, caught by the photographer twenty-seven years ago at the bright blissful beginning of their marriage.

He lowered the revolver and reached down to turn the photograph away, aware somehow that he could not kill himself with his parents watching. Every death in the German Army, he recalled, entails a formally worded message to the family. Tonight, when his soldiers found him, the details of his own death would be recorded: suicide. The message to his parents would, of course, merely say that he died in action, but the true details would be recorded in the files of the German War Office. His father's pride in him as a soldier would lead him to the files: Walter would look for the record of a hero and would find, instead, the indictment of a coward.

Kruger's hand began to shake, holding the heavy pistol. Suicide: his parents would be the ones to bear his pain. For his mother, a practicing Catholic, it would mean finishing out her own life with the knowledge that he had damned himself eternally to hell. "There is no way God can forgive the sin of suicide," she had once said to him. "God's mercy is infinite, but the dead cannot repent." She had said that, he recalled, the evening his father announced that the Führer's niece had committed suicide.

Fingering the pistol, Kruger glanced at the other two photos in the triptych: one of himself and twenty-five young Wehrmacht officers, the other of their Supreme Commander. More than half the men on the left, he realized, had died for the man on the right: died believing that their Führer's promise of a Thousand Year Reich was good and noble and worth the expense of death. He stared at the Führer's portrait: the rigid mouth, the ordinary jaw thrust forward in that familiar attitude of exaggerated inspiration and nobility, as if by mimicry he could acquire in his face what, he knew, perhaps far back in his mind, he had never won in his soul. Relaxed, it would have been the jaw of an Austrian peasant. The little clipped moustache: perhaps a touch of male vanity to cover a weak upper lip. And the small eyes glaring out at the world: they looked up at you, but unlike Walter's and Elizabeth's eyes, they seemed to be looking at nothing. Before this, he had always seen in them the dark intensity of vision and prophecy. But now he saw something new: madness and fanaticism (Oster's eyes that afternoon had burned with that same kind of fierce absence); and lurking behind that, the vindictive cruelty of a disappointed, mean little man.

In the moment between decision and action, Kruger realized that the will had gone out of the deed. He stood now, arrested between the knowledge of his parents' future pain and the satisfaction of the Führer's revenge. He bent down and returned the pistol to its holster, saying to himself, no. It will come in its own way, in its own time. Perhaps tonight or tomorrow, in the merciful form of an American bullet. Perhaps later, in the last battle of our defeat. But not this way. This is too easy. And it leaves behind for the living all the wrong things: pain for those two, satisfaction and revenge for the other. Perhaps Anna alone would have known and understood the real reason.

Again there was the sputter and groan of a transport heading toward the Piazza Nazionale. By his watch it was 9:43. Loaded in transports, the entire company was to assemble in the piazza with the equipment and supplies they would take with them to Vergato. The convoy would depart at 10:30. Oster had promised a swift, efficient evacuation. All that remained to pack now was the second uniform and the second pair of boots.

Kruger opened the big wardrobe to remove the uniform and boots. They would be, of course, little use to him now. One way or the other, it would be over for him in a few days. He left the uniform but removed the Iron Cross attached to the jacket's lapel. This he would take. Before the end came he would manage to send it to his father in Munich. In the days to come, after Germany's defeat, when the bitter humiliations returned, Walter would have this, at least, to hang his pride on. At the bed he stuffed the few remaining articles into his duffel bag and then reached for the triptych of photos. He removed the photograph of the Führer and dropped the triptych into the bag. He found a match in the drawer of his bedside table and struck it. The photograph of Hitler caught fire at the corner. Holding it over an ashtray, Kruger watched the flames darken the Führer's face and curl the stiff white paper until the photo dropped, a pile of gray ash, into the tray. It was a small but satisfying gesture, and he felt curiously free as he slung the duffel bag over his shoulder, turned out the lamp on the bedside table, and felt his way through the darkness for the door, realizing he was the last soldier to leave the hotel.

On the ground floor he pushed open the blackout drape over the front door and stepped out into the Via Benedetto. Toward the south, where an hour ago the sky had been lit with the pulsing red light of artillery explosions, there was now only a wavering red nimbus along the horizon, the guttering firelight from the battle for

Spedaletto. It was over and Kleisner had begun his retreat north-ward.

He swung the duffel bag to his right shoulder and hurried ahead. The *ammasso* where he had met Anna yesterday was shuttered for the night. Again, this time with uneasiness added to guilt, he remembered she had insisted on telling him something important, and he had promised to meet her at four that afternoon in San Tommaso. His duty to her had been lost and forgotten among the duties of war. He would never know what had so frightened her.

Suddenly a small muffled explosion came from the square. He slowed and saw a bright yellow light rise up the facade of the bank building across the square. There was another, and then a third, burst of light; a second, then a third, explosion. He knew at once: Palestrina, Bassano, San Miniato—to leave nothing of use behind for the Allies. Their armies had burned towns all the way up the Italian boot in the wake of their retreat. But *this* town—there's no *reason!*

Ahead, in the brightening firelight, soldiers hurried from the transports toward the post office and the Fascist headquarters. They carried boxes of explosives.

He recalled Reiger's mention of Lemelsen's order to burn public buildings. Angrily, he broke into a run. He had left the evacuation procedures in Oster's hands and the procedures were standard! There was nothing in the standard procedures about burning! As he reached the corner of the Via Benedetto and started across the square, he saw flames rise from the door of the post office. German soldiers and Fascist *carabinieri* raced by toward the Fascist headquarters, carrying canisters petrol. Fires had already ignited on the first and second floors of the building. Four military transports filled with soldiers were drawn up in the square. There were shouts in Italian and German from the direction of the two burning buildings. Kruger slowed his pace, heading in the direction of the Municipio, where soldiers hurried in and out of the building with cartons. Oster, Weiss, and Haldner supervised the soldiers as they emptied the cartons into a pile of papers on the pavement.

"Ah!" Oster saw him coming. "Herr Oberleutnant!" He saluted, looking pleased with himself.

There was another explosion inside the Fascist headquarters. Kruger dropped his duffel bag. "What's going on here, Sergeant?"

"We're carrying out the general's orders, Lieutenant," Oster replied. "As you yourself ordered me to do."

Another explosion reverberated through the square, this one from the direction of the river. He had left the final order of retreat on his desk unread and returned to the Montecatini.

Oster said, turning to admire the light in the sky, "I assumed you read the general's order, sir. He directed us to burn the public buildings—government offices, post office, telephone, telegraph, power installations—and whatever records we had no use for."

Still another explosion, this one from the post office. In the glare of light Kruger saw Oster register the look of outrage in his face and smile, confident of his responsible obedience.

"Where's Reiger?" Kruger asked.

"In the radio room, Lieutenant, sending a message to Kleisner." He went on, as if talking to a delinquent child. "I've radioed Kleisner that we will destroy the bridge once he has crossed over." The soldiers dumped the last carton of papers into the pile. Among them Karl saw the small framed Dürer print that had hung in his office. He had carried the print with him from Germany three years before and had intended to return with it after the war: it had reminded him in foreign places of the spirit and genius of his German culture. "Kleisner will join us north of town," said Oster, striking a match.

Reiger came toward them from the Municipio building.

Oster dropped the match into the official papers heaped on the pavement. They were soaked with petrol and instantly burst into flames. Kruger looked up. On the far side of the bonfire Reiger stared back at him, mutely reading his mind.

IV

"Hail Mary, full of grace . . ." Don Alessandro began the first prayer of the fourth decade of the rosary.

"The Lord is with you. Blessed art thou among women . . ." Anna added her voice to the murmur, trying to give prayerful meaning to her words, but once again her thoughts detached themselves from the memorized phrases and settled on the two faces protruding from the crude wooden boxes at the opposite end of the living room. Against the blue-gray skin, her father's neat black moustache looked strangely artificial. To hide the bullet hole, Carmella Filipetti had draped a white cloth over the top of his forehead. The coffins, resting side by side on kitchen chairs, were plain rectangular boxes constructed from barn planking. In the wet Tuscan soil, they would crumble in a very short time. Piero's box, made of short, unmatched planks, was held together by narrow perpendicular strips of wood.

Someone, obviously not a member of the family, had tried to comb Piero's beautiful curly black hair, but they had parted it on the wrong side, making a cowlick of his crown. Like her father's face, Piero's was grayish-blue in the flickering light of the candles placed on tables at either end of the coffins. In death, their noses looked even more identical than in life. Piero's lips were parted slightly, which, despite the frightening color in his face, made Anna now and then think that he was about to speak.

"Hail Mary, full of grace . . ." Kneeling on the floor between the coffins and his little congregation, Father Alessandro began the second Hail Mary in the fourth decade. In her place at the back of the room (she had come down after the rosary had begun), Anna let her gaze rest on her mother's profile. During the entire recitation of the rosary, she had not taken her eyes from the two faces. Luisa's own face, drained of any expression, was the face of a stranger isolated in some very private world to which she alone had access. In her black dress and black scarf pulled back from her face, kneeling upright without the help of any support, she looked curiously noble and strong for a woman accustomed since birth to think of herself as second-best. Love, fidelity, and devotion had been her mother's strength for twenty-one years.

"Hail Mary, full of grace . . ." Again the priest's deep voice filled the room. Livia covered her face and began to cry. Luisa circled her body with her arm and drew her close. *Nonna* Adelaida's high, brittle voice rose above the others, ". . . Blessed art thou among women."

Anna looked down at the floor, ashamed for not forcing herself to kneel with the family at the front of the group. Suddenly, over the drone of voices, came the sound of a muffled boom. Startled, she glanced at the others in the room. A few minutes ago thunder had reverberated across the mountains to the northeast. This time, though, she was sure it was not thunder that she heard. Carmella Filipetti whispered to Signore Cimoni. Luigi and Maria Cimoni, kneeling with their two teen-aged sons on the far side of the room, looked at each other, alarmed. Angela Guardini, her mother's best friend, remained wrapped in prayer, oblivious of the sound. "Holy Mary, Mother of God . . ." Father Alessandro lifted his voice, ignoring the commotion behind him.

"Pray for us sinners . . ." Anna went on with the prayer, glancing apprehensively at the window covered with the blackout drape. The Americans are five or six kilometers south of Montefalco, she thought, nervously rolling the beads of her rosary in her fingers. An air strike at this hour of the night in a thunderstorm would be impossible!

Again, over the prayerful voices, another boom rolled through the room. For a moment the entire room went silent. Against the far wall the small electric lamp suddenly flickered, then went out, leaving the room illuminated only by the candles at either end of the coffins.

"Please remain kneeling," Father Alessandro said, "we will continue the rosary. Now we must pray for the living."

Luigi Cimoni reached up and drew his wife close to him.

"Hail Mary, full of grace . . ." the priest began, and in hushed frightened voices, the small congregation of mourners took up the prayer.

Quietly, trying not to draw attention to herself, Anna rose and hurried, tiptoeing, to the front door. Quickly, she let herself out and closed the door behind her. A flickering yellow glow illuminated the trees in front of the house. At once, before she stepped clear of the doorway, she knew that Montefalco was burning. Flames licked the sky above the dark forest between the farm and Montefalco. Two fires burned, one in the vicinity of the Piazza Nazionale, another higher up in the town where the building housing the power station stood. Brilliant orange and yellow ribbons streamed up into the dark skyline above the Piazza Nazionale. The rosary hanging from her right hand rattled in the wind blowing up the hillside from the river. The Americans, she thought, trying to evade the horrifying thought that came to her.

In the mountains across the valley, a bolt of lightning struck, followed by shuddering thunder.

"Carlo," she heard herself say.

On the far side of the river, from the direction of the new town, a burst of light illuminated the darkness between the trees. A ribbon of fire rose up into the sky. The dull boom of the explosion echoed up the valley. And now, she thought, the telephone and telegraph.

Something brushed her face. A drop of rainwater. It ran down her cheek in a thin, chilling thread. The small shock of the cold water on her face focused her thoughts. Papa and Piero. Fifty innocent men. Murder. And now this.

A second drop of rain struck her face. She moved forward to the edge of the pine grove and leaned against the trunk of a tree. She tried to grasp and hold a single thought, but they raced by too fast. "Oh, Carlo." She looked down at the dark earth at her feet and forced herself to picture the man's face. The image that came to mind was the face in the darkness two nights ago when they stood by the river, a moment before they parted: a face filled with pain, fear, love, and gentleness. "No," she said, then realized she was on the verge of laughter. Between *this* man and *that* man—she tried to fit the face by the river to the body of the German who had stood over her father in the square that afternoon, but the images would not come together. She leaned against the tree and gripped the trunk with both hands.

Another drop of rain fell on her neck, another one on her arm, still another on her cheek.

A sound floated up the hillside from the direction of the road below. At first she did not reflect on the sound. Then it came closer and took on the familiar groan and chug of a truck's motor. She lifted her head, listening intently. Presently, a truck drew alongside the farm and passed, heading north on the road to Vergato. A second truck followed, then a third.

"So," she said mechanically to herself, "he is leaving now. He has finished."

A fourth truck came up the road from the south and passed by.

Through the leaves overhead, the rain began to fall, peppering her skin.

Gripping the tree for support, she leaned forward and felt a violent spasm coil in her stomach, felt the nausea of it rise. She thought of the child in her belly—their child.

Another motor went by on the road below.

And now, she thought, not caring for what he has done to us in this little mountain village, taking what was useful and leaving nothing behind but death and misery—a bastard child that will be with me for the rest of my life—he goes.

Another smaller truck passed, the last of his convoy, and then there was silence. Above, the rain came down hissing through the trees.

She realized for the first time that the future for her had already been fixed: she, too, would have to leave Montefalco.

Across the mountains there was a glitter of lightning. She waited for the thunder, counting off the seconds until the boom rolled through the valley.

She closed her eyes. Beyond the Reno Valley, beyond the mountains of Tuscany, the world was immense and dark. All she knew of it was what she had read and what she had dreamed.

The boom of thunder rolled across the mountains. Even the mountains were immense.

She opened her eyes, took a deep breath, then gave herself up to a sudden and exhilarating feeling of unbounded hatred. If for nothing else, she could live for the satisfaction of revenge.

Overhead, through the dense leaves, the heavens opened. It came down now in a cold, wonderful flood: the rain.

II
1945

CHAPTER 1

I

Showered and changed from the fatigues he had worn for his work-day in the PW camp's German Administration Office, Lieutenant Kruger hurried down the dirt avenue between the enlisted men's barracks toward the officers' mess hall. Camp Windsor's veteran prisoners had warned him about the seasonal heat and humidity of this remote corner of America called the state of Louisiana. Tonight, as a concession to the April humidity, he wore a short-sleeved uniform shirt. Here and there along the checkerboard lanes connecting the camp's three fenced compounds, other tardy soldiers scurried toward their allotted mess halls. As Kruger passed the officers' latrine, the camp's streetlights came on, followed by the lamps high up in the four guardhouse towers.

He was late for dinner. The first time in five months. The lights always came on at six.

"Lieutenant Kruger!" a familiar voice called from the direction of the compound storehouse. A door slammed. Kruger kept moving and silently cursed. Sergeant Jürgen Weingaertner joined him three buildings from the mess hall. "Good evening, Lieutenant."

"Sergeant." A hulking ox of a man with a Middle European peasant's face that still bore the leathery scars of the North Africa sun, Weingaertner was one of Windsor's six veteran officers of Rommel's North Afrika Korps, a fanatical group of Nazis Kruger had thus far taken pains to avoid.

"You're late, Lieutenant."

"I had work to do."

"That's good." Weingaertner chuckled. "We like responsible commitment in our men."

We. Kruger grimaced at the reference. It was no secret, even from the Americans, that Weingaertner and his Afrika Korps controlled the internal machinery of prison-camp power. Weingaertner, a noncommissioned officer, had appointed himself camp spokesman to act as liaison between the prisoners and their American captors.

The sergeant kept pace with him. "By the way, Major Dorf asked me to give you a message."

"I finished his storeroom inventory a few minutes ago. I left it on his desk."

"Not that, Lieutenant. Colonel Peterson sent word we're getting a new shipment of prisoners tomorrow. Kramer's sick. Major Dorf wants you to take Kramer's place as interpreter for the incoming prisoners."

Kruger drew up at the mess-hall steps. "My English is rotten, Weingaertner. Dorf knows that." Three months ago, when it was clear that Germany would lose the war, he had started taking English lessons.

"Your English is better than Colonel Peterson's German." Weingaertner grinned.

"I speak a few phrases. That's all."

"Relax." Weingaertner jostled his shoulder. "You won't be alone. Your choir boy friend Metz is going with you. Between the two of you, you'll get by."

Your choir boy friend. The feeling of panic was immediate and familiar. Kruger continued up the steps. Metz, a newcomer to Windsor, was one of the camp's open and fearless anti-Nazis. They had met two months ago when Metz offered to serve Mass at the camp's Catholic chapel. Their shared Catholicism had been the basis of a secret friendship. Fearing the dangers of anti-Catholic Nazi reprisal, he had carefully steered clear of public association with Metz. He turned at the door. "Corporal Schuster's English is better than mine," he said, regretting his decision to learn English.

"Dorf wants *you,* Kruger." Weingaertner looked at him meaningfully and held the door open for him to pass.

He and Weingaertner were the last of the thirty-three officers to arrive. Kruger took a tray and moved along the counter where an enlisted man was dispensing food. *Dorf wants you, Kruger.* Dorf, Windsor's ranking German officer, held his position of authority in name only. Kruger held out his plate for meat loaf, potatoes, and hard-boiled eggs. The order had come not from Dorf but Weingaertner and the Afrika Korps. But why him? From the beginning, to survive this war, he had decided to vanish into the background of

prison-camp life. He had been scrupulous in his efforts. He moved
down the counter to take bread and milk.

Weingaertner joined him. "Another thing, Lieutenant. The major
wants you to make out a report on the newcomers."

"What kind of report?" Kruger reached for silverware.

"We want you to talk to them. Get some personal information.
For instance, we'd like to know who the deserters are."

Kruger dropped his knife on the floor. He quickly stooped to pick
it up, feeling a chill run up his back.

"Something wrong?"

"I'm tired, Sergeant, that's all."

"We want—the major wants the report typed in triplicate. One for
him, one for us, and one for our general files."

Triplicate, Kruger thought. Just like they do in Berlin. "Whatever
you say, Sergeant."

He left the counter and began zigzagging his way through the
tables. The only empty chairs were at the Afrika Korps table. *We,*
Kruger thought again. He meant, of course, the Afrika Korps
Lagergestapo. Father Straub had been the one who first warned him
about Weingaertner's Lagergestapo. Six months ago, the afternoon
he went to the priest and confessed his crime in Montefalco. Until
then, he had kept the nightmare of his sin secret from everyone. He
had told Straub everything in confession: how after the retreat in
September he had deserted the army near Vergato, wandered south
behind enemy lines, and surrendered, not knowing or really caring if
the Americans would shoot him or take him prisoner, never dreaming they would ship him to North Africa and from there, finally, to
America to spend the rest of the war in a prison camp. Living in terror that the curse of Montefalco would follow him to the swamps of
Louisiana, he had forced himself to become a prison-camp
wallflower.

He passed Lieutenant Metz seated at a table in the center of the
room. In his mid-twenties, reputedly the son of a German general,
Metz had served with the Wehrmacht in Russia and had been captured in early '45. He had warned Metz repeatedly about making enemies of the AK Lagergestapo. He had repeated Straub's stories of
quiet after-dark meetings, beatings down by the latrines, and
Straub's account of the mysterious death last year of a prisoner
whose body was found hanging in the latrine, a death that the Americans dismissed as suicide but which the prisoners knew to be
murder. It had happened, others later told him, in almost all the two
hundred PW camps in America.

Metz glanced at him as he passed, but Kruger pretended not to see.

"You're late, Kruger," Lieutenant Loeb said as he reached the Afrika Korps table.

"I had work to do for Dorf." Kruger seated himself, aware that Loeb was eying him suspiciously. A big man with a spoiled soft face and watery blue eyes, Loeb was rumored to be fourth in Lagergestapo command. The other AK officers, Pabel, Richter, Shinker, and Knabe, went on eating, ignoring his intrusion.

Kruger self-consciously cut into his meat loaf. He had carefully avoided the AK table before this, knowing that he had no court of appeal with the Americans against these Nazi fanatics. The Americans tolerated their internal rule, for they encouraged the prisoners to cooperate with the American PW labor program, and that was very much to the liking of Colonel Peterson, Windsor's American commander.

Metz had once openly mocked them about their work program. *"Arbeit macht Frei,"* he had said. Later, Metz had accused him of cowardice for not having joined in his game with the Lagergestapo. But after his brush with suicide in Montefalco, he had decided that if punishment was to come, it would come in Italy after the war. Not here, not now—not from Germans or Americans. Like a man walking a tightrope between two ends, he had kept his desertion secret from the Germans and his reprisal execution secret from the Americans.

"We have guests arriving in the morning," Weingaertner announced, seating himself opposite Kruger.

Sergeant Pabel, the youngest AK officer, looked up. "Where are they from?"

"Ask Kruger there," said Weingaertner. "Kruger drew up the allotments this afternoon."

"Where are they from, Lieutenant?"

"G-thirty-one," Kruger muttered. For a moment the table fell silent. The incoming prisoners were identified by letters and numbers. The letter stood for the country in which they had been captured, the number for the military zone. G-31 stood for Germans captured in western Europe. Since the collapse of France, Belgium, and Holland, there had been a steady stream of prisoners arriving from Germany itself. The AK had refused so far to believe the news that the new arrivals brought from Europe, that the Reich was on the verge of total collapse.

Pabel spoke up. "Those guys they're sending us now—they're not soldiers! They're civilians! Boys and old men! Pigshit! Civilian pigshit!"

"You're right, Pabel," Weingaertner encouraged the boy. "Sending us that pigshit is the American way of demoralizing us. It's a propaganda trick. They want us to write back to Germany and tell our families we're losing the war."

Kruger thought of his mother and father waiting for the end to come in the bombed city of Munich.

"By the way, Kruger," said Loeb, "aren't you having ice cream? I thought you liked American ice cream."

"No. Not tonight." He fought the flush rising in his face. It was a private thing with him, passing up the ice cream. Father Straub, his confessor, had encouraged his small secret acts of penance. His only compromise with anonymity had been his return to Catholicism and his attendance at Sunday Mass. The only freedom from guilt he had found these last seven months had been spiritual: God, Straub had assured him, had forgiven his sin.

Someone rattled a piece of silverware against a glass. When Kruger looked up, Lieutenant Metz was already on his feet. Next to his plate lay a small stack of newspapers. Metz had been given the task of translating the American newspaper articles and summarizing the day's events at the evening meal. The noise in the room died away. "Gentlemen!" Metz looked around. "I assume you saw the American flags at half-mast today." He lifted one of the newspapers. "I have here an evening copy of the Windsor *Chronicle.*" He held up the front page. "For those who don't read English, the headlines of this April 12, 1945, issue announce the death today of President Franklin Roosevelt." He swung the front page toward the Afrika Korps table. The huge headline read, ROOSEVELT DEAD.

For a moment, the only sound in the mess hall was the clatter of dishes and pans from the kitchen.

Pabel turned to Weingaertner, his face illuminated from within. "We did it!" His cry shattered the silence. "The bastard's dead! We did it!"

Like gunpowder, the room exploded. There were shouts, "We've won! He's dead! They admit it! We've won!"

Kruger sat back. Roosevelt had been Hitler's biggest stumbling block, larger than even Churchill or Stalin.

A sound of banging commenced, someone beating a coffee mug on a table. Pabel, then Loeb, Weingaertner, Shinker, Richter, and Knabe joined in. The response of the Afrika Korps was like a signal to the rest of the room. Mugs—even Major Dorf's mug—took up the wordless chant of victory.

Kruger's astonishment gave way to sadness. He thought, we're like desperate orphaned children with a piece of Christmas candy.

Weingaertner saw that his mug was empty and idle, and he glared.

Obediently, shamefully, Kruger took his mug and joined the banging, thinking how pathetic his unconditional commitment to the Thousand Year Reich had become.

"Gentlemen!" Metz called out.

One by one the mugs were laid down.

"Now, gentlemen"—the lieutenant took another paper and sighed heavily (Kruger saw that the gravity was a studied performance and felt a chilling dread come over him)—"now for the rest of the news. The second lead stories in the other American papers today tell us that the U.S. Fifth and Sixth Armies under Eisenhower have crossed the Rhine River and have now advanced to the Elbe." He looked around, observing the effect of his words.

Shinker, a second lieutenant with an innocuous Rhinish-looking face, Weingaertner's toad, murmured something under his breath.

The lieutenant, meanwhile, paraphrased the newspaper articles. "The armies of Weitengoff and Rundstedt have been forced to retreat eastward toward Berlin. Zhukov, against Heinrici's army in the East, has drawn up his Russian XIV Army on the banks of the Oder, gentlemen." Weingaertner's cheek twitched uncontrollably. Kruger averted his gaze, stunned by the limits of Metz' reckless disregard of Nazi passions. "It says here that Zhukov's forces have encountered little resistance from Heinrici in eastern Prussia."

Weingaertner's fist struck the table, shattering the pallid silence. "Lies!"

Unruffled, Metz turned to Weingaertner. "Perhaps, Sergeant. I didn't write the articles, I merely translated them. I'm merely doing my duty." He took up a third newspaper. Heretofore, he had translated only innocuous articles at the dinner table and judiciously posted the gloomier ones in the PX. "Another article here in the New York *Times* says that Japan yesterday surrendered the island of Okinawa to the Americans."

Weingaertner stumbled to his feet, knocking over his chair.

"I repeat, Sergeant." Metz smiled pleasantly. "I did not *write* the articles."

Kruger realized that young Metz had planned the entire performance.

Pabel broke the paralyzed silence. "Traitor!"

The magic word galvanized Weingaertner. He left the table and moved toward Metz. "American propaganda lies. Lies, Lieutenant. And you are a traitor for repeating them here."

"It's over, Weingaertner. Finished." Metz addressed the hulking Afrika Korps sergeant as if speaking to a retarded child. "Let's stop kidding ourselves. In a few days they will have Berlin." He shifted his gaze toward Kruger and smiled, ruefully. "All that's left for Germany now is the reckoning."

Kruger recalled Metz' chilling prophecy after Mass last week of postwar trials for those who had set blind obedience above morality.

"In Germany, Lieutenant, you would be shot," Weingaertner said.

Fired by the example of his superior, Pabel lunged to his feet. "He's a traitor!" He looked around at the bewildered faces. "A coward and a traitor! He should be shot! *Here!*"

Something suddenly hurtled across the room—a cereal bowl. It struck Metz in the chest and sent him catapulting backward against a support post. The bowl clattered to the floor. As Metz steadied himself and looked down at his uniform shirt splattered with vanilla ice cream, Pabel and Weingaertner moved forward. Kruger saw the glint of a table knife in Pabel's hand.

"Weingaertner! Pabel!" The short fat Major Dorf lumbered to his feet, his face hemorrhaging with panic. "That's enough! Stop it! Do you want the Americans down on us?" Weingaertner and Pabel drew up. "You will leave the mess hall! All of you!" It was an order, everyone knew, without the weight of real authority. "That's an order! Everyone! Out!" Dorf said, trying to salvage some vestige of the lost power of his rank. The remaining officers turned toward Weingaertner for a signal. He acquiesced and motioned for Pabel to leave. The officers began rising.

Dorf said to Metz, disgusted, "Go to the barracks, Lieutenant, and clean yourself."

On the way out, to avoid any accusation of guilt by association, Kruger kept close to the wall, away from Metz. After seven and a half months, the guilt, shame, and the cowardice had become second nature. Outside he turned in the opposite direction from the officers' barracks in the direction of the PX. The officers had paired off for their usual evening walk.

"Lieutenant." Weingaertner's voice came from behind. Kruger kept moving, but Weingaertner caught up with him. "You in a hurry, Lieutenant?"

Kruger dropped back to an even pace. "I have things to get at the PX."

"Your choir boy friend Metz—that was a foolish thing to do."

An impulse to deny friendship with Metz came and went, checked suddenly by a larger sense of shame. "Yes, it was," he said.

"Why do you think he did it?"

"I don't know."

Weingaertner grinned at him in the darkness. "We should find out, don't you think?"

"Find out what?" Kruger's throat tightened.

"I mean, some of the men seem to have left their loyalties behind in Europe."

"I wouldn't know about that, Sergeant. I'm an ordinary soldier."

"Good. Then as an ordinary soldier you will understand what I mean by *duty*. Come, let's have a little chat."

II

"Dr. Hutton asks how long you've been here at San Paolo, Signora Lamberti." The Red Cross nurse gently but firmly loosened Anna's grip on the lower part of her dressing gown.

"Five months. Almost six." Anna felt the doctor's hands touch her naked skin below the huge bulge in her stomach. She winced and turned her face toward the wall of the examination room as the nurse translated her reply into English.

"The doctor asks if you intend to return to your home after the baby is born."

"No." Anna swallowed thickly. "I'm going to take the baby and move to the city—to Florence."

"Relax, Anna," the doctor said in English.

"Firenze is crowded now, signora," said the nurse. "Until the war is over, you won't find a place to live there. At the moment, there's no food for civilians in Florence, and no work to be had."

Anna closed her eyes. She had been through this conversation with the Displaced Persons authorities a hundred times before. From November, when she arrived at the DP camp, until now, there had been no question of going *anywhere*. Last winter, the Americans and English had come to a halt in their advance up the Italian peninsula. From October until now, Florence had remained a restricted war zone. Italian refugees like herself had been placed in holding camps like San Paolo to wait out the end of the war.

"The doctor says for you to sit up, Anna."

Repatriation: that was the English word they had used. Everyone in San Paolo was talking about repatriation: returning home to their farms, their villages or cities—to their families. She, on the other hand, had decided back in December, when she left Montefalco, never to return. She sat up and swung her legs from the table, drawing the dressing gown around her body.

"... *is normal* ... *good condition* ..." The young American army doctor spoke to the nurse in English. He was shorter than Captain Fitzgerald, the American officer who had made the appointment for her that morning. The nurse addressed the doctor as "Major Hutton."

"The doctor says everything is normal." The nurse smiled. "Despite the rationed diet, you seem healthy. If everything goes on schedule, you can expect the baby at the end of May or in early June. In the meantime"—she followed the doctor to the door—"he wants you to come back for another examination next week."

"All right," Anna said in English.

Major Hutton chuckled. "I see Captain Fitzgerald has taught you some English."

"A little." Anna looked down and blushed.

"Next Tuesday, Signora Lamberti?" the doctor asked, using, as they all did, her adopted married name.

"*Sì.* Next Tuesday."

"You can dress now, signora," said the nurse, leaving with the doctor.

Anna hurriedly drew on her underclothes and her dress. She had promised to meet Captain Fitzgerald by her barracks at nine-thirty and give him the doctor's report. It was almost ten. Perhaps after the baby was born she would ask Captain Fitzgerald to help her find a room in Florence, maybe a job. As head of the Displaced Persons subcommission of the Allied Military Government in the entire region around Florence, Captain Charles Fitzgerald could arrange almost anything. Otherwise, for a woman like herself—a woman with a child but no husband—it would be difficult to survive in a city like Florence after the war. Difficult even for a woman who had been married to an Italian soldier, a hero who had given his life for Italy in the war as she had claimed when she arrived pregnant at San Paolo.

Anna squeezed into the tight pair of women's American army shoes Captain Fitzgerald had given her to replace the worn-out shoes she had arrived with. She had walked all the way from Montefalco to Pistoia in those shoes back in December of last year, and then from there to Florence and San Paolo, certain of only one thing: she and the baby were going to survive this war, and the responsibilities for that were hers and hers alone.

Anna grabbed her sweater and hurried out of the small refugee clinic. It had rained heavily yesterday and the supply trucks had churned the road into deep muddy tracks. She kept to the edge of the road and passed the three-story stone building which housed the American military headquarters. Below, spread out over the field which had once been a dairy pasture, were hundreds of army tents shrouded in a gray blanket of smoke from their heating stoves. Situated off the Siena road south of Florence on an abandoned dairy in the Tuscan hills, San Paolo had been constructed as a temporary receiving station for war refugees, but had become in the last year a permanent settlement. San Paolo looked for all the world like a huge gypsy encampment—except gypsies would have abandoned it long before it became a squalid slum.

Some new refugees, peasants by the look of their clothes, stood near the reception building. Among them a squat woman in a voluminous black shawl drawn over her pregnant stomach. The woman grinned as Anna passed. In San Paolo there were many pregnant women. The war had bred lots of babies. Some of the pregnant women came to the camp with their husbands, but most came alone: wives of soldiers or partisans or abandoned widows. None, of course, admitted that they were the abandoned victims of passing affairs with German soldiers. No Italian woman would or could admit to that crime. Hopefully, in the wreckage of the war, the lack of documented proof of her marriage to an Italian soldier would be accepted, if not by the American and Italian authorities, then at least by the ordinary people around her. The Florentines, she was confident, would never know that her child belonged to the most hated man in western Tuscany: to the man they now, at home, called *Il Macellaio di Montefalco,* the Butcher of Montefalco.

Captain Fitzgerald's American army jeep was parked before the first of the three barracks. He sat in the driver's seat with his back to the road. As always, Anna felt nervous in the big American's presence. For the four thousand souls at San Paolo, Captain Fitzgerald's authority was absolute. It was he who decided who was to live at San Paolo and who was to be sent farther south; he who decided what food and clothing and accommodations they were to have and how long they would remain.

At the sound of her shoes sucking through the mud, he turned and swung himself from the jeep. He stood waiting with his hands on his hips, grinning. In his khaki American officer's uniform and cap, he looked imposing. Lean, over six feet tall, he towered over most Italians. "Slow down, little mother," he said in English, then lapsed into perfect Italian. "There's no hurry, Anna. I've got all the time in the world."

She stopped a few paces away and nervously fidgeted with the loose ends of her unkempt hair. Since her arrival at San Paolo, she had met with Captain Fitzgerald many times. He had been the one to order her to move from the tents down in the meadow to the barracks here on the hill. He had visited her regularly on his inspection tours of the camp, had quietly supplied her with food and clothing not available to the other refugees, and had on several occasions driven her to Florence in his army jeep and bought her little presents in the shops. At first, she had shunned his attentions, convinced that she was expected to be like other women at San Paolo, the object now of an American soldier's sexual satisfaction. It was a common joke among the other young women in the camp that the American liberators were even more libidinous than their German captors. Except, as Anna soon began to realize, Captain Fitzgerald never ventured beyond affectionate politeness. He seemed somehow older than his thirty-one years, almost paternal and protective. Perhaps it was the fact that he had confessed to being, like her, once married. His being a widower had seemed like some kind of protection.

She saw that his green eyes—normally sharp and intuitively alert —were withdrawn and anxious this morning. "What did the doctor say?" he asked.

"Everything is normal. He says I will have the baby at the end of May or the beginning of June."

He nodded. "I gather he said nothing to you about where the delivery will take place."

"No."

"Normally, the women have their babies here in the camp. But I've made other arrangements for you. You'll have the baby at the Misericordia Hospital in Florence."

Anna recovered from her shock and said, warily, "But how? The rules say that we—"

"Never mind the rules. It's within my power to change the rules. I've made some other changes regarding you, too." He smiled, mischievously.

Anna glanced away, reminded of her and her child's helpless dependence on the captain's good favor. She had vowed before leaving

Montefalco never again to put trust or faith in anyone outside herself, least of all in any man.

He went on, "On the evening of April ninth, Anna, we opened our offensive on the German winter line." Anna took one step backward. "Yes, I know. Your family lives just south of the line, but I'm sure they're safe. We're already beyond the Apennines and within range of Bologna. It looks like we'll be in the Po Valley very shortly."

"How long?"

"I can't say. Days, maybe a couple of weeks. The point is, we expect a huge number of refugees to move south. The first will arrive here in Florence in a day or so. Which means that San Paolo is going to be filled beyond capacity. A lot of these people will be sick when they arrive. Until we can inoculate them, there'll be danger of disease. Malaria, typhoid, the kind of thing we had last year. I've decided to move you to a private home north of Florence, to Fiesole. You'll be safe there and well cared for."

Anna nervously fingered the bodice of her dress. The thought of change after five months was terrifying. Out there, beyond the familiar confines of San Paolo, was a dark world of guns and death, of starvation and disease and homelessness, where the death of any one person meant nothing, where people fought like animals for mere survival. The darkness out there was undeniably real compared to the darkness she had imagined as a child. "But—" she said.

"But what? You'll have the baby in the best hospital in Florence. In the meantime, you'll stay with a close friend of mine. A woman. She'll take good care of you."

Helpless, Anna began to cry.

"*Anna.*" He took her hands, "I promise, everything will be fine. I will not abandon you." He pressed her fingers to emphasize his words. He had never held her hands before this, she realized. "When the time comes, I will take you to the Misericordia myself, do you understand?"

She nodded, knowing that protests were useless. "I . . . understand." But she did not understand.

"You'll be very comfortable with my friend. She's rich and everything you need will be provided. I've known her for many years, long before the war. It's all been arranged." He led her toward the door of her barracks. "I'll drive you to Fiesole myself."

She withdrew her hand. "You don't have to explain, Captain. I will do as I am told."

III

Four olive-drab army transports pulled into the gravel parking lot alongside the red brick Windsor train depot. Sergeant Matthews, the American MP in charge of transporting the incoming shipment of PWs from the downtown station to the camp outside Windsor, jumped from the rear of the first truck. Kruger and Metz, along with twelve American MPs, joined Matthews at the edge of the parking lot near the double line of railroad tracks. "Okay, you guys! We've got fifteen minutes! This is gonna be a passenger train with one coach attached to the rear! I want you MPs down at the end of the platform. There'll be seventy-six PWs on the train. When the prisoners unload, I want them lined up along the platform double file, regardless of rank. We'll move 'em down the platform to this end. You, Gutierrez"—he jabbed a finger toward a young MP holding a clipboard—"check off their names as they board the trucks. And you, Kruger and Metz, I want you guys down at this end with me. If I give an order to the PWs, translate it loud and clear. You got that?"

"Yes, sir," Kruger replied in English.

"Yes, sir," Metz followed suit.

Matthews went on, "In the meantime, the rest of you guys make sure the platform is cleared of civilians."

There were "Yes, sir's" as the MPs saluted and moved off along the concrete platform.

"Kruger and Metz, you wait over there while I check if the train's on time." He pointed to the end of the platform near the parking lot and walked off toward the station.

Alone with Metz for the first time since last night's mess-hall debacle, Kruger seized the opportunity as they reached the station platform. "I want to talk to you, Werner, about last night."

"What about it? My duty is to report the news at dinner." Metz shrugged. "It's time those assholes were told the truth in public."

"You could have posted those articles in the PX. You knew what the AK would do. You planned it. If you're trying to commit suicide, my friend, there are quicker and easier ways."

"You don't understand, Kruger." Metz thrust his hands into his pockets and began pacing back and forth across the platform. "Tell me, what do you know about my father?"

"Your father? Only what you've told me. Why?"

"I told you he was a general."

"So? What of it?"

"The name's not Metz, Kruger, it's *von* Metz. Friedrich von Metz. Does that ring a bell?"

Metz had never affixed the von to his name before. General Friedrich von Metz, if he remembered correctly, was a high-ranking Waffen-SS general, a man rumored to be very close to Hitler. "Hitler's friend?" he said, annoyed.

"The very one."

"You never told me."

"You never asked. What I'm saying is, as long as the Führer is alive, I've got nothing to worry about from Weingaertner's Lagergestapo. If my father's not with the Führer at this moment, Karl, he's probably with Himmler. For the time being, the family of Herr General von Metz is beyond the reach of the Gestapo."

"I see. Does Weingaertner know?"

Metz nodded. "Sure. Weingaertner knows everything."

At the far end of the long stretch of tracks a small black dot appeared on the horizon. Kruger hesitated, then said, "I think you're wrong about Weingaertner, Werner. Last night after dinner, he questioned me about you. He knows we're both Catholics. He's seen us in chapel together. He asked me—ordered me—to find out things about you."

"What things?"

"He says you're a deserter."

"I see." Metz turned away toward the approaching train.

"There's no immunity for deserters, Werner. Even for the son of a Waffen-SS general."

"And if I am—what are you going to do about it?"

"Nothing. I'll tell Weingaertner I couldn't find out."

"You were ordered to find out, it's your duty."

Kruger saw the light in the center of the black engine and above it a whiff of black smoke across the sky. He said, "I can't turn you in. I'm a deserter myself." The confession after seven and a half months of silence and secrecy, the sudden relief, made him feel suddenly light-headed.

"The fact is, Karl, it doesn't matter if you tell them or not."

"What do you mean, *doesn't matter?* The war is almost over, man! If you keep your mouth shut, if you lay off the AK, they'll leave you alone! All you have to do is stay alive for a few more weeks—a couple of *months!*"

"You're wrong."

The hot humid breeze chilled the sweat on Kruger's face. "What does that mean?"

"You know I was in Russia, don't you?"

"So?"

"You ever heard of a town called Minsk?"

"I've heard the name."

"Four years ago, my Wehrmacht unit was assigned to a mission in Russia. My father arranged my assignment. We accompanied one of his *Einsatzgruppen* units into Russia." Metz began pacing again. A whistle like a wail rose up in the distance. "For the mission he got me promoted to *Oberleutnant*. My orders came from the Waffen-SS —from my father. He assigned us to the area around Minsk. Our job was to assist the Waffen-SS in solving the final question of the Jews in Minsk. *Endlösung,* he called it. I followed my father's orders, Karl, to the letter. We had the Jews dig a pit outside Minsk. We helped the SS exterminate the Jews of Minsk. When it was over —when the shooting was over—the pit was full. A hundred thousand. More, maybe. I don't know how many. I couldn't . . . I didn't count. I sent back a rough estimate to my father. He was very pleased." There were shouts at the far end of the platform from the American MPs. "So you see, it makes little difference if Weingaertner knows I deserted or not. When it's over, they're going to send us all back. There'll be trials. I can't go back, nor can I stay. Either way, Gestapo here or Russians there, I'm going to hang."

Kruger said, thinking not of Minsk but of Montefalco, not of Metz' hundred thousand Russian Jews but of his own fifty Italian Catholics, "I can't go back, either, Werner." But his words, he realized, had been drowned by the train's final whistle.

Metz said when the whistle ended, "You have nothing to hide but desertion, Karl. When it's over, you can go back. You were an ordinary German soldier."

"Metz!" Sergeant Matthews barreled toward them from the station. "Get over there with Gutierrez by the trucks! Make sure he gets their names right!"

Metz started toward the parking lot.

"Werner—!" Kruger called after him.

"Kruger!" Matthews cut him short. "You stay with me! Translate everything I say into German!" Matthews joined him on the platform as the huge locomotive lumbered into the station with its seven passenger cars. The MPs had stationed themselves at the far end of the platform. As the train stopped, Negro porters jumped from the first six cars to prevent the civilian passengers from leaving or boarding the train while the prisoners filed down the steps to the platform. The soldiers emerging from the train, Kruger saw, were younger than the average prisoner at Windsor, most not more than eighteen or nineteen: the tired, grimy scrapings of the Führer's replacement army.

He glanced toward Metz with Gutierrez at the trucks. A hundred thousand Jews. Father Straub had once said that reprisal executions were sometimes legitimate under the Geneva Rules of War. Surely Montefalco was not the same as Minsk.

A double-file column of faded, disheveled Wehrmacht, Luftwaffe, and Schutzstaffel uniforms formed along the platform. At the far end of the column Kruger observed several Wehrmacht officers' caps emerging from the rear of the coach.

"Okay, Kruger," said Matthews, "I'll give the orders. You translate."

"Sir." Kruger snapped to attention.

"'ttension!" The sergeant's shout brought the PWs in the front of the line to rigid attention.

"Achtung!" Kruger shouted.

In a chain reaction down the line, the others followed suit. Kruger studied the passing faces: exhausted, frightened, confused, and wary.

"Right face!" Matthews shouted as the front of the column came alongside.

"Rechts!" Kruger imitated Matthews' tone.

The column swung right toward the trucks.

"Now tell them to have their PW I.D. numbers ready to give."

"Seit bereit, eure Nummer anzugeben!"

They had given it a thousand times in the last few weeks. Their faces looked aggravated but resigned.

A few moments later, as the middle of the column reached the turning point, Matthews said, "Repeat the I.D. order."

Kruger did so: *"Seit bereit, eure Nummer anzugeben!"* Matthews, he thought, must think they're idiots. For American soldiers, ignorance of English was equivalent to mental retardation. Over the head of the enlisted men, toward the rear of the column, the officers' caps came into view. Kruger moved his head to see if he could identify their ranks. Through the closely packed column, he saw a pair of pale eyes behind gold-rimmed spectacles. Under the lowered bill of the cap, the sharp nose and the thin mouth looked familiar. For a moment, the passing column blocked his view. When the face came into view again, the steel gray eyes behind the spectacles sent a tremor through Kruger's body. He took a small step backward and, for an instant, heard himself silently deny what his eyes had told him. Under the cap, Sergeant Rudolf Oster's narrow lips spread into a cold, satisfied smile. Kruger watched the face advance, saw that Oster now wore the uniform of a Wehrmacht captain. The eyes were laughing, he saw.

"Come on, Kruger, repeat my order," Matthews said, "I want these guys outta here in five minutes. This train can't load until we're outta here."

Kruger looked back toward the column as Oster made a smart right turn and started away. *"Seit bereit, eure Nummer anzugeben,"* he said, trying to steady his voice.

IV

On the road north to Florence, Captain Fitzgerald drove slowly to avoid the pockmarks and holes left from last year's Allied bombings. For the first three quarters of an hour after leaving San Paolo, he and Anna had talked of little more than the Tuscan scenery: the villages dominating the hilltops, the monasteries and villas perched among the green cypresses and silver-gray olive groves. Captain Fitzgerald had succeeded in astonishing the young Italian woman with his knowledge of Tuscan history.

She glanced at his handsome, angular face next to her in the army jeep's driver's seat, seeing he had once again withdrawn into himself. "I know something is wrong, Captain. Do you want to tell me?"

"I was thinking about the war, Anna." He sighed heavily. "President Roosevelt is dead."

She swung in her seat. "When?"

"Yesterday. We got word this morning."

"How?"

"A stroke. The Vice-President has taken over. A man called Truman. I don't know much about him, except he comes from Missouri. I think we're in trouble."

"But you've already won the war."

Fitzgerald shifted down on the steep upgrade. "Here in Europe, yes. But not in the Pacific. This guy Truman will have to pull something fast to win in the Pacific. Not only that, Roosevelt was going to use the war to reshape the balance of power after the war. If I'm right, Truman will have problems after the war—not only here in Europe, but also in Asia."

Anna shook her head. "I'm a Tuscan peasant. I don't understand politics." She thought of Kruger's German politics and its effect on her life. "All I know is, the Germans will leave us in peace now."

Fitzgerald chuckled. "I'm not a soldier by profession, Anna, I'm a lawyer. International law. Politics, not guns, is my profession."

"I didn't know."

"You never asked."

She looked away. It was true. She had never asked because she did not want to appear vulnerable to his charms. "I'm sorry."

"Five months is a long time to know a man and not know what kind of person he is. I think I know why you've avoided me, though."

"Why?"

"For the same reasons I avoided women after my wife died. Your husband was killed what—six months ago?"

"Yes." She felt suddenly trapped again. Three months ago she told the captain her fictitious story about her husband's fictitious death. She had not dreamed at the time that her lie—her alibi— would come back in this personal way to plague her.

"You loved him very much, didn't you?"

She hesitated. *Loved him*. Trapped in a miserable half-truth between the past and the present, she said, "Yes."

"Take it from me, it will get easier as time goes by. What's more, he didn't leave you entirely alone, like Sylvie left me." There was a frank note of pain in his voice. "You have his child," he added.

"Yes. I have his child."

"Sylvie and I were going to have children, but she died before we had the chance. You see, I married her right out of law school. We moved to New York City and I joined my father's chemical firm as an attorney. During the four years we were married, I was too busy being a gifted Ivy League lawyer to be a father."

"I gather you loved her very much."

"Yes. More than I knew at the time."

His ready admission felt like a reprieve. She went on. "Your wife —Sylvie—was she young?"

"Twenty-seven. She died of leukemia. Her real name was Silvanna, but I called her Sylvie for short. She liked the American form of her name."

"Silvanna? She was Italian?"

"A Florentine. I met her here in Florence in 1935. Her parents were friends of my parents. My father collected art. So did Silvanna's. She came to school in the United States in 1936. We married at the end of '37. She died in 1940." As they reached the summit of the hill, the town of Impruneta came into view, dominated by the shattered church tower of Santa Maria dell' Impruneta. "Her maiden name was Silvanna Agnoletto-Patini. Her father, Giuliano, was arrested by the Germans in '43 and shipped to Germany. He was a Jew. He has not been heard of since. Her mother, Lucrezia, lives in Fiesole."

The puzzle came together. Anna repeated the name of the villa he had given her yesterday. "You mean, the Villa Patini?"

"Yes." He smiled. "The marchesa lives alone now. She's sixty-one years old. She was delighted when I asked if you could come and keep her company."

Anna looked out across the ragged Chianti landscape toward Florence and the smoky outline of the Tuscan mountains beyond, speechless.

For the next hour, until they reached the foothills above Florence, she avoided the subject of their personal lives, wondering if she had allowed herself to be led into yet another inescapable trap. On each hairpin curve ascending the foothills north of Florence, they came upon a fresh view of the ancient city: the Palazzo Vecchio with its crenellated double tower; the Duomo with its red-tiled, marble-ribbed dome; the small dome of Santa Croce; and rising out of the city's red-tiled roofs, the massive tops of palazzi and churches Anna did not even know.

"When I was eleven," she said, "my *nonno* took me, my sister, and my brother to Florence. That was my first encounter with the world. I decided then that I would one day leave Montefalco and make something of my life." She looked down at her bulging stomach under the gray maternity dress the supply officer at San Paolo had scrounged for her. "I've come quite far in nine years, haven't I?"

"You've become a woman, Anna. A beautiful woman."

Anna made a face. "Among other things, Captain, I have lost all illusions in this war."

He rounded another hairpin curve, nearing the town of San Domenico de Fiesole. "Considering you lost a husband and a home, I think you've done pretty well."

"When the war is over, I am going to make a life for myself and my baby. If nothing else, I have a good education. I will find work in the city. In Montefalco, I was a child. The war changed that. I will never allow myself or my child to become anyone's victim. Ever again."

The captain gave her a questioning glance. "The Florentines have a motto for themselves—*Più bello che si può*. You make yourself as beautiful as you can, under the circumstances. The Florentines, if anything, are realists."

A hundred meters before the town, they left the highway and turned along a dirt road between the walls of two imposing villas. The captain pointed. "The Villa Patini." He turned through a gate into a circular drive that led to a huge, three-story rose-tinted villa and drew up at the door. "Well?" He swung himself from the jeep. "What are you waiting for?"

As Anna stepped from the jeep, she looked down at her shoes, still streaked with the DP camp's mud. Straightening the skirt of her ugly maternity dress, she gaped at the austere palatial surroundings, feeling suddenly ashamed of herself.

The captain intercepted her when she turned to the jeep for her bag. "I'll take that."

"I look dreadful."

"You look fine. Relax. She knows where you're coming from." He led her to the massive front door and pulled the bell chain. "For the last five months, I've avoided describing you to the marchesa," he said. "All she knows is that you're twenty years old, the widow of an Italian soldier, and a pregnant refugee."

The great door swung open on an old woman in a long black peasant's dress. Her hair, parted down the center, was snow white. "Ah! Signore Capitano!" She turned to Anna and a look of shock came over her face.

"*Buon giorno, Marina*." The captain took hold of Anna's arm. "This is Signora Lamberti." He drew her into a marble vestibule. "Marina is housekeeper for the marchesa. She's been here at Villa Patini longer than the Agnoletto-Patinis. Right, Marina?"

"*Sì, signore*," she replied without taking her eyes from Anna, "this way, please." She pointed down a long hall stretching the width of the villa. "The marchesa is waiting for you in the *salotto*." Except for a carved table of dark rich wood along one wall, the hall was entirely empty of furniture. The patterned marble floor glistened with the damp patina of a recent mopping. "The floor," the housekeeper said, leading them to oak doors at the far end of the hall, "be careful." She glanced again at Anna. At the doors, she turned. "I will be in the kitchen if you want something, signore." She glanced again, this time with a look of astonishment, and hurried away.

"Relax, everything will be fine," said the captain, opening the doors into a large, richly furnished parlor. He drew her inside as a soft female voice called from the far end of the room.

"Carlo!" The woman came toward them with her arms out-stretched in a gesture of welcome. She was small and fragile-looking, with reddish blond hair and fair Milanese-looking skin, and dressed in a plain black dress.

"Lucrezia!" The captain moved toward her and momentarily blocked Anna's view of the woman.

"You're late, young man," said the marchesa, more delighted than piqued.

"The traffic through Florence was terrible . . ." He bantered with the marchesa as Anna stood awkwardly by, surveying the assortment of antique chests, tables, and upholstered chairs. There were paint-ings along the walls in heavy gilded frames, masters, by the looks of them. The captain had said the marchesa's husband had collected paintings. On the far wall her eye rested on one small modern-look-ing painting—a portrait. She stepped back, stunned. The portrait was of a young woman, and the face bore a remarkable resemblance to her own. She thought, at once, of the look on the servant's face when she opened the door to greet them and suddenly realized the captain and the marchesa had stopped talking. When she turned, the marchesa was staring at her, and it was the same look of astonished recognition in her face.

"Marchesa," the captain said quickly, "may I present Signora Anna Lamberti."

The marchesa seemed momentarily flustered. "Forgive me, Anna, for a moment I thought—" She brushed the air and smiled. "It's nothing. Tell me your name again. Anna—?"

"Lamberti, signora," she replied, but the name sounded strangely hollow to her.

"Give me your hand, Signora Lamberti." The marchesa's com-mand was earnest and lacked any sign of condescension. She went on studying her face, though. "You are most welcome here, my dear. I have looked forward to your visit for weeks now."

"*Grazie,* Marchesa."

"Lucrezia, please. As we will be together now in this huge empty house, you will call me Lucrezia. And you will be Anna—*è vero?*"

"*Sì. È vero.*"

"This naughty boy here refused to tell me anything more than the barest facts about you, Anna." She smiled knowingly at him. "Re-fused, as a matter of fact, to even describe you."

The captain's wry grin was puzzling. "In English, we have an expression—*One picture is worth a thousand words.*"

The remark, she realized, was not directed at her grotesque appearance. Confused by their exchange of looks, thinking of the marchesa's daughter and the captain's dead wife, realizing the portrait was of her, she said, "I doubt that I know a thousand English words."

They laughed at her attempt in English. The marchesa said, "Now, come." She led them to a cluster of silk-upholstered armchairs near one of the French windows. "It's a long drive from San Paolo. You and Carlo must be starved . . ." She went on talking about the strain of a long drive, but Anna no longer listened.

Carlo: for the second time, the name brushed by her with chilling familiarity. *Charles:* she had never used the captain's first name or thought to translate it into Italian. How could she have missed the connection?

"Anna?" the captain asked, puzzled by her momentary lack of attention. "Lucrezia asked if you're hungry."

"No. No, thank you."

"Sit down then, my dear. I'll make you both drinks." When the captain and Anna had seated themselves, she said, "Now. What would you like, Anna?"

"Anything."

The marchesa went to a marble-topped table against the wall where bottles of liquor and glasses were arranged on silver trays. "Come now, Anna, you must treat this house as your own from the start." The captain smiled. "You will be living here until the child comes," she said, rummaging through the bottles, "and then you and the child will come back and stay with me until Carlo has arranged everything for the three of you." The captain looked toward the marchesa and started to speak. "I have only one servant left at the villa now," the marchesa continued, "so you and I will have to make do for ourselves, like a family." The captain's face colored and he looked down at the floor, mortified, as the realization flooded over Anna. "Now, I have fruit juice, mineral water, wine, and a variety of liquors." She drew out a bottle and turned. "And here. A bottle of French champagne. For this occasion, I think we should have the champagne." Anna sat looking at the captain's crestfallen face, feeling the room shrink around her. "It isn't chilled, but no matter." She began unwrapping the seal on the bottle, oblivious of the deathly silence across the room. "In wartime, when there's love to celebrate with champagne," she said, compounding her dreadful mistake, "one does not quibble about temperatures."

"Lucrezia," the captain broke in, anger surfacing in his voice, "please don't open the champagne. It isn't necessary." He looked up with a silent plea for forgiveness from Anna.

The marchesa stopped fussing with the foil wrapper on the bottle. For a moment, no one moved. Anna stared vacantly at her lap, and the captain looked at the floor. The marchesa turned back to the table and set the bottle down. "I see. I'm sorry. I . . . I didn't realize. I didn't know. I thought—" She left the thought unfinished.

"It's my fault," said the captain, "I should have explained." He stood up and nervously looked at his watch. "I must leave now. I had no intention of staying this long. I have a dinner appointment with Brigadier Upjohn in Florence."

"Carlo," the marchesa appealed, "forgive me. I was certain you had already—" Again, compounding the error, she left off.

"No, Lucrezia. I didn't. Anna, you see, is still in mourning for her husband. He died only six months ago." As he moved toward the door, he glanced toward the small oil portrait of the woman and seemed distressed. "You know yourself, Lucrezia, how long grief can last." He turned back to Anna. "You'll be very comfortable here. We've sent supplies up from the storehouse. I promise, you'll be no burden at all to Lucrezia."

"None whatever," murmured Lucrezia.

The clues, she realized, had been there in front of her for five months. How could she have missed them? His constant, though guarded, attentions, the way he singled her out from the other female refugees, the way he treated her like a woman for the future rather than one for the present—how could she have translated his behavior into nothing more than the usual passing lust of a soldier? The room was suddenly stifling. Anything but this, she thought, unable to pronounce the word *love* to herself. "Captain." She got up as he opened the door. "Wait. Please. I'll go with you." She thought, I must get out of here! Now! Before it's too late! Back to San Paolo— Florence, *anywhere*. "I'll walk you to the door." She hurried to join him, thinking, I'll get out of the house, then tell him.

"Yes, Anna, do that," said the marchesa. "Walk Carlo to the car. I'll wait here."

In the hallway, she realized she had handed over the duffel bag with her clothes to Charles. "My clothes. You brought the duffel bag in with you."

"I gave it to Marina. I imagine she took it to your room."

She kept up with him down the hallway. "Captain Fitzgerald—"

He cut her short. "I know what you're going to say. You want to go back to San Paolo."

"Yes." She thought, if I don't, it will happen all over again. It's the same trap.

"That would be a terrible mistake, Anna. In San Paolo, you'll run the risk of a malaria epidemic."

"I'm not afraid of malaria."

"Perhaps not, but it's not worth the gamble."

"I don't want to stay here."

"If you're not afraid for yourself, then think of the child."

"It's *my* child, Captain, not yours!"

"It's yours, Anna, to give life to, but not yours to selfishly endanger."

When the war is over, I am going to make a life for myself and my baby. His truth silenced her. She followed him into the darkened vestibule.

"I don't know what you think this war has done to you, or why you're so determined to take the world on by yourself, but you have one more illusion, as you call it, to lose, Anna." The anger in his voice sounded huge in the darkness. "From now on, you're not free to choose for yourself alone. Your share of the future when this war is over belongs to two—at least, two. Your baby has no father, and you have no visible means of support, and probably no hope of any for a long time to come. What are you going to do about that?"

"I don't know. I'll manage." Unable to see more than the faintest shadow of him, she stepped back into the darkness.

"How? Where?" He made no move to open the door.

"I'll get a job. In Florence."

"And live alone with your baby?"

"Yes." Their voices reverberated from the walls and sounded deafening in the enclosed space.

He let go of the doorknob and took a step toward her. "What happened to you, Anna? Tell me."

An absurd thought came to her: that he would try to touch her where she stood against the wall, or worse. "Please," she said, breathlessly, "let me go."

"Back before San Paolo, something happened to you. I want you to tell me. I want to help you."

She tried to breathe, but could not. "The war—my husband—" She started to tell of the reprisal and her murdered father and brother, but dared not speak of it.

"The war has hurt everybody. You are not the only woman to have lost a husband." He was suddenly the commanding officer again, drilling her as a refugee. "I've seen grief in this war, I've seen anger and bitterness, and I've seen women determined to survive with fatherless children. But I've not seen this other thing—this determination to live apart from the world—to hide yourself from everyone and everything. Why, Anna?" She turned her face against the cold wall and began to cry, running her hand over the polished stone. His voice was soft when he spoke again. "Tell me what they did to you, Anna, I can help you."

For the first time in eight months, she let the truth flood her mind with the memory of that annihilating trust and its murderous rewards—her father and brother, a child to be born in her own self-imposed damnation. "They took everything . . . I gave them everything . . ."

"Who, Anna?"

"The Germans . . . the war." She gave in, wept, and felt her legs give way. With nothing to grip, her hands slid down the wall. "I cannot stay here." He caught and held her. "I'm afraid of the *world*." The word sounded huge.

He drew her up, holding her by the elbows, but made no move to draw her closer to him. "I know that fear, Anna. Even without the war and the Germans. It will take time, but it will pass. Trust me. I know." He led her toward the door. "In the meantime, I cannot and will not let you go back to San Paolo. You will be safe here from the world. Lucrezia understands the world more than most. Observe her while you're here. While you wait for the baby, I'll stay away. When it's time for the Misericordia, I'll come back for you." He took hold of the doorknob. "Look at me, Anna."

She did as she was told, but in the darkness he could not possibly read the terror in her face. "I can't tell you any more."

"Then don't. I'm sorry you learned about my intentions this way. I wanted to wait until after the baby. Lucrezia figured it out for herself. I thought maybe after the baby you'd let go of the past and start thinking of the future. Yours and the baby's. I know you loved your Lamberti, but he's dead. He belongs to the past now." He released her arms and opened the door, flooding them with blinding sunlight. "What's more, you'll find I'm a very patient man." He left her at the door and walked out toward his jeep.

She thought of Kruger living on in comfortable indifference somewhere in his native Munich after the war, then remembered the portrait in the *salotto*. "It's the same, isn't it," she said, "whether they live or die?"

He looked back, questioningly. "Who?"

"The ones we love. They stay with us in the mind, either way, don't they?"

He seemed to realize what she meant. "You mean—"

"Yes. The portrait in the *salotto*."

"Then you saw it."

"Yes."

"I see." His face slowly softened with a faint smile.

She left the door and walked out onto the gravel drive. "Did you think I wouldn't eventually see it?"

"I was going to ask Lucrezia to take it down. I forgot."

"Was she like me as much as that?"

"Yes. Almost in everything. Except, she loved the world."

"You still love her, don't you?"

He nodded. "But she's dead, Anna."

"Is she?"

He considered her question and then nodded. "You're right. I guess they do stay with us in the mind, either way."

"Yes. Living or dead, they stay."

"We can't—either of us—go on like this, you know. It may not be perfect, but it may well be the best we'll ever have." He rounded the jeep and swung himself into the driver's seat. "What do they say? *Più bello che si può?*" He smiled.

Your share of the future when this war is over belongs to two—at least, two. "I am myself. I am not another," she said.

"Nor am I, either." He started the motor, then motioned her to come closer. "What belongs to you is yours—the good and the bad of it. What belongs to your child is his—or hers—or will be when the kid's old enough. Until then, it's a question of providing. Some things I have and I can give, others belong entirely to me. The portrait, for instance, and its past. There are a few things you should know about me in advance. For instance, I'm a very rich man at home. I have too much for one, and it's all rather meaningless if I don't share it." He grinned. "And another thing. As you see, I don't give up easily. Nor am I above bribes. After the war, America might be a good place for someone who doesn't like this rubble of the war." He winked playfully. "For you and that soldier's baby, I mean." He threw the jeep into gear and pulled away. "Just think about it."

CHAPTER 2

I

While Father Straub unvested in the sacristy, Kruger extinguished the altar candles and gathered up the cruets and the *lavabo* dish. As acolyte for Sunday Mass that morning, it was his duty to strip the altar afterward to make way for the Protestant service to follow. On Sunday the chapel at Windsor served all denominations.

"We had a good showing this morning, Lieutenant," the mild-mannered, ascetic priest said at the table in the sacristy where he was unvesting.

Kruger set the cruets and *lavabo* dish down. "Yes, Father. Better than last Sunday."

"How many German soldiers did you count?"

"Twenty-two, Father. Not counting myself."

"I consecrated seventy-five hosts for Communion, Karl. I had only ten left over to consume. That's a good fifty percent improvement over last Sunday."

"Yes, Father." Kruger poured the unconsecrated wine left over in the cruet from Mass back into the bottle.

"I think we both know why, too."

"The men have taken the news from Germany pretty hard, Father." In the last week alone, there had been the fall of Berlin and the announcement of Hitler's death.

"There must be what, Karl—a couple of hundred Catholics among the prisoners?"

"I don't really know. Those who don't practice their faith never talk about it."

There was a sigh from the vestment table. "You mean, they don't *dare* talk."

"Yes, Father."

"Is it still the Lagergestapo?"

Kruger knew where Straub's question was leading. During Mass, Rudolf Oster had come into the chapel. He had sat down for five minutes directly behind Werner Metz. Then he had gotten up and left. "Yes, Father. They're as determined as ever."

"That officer you told me about last week—Captain Oster. He came in during my sermon."

"He came in, Father, to take names of the guys at Mass. He now works for Weingaertner's Lagergestapo. Now that Hitler's dead, they're making lists."

"Stupid little men." Straub pulled the alb over his shoulders. "What difference will it make now, knowing who is and who isn't loyal?"

"A military defeat isn't the same as a political defeat for those guys, Father." Kruger took the wine and water cruets to the sink to wash them.

"Have they threatened you, Karl?"

"No, Father. I keep my mouth shut. It's not me they're after. It's Lieutenant Metz. He's been talking again around the camp."

"I see." Straub left off questioning and busied himself folding the long white alb.

Kruger ventured where until now he had never gone with the priest. He asked, "Tell me, Father, what do you know about Lieutenant Metz' background?"

"Some. Not much."

The priest's reticence, knowing his vigilance around the camp, puzzled Kruger. "Nothing more?"

Straub did not reply.

Kruger returned the cruets to the small table by the window. He ventured one step further. "Metz and I have certain things in common, Father."

There was no response from Straub.

He had vowed never to speak of either Metz' desertion or what Metz had done in Minsk. He had wondered, though, if Metz had ever spoken to Straub of his past. "Now that Hitler is dead, Father," he said, "Lieutenant Metz is at the top of the Lagergestapo's list." Still, no response. "I should have said something to you before this, I guess. I just didn't want to get involved." He hesitated, waiting for some sign, then said, "Have you heard of a prison camp called Ruston, Father?"

"Yes. It's where prisoners who are openly anti-Nazi are sent."

"I think Metz should be sent there. Immediately, in fact. I told him a couple of days ago he should go to Colonel Peterson and ask for a transfer, but he refused. I think you're the one who should speak to Peterson, Father."

Straub placed his chalice and the ciborium in their black leather cases and snapped the lids closed. "There's nothing I can do, son. I'm sorry."

In the priest's resigned withdrawal, Kruger read the mute obligation of confessional secrecy. "I see." He weighed suddenly his own resolution to survive the war in neutral silence against the danger of himself speaking to Colonel Peterson. The Lagergestapo kept close watch on who visited the American commander's offices outside the prison compound. He said, "Do you think I should speak to Peterson myself?"

"You should do what your conscience tells you to do, son."

The word *conscience* brought back memories of Montefalco and Anna Miceli. "Right, Father . . . I guess I should ask for an appointment myself." He heard the halfhearted note of cowardly indecision in his voice and compared again the prospect of a meaningless death here in Windsor to the one maybe awaiting him in Italy after the war. Metz had talked about the certain trial and death awaiting him in the months to come.

"Have you finished, Karl?" Straub turned from the table with his cases.

"Yes, Father."

"I'll walk you to your compound."

They left the sacristy and followed the eight-foot fence separating Compound Two from Compound Three. The avenues were crowded with soldiers hurrying toward their mess halls for breakfast.

"How long have you been acting as sacristan for me, Karl?" Straub asked.

"Two months. More or less."

"And how long have I been your confessor?"

The priest knew the answer. He was leading him. "Four and a half months."

"Then perhaps you'll give me credit for knowing a little about you. I've been watching you over the months. You spend some of your time alone in the chapel."

"A little."

Straub waved toward the American guards posted at the gate to Compound Three as they passed through. "Now that the war is over, I've begun to see despair in some of the men."

"Despair, Father?"

"I know it's a bitter thing to face the prospect of death *after* defeat, Karl."

"You mean, Metz?"

"Perhaps. But let's talk about you. I also know that despair is not the sin of a man who prays."

"After what I've done"—again, Kruger thought of Montefalco, Anna Miceli, and his twofold betrayal—"who else but God's going to listen?"

"Listen to me, Karl. You have served your country as a soldier. Your country—my own country—was responsible for this terrible war and has, in God's justice, suffered the punishment of defeat. Where responsibility, as you call it, ends, I don't know. War condemns everyone who fights and loses. What you did in Italy was morally wrong, and perhaps you will be punished. You won't know until you are accused."

Kruger started to turn away toward the officers' mess hall.

"No, Karl, walk this way for a minute." Straub pointed in the opposite direction of the crowd. Kruger followed. "As far as God is concerned you have accepted moral responsibility. Who will and who will not be punished for following the orders of their superiors is a question for the victors to answer. I know, for instance, what happened after the Great War."

Kruger drew up. A piece of Straub's puzzle fell into place in his mind. "You fought in that war, Father?"

"On the side of Germany. I was a corporal. I fought in France in 1917." He motioned for them to continue walking. "My commander put me in charge of a gas battery. We were ordered to shell the enemy lines with mustard-gas bombs. Hundreds, maybe thousands, died. I never knew. We had our orders from above, and our duty was simply to obey. After the war, I waited for retribution for what I had done. But nothing happened. In 1922 I got permission to immigrate to the United States. In 1923 I entered a seminary in California. I was ordained in 1930." They continued on down the main avenue.

After an interminable silence, Kruger asked, "Why are you telling me this, Father?"

"As you get older, Karl, you will discover that the Providence of God has to work in the most appalling conditions. The choices, you see, all belong to us. God's Providence seems to be always one step behind." Kruger recalled his mother's childhood story of God's providential rope. Straub went on, "As a soldier, you loved your country, trusted your leaders, and obeyed. Faith, hope, and love are virtues that can be turned in any direction. They are also virtues not easily found in most men. In God's Providence, we are free to use them to serve a man like Adolf Hitler or . . ."

Kruger watched Straub amble ahead. "Or what, Father?"

Straub looked back and smiled mischievously. Then he shrugged. "Think about it."

Instead of heading to the mess hall, Kruger turned toward the company PX. *Think about it.* He *had* thought about it. But the notion of that kind of reparation—spiritual reparation—had always seemed somehow second best. The choice, at any rate, was not his to make. Others—Montefalco—would decide his fate.

At the PX he bought a copy of *Der Graf,* the German newspaper printed by the prisoners of Camp Kearney, Rhode Island, and circulated among the two hundred PW camps in America. The lead story told of the reputed suicide of Hitler in the Berlin Chancellery. He paid with a PW five-cent coupon and turned to leave.

"Herr Oberleutnant Kruger." Captain Rudolf Oster stood in the doorway, blocking his exit. "Heil Hitler."

The salute was that of a superior to an inferior officer. Kruger returned the salute and moved toward the door. "I gather, Captain, the proper salute now should be Heil Doenitz."

Oster's eyes narrowed. He motioned Kruger out. "I think it's time, Lieutenant, we had a talk."

"I'm on my way to breakfast, Captain."

"Good. We'll eat together." He joined him on the avenue outside. "You've been avoiding me these last couple of weeks."

"I've nothing to say to you, Captain."

Oster chuckled sourly. "But I still don't know the true story of your capture by the Americans." Kruger made no reply. "The morning we found you missing—you and the command car—I assumed you'd been captured on your way to see Major Raeder in Vergato. But, of course, Major Raeder was not in Vergato at that time."

"As it turned out, he wasn't."

"Some days later we found the vehicle you had used. There was very little left of it. We assumed you had taken a direct hit from a mortar shell. We found bits of your personal effects in the debris. I informed the War Office that you had been killed in action. Imagine my surprise when I found you here in America. Alive."

He had purposefully left his helmet, gun, and keys behind in the command car when he set fire to it and then blew it up. He said, "I survived the explosion."

"The War Office thinks differently. As yet, I have not informed Berlin that you are here in America, a prisoner of war. I will do so, of course. Otherwise, there will be some confusion when the war is over. Both in Germany and in Italy, as well."

"If you must know, I was taken prisoner south of Vergato."

"*Behind* enemy lines, Lieutenant?"

Kruger made no reply.

"Desertion is a crime punishable by death—even here in America."

"And for those who surrender, Captain?"

"I didn't surrender, Kruger. I was overrun. The Führer ruled on surrender, too. The punishment for desertion and surrender are the same."

"You mean, Vietingoff should have kept on until his men were all killed?"

"Cowardice is no respecter of rank. Colonel-General von Vietingoff-Scheel is a coward and a traitor. And he, like all the others, will die a traitor's death. Our military defeat in Europe is only a passing phase."

Kruger realized he was in for another Nazi homily. He said, "Tell me, Captain—after Himmler is gone, from whom will the Gestapo take orders?"

"The Gestapo?" Oster feigned innocence.

"Yes, Rudolf. The Gestapo."

"You seem to know a lot, Lieutenant."

"I knew back in Montefalco."

Oster shrugged. "The authority will undergo some changes, of course. But like your Catholic Church, the chain of power will continue unbroken."

"You seem to know a lot, too."

"We have a complete dossier on you, Kruger." Oster's voice became suddenly businesslike. "Dating from Montefalco. Your visits to the church of San Tommaso, for instance. Your affair with that Italian girl. I remarked at the time how you seemed to make a habit of treason and disloyalty—fornication one day, Mass the next. Your desertion will come as a surprise to no one."

"Enough people had died under my command; I wanted no more blood on my hands."

"You have parents, I gather, in Munich."

Kruger felt a hot flash across his face. "They know nothing. They think I'm still in Italy."

"Then you will not want our people in Munich to disillusion them. Sergeant Weingaertner tells me the Americans have a PW camp set aside here in Louisiana for anti-Nazi traitors."

"And a camp in Oklahoma for Nazi fanatics."

"He tells me some of the men have gone to the American commander here and asked for asylum in this camp—what is it called?"

"Ruston." Sweat prickled his forehead.

"Your friend Metz, for instance. I gather he's a likely candidate for Ruston."

"Leave the boy alone, Oster." Kruger's anger surfaced in his voice. "He has troubles enough."

"As far as we know, you and Metz are the two most likely candidates for Ruston." They were a few yards from the mess hall. Oster came to a halt and waited for a group of officers to pass. When he spoke, it was a flat statement. "You will remain here at Windsor, Kruger, until we decide what to do with you. You will do nothing, moreover, to influence Colonel Peterson on behalf of Metz. If you ask for asylum—for either of you—I will inform the authorities here about your military reprisal in Montefalco. So far, I gather you've said nothing about that to the Americans. I myself, of course, was not responsible for your actions. I have nothing to lose in informing the Americans. Moreover, if you leave Windsor or interfere on behalf of Metz, I will inform the authorities in Germany through the Red Cross that you are alive and that you deserted, and your parents will suffer the consequences. Do I make myself clear?"

"Quite."

"Good." Oster moved toward the mess-hall steps. "Now we will enjoy some of this American—I believe they call it *breakfast.*"

II

"Wake up, Anna." His voice was closer, gentle and soothing.

She rose up out of darkness.

And saw images hovering above her: something white. A dress, a woman, and a man she could not, for the moment, name.

"Che fai . . . ?" she asked, bewildered. "Where am I?"

"The Misericordia, Anna." It was the captain who spoke. "Everything's fine. Now lie back." He arranged the pillow behind her head and she obeyed. She saw the bed, the cream-colored stucco wall with the little picture of the Madonna and Child, the beds across the way filled with women, and a window: it was dusk.

The nurse by her bed said, "You had a rough delivery, dear, the baby was long overdue; but it's over, and you have a wonderful little child." Under the starched white cap her wrinkled face smiled mechanically. "A boy," she said. The voice was like that of Sister Louisa, her history teacher at the Santa Cecilia convent school.

"He's beautiful." The captain grinned at her.

"And quite healthy. How much did you say he weighs, Sister?" The nurse turned toward a second nurse at the foot of the bed who held a small bundle in her arm.

"Thirty-five hundred grams, Matron."

"Do you want to see him?" the captain asked.

"Yes." Anna started to lift herself from the pillow.

"Lie still," the matron said.

"Here, Sister, let me," said the captain to the nurse with the bundle.

The nurse hesitated.

"Let the father do that," the matron said, "it's the custom here."

"But, Matron—"

"Actually, Sister Tabarelli"—the captain winked at Anna—"I'm not the father. I'm only a friend."

"Oh. I see."

Fitzgerald took the baby from the young nurse and turned the bundle with the open end toward the head of the bed. "Lie back," he said in English, "hold him in your left arm."

Anna rolled onto her side to form a natural cradle with her arm.

"You may feed the baby for ten minutes, Signora Lamberti," said the matron, "then he must go back to the nursery."

Anna saw the top of the baby's forehead through the opening in the blanket and felt delicious pleasure spill through her body. The soft skin was mottled red. There were wisps of dark hair under the white cotton tuck.

"Well, *look* at him." The captain laughed.

She lifted the cotton fold, saw a tiny squirming face, a mouth puckered into an irritable look of hunger, and a bubble of spittle in its center like a raindrop. And his nose—not much of one—with just the hint of straight chiseled bone where the bridge would be. Like— She brushed away the image of another nose before it took shape in her mind and looked at the doll-like fingers curled into two little agitated fists beating the air. "He's hungry," she said, instinctively reading her son's face.

"Does she know how to breast-feed?" asked the matron, critically.

The captain and the two nurses began talking but Anna did not care to listen.

Her son's eyes were the color of deep water. He looked at her, but she knew that he could not see, or if he saw, did not understand this strange new world.

"I spoke to the administrator this afternoon, Sister," she heard the captain say. "I want Signora Lamberti moved to a private room; she needs rest, and you've put her here in a ward with a lot of wounded women . . ." He went on lecturing the matron.

Anna suddenly remembered the war. The feeling of delicious security and perfection suddenly dissolved. She remembered waiting that morning in the reception room while the captain filled out the forms, watching the other patients pass by. Her labor pains had started an hour and a half before in her room at the Villa Patini. Lucrezia had sent Marina to the nearest phone to call the captain in Firenze, and he had driven out to the villa in a staff car to take her to the Misericordia. She had not seen him for six weeks. As he had promised, he had stayed away. Though in labor, she had felt glad to see him and ashamed of herself for the pain she had caused him. By the time they reached the reception room of the Misericordia, her pains of labor had become excruciating, but they were good pains, unlike the pains of those around her: a man, a partisan brought in from the mountains (the grief of Piero's murder had come back) with a bullet in his side; a woman whose husband had died only moments before from a German land-mine explosion. Her pain, she remembered thinking, had at least a future. Theirs had only a past. The war was over, Hitler was dead.

"For you and Signora Lamberti, Captain, the war is over," the matron said, "but for these women, it's only just begun."

"All right, then, she will *share* a room." The captain compromised.

"I will do what I can to find a double." The matron went away, gesturing to the other nurse to follow.

Anna turned back to the baby and smoothed his chaotic wisps of dark hair. No one had bothered to do that. The skin of his head was warm and very tender. A thought came to her from nowhere: Kruger had parted his hair on the left side. She moved the hair, making, she realized, her first decision for the baby's future life: on the right. She looked again at her son's eyes. And again a painful image intruded on her pleasure: Kruger's watery blue-green eyes. If the boy's eyes changed color, even slightly . . .

The captain sat down cautiously on the edge of the bed. "How do you feel?"

"Tired." She smiled, wondering how she could share this other feeling with an outsider. It was a pleasure of the blood.

"Do you like him?" The captain opened the folds of the blanket.

She tried to imagine a word that would contain everything. "Yes," was all that she could say.

"He's got your hair and coloring."

"Yes, he does." But Kruger had also had dark brown hair, she thought.

The captain touched the baby's arm and stroked it affectionately. There were shadows of exhaustion around his eyes. "We're moving you to a semiprivate room."

Far down the line of beds, a woman groaned.

"I don't need a room. I can rest where I am."

"Maybe you can. But I can't." He smiled. "You don't belong in here, Anna. You have a baby to feed. These women are wounded, some of them have diseases."

His protective solicitude for the two of them was like the warm eiderdown on her bed at the Villa Patini. She said, "I don't think we should stay in the hospital now. They need every bed they can find."

"For a day or two. Then you and the baby can come home."

Home. The word sounded strange but inviting. "A day or two?" She lifted her head, frightened suddenly. "Is something wrong? Charles!"

"Nothing is wrong. He's fine." He smiled.

She realized she had inadvertently and for the first time called the captain by his Christian name. He went on smiling, silently enjoying the pleasure of her little surrender. The baby squirmed in the pod of the blanket and struck the air with both little fists. She pretended to fuss with the blanket. In all these weeks away, Charles had communicated with Lucrezia by phone. He had sent food and provisions to the villa, but had not visited. Nor had Anna given any sign to Lucrezia that Charles would be welcome, for fear he would think that she had surrendered. Secretly, though, she had missed the man's protection—the spoiling care he had given her all those months at San Paolo. In her artful way, Lucrezia had taken every opportunity to drop hints about the captain's unrelenting affection (never the word *love,* though) and the value of his presence here in Florence for her and the baby, implying there were far larger values awaiting them after the war. "You're the one who needs rest, Charles," she ventured, "not me. Lucrezia told me thousands of refugees have come to San Paolo since the war ended." She allowed herself to look at him. "You're exhausted, aren't you?" It was her turn now to care for the tall handsome American Irishman.

"It's not the refugees. I'm used to those problems." He gave vent to a laugh. "What I'm not used to is sitting around a hospital waiting room for five hours. You had me worried!"

"You were here the whole time?"

"Of course. The nurses thought I was the father."

Sylvie and I were going to have children, but she died before we had the chance. His inadvertent admission of having borrowed from her his own lost fatherhood touched and saddened her. "Thank you for staying with me, Charles," she said. The sadness gave way to something much larger than gratitude, but something less than love.

The baby's face reddened and corkscrewed into a look of furious temper. A little cry broke from his mouth. "He's hungry," she said.

"He also has your temper."

The infant's shrill cry shattered the silence of the ward. Anna opened the laces of her gown. Somewhere in the ward a woman cursed as Anna lifted the baby to her breast. She was shamefully ignorant of the ways of child care, but tried to look as if she knew what she was doing. Abruptly, the screaming stopped as the baby found her—instinctively recognizing what he wanted and what she offered—and closed his mouth around her nipple.

"He must be starved," Charles said, "you were asleep for hours."

"They gave me drugs. He didn't want to come out."

"Obstinate, too. Like his mother."

"Not obstinate." She looked up. "Afraid. He must have guessed what kind of world I had in store for him."

Charles sat back and nodded thoughtfully. "I said it weeks ago, Anna. You can change all that."

The old familiar dangerous feeling of being closed around again by a man came over her. In his absence she had postponed the question of his proposition. It was too soon for answers. She turned to the baby contentedly suckling her. "He's smaller than I thought he would be," she said, changing the subject.

"He?" Charles chuckled softly. "You can't keep calling the boy *he,* you know. Have you thought of a name?"

"For a boy, I chose two Christian names. Angelo and Piero. Angelo Piero Lamberti."

When she looked up, he met her with an approving smile. "Angelo Piero. I like that."

"I'm naming him after my—"

"I know." He fixed her with a silencing look of comprehension. "After your father and your brother."

Anna stared at him, stupefied. She had never spoken of her father and brother to anyone—save Lucrezia—and had never given their Christian names.

"Two weeks ago, I looked at your identification file in the Control Commission office. You listed Montefalco as your place of birth.

The information on the refugee forms is pretty scant. For the future, I thought you'd need such things as your birth and marriage records, so I used my influence and sent to the authorities in Montefalco for copies. They got your birth record from the local church and the names of your relatives from the civil authority. I didn't know until then that you'd lost both your father and your brother in a reprisal execution. You never told me that, Anna."

"No." She turned away. "I didn't think you needed to know such things." She thought back to her reasons for secrecy with Charles. To help her, he would have opened an investigation into the deaths of her father and her brother. From that to Kruger, and from Kruger to her, was only a short distance.

"Why?"

"That's in the past. There's nothing to be done about it now." She remembered her vow, though, the night Kruger retreated and burned the public buildings.

"It would have explained to me why you were always so unapproachable. Why you seemed so bitter toward the Germans. Why you seem so protective—even a little possessive—with little Angelo Piero Lamberti here." He smiled.

"He's the only good the war left behind for me."

Charles nodded. "Did you think he wasn't included in my bargain?"

"Whatever there is of me, the largest share will always belong to him."

Charles thought for a moment, then nodded his assent. "At any rate, they had everything in Montefalco but your marriage record. I gather you weren't married there."

"No." Having to elaborate on her lie at this moment sickened her. "I went to the town where my husband was stationed. To Borgo San Lorenzo."

"Borgo San Lorenzo was burned last October."

"Yes. Three months after we were married. By the Germans."

"Then the records are gone."

"I suppose they are. They burned everything." She had chosen, of course, a town where she knew everything had been lost. She thought suddenly ahead to the distant future and the trap she had laid for herself with that one small lie to the Displaced Persons Commission: if she did not tell the truth now, if she postponed it further, she would not be able to go back. She would go on telling the lie: to herself, to Charles . . . and eventually to him—Angelo

Piero Lamberti. She sat up. "Charles," she said in a misery of panic and doubt.

"Never mind the records. It doesn't matter. Later, if the authorities need information, you can simply tell them yourself."

Deprived of her nipple, the baby began to cry.

"All the authorities need are a few facts for your papers. Now lie back and relax. The kid's hungry," he said in English. He smiled. "Eventually, you and Angelo here will have a whole new set of papers. And—who knows?—a whole new life, as well."

III

Outside the American commander's office door, Kruger glanced again at the reception-room clock: 7:55. He was twenty-five minutes late. Major Dorf had sent word through Shinker at dinner that he was to appear at the major's office in the German Administration building at 7:30. Given the fact that a movie was playing that night in the officers' mess hall, Dorf must have had urgent reasons. Major Dorf never missed the twice-a-week showings of American movies.

"All right!" the familiar voice shouted from behind the door. "Come in!"

The American sergeant at the reception desk nodded. The sign stenciled on the door read: COL. ALBERT M. PETERSON.

Kruger opened the door. The colonel sat behind a plain wooden desk covered with neat stacks of papers. "Sir." He saluted, American-style.

"You wanted to see me?" Peterson lifted his bullish steel-gray head and frowned.

"Yes, sir."

"You're—" The colonel gestured, fishing for his name.

"Lieutenant Karl Kruger, sir."

"Right. Sit down."

Kruger took the straight-backed chair in front of the desk.

"Now what's on your mind, Lieutenant?" Peterson suddenly assumed a fatherly tone.

"I asked for an appointment with you to discuss one of my fellow officers, sir." The decision to confront Peterson had been four days in the making. Given the dark mood of the Lagergestapo since Oster's appearance, he had realized yesterday that he could no longer postpone taking action. The opportunity had come this morning when the notice went up in the PX announcing the movie that night. Everyone attended the movies, even the Lagergestapo. The colonel was waiting for him to go on. "It concerns a Lieutenant Werner Metz, sir. Do you know the man?"

Peterson's face soured. "Vaguely. He's a newcomer. A trouble-maker, I'm told."

"Were you told that by Sergeant Weingaertner, sir?"

The eyes widened, warily. "What are you implying, Lieutenant?"

"I don't want to imply anything, sir. I want you to know the facts."

"Go on."

"I gather you've heard of what we call the Lagergestapo."

The face suddenly clouded. "Rumors."

"Rumor or not, sir, the Lagergestapo is a fact. The same men who control your labor program control our local Gestapo. Like the Gestapo in Germany, sir, they make lists. Lists of men to be punished. Anti-Nazis, deserters, anyone they think has turned against the Reich. Metz, sir, is now at the top of their list." He hurried on, seeing Peterson about to interrupt. "I think you should have Lieutenant Metz transferred to Camp Ruston, sir, before you have a murder to answer for."

"I see." The threat of another investigation this late in the war gave pause to the colonel.

"I mean, at once, sir."

"Has he been threatened?"

"Yes, sir."

Peterson considered his forthright reply. "In that case, why hasn't Metz himself come to see me?"

"He won't do that, sir." He thought of Minsk and Metz' choice— almost his wish—to die.

"Why?"

"I can't explain that, sir." He took a different tack, seeing the colonel's belief waver. "It's enough, sir, that you know he's a deserter."

Peterson's eyes betrayed his knowledge. Like Father Straub, he was bound to secrecy. The Americans alone had access to prisoner files. "So you want me to arrange the transfer?"

"Yes, sir. Immediately."

"I'll talk with the boy in the morning, Lieutenant, and hear his side of the story."

"I beg you, sir. He won't agree with me, and there isn't time. The Lagergestapo— They hold secret meetings—trials. Courts of Honor. They try the accused in secret and then—and then they hang them. Kholer, for instance."

"That was suicide, Lieutenant."

Kruger looked up at the clock, exasperated. "It was murder."

"Are you in a hurry, Lieutenant?"

"Sorry, sir, I was ordered to report to Major Dorf's office a half hour ago."

Peterson gave a snort and chuckled. "You must be mistaken. Major Dorf has gone to the movies. They're showing *Watch on the Rhine* tonight in your compound. Major Dorf would cancel a meeting with Hitler before he'd miss *Watch on the Rhine*."

He felt a sudden prickling chill run through his body, thinking of Shinker's announcement at dinner. Shinker was Lagergestapo. He sat back. "I didn't realize he went to the movies, sir." He thought of the possibility of Oster and his men waiting in the darkness outside the German Administration building. It was an accident that he had decided to come to Peterson first. He was reminded suddenly of the fragile balance between his own human luck and Straub's Divine Providence.

"If you've nothing more to tell me, Lieutenant, then I think we'll call it a night."

"I have nothing more to add, sir."

Peterson motioned. "You may go, then, Lieutenant."

Kruger left the American Administration building escorted by two American MPs. The colonel's aide had provided transportation for him back to the compound. He got into the back seat of the army jeep. As they swung toward the gate, he saw high in the guardhouse tower the beam of the searchlight sweeping the roofs of Compound Three.

"What's going on, Lenny?" asked the American MP at the wheel of the jeep when they drew up to the guard at the main gate.

"Trouble in Compound Three. There's been a fight over there." The sentry turned his flashlight to the back seat. "Who's this guy?"

"One of the officers from Number Three. Sanders ordered us to drive him back to his compound."

Just inside the fence, a jeep carrying four MPs sped past in the direction of Compound Three.

"Carson says there's been a knifing. The medics have gone over. They've got it under control now." The sentry waved them on.

The driver turned down the road toward the compound. Ahead, at the northeast corner of the compound, another searchlight swept the roofs. Kruger traced the beam. It came to rest on the area between the prisoners' workshop and the Administration building.

"Let's check it out." The MP in the passenger seat motioned the driver to turn, and they swerved across the avenue toward a crowd assembled in the space next to the Administration building. Three jeeps were drawn up in the darkness next to the building, adjacent to the workshop.

"Looks like those fuckers have had another one of their brawls," muttered the driver, pulling to a halt beside the other jeeps. Kruger caught sight of two medics just beyond the searchlights. He swung out of the jeep, following the MPs. In the space between the workshop and the Administration building someone squatted over the figure of a prisoner stretched out on the ground. Blinded by the searchlight beam, he could not at first recognize either man.

"Hey, you!" An American MP motioned for him to keep back.

He pretended not to see the MP and continued out of the light. A few yards from the workshop, he came to a halt. It was Father Straub kneeling over the figure. He lifted his head and nodded toward him, then bent down to the outstretched prisoner.

He felt the blood drain from his body.

Straub was lifting the head of Lieutenant Werner Metz in his hand. Werner's face was ash-gray in the bright white searchlight.

He took a step forward, then stopped, seeing Straub bend his ear to Werner's mouth. He was hearing the man's confession.

Two soldiers hurried by, carrying a stretcher. Then he saw what they were bound for: a second prisoner lying in the darkness next to the workshop. The soldiers dropped the stretcher on the ground. By the way they lifted the prisoner and slung him onto the stretcher, he knew that the man was dead. The blade of a knife glinted in the man's chest, and the head fell back as the soldiers lifted the stretcher. A pair of gold glasses slid from the face. Kruger made an inane gesture with his hand, seeing the face of Rudolf Oster: lifeless, the mouth frozen open in a grimace of rage.

He looked back toward Father Straub and saw the priest shift his weight, balancing Werner's head in his left hand. There was an expression of intense struggle on Werner's face as he tried to move his lips. "I killed him, Father," he muttered, "I followed him here, and I . . . I killed him."

An enormous stain widened across Werner's chest. In the monochromatic light the blood looked black.

Werner struggled to lift his head. A word hovered on his protruding lips. The left eye, directed up to Straub, widened with terrific effort. "Minsk," he said. Then his head sank down into the priest's hand. Blood came from the open mouth and ran down the side of his face.

The open left eye, Kruger saw, had been fixed in death. He remembered telling Werner in the shower that evening about his fears of a Lagergestapo reprisal against him. Oster had again threatened him that afternoon with retaliation for his desertion. Metz had promised to meet him outside the movie theater, and he had seen Shinker call him aside to tell him about Dorf's order to meet him at the Administration building. He had told Metz about the appointment and dismissed the lieutenant's warning not to go.

Father Straub closed the dead man's eyes.

He remembered another eye fixed in the death of another execution, remembered how the Italian had looked up at him with sadness, not for himself, but for his executioner. Metz had said it made little difference to him whether he died here or later in Germany when the war was over. He touched his forehead, thinking of the long unbroken rope of responsibility.

As you get older, Karl, you will discover that the Providence of God has to work in the most appalling conditions.

"*Deinde, ego te absolvo de peccatis tuis* . . ." Father Straub began the words of the absolution and raised his right hand, drawing a Cross through the air.

III
1955

CHAPTER 1

I

"I repeat," the voice said over the terminal PA, "due to low ceiling visibility at Los Angeles International Airport, all incoming and outgoing flights will be temporarily delayed."

Low ceiling visibility. Fog. Kruger counted four idle planes outside the window of TWA's Gate Six. He looked at the terminal clock —12:46—calculating: the flight from Munich would have arrived in New York at 5:15 that morning, they would have cleared customs there, then changed planes for the 7:30 flight to Los Angeles. It was maddening to have the whole carefully worked-out plan come apart in the final lap.

He started through the crowd toward the public telephone booths.

In his last letter home he had described what they must do at every stage of the trip so there would be no confusion or panic.

He maneuvered around a woman fussing angrily with her hand baggage. "Excuse me, ma'am."

She looked up and stepped aside, embarrassed by her language. "Father," she said, flustered.

And now, Kruger thought, moving on, what if the airline rerouted the plane to another city, San Diego perhaps? There would be no one to meet them: strangers in a strange land.

Kruger pulled the telephone-booth door closed and dropped the coin in the slot. *God's will.* He thought ahead to the awesome miracle about to take place two days from now: his ordination to the priesthood, the culmination of eight long years. He dialed the South Los Angeles number of the San Felipe parish rectory. Nine years, counting that long year of indecision and doubt following his release from the prisoner of war camp in Louisiana.

The phone rang a third, a fourth time. If both Father Straub and Father Mendoza had been called out, there would be only one car between them. He had assured Father Straub, San Felipe's pastor, that he would have the parish car back to the rectory by midafternoon.

The line connected. "San Felipe," Straub answered with a German-Spanish accent.

"Father Gunther. This is Karl. I'm out at the airport now."

"Great! Have they arrived?"

"We've got fog out here. They're circling, waiting to see if it's going to lift."

Straub laughed. "Relax, my boy. Don't worry about the car. I'll get a ride if I get called out."

"Sorry about the delay, Father."

Straub was silent for a moment. "It's not the fog, is it, Karl? It's your parents."

Straub, of course, could read his mind even over the phone. Last night, when he arrived from St. John's seminary to stay with Father Straub for the two remaining days before ordination, they had talked about his anxiety at seeing his parents for the first time in fourteen years. "Yes, Father. I'm nervous."

"How do you think they feel?"

He had a point. It was he, not his parents, who had chosen to stay apart all these years. It was he who had chosen to go to France for those two years after the war; he who had written letters with a hundred excuses for not coming home. "You're right, Father." He saw a man pacing outside the phone booth. "I'd better hang up, there's a guy waiting for the phone."

"A little advice from an old friend, my boy." Straub chuckled. "While you're out there fighting with God over the accident of fog, try to have a little faith in Providence."

"Right."

"When they get in, take them to the hotel. Don't worry about the car."

"Thanks, Father."

"You're welcome, Father." Straub hung up.

Kruger left the phone booth and took a seat near the lounge window. He could use the time to fulfill his daily obligation of reading the breviary. He took the small black-leather book from his suit-coat pocket and opened it to the place where he had earlier left off. After months of practicing, it was still difficult to snatch a moment here and there to read the daily Latin prayers. The breviary had not yet become a habit with him.

Elizabeth and Walter: the picture of his parents as he last remembered seeing them crowded out the Latin prayer he had started. 1941: he remembered quite clearly. He came home for a two-day leave after graduating from *Offiziersschule*. His father had not yet taken over the bicycle shop, and they still lived in the working-class tenement he had known as a boy. His mother, he remembered, had tried to make his visit—the first in almost three years—as festive as possible, but with Hitler's war in full swing, food was even more scarce than it had been before the war. His father, an ardent Nazi, had dismissed their lack of food and fuel as a welcome self-sacrifice for the Fatherland, but had spent a week's worth of rations to celebrate his graduation. During the war, while he was in Norway, France, and Italy, and then later, when he went back to France after the war, his mother had regularly written him. Toward the end of his second stay in France, her letters had been filled with thoughts of his homecoming. But by then, at the end of '47, he had known he would not go back to Germany; had known, too, that he could not tell her why, for a confession of his war crimes in Italy would have destroyed his parents. From the end of '45 until '47, when he immigrated to the United States, he had kept silent, waiting for accusations to come from Italy. But none had come. At the end of '47, with the approval of the Los Angeles Catholic Archdiocese, Father Straub had made the necessary arrangements for him to immigrate to the United States and enter an American seminary to study for the priesthood. His letter home to his parents, so he gathered from the reply he received later in America, had caused as much dismay as it had pleasure, for the question still remained unanswered: why had he not entered a German seminary?

"Attention, please," the voice came over the intercom. "We've been informed of a temporary improvement in runway conditions. We now announce the arrival of TWA Flight Thirty-four from New York at Gate Six. Passengers departing on Flight Twenty-six . . ." The voice went on with instructions for the other waiting flights as Kruger rose and maneuvered his way to the arrival door. Would he recognize them? he thought. They would both have aged in the last fourteen years. His mother had sent photographs only last year, taken in front of their new house in the more prosperous Bogenhausen section of Munich. His father had done well with his bicycle business. From a simple shop he had expanded into manufacturing bicycles and now owned a factory on the outskirts of Munich.

Remembering Walter's grueling hardship between the two wars, he had looked forward to hearing firsthand how his father had come to be the owner of his own factory.

The passengers filed from the plane toward the terminal door. None, as yet, resembled a middle-aged German couple.

He thought to himself, perhaps Straub was right after all; perhaps for designs still unknown to him, God had planned it all this way for them. Fourteen years—the interval had seemed like an eternity.

In the turmoil, Kruger did not recognize the very average-looking couple standing just inside the arrival door. The balding man, a little plump for his height, wore a wrinkled brown business suit; the woman, with graying hair curled in the neat American Mamie Eisenhower fashion, wore a dignified navy-blue suit and white blouse. Then her face broke into a familiar girlish smile. "Walter! Here's Karl!" his mother called in her soft Bavarian German and started forward.

Relief broke across his father's ample round face.

"Karl!" his mother cried. *"Liebchen!"* The word—the voice—came back from his childhood, still fresh.

"Mamma!"

They embraced. She felt smaller and more fragile than he remembered. Her hand fluttered excitedly over the lapel of his black suit jacket as she drew back and looked at his Roman collar. *"Liebchen,* you look wonderful!" she said in German.

"You, too, Mamma." He beamed. Hearing German, a woman next to them glanced in their direction.

"Son!" The deep resonant voice had not changed. His father grabbed hold of his arm.

"Papa!" Karl pulled his father forward and hugged him. His father's embrace, always bullishly awkward, had not improved over the years. "You look great!" Kruger said in English, then caught himself and went on in German, "You haven't changed a bit!" He thought, on the contrary, he has changed a lot. He was no longer the trim tough man of fourteen years ago: the bicycle repairman. His father, meanwhile, was saying how much he, on the other hand, had changed. "You look older, my boy! More mature!"

Kruger noticed how tired his mother looked. "Let's get your baggage."

"Ja! Good!" his father exclaimed. As always, a man of few words.

Kruger took them by the arm and led them through the crowd. They followed docilely like children, grateful for his guidance. He could see they had found America and the English language bewildering. A sign overhead read, BAGGAGE CLAIM.

"There!" His father pointed. "That sign says 'baggage claim,' no?"

"That's right, Papa."

His father gave one of his good-natured Bavarian laughs. "I take it your mother didn't tell you in her letters"—he broke suddenly into English—"I can now speak and read some English! Your mother can speak, too!"

"Listen to you, Papa!" Karl jostled his father, playfully.

"Elizabeth! Speak English to Karl!"

"Papa," she admonished, smiling.

"She speaks English!" his father insisted.

Karl said in English to his mother, "Did you have a nice flight over, Mamma?"

"Yes. Nice. But long."

"There!" Walter interjected. "You see?"

Karl continued in English, "You two have been studying! Why didn't you tell me?"

"Papa has studied." Elizabeth returned to German. "He needs English for his business."

"I have businesses all over Europe now, son. In England, too. And now even in America."

"Mamma wrote me about the factory. You have your own bicycle factory now, don't you?"

Walter beamed. "A big factory! Near Passau. You remember Passau?"

"Sure. I remember Passau." He remembered passing through Passau on his outings with the Hitler Youth groups.

"We make our own bicycles. Racing bicycles."

"I want to hear all about it, Papa," Kruger said as they reached the baggage-claim area. "In the meantime, let's find your baggage." He led them through the crowd toward the baggage dock.

"We have three things, Karl," his mother said, "two bags and a big parcel."

His father surveyed the chaos around the baggage dock. "Now in Berlin they have a *good* system for baggage," he announced in German, "very efficient. You wouldn't recognize Tempelhof now, my boy, it's been modernized." Walter moved ahead, pushing his way through the crowd. Elizabeth dropped back, leaving the problem of baggage to Walter. Kruger realized that nothing except circumstances had changed. He remembered how his father had always bullied his way through crowds in Munich to get close to the speaker's stand at the Nazi rallies. Then, as now, his father had abhorred the feeling of being only one of many.

"Papa needs help," said his mother. She started after him, looking alarmed.

"*Mamma.*" Kruger took her arm. "Now, relax. You stand over there out of the way and I'll help Papa. Okay?"

"Yes. You help him." She smiled submissively.

"Son!" his father called. "Here! I have them!" The sound of German and the way his father pushed his way through with the bags brought looks from the crowd around him. Kruger met him halfway. "I have the two suitcases, son! There's only the box left!"

"Let's wait until the crowd thins, Papa."

Flushed, his father frantically turned away without listening. "While I'm getting the box, son, you find a porter! We need help with these things!" He hurried back into the crowd.

Kruger reached down to move the two large bags. His eye rested on the smaller one: an old-fashioned gray box with leather straps. He recognized it at once—the suitcase he had taken to *Offiziers-schule* in 1939 and returned home with in 1941. He had left it behind in Munich in exchange for his army-issued duffel bag. The right-hand metal lock was dented where he had once forced it open with a bayonet point. He gaped at the old relic, mortified, then saw— catching his breath—the faded remains of two luggage stickers. Someone had made a halfhearted attempt to peel them off, but had left the fragment of a word, WEHRM, and the red and white center of the Reich flag with one broken arm of the *Hakenkreuz*. Kruger looked around with sudden panic. No one was remotely interested, no one had seen the evidence on the side of the bag.

"Karl?" his mother said.

"Papa's gone to get the box."

"Is something wrong?" She saw the expression on his face. "Did they lose Papa's box?"

"No, Mamma. Everything's here." He lifted the bags and turned the luggage stickers toward the wall. "Papa wants a porter, but I think we can manage."

"Karl!" His father came through the crowd pulling a big oblong cardboard box across the floor. "Did you find a porter?" Hearing the German and seeing Walter struggle with the outsized cumbersome parcel, people turned to stare.

Karl hurried to help him. "We can manage, Papa. The car's not far away."

"They promised! In Munich, the American agent for this airline promised there would be people to help!" Walter set his end of the parcel on the floor and looked around. "I paid money to have this delivered!"

"*Walter.*" Elizabeth gently took his arm. "Never mind, *Liebchen.* We're here. We'll manage."

Walter yielded to her—helpless, as always. He turned to Karl and beamed like a child. "I brought it for you, son," he said meekly.

"It's one of Papa's bicycles," said his mother.

Kruger flushed. "Papa."

"The priests in Germany ride my bicycles," his father said, "they're all over Munich."

The name was printed on the side of the box in tilted red letters to advertise speed: KRÜGERCYCLE. And below that, in smaller German letters, *Eine Wertmarke.* "Thanks, Papa." Karl squeezed his father's shoulder affectionately.

"You're welcome, son."

"You and I can manage this. We'll take one thing at a time."

"Yes, *Liebchen,*" his mother encouraged Walter, "let's do it Karl's way."

II

"Miss Fitzgerald!" Weidenfeld called from the direction of Columbia's Ferris Booth Hall. Anna kept moving across the mall. If he cornered her now, she would be late picking Angelo up at his school Midtown, and the stores would be closed. "Oh, Miss Fitzgerald!" Professor Weidenfeld caught up with her as she passed the statue of the Alma Mater in the center of the campus mall.

"Good afternoon, Professor." She feigned surprise but kept moving down the walk toward Broadway.

"I've read your final paper, Miss Fitzgerald." The professor wheezed from his dash across the campus. "It's good. I'm impressed."

"Thank you, Professor. That's encouraging."

The burly ill-kempt undergraduate professor of history kept pace with her, struggling to remove her term paper from the papers under his arm. "You chose an interesting subject, Miss Fitzgerald," he said, "perhaps a little specialized for an undergraduate, but interesting." He returned her term paper. "My only objection to your conclusions is that you reduced yourself to conjecture in your political analysis of Indo-China."

Her final fourth-year term paper in history had been Charles' idea. She said, pleased with her A+ grade and her efforts, "I chose a subject I thought would be useful for the future, Professor. For my graduate studies."

"I gather you've applied to our graduate law school, Miss Fitzgerald."

"*Mrs.* Fitzgerald, Professor," she said, correcting him for the hundredth time that quarter. "Yes, I applied six months ago."

"Excellent." They passed the iron gates on the west side of the campus and crossed Broadway at 116th Street. The professor waved to a student. "You will, of course, need recommendations, Miss Fitzgerald. Now, Professor Greene, the dean of the Law School, is a close friend of mine." His bright paisley tie blew up into his face on the wind from the Hudson River.

Anna smiled. The professor's reputation for pursuing the undergraduate girls was a notorious joke around campus. This term, *she* of all people. "My husband was associated with Columbia after the war when Eisenhower was president of the university. Charles is an attorney here in New York now. He works with the United Nations, but he keeps in contact with faculty. I doubt there will be any problem with recommendations."

Weidenfeld, the proverbial absentminded professor, adjusted the horn-rimmed spectacles on his nose, flustered. "I was only trying to be helpful."

"I appreciate the offer, Professor. And I appreciate your attention to my term paper. But I'm used to doing things my way—on my own."

"Of course. I understand." Weidenfeld's face turned crimson. "I take it you need a taxi."

"Yes. I have to pick my son up at school, and I have shopping to do in Midtown." The light changed.

He kept pace with her across the street. "Taxis are hard to find at this hour, I'll help you."

"That's very kind of you."

On the southbound side of the street the professor flagged an approaching taxi. He said, "I'm very impressed with a woman your age going to graduate school. And you're a mother, too?"

"Yes. I have a ten-year-old son."

The taxi swerved to a halt. "Here. Let me help you inside." The professor opened the rear passenger door.

She shifted her briefcase to her left hand and allowed Weidenfeld to take her arm. "Thank you."

"Good-bye, Miss Fitzgerald."

"Good-bye, Professor."

"Where to, lady?" asked the driver, impatiently.

Anna waved back to the professor as the taxi pulled away. She sighed and sat back. "We're going to the Dalton School on the East Side. Eighty-ninth Street."

"Right."

Anna turned her thoughts to Angelo, the Dalton School, and her shopping errands. She looked at her watch: 3:50. There would be time to pick Angelo up, drop him by the apartment on Fifth Avenue, and reach F.A.O. Schwarz before closing time. Provided the driver took a direct route through Central Park. "Take Ninety-sixth Street across, please," she said. The man was short, heavyset, and balding. She looked at the name printed on his hack license: Caselli. The trimmed black moustache, the ruddy complexion: a typical New York Italian taxi driver, she thought, settling her briefcase in the seat. She looked at Angelo's birthday list and smiled.

He had carefully printed and numbered the presents he wanted for his tenth birthday:

1. A racing bicycle.

He had badgered both her and Charles for months about the bicycle. The city, she had repeatedly explained, was no place for a child on a bicycle. Central Park, the only place where he could avoid traffic, was a dangerous place, even in daytime. She had forbidden him to play alone in the park. Charles had been an easier target for Angelo's appeals. Accustomed to lavishing *things* on the boy to make up for what was missing in the *blood,* Charles had conceded to Angelo's argument that he was now old enough to fend for himself. She had taken Charles aside and begged him not to let the child manipulate him so. By now, she had said, Angelo was well aware of the power he had over his stepfather, and was using him to get what she could not allow. Charles, in defense of his case for Angelo's maturity and approaching adolescent independence, had returned to the old themes of possessiveness and overprotection, but had, in the end, backed off.

2. A chemistry set.

On that, they had both agreed. A chemistry set was out of the question, living as they did in an old unfireproofed building.

She wondered if Angelo had not purposefully put the bicycle and the chemistry set at the top of his list as a challenge to their authority.

"You want to take Ninety-sixth across, lady?" asked the driver.

"Yes, please. Then down Fifth, if it's not crowded."

"You sound Italian, lady. Are you Italian?"

"Greek." She returned to the list. She had been through this scene countless times in countless New York taxis. The questions were invariably the same.

He laughed. "I know the Greek accent. You sound Italian."

3. A football.

The football she could get at F.A.O. Schwarz.

"You even *look* Italian, lady," the driver persisted, playfully. "You remind me of that young Italian actress—the new one—you know—" He snapped his fingers, appealing to her vanity. "What's her name, Sophia—?"

"Loren."

"That's the one. Sophia Loren. You look like her."

"Miss Loren is younger." She thought, Angelo is already ten, and I'm already thirty!

"You're Italian, aren't you?"

"Yes." She forced her attention to the list:

4. A hoop.

It was a silly toy. She had seen kids playing with them in the park across the street, twirling them around their hips. He had wanted one for months. Maybe at F.A.O. Schwarz, too.

"Where you from?" came the inevitable question.

"Tuscany."

"No foolin'!" He swung into Ninety-sixth Street and started through Central Park. "That's where I'm from! Pistoia. You know Pistoia?"

"Yes. I've passed through it." She looked away toward the patch of sloping green meadow at the end of its spring bloom. She had passed through Pistoia in late October of 1944 as a refugee.

"How long you been in the States?"

She had the answers ready to satisfy curiosity and, at the same time, avoid the painful subject of Montefalco. "I came after the war."

"You were there for the war?"

"Yes."

"Me, too. Where were you?"

"In Florence." Florence had always worked in the past, for it was large enough so that she was not drilled about particular events and particular people.

"I was in Pistoia. I was seventeen." The driver let up on the accelerator behind a slow city bus. "When the Americans got to Pistoia in September of '44, they shelled us. The place was swarming with *tedeschi*. My parents, both of 'em, got killed in the bombing. Me and my brother, we went east after that, over to Florence, where you come from. We spent the rest of '44 and the winter of '45 in a refugee camp near Florence. San Paolo. You heard of San Paolo?"

"Yes, I've heard of San Paolo." Its makeshift wooden barracks and the squalid tent city erected in the dairy pasture came to mind, and with the picture the memory of five months and three weeks of grubbing poverty, helpless terror, and relentless dread as she grew huge with Angelo.

"A stinking hellhole of a place, lady. Anyway, like me you came here after the war."

"Yes." She wished she had taken the subway down to Ninety-sixth and crossed over on a public bus, as she frequently did when she had more time.

"You been back since?"

"No. Never." She heard the inadvertent tone of bitterness in her voice and, before she could prevent herself, pictured the despised face of Lieutenant Karl Kruger.

"Me neither. Never had the money." The driver looked at her in the rearview mirror as he swung from the park and raced for a green light at Fifth Avenue. "I'll take Fifth down and then cross to Madison on Ninetieth."

"Whatever." She thought of Charles' generous and innocent offers to take her and Angelo back to Italy those first two years of marriage, after they moved to New York. For a while, as the taxi moved with the southbound Fifth Avenue traffic, there was a welcome silence.

By 1948, Charles had given up suggesting she return to Italy and visit her family. He had also given up asking why she never wrote letters to her mother and sister. She had written twice to her mother, at the end of 1945, to say she had married an American, Charles Fitzgerald, and had moved to New York City; and again in 1946 to say she had given birth to a son named after her father and brother, Angelo Piero Fitzgerald. At the same time, she had written Livia, hoping her sister had kept her secret about Angelo's real father, and had suggested it would be better for all of them if they let her mother and grandmother go on believing that Angelo had been born in America in 1946, for there was no good to be gained now "with the truth."

The driver swung east on Ninetieth.

Livia had written back from Pisa, agreeing with her. She had married, the letter had said, a man from Pisa and had given birth to two children, a daughter and a son. With her husband, a man who worked for a northern Italian industrial company, she had apparently settled into a comfortable middle-class life in Pisa. It was in that letter that Livia had given her news of Kruger. "It's certain to us here," she had said with a hint of satisfaction, "that he's dead." A postwar investigation by the people of Montefalco had led to German war records. Apparently, Kruger had been killed in the late fall of '44, south of Vergato. Consequently, no charges against him had been filed in Italy.

Anna tried to turn her attention to the birthday list, but old dormant feelings came back.

From 1945 until late 1946, when she learned of Kruger's death, she had lived in the hope of finding him and bringing him to justice. Livia's news had unleashed a turmoil of conflicting feelings: an unwanted and unexpected grief, on the one hand; and on the other, relief. For it was now clear that she would no longer have to debate with herself the issue that had plagued her since the war: faced with the choice, if she found Kruger, would she speak out and bring him to justice with a public trial in Italy, or would she keep silent and thereby protect Angelo, Charles, herself, and the security of their life here in America? From Livia's letter, it was clear that she was the only survivor from Montefalco who had gone on looking for Kruger. After the letter, she had gratefully let go of that responsibility.

The driver swung back west on Eighty-ninth, heading for the Dalton School.

The price she had paid for Angelo's security and future had been high. She had given up communication with Montefalco and her family. Not only could she never take Angelo to her home in Italy, she could never let Italy come to America. Worse, she had allowed both Charles and Angelo to conclude that she simply disliked her family. She had never shown Livia's and her mother's letters to Charles, nor had she spoken to Angelo of his grandmother, except in passing. The price for safe anonymity had been very high.

"*È lei sposata?*" The driver finally spoke as they approached the school.

"*Sì,*" she replied, then continued in English, knowing that her Tuscan mountain accent would betray her. "I married an American and moved to New York. We have a son," she added, going further than she had intended.

The driver pointed ahead. "You mean, the kid here at the Dalton?"

"Yes."

"Was he born here or in Italy?"

Anna ignored the question, pretending to study Angelo's list.

5. A cowboy pistol.

She sighed. Neither she nor Charles permitted him to play with even toy guns. As a result, Angelo had sought every opportunity to play with other children's toy guns, and placing the gun on the list was one more act of defiance to test her.

"I say, lady, was your son born here or in Italy?" the driver insisted.

"In Italy." She saw the youngsters playing on the sidewalk in front of the school and sat forward to look for Angelo.

He appeared from behind a parked car, saw her, and made a dash toward the oncoming taxi. "Hey! Mom!" He waved.

Anna grit her teeth as the driver braked and swerved to avoid Angelo.

"That him?" He pointed.

"Yes. That's him."

Angelo hurried to the back door. He was tall for his age, lean and gangly—caught in that shapeless interval between childhood and adolescence—all arms and legs. "Darn you, Angie," she muttered, seeing the boy's school blazer tied around his waist by the sleeves and his tie yanked down from the collar. She moved her briefcase to make room.

Angelo yelled back to some boys loitering near the school. "It's the day after tomorrow, you guys!" He threw open the door. "Mom," he complained, "I could have walked home."

"Get in, Angie, we're blocking traffic." Grumbling, he tossed his book satchel onto the seat and got in. "Seventy-ninth and Fifth, please," Anna said, then turned to Angelo. "Untie your blazer, Angie," she chided, "and don't sit on it that way."

"Are we goin' shopping?" He untied the sleeves and tossed the blazer on the seat.

"I'm going shopping, you're going home. Janet will be there. She'll stay with you until Dad gets home."

"Aww, Mom! Lemme go! I want to look at bikes!"

"Bikes? What are you talking about, *bikes?*"

"Dad's getting me a bike."

"No, Dad is *not* getting you a bike. We've been through this before. Now settle down."

"*Jeez.*" He rolled his eyes and flopped back against the seat.

"Now, straighten out, Angie!" she shouted, at the end of her patience. The driver glanced back through the mirror. She checked her temper and ran her fingers through the boy's thick dark hair to smooth it. "Look at you. You've been fighting again."

"Fighting! I haven't been *fighting!* Jesus, Mom!"

"Don't use that name, Angelo."

The driver smiled, speeding up toward Fifth.

"I want you to take a bath, wash your hair, and put on clean clothes before your dad gets home. Is that clear?"

"You're doing my birthday shopping, aren't you?" He grinned.

"Never mind what I'm doing." She saw the knowing twinkle in his bright blue-green eyes and softened. "You take a bath, young man, and leave the surprises to me."

"Janet," he moaned. "I can't take a bath with *her* there!"

Janet, the young nineteen-year-old college student she had hired two months ago to sit with Angelo during the hours she was away at Columbia, had replaced Marissa Lewis, another unreliable college student. "And why not, may I ask?"

"She comes in while I'm in the tub and watches." He glanced up, testing.

"Nonsense. Do as I say. If your dad comes home and finds you like this, he'll bathe you himself."

As they crossed Park Avenue, Angelo sighed and looked through the window. "I want a racing bike," he said, "not just a regular one."

The determination in his voice took her breath. "You'll be lucky, at this rate, to get anything at all, young man."

The driver smiled to himself again.

"I asked Hudson and McKinsie to come to the party," Angelo announced, flatly.

I've raised a brat! she thought to herself. The taxi bounced over a pothole. If Charles had spoiled the boy with things, she had spoiled him with affections. Charles had once said that she cared too much, that she had taken on the burden of two in her affections: meaning, of course, the boy's dead father, the dead soldier, Lamberti. She thought back, suddenly, to San Paolo and the Villa Patini: from the beginning, Charles had neither wanted nor tried to compete with what he thought were her lingering feelings for the dead Italian soldier. Nor she with his for the dead Silvanna Agnoletto-Patini. They had both played parent to Angelo, and they had laid out the terms of their marriage when he was still a baby and too young to understand.

The driver turned south on Fifth Avenue.

"I've told you, Angie, eight's the limit for the party," she said.

"McKinsie makes eight."

She had made endless resolutions not to succumb to his manipulations, but her decisions were useless long-term resolutions. "We're taking eight to the band concert in the park; so if you ask anyone else, *you* will be the one to stay home."

"McKinsie, I told you, makes eight, Mom."

She had failed in the daily short-term resolution. The boy's power over her (and he knew it in his child's way) had the force of seduction. "All right," she said, "but just remember."

Angelo brightened. "Dad says there's going to be fireworks!"

"That's right." The outdoor high school band concert in Central Park had been her idea.

"Wow! Neat!"

The driver had slowed, stalled in rush-hour traffic. "How old are you going to be, son?" he asked.

"Ten."

"Angelo? Is that your name?"

"Yes, sir."

"I got a cousin in Italy named Angelo."

"That's my granddad's name."

"Your mom says you were born in Italy, right?"

Mildly surprised, Angelo looked at her. "Yes, sir. In Florence."

The traffic moved ahead. "And your dad's an American, right?"

Angelo again looked at her, puzzled and annoyed. "No, sir. My dad was Italian. He was a soldier. He got killed in the war."

The driver's eyes were in the rearview mirror. "Oh. I misunderstood. I thought your mom said your dad was alive."

"That's my stepfather. He's not my real dad." The boy looked down and fidgeted with his sleeve.

Anna's feeling of helplessness was instantaneous and familiar. She said, "My first husband, Angelo's father, died in the Second World War. Just before the boy was born." And on the heels of her regret came the suffocating thought of the old self-propagating lie. "When you get to Seventy-ninth, driver, just stop at the park side of the corner." To forestall further talk of Angelo's dead father, she said, "When Dad"—the word sounded strange in her ear—"gets home, tell him I may be late for dinner. There's food in the fridge. You two go ahead and eat."

The taxi passed Eightieth Street. F.A.O. Schwarz was another twenty blocks. She made a quick decision. "Stop here, driver." She opened her purse. "I'll walk my son across the street and get another taxi downtown."

"Mom," Angelo complained, "I can walk *myself* across the street."

The driver pulled into the curb as Anna handed him a ten-dollar bill. "Get out, Angie. Take your satchel and your jacket and get out."

The driver handed her change back. "Happy birthday, son."

"Thanks."

Anna tipped a dollar, grabbed her briefcase, and joined Angelo on the sidewalk. She took a deep breath of the sweet air blowing across the park, relieved to be out and free. They walked in silence to the streetlight. The apartment building, an eighteen-floor granite monolith built in the early twenties, was directly across the street. She said, "Okay. I'll leave you here. You can cross on your own. I'll get another taxi."

"Jeez, Mom." He looked at her quizzically. "Big deal."

She stooped and kissed him on the forehead. "Tell Janet she can leave when Dad gets home. And here, take my briefcase up with you."

He grabbed her case and made a dash for the green light. "Remember! A racing bike!"

III

"The party isn't until the day after tomorrow, Paul, so keep it down here for the time being," Charles said, wheeling the bright blue racing bike into the lobby of the apartment building, "you know what a snoop he is."

"Yes, Mr. Fitzgerald." The doorman chuckled. "We'll keep it here in the office and bring it up before your party."

"By the way, it's a secret from everyone. So don't say anything to Mrs. Fitzgerald." He winked.

"You leave everything to me, sir."

Charles pressed the up button at the elevator in the rear of the marble lobby and caught sight of himself in the mirror. He smiled. The debate with Anna over the bike on top of his two days with Dulles' Defense Department had left bags under his eyes. He looked older than his salt-and-pepper forty-one years.

The bike. He sighed. He would tell Anna of his decision tonight, after dinner. He had weighed the pros and cons and reached a verdict in favor of the bike. There was more here at stake, he had told her, than a kid's bike. Angelo was approaching adolescence. It was time she let go of the child and gave the boy a taste of freedom, choice, and responsibility. "If you hold on like this much longer, protecting him from the world," he had said yesterday, "the world's going to take its revenge on you both."

The elevator door swung open. "Afternoon, Mr. Fitzgerald." John, the small, wizened Irish elevator man stepped back. "You're home early, sir."

"Yes, John. For once, the war merchants let me off early."

They started up to the fourteenth floor. Normally, on the ride up, they bantered about politics and the UN. Charles leaned against the wall, too exhausted to make the effort.

Dulles' Defense Department had drained him. Despite the obvious military chaos in the Vietnamese capital of Saigon, his suggestions at the UN for reshaping America's Asian foreign policy had fallen on deaf ears. By the end of today's meeting with President Ngo Dinh Diem's counsel, he had wanted to throw in the towel and resign from both his advisory position on the National Security Council and the Southeast Asian Treaty Organization. In his opinion, unless Eisenhower forced the Diem regime to reform its Vietnamese domestic policy at the level of the local peasant farmer, until civil freedoms were restored and political nepotism checked at the local government level, the Vietnamese were going to throw their eggs into the Chinese Communist basket before the decade was out. He had seen the handwriting on the wall as far back as the Second World War: in Roosevelt's, Churchill's, and Stalin's geopolitical decisions at Yalta. He had warned Truman's foreign policy advisors at the time: The mistakes and failures we have made in the past and those we overlook in the present will only propagate in the future. The West had won the war, but had lost the peace; and twelve years later, Eisenhower had inherited the winds of Roosevelt's Far East compromise with Stalin.

"Your son came in about an hour ago, Mr. Fitzgerald," said John.

"And the young lady, Miss Mumford?"

"She's been here maybe a half hour."

Anna had said she would go shopping after school and not be back till late. "You mean, Angie was up there alone?"

"He first went up to the apartment, then went down to see the Clemons boy on the ninth floor. He was there a few minutes, then went back up." The elevator came to a rest. "I think he got into a little scrape with young Jeff Clemons, sir. He came back with a bloody nose."

"Christ." Charles left the elevator. "Thanks, John." He turned back, exasperated. "If you see Jeff, ask him to come up and see me."

"Yes, sir."

Charles fished for his key on the ring. Anna's sitter, Janet Mumford, should have been present when Angie got home from school. Like the others before her, she was not going to last. Angie had been through countless sitters in the last four years.

He rattled through the fifteen keys, trying to find the apartment key.

God knows, too, he had encouraged Anna's ambition for a college degree and, more recently, her decision to continue into law school. The problem was Angie: divided responsibilities. She had said it ten years ago back in Florence: she would never again hand over responsibility for herself to anyone. *Ever,* she had said.

The key ring fell from his fingers. "Damn!" He stooped for it.

In the aftershock of Hitler and Mussolini, he had seen the same kind of resolution in other victims of the war. As with the others, he had thought her resolve would soften after the war. But the fear implicit in her resolution had lingered on: that someone someday would come along and take away her means of survival or, worse, deprive her of the one prize she had salvaged from the war, her son. Trust and faith were not Anna's strong points.

We've got too many goddamn *things!* he thought, fishing through the keys. Car keys, office keys, keys to the safe, keys to the house in Connecticut! God knows, she had nothing to fear from *him!*

He found the key he was looking for and turned it in the lock.

Fear of becoming a victim again, an obsessive sense of responsibility was one thing. With Anna, though, he had always sensed a dark side to that coin: blame. She had always explained that lingering undercurrent of blame by pointing to her family's tragedy. But the other side of Anna's self-responsibility was self-blame.

In the foyer he heard voices in the living room at the far end of the passage. The radio was going: the frenetic raucous screams of Angie's favorite singer, Elvis Presley. He set his briefcase on the floor. Miss Mumford's key lay in the silver dish. He pocketed the key and turned down the hall toward the living room.

Accepting this exaggerated need for self-reliance and independence (even the attendant self-blame) as one of those unhealed wounds of war, he had been the one to encourage her college degree and her notion of a career for herself. He had been the one, too, who suggested nannies for the boy during her school hours. The trouble was, the independent career woman had run aground against the protective and caring mother.

"Dad!" Angelo jumped up from the floor where he sat playing cards with Miss Mumford. "Did you get the bike?"

"Bike? What are you talking about?" He saw the girl's school books open on the table next to the bookcase as he turned off the radio.

Angelo bounded across the room. "Oh, Dad." He laughed and playfully punched him. "Come on, you promised."

"I promised nothing of the kind." He took hold of the boy's chin. "What's this with your nose?"

Janet got to her feet. "He was that way when I came in, Mr. Fitzgerald." She was dressed today in a flouncy skirt and NYU college sweater, with penny loafers and thick turned-down socks. She had taken care to emphasize her ample breasts under the sweater. She came toward him, fixing Angelo with a cunning smile. "Tell him what happened, Angie."

"I got beat up by some boys after school."

"Oh? Where?"

"On the street." The lie was so transparent that the boy started to color.

"That's not what you told me, Angie," said Miss Mumford.

"You promised!" Angelo shouted, pulling his chin away.

"Promised what?" Charles let the boy flounder for a moment in his own dilemma. "Miss Mumford?"

The girl's tiny hazel eyes darted between Angelo and him, assessing where her advantage lay. "I got here on time, Mr. Fitzgerald, but he didn't show up. So I went downstairs and waited in the lobby. When I came back up around four, he was here. He'd gotten into a fight with Jeff Clemons on the ninth floor."

Angelo glared at the girl with cold calculating hatred. In the momentary look, Charles read a chilling cruelty in the child's expressive blue-green eyes. "I think we'd better call it a day, Miss Mumford. You can phone later this evening for Mrs. Fitzgerald's schedule tomorrow."

The girl circled wide of Angelo and gathered her books. "All right."

"I'll see Miss Mumford to the door," he said to Angelo. "You pick up those cards from the floor and put them away. When you've done that, go to your room, take a bath, get into some clean clothes, and come back here to the living room. I want to talk to you."

Angelo sighed.

"I've got so much *work* to do, Mr. Fitzgerald," Miss Mumford said, clutching her school books to her breasts as they walked toward the foyer, "what with final exams and all."

He would let Anna take care of the firing as she had taken care of the hiring. Besides, until her law studies began again in the fall, she could go back to being a mother again.

"I'm almost certain I left my key here." Miss Mumford pointed to the silver dish.

"Never mind. The doorman will have one." He opened the apartment door and waited while she combed her shoulder-length pageboy blond hair, studying herself in the mirror as she worked.

"It's really a *drag* having to do classes all day, baby-sit in the afternoon, and then study all night."

Her childish imitation of world-weariness brought a smile to Charles' mouth. "I'm sure you manage, Miss Mumford."

The telephone began ringing in the living room.

Angelo dropped the deck of cards and hurried to the phone table near the window. "Hello?" He listened, puzzled, to a weird crackle and clicking noise at the other end. "Hello?"

There were garbled women's voices at the other end, voices from a great distance, speaking in a foreign language which sounded something like his mother's Italian.

"Hello!" a voice broke in, this one closer, sounding American.

"Hello," he repeated.

"This is the transatlantic operator. I have a transatlantic call for Anna Fitzgerald."

"She's not here."

"Just a minute, please." The woman raised her voice. "Hello! Italy? Montefalco?!"

"*Sì! Pronto!* Montefalco here!"

"The party you are calling is not at the number at this time." The American woman said her words slowly. "Do you wish to leave word?"

Far off, women talked in Italian all at once, and then the Italian operator came back, "Hello! We will talk to the party you have on the line."

"Go ahead," said the American operator.

"Hallo!" a different Italian woman shouted.

"Hello!" Angelo shouted back.

"Anna?"

"No! This is Angelo! Anna's my mom! She's not here!"

"You are Angelo?"

"Yes, ma'am." He wondered if he could be talking to the grandmother he had never seen.

"I am—" She seemed to have difficulty with English. She started again, "I am Luisa Miceli. I am Anna's mother. Your *nonna.*"

Angelo knew the word *nonna.* "Yes, ma'am." He felt suddenly frightened. He thought of his grandfather and his uncle who had been shot by Germans in the war. His mother's silence about her family in Italy had always mystified him: something always present but ignored—and therefore of forbidden importance.

"Where is your mamma, Angelo?" his grandmother asked. She, too, sounded frightened, but also kind.

"She went shopping, ma'am."

"Che? What? She is where?"

"Shopping! She went shopping for my birthday presents! It's my birthday the day after tomorrow, and she went to buy presents!" He realized he had said more than he needed to say.

"Your *birthday?"* The *nonna* said the word with a funny kind of gentleness like the grief of having missed something.

"Yes, ma'am."

"How old are you, *bambino?"*

"Ten."

There was a pause at the other end. "I don't speak good English, Angelo *bambino,* but you are only *nine* years old now!"

"No, ma'am. I'm ten."

Again, a pause. And now he could hear another woman's voice in the background, talking to his grandmother. The *nonna* came back on. "Is your papa there, *bambino?* Let me talk to your papa."

Angelo saw his stepfather hurry into the room. "It's my grandmother in Italy," he said. "She called to speak to Mom."

Charles took the receiver. Miceli—he had to think quickly for the woman's first name: Luisa, of course. In ten years of marriage he had never spoken to the woman. "Hello?"

"Hello! Signore Fitzgerald?"

"This is Charles Fitzgerald, Signora Miceli! I'm Anna's husband!"

"I am Luisa Miceli, Anna's mother! I am calling from Italy—from Montefalco!"

"Anna isn't here, signora. Can I help you?"

There was a pause at the other end and the sound of women's angry voices arguing at once: he could make out the Italian word *padre:* father. Angelo had meanwhile gone to sit on the sofa against the far wall, looking worried.

Signora Miceli came back on the line. "I call to give Anna news of her *Nonna* Adelaida."

"Yes, signora. *Di me, signora, parlo Italiano.*"

The sound of Italian suddenly unleashed a flood of words interrupted by choked sobs. "Tell Anna for me that . . . that her grandmother is dead. She died two days ago—here in Montefalco. . . . She was seventy-five years old . . . before *Nonna* died . . . before she died she asked me to find Anna in America and tell her . . . tell her that all is forgiven. With *Nonna* Adelaida, all was forgiven, tell her that, signore. Tell Anna that her *Nonna* Adelaida loved her very much . . ." She paused, recovered, and went on, "She died in peace here at home—a stroke. *Colpo.* Do you understand?"

"*Sì, signora. Capisco. Uno colpo.*" The word *blame* came to him as he spoke.

"We buried her yesterday in the cemetery of San Tommaso."

"I will tell Anna, signora. I'm sure she will want to call you back." He reached for the pencil and pad on the telephone table. "Will you give me your telephone number there in Montefalco? I will have Anna return your call."

"No. It isn't necessary to phone. Just tell her what I have said."

"As you wish, signora." Again he thought of the long unexplained expanse of responsibility and blame.

"One thing more, signore—" The woman hesitated. "The boy who answered the phone. He is your son, no?"

"*È mio figliastro, signora.*" Angelo knew the word for stepson and looked at him, puzzled.

"I don't understand, signore. He was born in America, no?"

"No, signora. In Italy."

"When, signore?"

"In 1945."

Again, she paused. "Anna wrote to me after she moved to America—in 1946. I know the year. I have only two letters from Anna, both from America. She told me you were married in Italy in 1945. In Florence. She told me she gave birth to your son in America the next year."

Charles stared at Angelo, wondering what, if anything, the boy had learned from his grandmother. Like fragments of a turning kaleidoscope, the facts at the end of the war shifted and moved in his mind, but would not come together. He said, dreading the blind path he was taking, choosing his Italian carefully so that Angelo would not know the words. "The boy is the son of your daughter's first

husband, the Italian soldier who was killed during the war in Italy—
in the fall of 1944, signora."

"I don't understand. A husband? 1944? That's impossible! Anna
left home at the end of October 1944. She was not married then,
and she was not married before. There is some mistake. You must
ask Anna yourself, signore."

Charles had stepped to the window with the phone. He stared
down at the sidewalk fourteen floors below where a young man on
roller skates was weaving backward through the pedestrians by the
park. "Yes, signora. There is some mistake. I will speak with
Anna." There was, of course, no mistake, and both he and Signora
Miceli knew it.

"Tell Anna that her *Nonna* Adelaida has left her a ring. Her own
wedding ring. My daughter Livia will send the ring to her there in
New York. For my part, signore, I have done what her grandmother
wished. I do not have more to say."

"I understand. I will give Anna your message. Please accept my
condolences. I am very sorry. Truly, I am." He looked at Angelo
and saw that the boy was doodling with a ball-point pen on the
cover of a copy of *Life* magazine.

"Grazie, signore. Addio."

"Addio." The line disconnected abruptly. Charles returned the
receiver and stood for a moment looking at the setting sun behind
the jagged skyline of Manhattan's West Side. Across Central Park in
the darkening silhouette of a building fronting the park, he saw a
light go on.

"Did Mom's grandmother die?" Angelo asked.

"Yes, son. The day before yesterday." He crossed the dark wood-
paneled living room and turned on the lamp at the far end of the
sofa.

The boy dropped the magazine on the coffee table and pocketed
the pen. "How did she die?"

"A stroke."

"Was she old?"

"Yes. In her seventies."

"Mom's mom thought I was going to be nine."

"She made a mistake, son."

"She said I was born in America."

"She's confused, that's all. You were born in Italy, in 1945. I was
there. You know that." He sat down next to the boy on the sofa.
"What else did she say?"

"Nothing."

The kaleidoscope fragments shifted in his mind, but still did not fall into place: the dead soldier, Lamberti; Anna's appearance at San Paolo, pregnant in the winter of '45; her ten-year alienation from her family. There were records of the American refugee camps in the military archives, but it would take time to trace Anna's personal file. Nor had he bothered to look at it carefully back in the days of San Paolo. He said, "Listen, son. Tonight isn't the time to tell your mother about this call from her mother. When she comes in, I don't want us to say anything about her grandmother. Okay?"

"Why?" It was a child's logic speaking.

"It wouldn't be kind just to tell her right off like that. She's been doing your birthday shopping. She'll be in a birthday mood." He smiled. "What's say we wait and tell her this bad news *after* your birthday. It won't make any difference if we wait. And that way we won't spoil her fun for the party."

Angelo thought for a moment. "Okay," he said.

"Good." He reached up and gently turned the boy's chin so he could see the bruise. "Now let's talk about Pinocchio's nose."

CHAPTER 2

I

Last night, before leaving his parents at their West Hollywood hotel, Kruger had made a safe calculation of the time it would take to drive from San Felipe in southeast Los Angeles to West Hollywood, and from there back to the Cathedral of St. Vibiana in downtown Los Angeles. He had told his parents to be ready at 6:00 A.M. The ordination ceremony would begin at 9:00. He had left plenty of time for the drive in case Straub's old '47 Ford gave out again on the freeway.

They passed Crescent Heights Boulevard, moving west on Sunset, winding along the flank of the Hollywood Hills. "The hotel's just a few blocks away," Kruger said. "We'll make a left turn down the hill."

"Are you nervous?" Father Straub chuckled.

They were five minutes late, already, and the carburetor on the old car had acted up on the freeway again. Fortunately, West Hollywood's busy Sunset Boulevard was deserted at this hour of the morning. "What did you feel the morning of your ordination?"

"It was so long ago, I can't remember."

The rector of St. John's had instructed the *ordinandi* to be at the cathedral by eight. Kruger said, "Ten to one the carburetor gives out between the hotel and St. Vibiana."

"Trust me, Karl." Straub laughed. "This morning, you're in God's hands."

"I hope God's hands are on your carburetor, Father."

"Have faith, my boy, have faith."

Last night, before going to bed, he had meditated on the virtue of faith, feeling the old uncertainties return. He had reminded himself that the step he was taking tomorrow morning was an irreversible one. Last night's question now returned: had he been called by God to the priesthood, or was he merely following the echo of his own voice? "Two blocks down," he said, pointing to a side street running downhill from Sunset between two Spanish-style apartment buildings, "make a left turn."

"Are you enjoying the visit?" Straub asked.

"To tell you the truth, no. Not really."

"Where did you take them last night?"

"My mother wanted to see Hollywood's Hollywood, and my father wanted to spend money, so I took them to the Brown Derby."

"Fourteen years is a long time. Have they changed?"

"Yes and no. My mother has aged, but she's still the same patient submissive woman she was in 1941. My father has made money, finally, so he likes to play tycoon. Otherwise, he hasn't changed. He still thinks Hitler was the best thing that ever happened to Germany."

Father Straub made a slow left turn down the hillside. The street was lined with two- and three-story apartment buildings. "Which one?" He indicated two bungalow-type hotels between the apartment buildings.

"The Spanish one with the palm trees." Kruger had booked his parents into a comfortable but modest Hollywood hotel so that his mother could get a taste of America's fabled movie capital and his father could feel comfortable with the bill. He had not counted on his father's penchant for spending beyond his means.

"You're not getting on with your dad, are you?"

"No. Last night, he brought up the war again. He wanted to talk about 'old times,' as he called them. He thinks I ended the war as some kind of Wehrmacht hero."

Straub pulled into the curb in front of the two-story Spanish building set back from the street behind a tropical display of banana trees. "I'll wait here in the car."

Kruger lingered for a moment to say, "He brought me one of his bicycles as a present. Last night after dinner, we came back here and he assembled the thing in their room. He even brought the tools with him. He had a lot to drink at dinner, so he talked. What he said brought it all back to me, Montefalco, everything. I left feeling wrong about this morning—my ordination. Like a man running from something. A fugitive. You know what I mean, you've heard me before."

"Then ask yourself again, have you ever been accused of a crime?"

"No."

"To your knowledge, has anyone ever filed charges against you?"

"No." Kruger thought back eight years to the time of his immigration. No charges had been filed against him in Italy, as far as he had discovered. He had assumed what Rudolf Oster had once told him was still true: Montefalco had concluded he was dead.

"You know as well as I do that there were legitimate military reprisals during the war, you've read the rules," said Straub. "If no charges were ever filed after the war, then you must assume what you did was maybe morally but not legally wrong."

"I've been debating that for eleven years."

"And?"

"Heads or tails, I can't seem to win. Would the charges have been filed if they knew I was alive?"

"Tell me this, Karl, do you want to be a priest?"

"Yes." He sighed. "With all my heart."

"Do you believe you have a vocation?"

"Believing, of course, is not knowing."

"In other words, it boils down to faith."

"Yes."

"Do you know any faith that's not blind?"

"No. None." He reached for the boxed orchid next to him in the seat. He had bought it yesterday for his mother and kept it overnight in Straub's refrigerator. "I'll only be a minute." He got out.

His parents were waiting in the small Hawaiian-looking lobby, seated in bamboo armchairs. "Son!" His father got up quickly as he came through the door. "We were worried!" he said in German, "You're late!"

"It's okay, Dad. We've got time."

His mother got up, beaming. "Look at you," she said, admiringly.

He was dressed, as yesterday and the day before, in the same black clerical suit.

He hugged his mother. "You look beautiful, Mom." He saw his father's expensive new suit. "You both look great." His father wore a blue summer suit and a white silk tie; his mother a two-piece white suit, pastel silk blouse, and a white brimless hat. They had obviously taken great care with their clothes, though they appeared to be dressed more for a wedding than for an ordination.

Kruger handed his mother the orchid. "Here. I thought you might like this."

"Karl! Look, Papa! An orchid!" She had, of course, never worn orchids in Munich. She opened the box and carefully removed the extravagant purple flower. "Imagine!" she said.

"He got you the real thing!" said his father.

Karl took his mother's elbow. "Now, come. We're going to be late. You can put the flower on in the car." He led them through the little Hawaiian patio with its banana trees and tropical plants to the car parked at the curb. Father Straub got out and came around to meet them. "Mr. and Mrs. Kruger." He greeted them in English.

"Mom and Dad, this is Father Straub. He's an old friend of mine."

"How do you do, Father Straub." Elizabeth offered her hand.

"Mrs. Kruger." Straub shook her hand warmly and turned to Walter. "Mr. Kruger, it's a pleasure. I've heard a lot about you over the years."

The implied compliment pleased Walter. "We are honored, Father." He gave Straub's hand a stiff formal shake.

"You ride up front with Father Straub, Dad," Kruger said, "I'll ride in back with Mom."

They struggled into the old Ford. On the way back down Sunset the talk in English revolved around Straub's ten-year friendship with Karl. "Father Straub is the man responsible for my coming to America," Karl said at last. "He was the first one to talk to me about the priesthood. We met back in '45, when he was chaplain—" He left the sentence unfinished, realizing he was leading back to the war.

There was a moment of uncomfortable silence. Karl thought of the still unanswered question about his failure to return home after the war. His father said in English, hopefully, "You are German, Father Straub?"

"I was born in Germany, Mr. Kruger, a village near Hamburg. I moved to America after the Great War, in the twenties. I've been here ever since."

Walter said in German, "You met Karl when he was a prisoner?"

"In 1945," Straub replied in German. "I was chaplain at Camp Windsor in Louisiana where Karl was interned."

"He was a Wehrmacht officer when the war ended," Walter went on, "an *Oberleutnant* when they captured him."

Captured, indeed, Kruger thought to himself and turned to his mother to divert the conversation. "Here, Mom," he said, "let's pin your orchid on."

"I'll take Fairfax down to Wilshire," Straub said, making a right turn, "and Wilshire down to the cathedral."

"That's the quickest." Kruger pinned the orchid to his mother's white lapel.

Walter said suddenly, "They decorated him during the war, Father. They gave him the Iron Cross First Class after he went to Italy in '43. Karl sent me the medal at the end of 1944, and I've kept it." He looked back at Karl. "Did you know that? I've kept it all these years." He laughed.

"No, Dad. I didn't."

His mother saw his embarrassment and gave a small apologetic smile.

"Tell Father Straub about your bicycle business, Dad," Kruger said quickly to change the subject.

"Your son says you make bicycles," Straub encouraged.

"That's right, Father. Racing bicycles. I've got a factory outside Munich now, and we make a good little racing bike. Maybe you've seen them here in California—we've started shipping them to America—the Krügercycle."

"I haven't ridden a bicycle in twenty-five years." Straub laughed. They passed Melrose Avenue heading south on Fairfax.

"I started off, you know, as a bicycle repairman. That was after the Great War—" Walter proceeded to narrate the story of his slow painful rise to success in the bicycle business. Kruger smiled at his mother and she returned the smile. He tried to turn his thoughts to the awesome change for him about to take place a short distance away at the cathedral. "I didn't have much success until after '41," his father said, "until after Karl came home from *Offiziersschule*. Up to that time, I'd only been an employee at the bicycle shop." He turned back to Karl. "You remember that shop, son? The one off the Kaufingerstrasse?"

"Yes, Dad. I remember."

Straub slowed as they started through the Fairfax Jewish district. The street on both sides was lined with small shops, delicatessens, a couple of bakeries, and a kosher meat market. A few elderly people moved along the sidewalk outside an outdoor non-kosher vegetable market open for early morning Saturday business. "I don't know Munich myself," said Straub.

Walter turned in his seat. "It was in the late winter of '41 that I took over ownership of that shop, Father. That's how it all began, I was given ownership of the shop in the winter of '41."

"Given?" Kruger asked, puzzled. He had always thought his father had bought the shop.

"That's right, son." His father glanced around at the passing shops.

Baumann. The name of the shop came back to Kruger, and with it a cold chill ran through his body. "I must have misunderstood," he said faintly.

"The old owners moved away," Walter went on. "That was in November of '41. It was wartime, the government—the army—needed bicycles for the troops, so I took over running the shop."

Baumann. Karl repeated the name silently to himself, and it slipped into place in his mind like the missing piece of a puzzle. "I see," he murmured.

His father was staring through the window at the shops with their signs written in both English and Hebrew, a few with Stars of David to advertise the kosher quality of the goods. Next to him in the seat his mother had turned away from the window to stare at her hands in her lap. Her face had flushed with the mute evidence. Kruger anticipated the question before his father turned to Father Straub and almost innocently asked, "What's this?"

"This is our Jewish neighborhood. These people all came here after the war." There was no indictment, though, in the man's voice. Straub, of course, knew nothing of the Baumanns.

"Ah," said Walter.

Kruger saw a look of tangled grief and shame pass across his mother's face. She closed her eyes for a moment.

II

"I thought you liked squash cooked that way," Anna said.

"I'm not hungry." Angelo toyed with his fork. The food on his lunch plate was untouched.

"You're not hungry because you've got tomorrow's birthday cake on the brain," Charles said.

Anna saw another meaningful exchange of glances.

"No I don't," said Angelo, "I don't have *anything* on my brain."

"What's going on between you two? Ever since last night you've been acting like a couple of Russian spies. What are you two plotting?"

"Nothing," said Angelo.

"Birthday surprises," Charles said. Again, they looked at each other.

Anna cut into the cold chicken breast she had prepared. Last night, she had arrived home a little before six-thirty. There had been a brief discussion about Angelo's bloody nose. She was an experienced enough mother and a good enough law student to know that something had happened in her absence that they did not want to talk about. For an hour and a half, while she warmed their uneaten dinner, set the table, and served the food, the two of them had gone out of their way to be helpful. In their forced conversation she had recognized the signs of a mutually concluded pact of silence. She now said to Angelo, "I thought it was your birthday secrets we're supposed to be keeping, not mine."

He reached for his milk glass and pretended to be thirsty.

"How was Columbia today?" Charles asked.

"I had an exam today, postponed from last Wednesday. Contemporary History. The Second World War."

Angelo suddenly inhaled and choked on the milk, splattering a mouthful across the table.

"Sweetheart!" Anna exclaimed. "Don't drink so fast!"

"I'm sorry." The boy set the glass down and wiped his mouth. "It went down the wrong way."

Charles asked, "What's for dessert?"

"Blueberry pie."

"Can I be excused?" Angelo said. "I'm not hungry."

"I thought blueberry was your favorite." Anna fixed him pointedly.

"I can't eat any more. I'm full."

"Full of what? You haven't eaten anything."

"I ate some chicken."

"And the squash? I fixed the squash the way you like it, the Italian way."

Angelo gave Charles a curious questioning look and then said to his mother, "How do you know it's the Italian way? Who says so?"

Anna sat back and laughed. "Of course it's the Italian way, silly. I ate it this way when I was a child! What are you talking about?"

"That was a long time ago. How do you remember? You haven't been in Italy since you were a girl."

"Angie," Charles cut in. "If you've finished, then excuse yourself and go."

"Excuse me."

"Where are you going, honey?" Anna asked.

"To my room."

She watched him hurry from the dining room. "What's going on around here, Charles?"

He looked up, feigning surprise. "What do you mean?"

"You know what I mean. What's going on? Something happened, and you're both afraid to tell me."

His face relaxed. "We'll talk after lunch. In the meantime, how about some blueberry pie?"

They ate pie, drank coffee, and talked aimlessly about the white paper Charles intended to write for the Dulles State Department on the subject of the American arms buildup in Indochina. Charles left her alone to clear the table and wash dishes. The maid had Saturday off. When she left the kitchen and passed Angelo's room, the door was closed and they were talking. She drew the glass curtains over the living-room windows to block the hot afternoon sun and went to the sofa to wait. Out of habit, she turned on the lamp at the far end of the sofa. Behind it—she stared, puzzled—the small ornately framed portrait of Silvanna Agnoletto-Patini, Charles' first wife, stood on the table, propped against the wall. She glanced back toward the wall where the portrait had hung unmoved for the last six years, surrounded by Charles' inherited collection of Italian masters. Odd, she thought, trying to connect the painting to last night's and this morning's mystery.

As she stood beside the table, Charles came into the room and went to the bar. "Do you want a drink?"

"No, thanks." She sat down, feeling uneasy, and watched him pour a brandy. He never drank liquor during the day.

He turned from the bar, rolling the snifter between his hands. "I just had another chat with Angie."

"What's going on here, Charles? Has Angie done something?"

He sat down in the armchair next to the sofa, sipped his brandy thoughtfully, then said, "I told him I wanted to wait until after the birthday to tell you."

"Tell me what?" she asked, alarmed. Where Angie was concerned, he had always come straight to the point with her.

He sipped again. "The first thing is Miss Mumford."

"Oh." Her relief was only partial. She sighed, realizing he had arranged his arguments, as always, with systematic logic and would not be hurried. She wondered if she would be brought to the stand this time as a witness for the defense or for the prosecution. She had known for some time that Miss Mumford would not last.

"When I got in yesterday afternoon, John was on the elevator. He told me Janet had come in late again. When I came upstairs, she was here with Angie. She lied to me about being late and tried to blame Angie for her negligence."

"I see. It isn't the first time. I've been holding back firing her for some weeks now. I'll phone her on Monday and tell her to pick up her check from Paul at the door."

"Sweetheart"—he tempered his impulse to reproach with affectionate patience—"you should not hold back doing and saying things when you know the problem is not going to go away."

She knew, somehow, that his reprimand touched on much larger issues. "I know, Charles. As usual, I was hoping that the problem would correct itself."

"It never does, Anna." He sat forward. "That's something you'll have to learn if you want to be an attorney. You can't postpone a piece of damaging evidence, for instance, if you know it's going to come out in the trial. This habit of hiding the truth is going to get you into trouble." He saw her larger shock and sat back. "At any rate, I took the key from her."

"I'll handle it, Charles. Now what else?"

"When I questioned Angie about the fight, he lied to me."

"You said he went downstairs to see Jeff Clemons."

"He did. But that's not what he told me when I came in and questioned him. He told me some boys had beaten him up after school."

"That isn't true. I picked him up at school."

"I know. I had a little talk with him last night. Apparently, Jeff has been razzing him."

"About what?"

"Calling him names. Yesterday, outside the building, he called Angie a dirty half-breed Irish wop. Angie went down later. They got into a fight. Angie got the worst of it, and the Clemons boy threatened him if he told."

"Why the name-calling?"

"Angie said he'd told some other boys that his real father was an

Italian soldier who'd been killed in the Second World War. A war hero. Jeff heard the story and accused Angie of lying—of making up the story to cover the fact that he's a half-breed. That I'm his *real* father."

"What difference does it make?"

"In itself, none. But the kids at school obviously know what difference it makes to Angie. He bragged about your Lamberti, and they saw through it. They saw the truth about *me*. Children have a cruel way of using those things."

"Charles," she said, "I'm sorry," reading his and not Angelo's pain at that moment, mindful of old wounds and old responsibilities.

"I'll come back to that subject in a minute, Anna." He sat back again. "Let's talk about Angelo's lie." He looked down into his glass at the dark finger of liquor at the bottom. "Like Janet Mumford, this isn't the first time Angelo has lied. Where do you think he's picked up the habit?"

She said, breathlessly, "You're saying, from me, aren't you?"

"Holding back or avoiding the truth is a way of lying, my love," he said.

She reached back in her mind across ten years to grasp just one single truth to give him, wondering where she could now begin. He waited for her to speak. But there was no single truth, she realized, except one, that she could offer. And that one truth was unspeakable. For in giving of it, she would bring down the whole safe edifice not only of their lives but of Angelo's life as well. She said, knowing that he already held one of her truths, "Please, Charles—you already know what you want to hear. What are you getting at?"

"Angelo is beginning to ask questions. He's reached the age when he wants to know things."

"*What* things?"

"About you, about me, about us together and us before we met. For instance, a little thing—he asked me when you had your portrait painted."

"I see."

"That's my failure. I should have told him the truth from the beginning."

They had told him as a child that the portrait was of her. They had considered telling him the truth about Charles' first marriage and had decided nothing would be gained in doing so. How could a child comprehend the mysterious ways of the adult heart?

Anna asked, finally, "Did you tell him?"

"No. It's too late. He would only despise me for it."

"What else did he ask, Charles?"

"He asked why we had never given him brothers and sisters."

She read a look she had not seen for years: grief and loss. *Silvanna and I were going to have children.* His words back in 1944 had stayed with her. "Dear God," she said.

"Yes." His gaze rested on the glass on his hand and his eyes glistened in the light from the window.

She left the sofa and knelt down beside his chair. The thought that he had finally told Angelo the truth about his lost fatherhood and her responsibility for the continuation of that loss filled her with a strange sensation of relief, gratitude, and grief. She gripped his knee. "You told him, didn't you?"

"Yes."

"Everything?"

"I told him the truth. I told him that he was the only child that we ever wanted. That he was everything."

"*Charles.*" She felt the old wound open. "That is not the whole truth."

"For you and me, together, it's the truth. Remember? I went into this marriage with my eyes open. Let's face it. You were honest with me from the beginning. Or so I thought. I may have wanted a child with you, I could have chosen to go elsewhere for children, but I chose to accept your terms. I have never regretted my choice or blamed you for the price of it. *Più bello che si può.* Remember?"

She nodded. "How can I forget?" Then her face clouded over.

He leaned forward, took her head in his free hand, and kissed her on the lips. "I told him there are many ways of loving. I told him some kinds, like yours for him, are in the blood. Others, like mine for him, are in the heart." He grinned. "Who was it who said, 'Like a flame—in the heart, ever burning'?"

"He understood you?"

"In his own way, yes."

She thought back to Angelo's avoidance of her last night and, again, his avoidance at lunch this morning. "What else, Charles? There's something else, isn't there?"

"Sit down, honey."

She did as she was told, guessing before he spoke what the next item was on his agenda. She caught sight of a new copy of *Life* magazine on the coffee table. On the cover was a photograph of a white-tusked elephant charging toward the cameraman across a grassy African savanna. Somebody had doodled on it with a ball-point pen. She said, "You think I've raised a liar, don't you?"

"I don't know. I'm merely asking where you think he's picked up the habit."

She recognized the wriggling doodle marks of Angie's hand: he had drawn a stick figure of a man facing the charging elephant. The man had a rifle drawn against his shoulder. Angelo had costumed the figure in clothes that looked vaguely like those of an Italian soldier. In a bubble above the figure's head, drawn like a cartoon, he had printed the words *"Viva L'Italia!"* Bullets streamed from the gun into the head of the charging elephant. Across the forehead of the enraged animal, he had drawn a Nazi swastika.

"Anna?" Charles said. "Did you hear me?"

"Yes." She caught her breath. "I heard."

III

The eleven St. John's seminary candidates for ordination to the priesthood began the solemn procession from the vestibule to the cathedral sanctuary to the slow rhythm of plain *a cappella* Gregorian chant. The men were ranked two across and five deep. They wore deacon's vestments: a long white alb tied at the waist with a white cincture, a white stole draped diagonally over the shoulder, a white maniple pinned to the left sleeve of the alb. They carried lighted tapers. Behind, following, came the diocesan clergy: *monsignori* and priests, the faculty of St. John's seminary, and the cardinal archbishop of Los Angeles, vested in a white cope and miter, accompanied by a deacon and archdeacon.

The front pews of the crowded cathedral had been reserved for the families of the *ordinandi*. Walter and Elizabeth Kruger were among those standing in the first pew. As Kruger passed, he smiled, and they returned the smile, proudly, and his mother's smile brought back the memory of the *Frauenkirche* in Munich and his early dream of the priesthood. As he started up the steps into the cathedral sanctuary, he saw Father Straub among the clergy and recalled the priest's admonition last night about the strange—sometimes almost appalling—circles of God's Providence.

The cardinal archbishop took his place at the altar facing the congregation, the miter was placed on his head, and he seated himself on the faldstool between the subdeacon and the archdeacon.

The priest acting as Notary stepped forward and addressed the semicircle of *ordinandi: "Accedant qui ordinandi sunt ad Ordinem Presbyteratus!"* he called out.

The words—Let those who are to be ordained to the priesthood approach!—gave Kruger a sudden feeling of panic. He thought of eight years of doubt and debate. Straub had said that morning, *Do you know any faith that's not blind?*

One by one, the Notary began calling the names of the *ordinandi:* "Paul Henry Anderson!"

One by one the candidates replied, *"Adsum!"* Present! and approached the cardinal to make the ritual genuflection of submission and obedience.

Waiting for his alphabetical turn, Kruger repeated to himself his long-thought-out motives for choosing the priesthood: I want to bring good into the world. The desire, he knew, was rooted in that deeper hope he had of future reparation for past evils. I want a life of service that offers as a reward an eternity of salvation rather than a mere Thousand Years of survival. An eternal, not a corruptible kingdom. I want these things and believe, in good faith, that God has called me to them.

"Karl Gustav Kruger!"

Kruger stepped forward. It is done, he thought. *"Adsum!"* He approached the cardinal archbishop and genuflected. The candle flame in his right hand wavered. Looking up, his eyes locked for a moment with those of Cardinal Boyle. In eight years of study at the archdiocese secular seminary, he had met his bishop only three times. Young for a man in his position, Francis Cardinal Boyle was in his late fifties, and his face was more like that of a corporate executive than a prince of the Church, with his pewter-colored hair and white silk miter. In the cardinal's stern eyes, he saw the challenge of a question. Then the prelate smiled, faintly. Kruger rose and returned to his place with the other *ordinandi.*

The archdeacon, Father McAdam, addressed the cardinal archbishop, *"Reverendissime pater, postulat santa mater Ecclesia Catholica . . ."* Most reverend Father, Holy Mother Catholic Church begs you to ordain these deacons who are present to the burdens of the priesthood.

"Scis illos esse dignos?" Do you know them to be worthy?

McAdam, the rector of St. John's, replied, *"Quantum humana fragilitas nosse sinit, et scio . . ."* As much as human frailty permits me to know, I both know and testify that they are worthy of the burdens of this office.

"Deo gratias," Thanks be to God, came the cardinal's response.

The formal question and the answer brought back an image to Kruger: Major General Hans Gloebel, the autocratic director of the

Offiziersschule, addressing the identical question to the Wehrmacht cadets that afternoon of graduation.

"Quoniam, fratres carissimi . . ." Cardinal Boyle exhorted the clergy and congregation to confirm or deny the worthiness of the candidates *". . . verumtamen memor sit conditionis suae."* If anyone therefore has anything against them, for God and on God's behalf, with trust, let him come forward and speak. Boyle paused and scanned the congregation, waiting for objections.

Kruger looked down at the marble floor. The request seemed to be directed at him alone. He pictured Anna Miceli and the fifty dead men in the Piazza Nazionale that autumn of 1944.

The cardinal went on, *"Consecrandus, fili delectissimi, in Presbyteratus officium . . ."* You wish, my dear brothers, to assume and carry out the office of the priesthood: he went on to remind them of their duties to offer Mass, give blessings, to be exemplary, to preach, and to baptize *". . . mortificare membra tua a bitiis, et concupiscentiius omnibus procures—"* To mortify their bodies from all vices and to safeguard themselves from all concupiscence.

Anna Miceli. He had never forgotten in either mind or body the feelings of completion and fullness he had experienced with Anna Miceli: those brief months with her in Montefalco when they had met and made love in the Adele Ravine. More disquieting than mere bodily temptation, the passing sexual urge had always been overshadowed by the memory of that perfect union of sex and love. The truth was, he knew, that had human circumstance been different for them both, they would have married and, perhaps by now, would have had children of their own. But he had burned that bridge eleven years ago.

The cardinal came to the end of the ritual sermon: *". . . nec tu de tanti officii susceptione damnari a Domino . . ."* Nor let us, by the performance of such an office, merit damnation from the Lord, but rather merit His rewards.

Kruger thought of the blind leap of faith he was making into future spiritual darkness—the gamble he was taking with eternal damnation.

The time had come for the last symbolic gesture of submission and renunciation before ordination. Kruger and his fellow *ordinandi* spread themselves out facedown on the sanctuary floor. With the ritual prostration, a profound silence came over the congregation.

Kruger closed his eyes and mentally vowed his total physical and spiritual renunciation of the flesh and the world. Henceforth, he thought . . .

"Kyrie, eleison." Lord have mercy on us. The seminary choir began the long chanted Litany of the Saints.

"Christe, eleison," the congregation responded in plain chant. Christ have mercy on us.

"Kyrie, eleison," the choir repeated.

Hearing his mother's soprano voice from the far side of the church, Kruger opened his eyes. She had always sung the Litany responses in the *Frauenkirche* with a clear fervent voice.

"Santa Maria." Holy Mary.

"Ora pro nobis." Pray for us.

The choir went on chanting, calling for prayers from the canonized members of Christ's Mystical Body: saints, patriarchs, prophets, apostles and evangelists, popes, confessors, martyrs, doctors, virgins, bishops, priests—those who had, in their own way, achieved perfection and sanctity.

"Sancte Matthaei." Holy Matthew.

"Ora pro nobis." Pray for us.

Kruger wondered at the astonishing human differences in God's saints: some—many—like St. Augustine, had risen to sanctity in the wake of terrible sin. In God's Providence and with God's Grace, anything was possible.

The choir reached the end of the Litany and chanted the Gregorian prayers for deliverance: *"A subitanea et improvisa morte . . ."* From sudden and unforseen death . . .

"Libera nos, Domine." Spare us, O Lord.

Kruger recalled his brush with the sin of suicide that despairing night eleven years ago in his Montecatini hotel room.

"Per crucem, et passionem tuam . . ." Through your cross and passion . . .

"Libera nos, Domine." Spare us, O Lord.

In His inscrutable wisdom and Providence, perhaps God had that night let him see how far down into the abyss a man alone, without God, could go, so that, for the rest of his life, he might never forget the power of divine Grace and the folly of human pride. *I, Karl Gustav Kruger, swear by God this sacred oath, that I will render unconditional obedience. . . .* There had been other vows, other promises, other fruits of obedience before.

"Ut omnibus fidelibus defunctis requiem aeternam donare digneris . . ." That you grant to all the faithfully departed eternal rest.

"Te rogamus, audi nos," he prayed, thinking of the fifty souls against the post-office wall.

Cardinal Boyle stood up with his pastoral crozier and blessed the candidates, asking God to sanctify and make them worthy of the sacrament about to be conferred.

The choir chanted the final supplication, and then there was silence.

The moment had come.

The master of ceremonies clapped his hands once, softly. The *ordinandi* rose from their prostrate positions and knelt. As the first candidate, Paul Anderson, approached the altar, Kruger glanced at his parents in the first pew. They were grinning at him. His mother toyed proudly with her orchid. He remembered the old wedding photo he had kept with him during the war. He had left it behind in the duffel bag the morning he deserted the army. Their expressions were the same, only their faces were thirty-eight years older.

His turn came. He stood up and moved to the altar. The linen amice around his neck was drenched with sweat. He ascended the steps and knelt before the cardinal. The air around the altar was pregnant with sweet spicy incense. He inclined his head, closed his eyes, and waited for the simple unceremonious gesture of ordination. The brief moment of waiting seemed like an eternity stretching before and after. It came: a gentle pressure of the cardinal's hands on his head. The hands held. It was done. Wordlessly. He kept his head bowed, his eyes closed, and felt the hands of the other assisting priests descend on his head, one by one, and confirm the irrevocable change.

When they finished, he opened his eyes. I am a priest now, he thought, forever.

He looked up and saw the cardinal's smile. He returned the smile, acknowledging his submission and responsibility, then rose and descended the steps. Turning mid-sanctuary, he gave in to an impulse and grinned at his parents. They looked for all the world like the other smiling parents around them, like proud, simple, modestly successful Americans.

He knelt down, seven new priests on his right, three waiting candidates on his left. *The end of one life and the beginning of another.*

His mother took out a handkerchief from her purse and held it to her eyes. Caught between embarrassment and solicitude, his father squeezed her arm. When the handkerchief came down, it was not the relief of joy he saw, but once again the pain of tangled grief.

Baumann: this time, the name sank through his mind like cold lead. *The owners moved away. That was in November of '41.*

He looked away toward the cross above the altar and read the agonized face of Christ crucified.

CHAPTER 3

I

"Hey, Mom!" Angelo cried. "What's this one?"

There were squeals and shouts from his nine little birthday guests in the living room.

"I don't know," Anna said, laughing, "that one's from Dad. Unwrap it and see!"

Charles smiled, rolling the bike quietly down the hallway.

"Where's your dad, Angie?" asked one little boy.

"I donno. Where's Dad, Mom?"

"He's gone to make a phone call, he'll be back."

He had left the room minutes before to get the bike from Paul, the doorman. It was to be the *pièce de résistance* of the birthday presents, a surprise. He was glad now that he told Anna last night about the bike. She had protested for a while, then conceded when he compromised with her and promised that the bike would be kept up at the country house in Connecticut. He stopped short of the archway leading into the living room. In the center of the room, surrounded by his guests, Angelo finished tearing the wrap from the big box.

"Mom!" he shouted.

"A 'rector set!" someone added over the squeals.

Anna caught sight of Charles at the archway with the bike, smiled, and drew back to the window.

"It's the one I *wanted!*" exclaimed Angelo, pulling the lid from the box, "The *big* one! Thanks, Mom!"

"You'll have to thank your dad, sweetheart, not me."

"Your dad gives *you everything,"* remonstrated one little boy.

Anna gave him a playful long-suffering look and motioned for Charles to come in.

"Leave the Erector set in the box, Jimmy!" Angie protested as Charles pulled the bell attached to the handlebar and wheeled the bike into the room.

There was a moment of silence as the ten youngsters turned to see the bright blue racing bike come rolling in.

"A bike!"

"Wow!"

"Look at that!"

Angelo got slowly to his feet, stunned, his mouth open with disbelief. Charles stopped a few feet from the boy and grinned.

Resigned, Anna shook her head and laughed. "Well?"

The kids hurried to the bike, leaving Angelo rooted to the floor. "It's a *racing* bike!" a freckled redhead shouted. A fat little kid in a baggy baseball shirt pointed. "Look! It's got everything!"

Anna laughed again, enjoying Angelo's thrill. "Well, go *look!*"

Angie made his way through the children, and they parted, waiting for his reaction. "Wow," he said, awed by the gleaming machine, wanting but unable to touch it.

"Is this what you wanted?"

He looked up. The disbelief gave way to a look of awkward unworthiness. "Yes, sir." He blushed with embarrassment.

Charles thought of the games the boy had played with them to get his way and pushed the bike forward. "It's yours, son. Take it."

Puzzled by their silent eye exchange, the other kids glanced at each other. Angelo took hold of the handlebars. "Look!" a lanky boy wearing thick glasses said, "it's even got a headlight!" The kids crowded around to inspect the bike's accessories.

Charles joined Anna at the window. "You were right," she said, affectionately circling his waist with her arm, "it's the best thing you could have done."

"You mean, he's not a child anymore?" he said, teasingly.

She conceded with a playful punch on the ribs.

"Look, Angie, it's got a silver bell!"

"And a taillight!"

"Is it what he wanted?" asked Charles.

"Exactly. That's all he's been talking about for months. Where did you get it?"

"At that bike shop near the UN."

Anna nudged him and indicated the Clemons boy, a big clumsy fellow, who had lingered behind at the fringe of the crowd, pretending to look indifferent. She smiled. "What did I tell you?"

Charles nodded. Anna and Jeff's mother had had a talk that morning and had decided to bring the two boys together. It was a question, Anna had said to him, of Jeff Clemons facing the truth about himself. He was jealous of Angie.

Someone began ringing the little silver bell as Angelo mounted the bike.

"Not in the living room, Angie!" Anna called over the shouts.

"Aww, Mom!"

"There are rules, young man!"

"It's going up to the country tomorrow," Charles added. "It's not for the city."

Angelo pretended not to hear but compromised, remaining in place and spinning the pedals furiously. "Rrrrrrr!"

"It's either feast or famine." Anna looked up and sighed.

"Look what it says, you guys," announced Jeff, whose voice was beginning to change. He moved a smaller boy aside and pointed. "It's a Krügercycle!"

Anna turned to the children, looking mildly surprised.

"What's that?" one of the boys asked.

"Don't you know what a Krügercycle is, dummy?" Jeff Clemons challenged.

Anna's face appeared curiously distressed as she stared at the bike.

Someone announced, "I know what a Krügercycle is! That's the newest kind! There's a guy in my building who's got one! He says the Krügercycle is the fastest bike you can get!"

"It's the best racing bike in the world!" shouted Angelo, spinning his pedals.

"Something wrong, honey?" Charles asked.

She seemed not to hear and moved slowly toward the children around the bike.

"Look, Mom!" exclaimed Angelo. "It's a Krügercycle. Dad got me a *Krügercycle!*"

She continued through the kids and looked down at the name printed across the fender guard. "Yes, honey," she said, faintly, "I see."

The children saw the look on her face and stopped shouting.

Charles left the window and covered for her strange mesmerized distress by playfully hugging her. "Relax. It's a perfectly safe bike." He laughed. "Angie's a big boy now, remember?"

"Right!" Angelo exclaimed and went on spinning his pedals.

"Listen, you kids," Charles called, "it's seven-thirty. The concert starts at eight. I want everyone to line up outside the bathroom and take care of business. There's no john in the park."

Four of the boys made a dash for the hallway.

Anna turned away and busied herself gathering the birthday wrappings. He took her arm. "Sweetheart, what's wrong?"

"It's nothing, Charles." She freed her arm and forced a smile.

"It's supposed to be the safest bike made today. I checked the consumer guides. It's got very good brakes."

"Never mind. It's nothing. I just—"

"Just what?" he persisted, thinking for the first time in hours of the painful announcement he had so far postponed and the questions that would inevitably follow.

"Who makes the bike?" she asked.

"Some German company. They're new. Why?"

She sighed and grimaced. "It's not important. Do you have the concert tickets?" She forced a bright smile.

"Yes." He thought of her habit of avoidance and postponement again and the frightening prospect of worse things, of lies all the way back to Florence: *He is your son, no? He was born in America, no?*

"You can ride it to the concert!" one of the boys exclaimed.

"We can take *turns* riding it," added Jeff Clemons.

Anna said, turning away, "You're going to leave the bike here, Angie. We're going to walk."

"Awww, Mom!"

"No! There's no place for a bike in the Sheep Meadow, and it's dangerous to ride in the park at night."

"He can keep it in the meadow *with* him, Mrs. Fitzgerald," the freckled boy piped up, "a lot of kids bring their bikes."

"Get off the bike, Angelo," said Charles, "and go to the bathroom. The bike stays here."

Angelo obeyed, then turned back, testing his mother with one of his downcast looks of seductive appeal. "Please, Mom. Lemme take it. I promise to be careful." His eyes watered. "It's my birthday. I'm not a baby anymore."

"The bike stays here, son," Charles said, "and tomorrow it's going to Connecticut."

Anna's resolve gave way. "What if someone steals it, sweetheart?"

The boy saw his opening. "I'll keep it with me! I promise! It's a Krügercycle, Mom, and I'll never let it out of my sight! Ever!"

II

"Hurry, children!" Anna called back to three children who had dropped behind to watch a young man giving a sidewalk violin performance. "We're late!"

The little Exler boy whizzed past them on Angelo's bike, weaving between the pedestrians on the sidewalk, heading toward the other children, who waited for him under a lamppost at the crest of the slope. "Relax." Charles took her arm. "It's perfectly safe here with all these people around."

"I know. I just don't like this section of the park." Here, the lamplit sidewalk meandered through a dense grove of underbrush and trees. It was an old and instinctive fear. "I can't help it. It's an old phobia, and I can't change it."

"From childhood?"

The pointedness in his voice puzzled her. "Yes."

The Exler boy turned over the bike to Jeff Clemons, and he started toward them down the slope, weaving dangerously.

"Only to the bottom of the hill!" Angelo yelled after him. "We're gonna be late!"

"Ten years," she said, "it seems like yesterday."

"What? Your phobia?" Charles glanced at her, teasing.

"Angelo's birth. It's hard not to still think of him as a baby." The bike sped past them. Seeing the name on the fender guard, she thought of Kruger.

"Babies don't ask questions."

The statement grazed her mind like the wind from the passing bike. She was thinking how often she had seen the name Kruger in these last ten years. It was a common name. Besides, the man was dead: but even so, the sight or sound of his name still frightened her.

"Hey, you guys!" Angelo yelled. "Hurry up! We're gonna be late!"

Anna picked up speed and Charles followed, holding her arm to support her on the steep slope. She thought back to the morning and the ongoing looks Angelo had given her. She had seen by the child's expression that something had been left unsaid in yesterday's talk with Charles. "You didn't tell me everything yesterday, did you?"

"What do you mean?"

"You know very well what I mean. I've been getting funny looks from Angie all day."

"We'll talk about it tomorrow. We're late as it is." Jeff whizzed past them on the bike.

This time the name on the bike sent a chill through Anna's arms and neck. The man is dead, she said to herself again, seeing within her the old and neglected but still limitless potential for hatred and revenge. In the next instant, telling herself she was absurd to even imagine it, the hatred swept back on her with a familiar horrifying fear. She said, dropping back, "I want to know now, Charles. I want to know everything. *Now,* not *tomorrow.*"

"*Mom!*" Angelo moaned.

The sound of band music floated over the hillside. "They've started, Mrs. Fitzgerald!" Alan McKinsie exclaimed. The other children broke into shouts.

"Later," Charles said. "We'll talk about it when we get home."

She acquiesced and followed him up the hillside, chiding herself for her momentary foolish fear. Angie's and Charles' behavior, the Krügercycle: she was imagining things. She had given up the old paranoia years ago after Livia had sent word of Kruger's death. This was one of those coincidences like the air crashes that she imagined always came in threes when she was about to travel.

Angelo took the bike from Jeff as they reached the crest of the hill. "I'm gonna ride down," he said, "I'll meet you guys at the bottom."

"Angie!" Anna exclaimed, but he had already pedaled off down the sidewalk leading into the meadow.

"I'll find a good place for us!" he called back.

"He heard me, Charles," she said, angrily. "That was downright disobedient." She watched the bike's red taillight grow small in the darkness.

Charles ignored her. "All right!" He addressed the nine kids around them. "Everyone keep together. Let's not get lost!"

Anna let the group start down the sidewalk, then caught up with Charles. "Please, Charles, tell me what's going on, I want to know."

"Not now." He took her arm again. "I'm sorry. Maybe it's time you had a taste of your own medicine. It's a lesson that will make you a better attorney later on, my postponing the evidence."

The decisiveness of his words and, at the same time, the pain in his voice silenced her. She dropped back and followed a few paces behind. Her breathlessness, she knew, was not from their rapid pace.

A large crowd of adults and children sat sprawled across the grassy floor of the meadow before a temporary wooden bandstand. The uniformed band, made up of various borough high school bands, was performing a medley of Sousa marches to the occasional explosion of fireworks set off in the clearing behind the bandstand. A roman candle, followed by a second, burst in the sky overhead, and in the light of their pink and silver sprays, Anna searched the edge of the crowd for the lights of Angelo's Krügercycle. For the moment, he and the bike were nowhere to be seen. She followed Charles and the children across the meadow, skirting the crowd. A barrage of firecrackers exploded. "Charles!" she called, suddenly panicky.

"Over here!" He motioned her to follow.

She caught sight of Angelo standing with his bike on the far side of the meadow. When they left the apartment, she had asked both Charles and Angelo to find places far back from the source of the fireworks display—away from the noise and smoke. They both knew that she was afraid of fireworks, for they reminded her of the war. The band began another Sousa march. As she reached the place Angelo had selected, she smelled the familiar but forgotten odor of burned gunpowder. "Charles," she called over the music, "please! I asked you and Angelo to sit farther back!"

"Aww, Mom," Angelo protested, "we can see *everything* from here!"

"Come on, you guys." Charles started toward an open area at the rear of the meadow under the trees. "We'll sit back here."

"This is the best place, Dad!" The other children echoed his plea.

"Mom was in the Second World War," Angelo explained to them. "She got bombed and shot at by the Nazis."

"Quiet!" someone shouted.

"Charles." Anna moved away. "Never mind." She motioned for the children to stay. "I'll move up there." She started toward the edge of the meadow.

"Anna!" Charles called after her.

"Shut up, you guys!" someone shouted from the crowd.

Anna thought again of Angelo's magazine doodle: in his child's mind, the Nazis had killed his father. She could not, of course, blame him for his feelings.

Under the trees bordering the meadow she sat down in the grass. A sweet smell of summer clover mingled with the stench of gunpowder. This time, with the odor, came an image: the vaporous cloud that had lingered over the bodies in the square that afternoon.

"Anna." Charles came toward her.

"It doesn't matter, Charles. Go sit with the children."

He dropped down beside her in the grass. "You okay?"

"Yes. I'm fine."

For a while, they sat in silence, listening to the rousing but off-key climax of the Sousa medley. Sprawled out in the grass fifty feet away down the slope, the kids appeared to enjoy the rare treat of an outdoor concert. The band was laboredly amateurish, but it did not matter. "This was a great idea," Charles said.

"I read about it last week in the *Times*. They're supposed to be the finalists in a city-wide high school contest."

Behind the band, arranged along a latticework, a giant American flag of red, white, and blue sparklers ignited. Cheers and applause went up. The kids screamed and rolled rambunctiously in the grass.

In the pause between musical numbers, Anna sat forward. "I want to know, Charles. What has Angelo done?"

He pretended to fuss with his pipe. "All this fire," he said, "and I didn't bring a match."

"All right then, I assume it was me."

He rested his arms over his knees and looked down pensively at the ground. The band began a clumsy rendition of the latest rock-'n'-roll hits. There was laughter and applause. "Angie and I were going to wait until after the birthday. I was going to tell you tomorrow."

"Tell me what?"

"The day before yesterday, while you were out shopping, there was a phone call—from Italy."

The word silenced her. She watched a thin vapor of smoke float across the meadow. "Go on," she said, finally.

"From your mother in Montefalco."

She took a breath. Livia had the New York number. She knew, before he spoke again, what he would say.

"She phoned to say that your grandmother died."

Something shot into the air, hissing. A barrage of brilliant explosions peppered the sky. "*Nonna* Adelaida," she said, then let go of her breath.

"I'm sorry." He gripped her arm.

"When?"

"Four days ago. Two days before she called."

"How?"

"A stroke. She died peacefully in her sleep. She asked before she died that your mother tell you that all is forgiven."

The statement silenced her again. Her mother knew, then. Livia had promised in her letter never to tell. They all knew, *Nonna* Adelaida, her mother, Livia. And now . . . ? The horrifying delayed realization now broke over her.

He spoke before she had the chance to ask her question. "What was forgiven, Anna?"

She replied, relieved, gambling that her answer would satisfy, "My running away and never returning."

"Angie answered the phone. He talked with his grandmother."

She remembered the doodle on the cover of *Life* magazine. "What did they say?"

"She asked for you. He told her you were out shopping for his birthday. It seems your mother was under the impression that the boy was nine instead of ten."

Her face went cold. She remembered the letter to her mother in 1946. "She gets things confused." But if her mother still thought that Angelo was Charles' son: she turned the welcome conclusion in her mind.

"I talked with your mother. She was also under the impression that Angelo was my son, Anna."

Her relief was short-lived. The truth closed in on her like the narrowing end of a trap. "That's ridiculous," she said, lamely.

"She said you told her in a letter you wrote that the boy was born after you came to America."

Below, the kids broke into shouts as the band began to play another of the new rock-'n'-roll songs.

Silently, she cursed herself as she said, "I told her that so she wouldn't think I'd spent that last year of the war pregnant." Given what she had told him ten years ago in Florence, the excuse sounded idiotic.

"She also said that you were never married before me. When you left Montefalco in October of '44, you weren't married, were you?" Another display ignited behind the band: a huge sparkling Catherine wheel of crackling white flares. "Is that true, Anna?"

She pulled a handful of clover from the ground and closed her eyes, realizing she had, after ten years of trust and generosity from Charles, run their marriage aground on that one single lie back in San Paolo. "Yes," she said, thinking how high the price had been for Charles.

"I don't understand. Why did you lie to me? What difference did it make if you weren't married to Lamberti?"

Lamberti is dead, she thought, Kruger is dead. Charles' assumption suddenly gave her a way out, a reprieve. But she needed time to think it through. "Please, Charles, don't ask me to explain," she pleaded, *"please."* She tried to imagine the damage she had accomplished over the years.

"You're the one who wanted explanations," he said. "Don't you think that works both ways?"

The smoke from the glittering pinwheel rolled toward them across the meadow. The children cheered.

She got to her feet, unsteadily, thinking but one thing: I must get away. "I can't explain now," she said. "I'm going home. You stay and bring the kids back."

"Anna!" There was anger in his command.

She walked on, letting the pull of gravity carry her down the slope. The band blared the final dissonant notes of a song. A string of popping firecrackers exploded. A fiery whirligig flew up into the sky, hissing. The crowd shouted for more, applauding.

"Anna!" Charles called again.

She began running toward the lamplit sidewalk on the far side of the meadow. Kruger was dead, Lamberti had never lived: she was beyond their reach. She began to cry. All along, it had not been what the truth could do to her, nor to her or Charles or both of them together, it was for Angelo she had lied! Once, twice . . . and then on and on until it was too late to go back!

She heard footsteps in the grass behind her. "Anna!" Charles caught up, took her arm, and angrily pulled her back. "For God's sake, stop running from me!"

They stood looking at each other in the darkness, panting. She got her breath and said, "Angelo. The children. We can't leave them."

"Never mind the kids . . . I want to know, Anna . . . I want to know the truth."

"You know the truth."

"I don't care if you were married or not when I met you. I don't care who Angelo's father is. Why did you lie to me? What difference did it make?"

"I lied for Angelo . . . for his sake."

"To protect him from what?"

She saw that she had again run aground on the truth. She began to cry, helplessly. "From me. From the truth about me."

He came forward and took hold of her shoulders. "Who was the man, Anna?"

"A soldier."

"I know that. Lamberti."

She shook her head. "There was no Carlo Lamberti. There was no Italian soldier."

His fingers tightened on her shoulders. "I see. . . . What was he, an American?"

They flowed out like water through a broken dam: the old irreconcilable feelings of love and hatred, trust and betrayal, justice and revenge. "German," she said.

In the pale pastel light of a shimmering cascade of embers, Charles stared at her, speechless.

The man was dead. She saw suddenly, hating herself at the same time for the things she had done and would go on doing for Angelo, for choosing another safe way out. "There was no love in it. I was raped." She added, mechanically, "I was raped by one of the Germans who killed my father and brother."

He sighed. "Anna."

"Now you see—don't you?" She closed her eyes, sickened by the lengths she was prepared to go to protect the future against the past.

He drew her close and folded her up into his arms.

She went even further, propelled by the old and familiar force of her lifelong flight and her habit of motherly protection. She swallowed back the bitter taste of gunpowder in her mouth and said, "Promise me something, Charles."

He responded with a gentle pressure of his hands.

"Promise me you will never tell Angelo."

"I promise."

The reprieve in his words flooded her with a sudden but short-lived feeling of freedom. She let go of the tears, holding onto him, knowing and hating that for which she was really crying, the things lost and now beyond reach.

Behind them, the crowd applauded.

IV
1964–1967

CHAPTER 1

"I spoke to Dr. Grasser a short while ago, Mrs. Fitzgerald." The starched white uniform that came toward her from the third-floor nurses' station was a plump young woman with short permed black hair. "The doctor says your husband is suffering, at this point, from extreme dehydration." The round girlish face under the cap was not one Anna recognized from the normal midday shift. The voice came from a tiny rosebud mouth fixed in a patronizing no-nonsense smile. "We think your husband should be placed at once on a saline IV, Mrs. Fitzgerald."

The saline drip had been suggested repeatedly in the last two weeks. "We?" Anna challenged, trying to mask her exhaustion and impatience behind a pleasant smile.

"Dr. Grasser placed the order, ma'am." The nurse reached for her patient report board.

Grasser. She could not summon up a face to fit the name from the endless parade of hematologists, urologists, gastroenterologists, and radiologists who had passed through their lives in the last five months since January. She stepped back into the corridor to give the woman berth through the door. "My husband has already made it quite clear to Dr. Whitman that he wants nothing beyond his usual prehospital medications." She glanced at the name tag pinned to the woman's uniform. Fay Ballard, R.N. The title below the name identified her as head nurse.

"I have to follow Dr. Grasser's orders, Mrs. Fitzgerald."

"I don't know any Dr. Grasser, Miss Ballard. Dr. Whitman is in charge of oncology here at St. Joseph's, and he knows the conditions under which my husband checked into this hospital."

"Dr. Grasser is standing in for Dr. Whitman today."

"In that case, have Grasser phone Whitman." Distracted by a movement near the telephone booth at the far end of the corridor, Anna turned to see the man who had occupied the booth when she passed hurry off down the corridor. For an instant she wondered if she shouldn't retrace her steps and make the call to Angelo in Maryland without Charles' permission. Had the booth been empty when she passed, she would have made the call now, before returning to Charles, for it would have to be made before the day was out, with or without Charles' permission.

"Mrs. Fitzgerald," the nurse reprimanded.

"There will be no IVs, Miss Ballard, is that clear?" she said, now red-faced with anger.

"Then you'll have to speak to Dr. Grasser yourself. The order has been placed."

"Tell Dr. Grasser to phone me in the room. Excuse me, I have urgent business with my husband." She turned in the direction of Charles' room at the opposite end of the long baby-pink linoleum corridor, glancing at the clock in the nurses' station. Three-twenty. Walking swiftly, she took out the documents from her purse. She had assured Charles she could make the trip uptown to Gleason's office, have him correct the mistake in Angelo's trust fund papers, and return to him in the hospital within an hour and a half. The errand had taken three.

Miss Ballard's creosol shoes came squeaking up behind her. "Mrs. Fitzgerald, we are not allowed to omit a patient's basic and essential medications. Your husband is in need of fluids."

Anna slowed for the woman to catch up with her. "You're new here on the floor, aren't you, Miss Ballard."

"I took over this morning from Mrs. Oates." She went on, offering no explanation for the demise of kind Mrs. Oates, who, of all the nurses who had attended Charles for these two grueling weeks, had understood why he had allowed himself to be hospitalized. "Your husband's welfare is now my responsibility, Mrs. Fitzgerald."

The blood rushed back to Anna's face. "The manner in which my husband has chosen to die is his responsibility, young lady, not yours."

As always, the nurse withdrew behind the screen of authority. "I don't give the orders, I merely follow them."

Anna stopped abruptly. "Let's get a few things straight, Miss Ballard. My husband did not come here to recover, he came here to die with peace and dignity. He has known for five months that his cancer is terminal. He submitted to hospitalization two weeks ago to appease his doctors, and he did so on the condition that they would not try to prolong his life with a lot of useless scientific gadgets or mind-deadening narcotics."

"I'm trying to *explain*, Mrs. Fitzgerald—!"

"Let me finish!" She thought of Charles' statement that morning before she left on his errand, and tears spilled into her eyes. "My husband and I are both practicing attorneys here in the state of New York. So you do not have to instruct either of us on the legal rights of hospital patients. He has expressly refused to be plugged into machines or drugs. There will be *no IV,* is that clear?" She started off again.

Ballard followed. "I'm afraid, Mrs. Fitzgerald, that your husband is no longer in a condition to decide what is or isn't in his best interests."

The statement brought Anna to a halt. When she left him at 10 that morning, he was in pain, but his mind was quite clear. "What are you trying to tell me?"

"When I went in at noon to check on Mr. Fitzgerald, he was in extreme pain. I telephoned Dr. Grasser, and he came up to check. Subsequently the doctor ordered me to give your husband"—she blanched and stepped back fearfully—"a sedative."

"My husband has refused *sedatives.*"

"Dr. Grasser altered that order on the chart." She flipped through the pages on her clipboard. "He said your husband wanted the drug."

"I don't believe you." Again Charles' statement, his look, and the ominous feeling of panic she had felt as she left the room that morning came back.

"Then you must ask your husband, Mrs. Fitzgerald."
If he has asked for drugs to kill the pain, then . . . With a sinking sensation of defeat she said, "What did you give him?"

"The doctor ordered an injection of morphine."

Morphine deadens the mind, she thought with terror. "I see. When?"

"An hour ago, ma'am."

An hour ago, while she sat in Ted Gleason's office; when she finally reached the decision to tell Charles the truth. When she left his room that morning, she had sensed that time might run out in her absence. "Is my husband conscious now?" she asked, dreading the answer.

"He's resting nicely, I believe."

"Thank you. I'll go to him."

"If he needs anything, Mrs. Fitzgerald, just ring." The nurse hurried off cheerfully toward her station.

Anna moved on again toward his room. *I want you to know something before I die, Anna.* His words pounded in her head. *The fault between us wasn't yours. It was mine. I deceived you.* He had said that as she was leaving his room with the papers he wanted corrected. For the next three hours the words had rung in her mind like a death knell. During the interminable wait for Gleason, she had prayed that time, this last little reprieve of an hour, would not run out on her.

She stood at the door to his room, unable to open it. If he was drugged beyond consciousness . . . The words flooded her mind, this time with nineteen years of accumulated guilt. *It was mine. I deceived you.* Back in January, when they learned that he had contracted cancer of the liver and that it was only a matter of time, she had told herself that the time had come for her to revive the question they had both put to sleep nine years before; the unanswered question that had, in fact, hung around the neck of their marriage like a millstone. She had even wanted to bring Angelo back from his boarding school in Maryland, sit down with the two of them, and lay out the facts as they had been—all of them, all the way back to the beginning. But Charles had made her promise to keep silent about the disease, not only to his business associates but to Angelo as well. "There's plenty of time," he had said, "and I want Angie to finish his senior year at Stratton. I want him to graduate without having to worry about me. He won't make it if he knows, Anna." He had documented his case for silence with a long list of Angelo's troubles dating back to his freshman year in high school. They had spent three tortuous years moving him from school to school, psychiatrist to psychiatrist, trying to find stability for her son. After January they had lived suspended in a vacuum, pretending that Charles' death was a long way off while he went about arranging his business and financial affairs, securing the future for her and Angelo. She had welcomed Charles' reprieve and let herself revive her habit of postponement.

Funny, she thought, to be caught short like this—by nothing more than a three-hour lunch break.

She went into the room and carefully closed the door. The venetian blind was closed over the window, allowing only a faint glow of sunlit twilight into the room. He lay on his back with the cotton coverlet drawn up to his chest, just as she had left him that morning. He was sleeping. She tiptoed to his bed, listening to the labored sound of his breathing and the rattle of catarrh in his throat. His mouth was open. In the last month since he retired to his bed at home, he had steadily lost weight, and his long slender frame was nothing more than bone draped with sallow, bile-yellowed dry skin. His curly graying hair had fallen away in recent weeks. She had picked strands of it from his pillow when he wasn't looking. As the cancer spread through his body, she had watched it eat its way to the surface and turn his forty-nine-year-old body into that of an eighty-year-old man.

She set her purse and the documents down at the end of the bed. She would wait until the drug wore off and he awakened. She took out a Kleenex and dabbed her eyes. She would use this time to word her confession to him. Having thought about it so long, she could taste the feeling of cleansing relief that would come when she tore away the old illusions she had burdened him with all these years. She would tell it simply: To protect herself and Angelo, she had lied to him all those years until he gave up and stopped probing into her past. He had given up searching for answers to their sexless and passionless marriage back in 1955, that summer when she slammed the door on him with her lie about the German who had raped her, when she made him promise never to speak of her tragedy to Angelo. She had let him believe all these years that she had never loved any man before the German and would never love any man afterward either. She would tell him simply: I was not raped. I knew the man, I loved the man, and we had an affair. He gave me a child, Angelo. Then, in the midst of that, he murdered my father and brother, and the next day he vanished from Montefalco, only to be killed himself in the war. I have hated the man for nineteen years and hated, moreover, the idea of intimacy with any man after him.

His arm, she saw, was exposed on the bed. She moved closer and carefully drew the coverlet over it.

He gasped for air, sucking the catarrh into his throat. Alarmed, she reached for the suction device on his bedside table. He swallowed before she could insert it. His eyelids parted. He murmured something thickly. She waited to see if he would awaken, then laid the device back on the table. His head, meanwhile, moved again, and his eyelids parted further. "Tell him—" he murmured, then fell silent and opened his eyes dreamily.

"Charles?" she said softly.

He turned his face toward the sound and tried to focus his vision through the veil of drugs. "Anna?"

She sat down on the edge of the bed and stroked his forehead.

"Yes, honey. It's me. Anna."

He looked up, puzzled. "You—?"

"How do you feel?"

He swallowed, dry-mouthed, and tried to speak, "I'm not . . ."

"Here." She reached for the glass of water on the table and turned its plastic straw to his mouth. "Take some water."

He closed his lips around the straw and sucked on it feebly.

"Better?" She smiled.

"Yes." The look of puzzlement came back. "You must . . . you must go to . . . to Gleason now," he said, "Tell him . . . what I said."

She realized he was still where she had left him that morning. "It's already done, sweetheart. I went to Gleason. He made your changes. It's done."

He looked away toward the blind. "Is it nighttime?"

"No, darling." The sunlight through the blind, she saw with alarm, was quite plain to see. She thought of her promise when she left. "It's lunchtime. I told you I'd come back for lunch. We'll have lunch now. Are you hungry?"

"No." He tried to lift his head. "Did . . . did Gleason . . . do what I told him?"

"Yes. He made the changes. I have the papers. Do you want to see them?"

"No . . . Just tell me."

She sat back, smoothing the coverlet over his chest. "He inserted the clause you wanted. It says, if Angie gets sick—if there are any more problems with Angie—" The memory at that moment of those last three years momentarily rattled her. She stopped to remember the exact wording. "If any expenses are incurred for Angelo during the next three years, until he's twenty-one, the costs are to be paid from his trust fund."

"And not . . . not from yours."

"Not from mine."

"And you . . . you will decide . . . not Gleason."

"Yes, honey." She thought of the time slipping away. "It's all there. I promise."

"Anna—" He made an effort to rise and looked at her wide-eyed. "I want Angie to have anything he needs," he said, forcing himself to complete the sentence in one breath. A spasm of pain shot through his face.

"Charles!" She pressed him back against the bed.

"It's . . . okay." He smiled.

The time had come. She leaned forward and took his hand. "Now, listen to me Charles. Please listen. I want to talk to you."

He nodded.

"First, I'm going to call Angelo at his school this afternoon. You must let me tell him now. Do you understand?"

His face lit up with surprise. "You mean . . . he . . . he graduated?"

She sat back, hesitating, weighing how easy it would be to give him this little gift of comfort. Either way he would never know. "Yes, honey. He graduated."

His face flooded with delight and relief. "He passed . . . he passed math? . . . And English?"

In his junior year Angelo had flunked both subjects, and they had been forced to find a school outside New York that would take him. Stratton Military Academy had been Charles' solution, for he had influence there, and the boy had promised to pass all his courses if they let him go to school away from home. "Yes, honey. He passed everything." She smiled. But thinking of the report she had received at the end of his winter term, her voice wavered. "Even English."

"You see?" His cracked lips spread into a painful grin. "I told you."

"Yes, you told me."

"Then . . . phone him. Tell him . . . tell him—" He drew in air. "Tell him . . . I want him . . . to come home." Pain streaked across his eyes. He fought to lift his head. "Anna! . . . Tell him I loved him!"

She looked down, reading his meaning, and felt her tears spill out. "Oh, Charles." She shook her head. "There's something else." When she looked up, he was staring at her, transfixed.

"He didn't . . . believe that, did he?"

She bent forward and took him by the shoulders. "Listen to me, sweetheart—"

The words went by him. He said, "Tell him, Anna."

"Please, Charles, try to listen!" She thought of the absurd length of time it had taken her to reach these short moments left to them.

"Tell him what happened to us, Anna!" he said, and the strength he was forced to summon in lifting his head made his eyes look huge.

The breath that came from his mouth sickened her. She gaped, speechless.

"I knew," he went on, "back then, I knew what I was doing . . . I forced you . . . to marry me."

"Charles!"

He ignored her. "I knew you had no choice . . . no chance . . . to find the right man for you . . ."

She saw his excruciating need to finish. "And what, Charles?"

"I was not the man . . . I wasn't the man you would . . . have chosen, Anna." The little color in his face drained away. "I knew it . . . when we met in San Paolo." He let his head drop back to the pillow. "I used you . . . to make up for what I had lost."

"Oh, Charles—" She ran her fingers across his forehead. "I know that. I've always known. It made no difference."

"Angie." He looked up vacantly toward the ceiling. "Angie needs to know about Silvanna."

The name silenced her.

"Tell him, Anna, everything."

She hurriedly tried to think of a single sentence to contain everything she had kept hidden from both Charles and Angelo over the space of her lifetime. She said—and the words, as she said them, sounded like something one might hear in a ludicrously bad stage play—"I was not the woman you married, Charles."

"Tell him . . . tell him we tried . . . we did the best we could." His voice evaporated to a whisper. "If there was fault . . . it was mine."

She said slowly, clearly, "I lied to you back in Florence, Charles."

He did not hear her statement. He was looking up at something far away in the distance. *"Più bello . . . che si può,"* he said.

Suddenly blinded by frustration, she shouted at him, "I want you to know the truth, Charles! I want you to die with the truth!"

He did not hear. "When we get to the villa . . ."—the words were spoken with a curious mechanical ease—". . . I want you to sit . . . for your portrait."

"Charles?"

"The Arno . . . it's flooded now."

"Sweetheart, *look* at me! I'm *Anna!*"

For an instant his vision cleared and he looked at her. "Anna?"

"Listen to me. *Please.*"

"Your hair," he said in Italian, "you've . . . cut your hair."

She saw that he was not looking at her at all. The panic drained from her body. She sat back.

He said, "Your hair . . . it was long . . . I wanted it . . . long for the portrait."

She lowered her gaze, knowing, of course, to whom he spoke. For a moment she sat weighing the cost to herself of this second easy gift of comfort. She said in Italian, "No, darling. I haven't cut my hair." She was thankful suddenly that she had merely pinned it up all these years. She reached behind her head, pulled the clasp from her hair, and shook it free. "See?" It fell about her face and shoulders. "It's just as it was."

He tried to lift his hand, smiling.

She lowered her head, took his hand, and wound his fingers into her hair. "This is the way it will be for the portrait, Carlo," she said. She left his fingers knotted limply in her hair and buried her face against the bedclothes to muffle the sound that came rolling up through her mouth. For a while she lay still, listening to the steady but labored sound of his breathing above her. She recalled asking him the day he checked into the hospital, why he had chosen St. Joseph's. He had said, almost as an afterthought, that it was the hospital where Silvanna had died twenty-three years ago.

When she sat up, she saw that he had escaped into sleep. His mouth was open. She took the suction device from the table and cleared the catarrh from his throat. The failing sunlight through the blind had cast a monochromatic yellow glow over his face. She leaned down and kissed his forehead. "Rest, my darling," she said.

Turning away, she thought, *And now Angelo.* But there's no hurry. Nothing is going to change. She took her purse from the bed and walked steadily to the door. In the corridor, on her way to the nurses' station, she tried to summon up a single identifiable feeling, but the numbness now covered her entire body. She looked in at Miss Ballard bent over her desk in the station. "Miss?" she said.

The young woman rose up and instantly saw the look on her face. "Mrs. Fitzgerald!"

"I want you to phone Dr. Grasser."

"Is something wrong?"

She dismissed the question with a gesture. "Phone Dr. Grasser and ask him to come up."

Ballard came toward her. "What's happened, Mrs. Fitzgerald?" A hint of terror flickered in the young woman's face.

"Relax, Miss Ballard. The drug worked quite well. My husband is resting peacefully now." She turned toward the elevators. "Tell Dr. Grasser I'll meet him in my husband's room in a few minutes. I'm going to make a phone call to our son in Maryland now. I won't be long." She walked off down the corridor to the phone booth. Inside, she fished a coin from her purse, dropped it into the box, and dialed zero.

The voice responded after four interminable rings. "Operator."

She gave the number of the Stratton Military Academy outside Baltimore and instructed the operator to charge the call to her home phone.

A boy's voice came on the line. "Stratton Military Academy."

A momentary feeling of monotony came over her. She said, "I want to speak to Angelo Fitzgerald, please."

After a muffled exchange, the boy said, "I'm afraid he's in class right now, ma'am."

"I'm Mrs. Fitzgerald, Angelo's mother. This is an emergency. You'll have to get him out of class."

"Yes, ma'am . . . Do you want to wait, or should I have him—?"

"I'll wait, thank you." She settled back and pressed the door closed. The booth smelled of body odor and cigarette smoke. She closed her eyes, trying to remember the words she had formulated weeks ago to tell Angelo of Charles' condition. After five months of pretending that all was well at home, after five months of inventing alibis to keep him away from home (the Easter vacation had been hard to explain), it would be impossible now to retrace her steps and confess to him that she had lied to him all along for his own good.

She knew, somehow, it would sound like something he had heard before.

He would, she already knew, file it away in his mind amid the long list of grievances and accusations he had collected against her since childhood as evidence for the future. If she had bequeathed him anything of herself, it was the ability to harbor and nourish old hatreds.

The school's one outside phone was in a booth across the hall from the registrar's office. It was connected to the office through the switchboard. Angelo closed the door and adjusted the stool under him before lifting the receiver. She had never called him out of class to talk on the phone before this. He took the receiver down and listened for a moment before he spoke. She was breathing heavily at the other end. "Hello?" he said cautiously.

"Angelo."

The leaden drop of his name told him instantly that something bad had happened at home. "Mom?"

The moment of hesitation only compounded his dread. "Are you alone, Angie?"

"Yeah, Mom. Sure. What is it, what's up?"

She sighed. "It's your dad, honey." Again she stopped. It sounded like she was doing something with the receiver, covering the mouth-piece. She cleared her throat. "I called to say your dad is sick, Angie."

"Sick? Sick with what, Mom?" His stomach tightened.

"It's very serious, sweetheart. I want you . . . Charles and I want you to come home. As soon as you can."

He had thought for a moment that she would say he had died. He grabbed at that small relief. "What's . . . what's he got, Mom? What's he sick with?"

"Angelo . . . your dad . . . They've found he has cancer."

The skin on his cheeks and neck tingled at the sound of the word. It was his turn to be silent. He thought again of his suspicions over the last month and a half. When she had phoned each week, she had explained his dad's failure to come to the phone by saying he was away on business. He sensed he would have to be the one to speak. All he could think of to say was, "What kind of cancer, Mom?"

"Cancer of the liver, honey." Her voice fell away, and she began to cry. He wished she hadn't started to cry so soon. Before he had the chance to get his head together.

"Where—" His voice cracked. "Where is he? Where are you?"

"In the hospital, Angie sweetheart. I'm with him at the hospital."

He raked the side of his face with his hand, silently cursing her for forcing him to ask all the questions. "How long has he been there?"

"A while. A few days."

"Why didn't you let me know?"

She got control of herself. "Dad asked me not to tell you, Angelo. He didn't want you to worry. There was nothing you could do, sweetheart."

Sweetheart. The word, the way she kept saying it, irked him. He had suspected something was wrong all the way back in January, and she had always said, *Everything's fine, sweetheart.* "Has he got a good doctor, Mom? What does his doctor say?"

"He's seen the best doctors in America, Angelo. They've done everything"—her voice broke again—"everything they can."

There had been repeated *business* trips to Boston back in March when he phoned to talk to his dad. "You mean—" He felt a sudden emptiness, realizing she had taken away his last glimmer of hope. "You mean . . ."—he searched for the word people always used— ". . . it's *terminal.*"

"They've done all they can. We want you to come home now."

Home now. Now that it was too late. He thought of the need he had felt as a kid for the man to be a dad—a real dad—and the hole he had lived with in his soul all those years. "Mom?" he said, then caught himself on the brink of crying. He covered the mouthpiece, squeezing it with both hands, and stifled a whimper. He looked out through the glass window in the door to make sure no one was watching. When the urge had passed, he put the receiver back to his ear and said, "Tell me the truth. Is he . . . is he already dead?"

"No, Angie, he's not dead. But he's very sick."

He recalled the phone call he and his dad had gotten from his grandmother in Italy nine years before and the weird games they had played to keep his mother from knowing the truth and, afterward, the strange silence his mother had kept about her family when she learned of her *nonna's* death. "Which hospital is he at, Mom?"

"St. Joseph's. In Greenwich Village."

"I want to talk to him."

After a moment she said, "I'm calling from a phone booth, Angie. Your dad's in his room, he can't come to the phone."

"What's his room number? I'll phone him there."

"No, Angie, please, don't do that. He's sleeping now. He can't talk on the phone. He asked me to phone for him. He wants you with him, sweetheart." •

Like he wanted me around for the Easter holidays when they lied and said they were going off on a business trip, he thought. Frustrated, he pulled at the short stubble of his crew cut. His dad would be glad to know they had cut off his long hippie hair. He said, "I'll phone him later, then."

"Meanwhile, honey, I want you to look at your schedule and see when the next train leaves for Baltimore. You can take a taxi to the airport and . . ." She went on talking about schedules and plane reservations.

He didn't bother to listen. Instead, he took out his pocket knife and pulled open the smallest of its blades. He was thinking of another death she had lived through, one he had only heard about: his real father's death. He began carving on the wooden wall in front of him.

"Angelo?"

"I'm listening." That death—her first husband's death—had marred both his mother and his stepfather for life, though he knew not why or how. He worked the knife quickly, easily, carving the familiar U.S. Army's Infantry emblem on the wall. Other students had carved emblems before him.

She was saying, "I won't be home tonight, Angie. Make a reservation and leave word with your dad's secretary. I'll meet you at the airport."

A thought came to him. He asked, "What about dad's business, Mom? Who's gonna run the business for him?" He already knew her answer before she gave it.

"That isn't important now, darling," she said, postponing it.

"It is to dad."

She sighed. "He asked me to take over until things can be arranged."

He stopped carving and looked down, bewildered by the thought of the arrangements she must have been making all during the time he was dying. "I see," he said, but he was looking beyond those designs she had made for her future. He was seeing into the heart of her long, sexless, and ungiving marriage to the poor dying man. Rich and generous as he had been, Charles Fitzgerald had never held a candle to her dead Italian war hero lover.

"Please, Angie—" She began to cry all over again.

And the tears were contagious. His own eyes filled. He gripped the handle of his knife, hating the suggestion of their sentimentality. At least, he thought, she can find it in her to cry for the man. He dared not say more than a few words. "Right. I know."

The bell ending his class in contemporary military history rang. He had left in the middle of a lecture on Southeast Asia and that weird country Vietnam. A subject his dad had talked about.

"He loves you, Angie, very much," she said.

"I'm sure." Outside, the hallway filled with cadets on their way to their next classes. "I've got to go now, Mom," he said, fighting to hold back his grief until he hung up.

"All right, Angie." She gave up. "I'll wait for your call."

"Yeah." He lowered the receiver slowly, knowing in the back of his mind that he meant the gesture as something final. Boys passed by outside in the hallway. He stooped down so they wouldn't see him through the window.

He felt a part of his life, a part of himself, fall away into nothingness, into the past, into eternity.

He covered his mouth with his left hand to stifle the helpless cry of loss that came out of him, and with his right hand savagely drove the knife into the wall.

CHAPTER 2

I

"Hey—what happened?" Father Kruger called to the three sheepish-looking teen-agers who came through the front door of the parish hall. "You're late!"

"Sorry, Father, we got delayed at school." Martha Chung, the captain of St. Phillip Neri's High School Sodality, led the way, followed by two Sodality cell leaders, Pete Hodges and Luis Machado.

"Where are the others?"

"We figure they went to the antiwar protest out in Century City, Father," said Hodges, a junior at Phillip Neri.

"All six?"

"Yes, Father." Machado, a sophomore, looked to Martha for support. "I talked to Oliverez at lunch and he said everyone was going."

Kruger swung from the table at the front of the hall where he had been sitting for a half hour. "It's almost five. I've been waiting here a half hour for you people. Someone should have let me know the others weren't coming." He thrust his hands into his cassock pockets and walked irritably toward the window. "I've got a parish to run, you know. And a school to build," he added. He closed the window. There was no response from the youngsters. As pastor of St. Andrews, the parish church for Silverlake's Catholic high school, he had agreed to chair the weekly meetings of Neri's Sodality leaders. He turned to face the kids and, testing, said, "So what do you suggest we do?"

Martha spoke up. "We were supposed to vote on the Sodality summer picnic, Father. But since we don't have a majority, maybe we should cancel till next Friday."

"We think—" Hodges glanced at Martha. "We think the antiwar demonstration's more important than deciding the place for our summer picnic, Father." The tall gangly youth grinned. "We thought we'd drive out to Century City and join the others—make a show of Sodality support against the war in Vietnam."

Machado, a frail timid boy, one of St. Andrew's many Mexican parishioners, added, "We came over to ask if you wanted to come with us, Father."

Kruger ambled back to the table. "I see." He thought of his assistant, young Father Paul Gomez, and realized that his temper was not, in fact, directed at the kids at all. The young priest had failed to show up for a meeting with the grade school building committee that afternoon. He remembered suddenly at breakfast that morning how Father Gomez had talked about the antiwar rally scheduled to coincide with President Johnson's appearance that afternoon at the Century Plaza Hotel in Century City. He said, "I'm afraid I can't do that, Luis. The archbishop has forbidden the clergy of Los Angeles to demonstrate in political rallies." He thought of the canceled building-committee meeting, Gomez's absence, and the rally, and felt a momentary chill come over him. Only that morning Gomez had criticized the archbishop's directive, saying he thought the Church had a moral responsibility to publicly condemn the nation's involvement in the war.

Martha spoke up. "I know I shouldn't maybe say this, Father, but I think Cardinal Boyle's wrong to do that. I think the Church has a duty to protest the war."

"It's late, kids." Kruger motioned them to the door. "We'd better go now."

"We know you don't approve of the war, either, Father," said Machado, following him.

"Neither does Father Gomez," added Hodges.

"Duty for a Catholic, I'm afraid, isn't just a question of personal beliefs and choices," he said, leading the youngsters to the door. "Otherwise—" He turned, smiled, and held the door open for them to pass. "There'd be little need for faith, would there?" He heard the moral theologian in his voice and felt the pull of his own personal conscience. Privately, in his own heart, he could not argue with their convictions about the Church's responsibility.

"I realize that, Father," said Martha. She stopped in the gravel drive outside and looked back, reluctant to concede, confused. Of Neri's young political activists, Martha was the most militant. She was also, he knew, one of the school's most fervent and zealous Catholics: a dilemma for him, a priest, Gomez had once said, in an age when religious piety was scorned by young people.

Locking the parish hall door, Kruger said, "For a Catholic, Martha, duty and responsibility have to be interpreted in the light of obedience and faith." He began walking slowly across the parking lot toward the parish rectory. "In other words," he added, knowing that his homily sounded forced, "we have a duty to obey the voice of God's representatives here on earth, the Holy Father and our bishop, even though we may not agree with them. That's where faith comes in. Do you understand?"

"Yes, Father," Martha replied, looking off toward the car they had arrived in together.

"It's all part of God's Providence," he said, quoting his own sermon at last Sunday's Mass. He had spoken about the Christian dilemma of responsible secular authority versus an individual's moral obligation to conscience, a subject that had perplexed him for the last two years, since 1965, when he first saw the signs of future social breakdown sprouting up from the seeds of righteous social protest and civil disobedience. Unlike Americans, he had seen firsthand in Germany how the poisonous flower of anarchy could grow into the beautiful but deadly fruit of righteous social order—with its inevitable backlash of intolerance.

"You're sure you won't change your mind, Father?" asked Machado, turning back.

Kruger smiled. "I'm sure, Luis. There's no reason why you shouldn't go, but I can't."

Young Hodges squinted up into the late afternoon sunlight. "Father Gomez said he was going."

The statement stopped Kruger cold. He looked down at the dry gravel. "I didn't know."

"He came by the school this afternoon and said he'd march with us under our 'Catholics for Peace' banner."

He forced a smile. "Maybe you misunderstood."

"No, Father. He's gonna meet us at the Cheviot Hills Park across from the 20th Century-Fox studios at five. That's where the parade's starting. He went ahead early to organize things. We're supposed to march down Pico to Century City. Father Gomez and some of the nuns from Neri will be there."

"I see."

Martha read his expression. "We'd better split now, you guys." She pulled at Machado's shirt. "We're late as it is."

"See you later, Father." Machado waved.

"Next Friday, Luis." Kruger waved, trying to appear calm. "And by the way—be careful. If there's any trouble, any sign of violence, you should leave. Immediately. Do you understand?"

"Yes, Father," Martha called back from the car.

Kruger left the parking lot and started across the vacant field between the parish hall and the rectory. He pictured Gomez in his clericals and the nuns from Neri in their habits marching down Pico Boulevard. He jumped one of the abandoned foundation ditches dug last year for the new parish grade school. The ditch had begun to cave in over the months. He hurried toward the one-story Spanish stucco rectory, thinking of Cardinal Boyle, Father Gomez, and the inevitable repercussions that would follow the young priest's flagrant disobedience. Gomez had said there would be television news coverage of the event. Two weeks ago Boyle had discussed with him Paul's appearance at a public antiwar rally two days before. He had summoned him to his residence downtown and ordered him to warn his young assistant about the repercussions of clerical disobedience.

Kruger jumped another foundation ditch.

The cardinal had reminded him of his request for financial aid to build his new parish grade school. The new school's future rested, he had said, on financial support from the diocesan building fund, and he, the cardinal, controlled those funds. Boyle had already announced last year that he was considering uniting St. Andrews with its neighboring parish, St. Anne's. The cost of maintaining two parishes in a poor racially mixed area like Silverlake, he had argued, was beyond the financial capacities of the diocese. "We'll wait, though," he had added at the end of the meeting, "and see what kind of pastoral work you and Father Gomez can demonstrate in the coming year."

Kruger jumped the last school ditch and raced toward the rectory door. The words *Damn you, Paul* came to mind, but he stopped short of saying them. In everything but this Gomez was an exemplary priest. Youth, inexperience, and headstrong idealism were his only faults. He had come to St. Andrews after ordination, in 1964, one of the new breed of priests caught up in America's current social and political revolution.

In the kitchen he saw the half-eaten remains of Paul's lunch on the table, a bologna sandwich. He glanced at the clock over the sink: 5:16.

This morning Gomez had seemed pleased there would be massive media coverage of the city's biggest antiwar rally thus far. Undoubtedly the cardinal would be watching the evening news.

Unbuttoning his cassock as he went, Kruger hurried down the hall to his bedroom. The demonstration was scheduled to begin around 5, Gomez had said.

This time, he thought, reaching his bedroom and tossing his cassock to the bed, I'll invoke the priest's vow of obedience. I'll go there, find him, and order him to leave.

In his four years as pastor of St. Andrews he had never been forced to invoke the vow of obedience with Paul. He had all but forgotten the vow and could not even remember the wording of it in the Church's canons.

Instead, the words of a different vow of equal force and weight came to mind, and with it the dark memory of its terrible fulfillment: *I, Karl Gustav Kruger, swear by God this sacred oath, that I will render unconditional obedience.*

He stood listening to the silence, trying to weigh spiritual and secular obedience on the same mental scale. *Duty for a Catholic, I'm afraid . . .*

He recalled the fervor of his obedience to the voice that had called him to that other war and the price he and others had paid: the fifty souls he had left in Montefalco's square, the dream he had broken that night when he retreated from the only woman he had ever loved, the only woman who, over the years, had made him question the vows of his priesthood.

Faith, the cardinal had reminded him to tell Paul, was a blind virtue in its highest form. He pictured Boyle seated at his television set that night, watching young Gomez pass by. He thought, *If I go there now, if I'm seen with Gomez—even if my intentions justify my presence . . .*

The choices coiled in his mind, tangled up with responsibilities, both human and spiritual, with sin and virtue, with his Catholic priest's faith and his Catholic personal conscience.

He would start out, at least, and make his decision on the way. He would wear mufti just in case. He took off his black trousers and his white clerical shirt. On the way to his closet he turned on the small television set in his bookcase. He could watch the five o'clock news while he dressed. He took a pair of corduroy trousers from the closet, and as he pulled them on the TV picture appeared, followed by a newscaster's voice. The camera was directed at a large crowd milling in what appeared to be a public park. ". . . and from here," said the newscaster, pointing, "the march is already in progress down Pico Boulevard, heading into Century City. Now we'll cut to Bob Greene over at the Avenue of the Stars. Bob?" The picture switched to a second newscaster standing at the intersection of Pico and the divided Avenue of the Stars. "Right, Alan!" The newscaster adjusted his earphone and pointed toward a long line of demonstrators marching six deep up the length of the boulevard. Banners and placards moved overhead.

Kruger reached for a short-sleeved sport shirt in his closet.

"We're here at the intersection of Pico Boulevard and the Avenue of the Stars," the voice said, "and as you see, the groups marching here range from students to professional organizations, even religious groups!" Kruger turned to see the camera close in on a group carrying a long banner that read "Catholics for Peace." He saw, dotted among the blur of young faces, the vivid black and white fragments of nuns' habits.

From the distant background, drowning out the chatter of voices, came a chant: "Hey! Hey! LBJ! Hey! Hey! LBJ! How many babies have you killed today?!"

Kruger left his mufti short-sleeved shirt fall to the floor.

". . . and we're told," the newscaster shouted over the chant, "we're told that the President's helicopter will shortly land on top of the Century Plaza Hotel!"

The camera kept moving in on the Catholics for Peace, singling out the faces of nuns among the demonstrators. The familiar face of a Phillip Neri senior, young Robert Kim, passed by on the screen, followed by that of a priest in a Roman collar.

Kruger stepped back against his desk top, watching the dark-haired, clean-shaven, smiling face of Father Paul pass by.

The announcer talked on about police and the threat of violence when the parade reached the confines of Century City.

The chant, "Hey! Hey! LBJ!" mingled with a second, angrier chant in the distance: "Peace now! Peace now! Peace now!"

Kruger stepped forward, pressed the off button on the TV set, and watched the picture dissolve to a tiny bright white dot.

He thought of Cardinal Boyle, the parish grade school, and Father Gomez in the same breath. The word *peace* reverberated in his ear as the dot vanished, leaving him standing half naked in his own shameful silence.

II

The foyer light was out. She was sure she had turned it on that morning when she left for the office, knowing she would not return home until after dark. Perhaps the bulb had blown.

Anna reached into the foyer and flicked the switch. The light came on.

Odd, she thought, fumbling with her keys, briefcase, and purse, I know I turned the light on. Whether she was at home or out, she had always left the foyer light on at night. Living alone as she did since Charles' death, she had made a conscious habit of the light.

She latched both locks, musing, I'm getting to be like one of those dotty New York widows in my middle age. All I need now is a poodle.

She dropped her keys on the foyer table, turned into the passage, and stopped dead. A light burned in the living room. That, she knew, she had not left on. With a paralyzing chill of terror, she thought of the robbery four years ago after Charles died, when she came home to find the lock picked and the place ransacked.

She whispered a prayer and began inching back into the foyer, thinking of the noise she had made coming in, the locked door behind her, the empty hallway outside, and the long soundproof solitary night ahead when no one would phone or visit.

But the door had been doubly locked when she came in!

A movement came from the living room, knocking the wind from her courage. "Mom?"

She stood still, caught between the falling terror of helplessness and the rising relief of joy.

"Is that you?" He came into view, silhouetted against the light from behind. "Mom?" He laughed. "It's me!"

The voice was Angelo's, but the specter of the body was not. His name spilled out with her breath. "Angie."

"Christ!" He came toward her. "You look like you've seen a ghost!"

She made a wordless sound, thinking of four long years of absence and silence and solitary grief in the same breath.

He came into the foyer light, grinning: not the gangly boarding-school youth of four years ago, but a full-grown man—a soldier in a military uniform. "Mom! It's *me!*" He laughed.

Her shock passed. She met and embraced him. "Angie!" The briefcase got in the way and she let it fall to the floor.

He was laughing, but his embrace was reticent and stiff. In that, he had not changed. He towered over her, immense and controlling. The sensation was vaguely familiar. She tried to attach it to Charles, but could not. She could only think, this is a man's body, not a child's.

He drew back, flustered by her momentary attempt to prolong the embrace, and laughed. "Surprised?"

"I—I had no idea!"

"I know. I planned it that way."

"Look at you!" She turned him into the light, ignoring the implication of his remark. "You've grown *up!*" His shaggy high school hair had been cut short.

"You think so?" He beamed. His face: the baby fat had fallen away, leaving a lean jawline that— Out of habit, she pushed away the image of another jawline. He spread his arms to demonstrate the change. "Boot camp! That's when this happened!" The gleam of pride she saw in his blue-green eyes, bluer and greener than she remembered from before, was something new. She remembered only adolescent confusion and sullen helplessness.

"You look wonderful."

"You, too." He pointed. "You changed your hair."

She laughed at the stumbling compliment. After Charles' death, she had worn it as she had in Italy years before, knotted behind her head. "Darling, when did you get in?"

"About an hour ago. I got Paul downstairs to let me in. I told him not to tell you I was here."

"I was expecting you next week! You should have phoned! I went out to dinner!"

"I decided to surprise you. It happened so fast, getting my papers, I had no time to warn you. I learned only this morning I was out, and I booked a flight outa San Francisco right away."

"Well, you're home, and that's—"

"You got my letter? The one I wrote before we left Nam?"

"Yes, of course. You said—"

"When we got to San Francisco, things were kinda hectic, I didn't know how long—" He went on talking, smiling, pacing through an explanation she neither wanted nor needed. After two years in Vietnam and three letters home, his need to explain his sudden arrival merely bewildered her. ". . . I guess I should 'uv phoned your office yesterday when I—" He left off, realizing he'd cornered himself into a lie.

"It doesn't matter, sweetheart. Let's go into the living room and sit down."

"Yeah. Let's." The hallway was too narrow for them both. She dropped back and followed, wondering why he had needed to lie at this point, after four years with no explanations. He looked back. "I see you've done the place over."

She detected disappointment. "Yes. Last spring. I wrote you, remember?"

"Right. I forgot." The TV was on, but the sound was off. He went around the living room turning on lamps. She had painted the dark paneling white and had bought new modern-looking furniture. She waited for some reaction. Last January, knowing he was reaching the end of his Vietnam tour of duty, she had written to say she wanted to redecorate and asked for his advice. To her surprise, he replied, telling her to do as she pleased but asking her to leave his bedroom alone.

"Do you like it?"

"It?"

"The apartment."

He looked around as if seeing it for the first time. "Do you want the truth?"

"Yes, of course." Her hopes collapsed even before he spoke.

"I kinda liked it the way it was."

"Oh." She had done it over thinking he would need a change when he came back. "I could always—" She left off, realizing it was too late to go back to what the apartment had been when Charles was alive.

"What difference does it make?" He tried to ease her with a laugh. "It's your apartment, not mine. Anyway, you didn't touch my room."

"Yes."

"That's all I asked. Now, go sit down, I'll make us something to drink."

"All right. I'll have what you're having," she said as he started past her. He chuckled. In the brighter light, she saw the startling change in his body for the first time. "Your shoulders! Look at you! You used to be so skinny!"

"That's the army for you. There's no room in Nam for skinny runts, Mom." He began mixing two drinks at the bookcase bar.

She sat down on the sofa. The late evening news was on and the face of the newscaster filled the soundless TV screen. She thought of the thousand questions to be asked and answered, but realized she was at a loss to begin. She lumped them all into one. "Tell me about yourself, sweetheart. I want to know everything."

"For instance?"

She drew one from the hat. "For instance, are you still a sergeant?"

He left the bar with their drinks. "No." The pride returned to his smile. "I got promoted. I'm a lieutenant first class now."

"Wonderful!"

He heard the ring of forced enthusiasm. "Here." He handed her her drink. "Do you like black russians?"

She grimaced. "It's fine."

"Anyway, *I* think it's wonderful. You don't get that rank for nothin', you know." He smiled, knowingly. "In fact, if I remember right, it's the rank my father had in the Italian Army, wasn't it?"

The remark caught her off guard. "As a matter of fact, yes, it was."

He remained standing. "Ask me another question."

She tried to steer around questions of war. "Have you been well?"

"Look at me." He spread his arms, demonstrating. "Do I look like I've been sick?"

She recalled the long nights lying awake and alone, wondering if his silence meant he had been wounded or killed. "You look *very* healthy."

"That's what discipline, regularity, good food, and exercise can do for you."

They were back to soldiering. She said, "Tell me what else you've been doing? Did you travel?"

"First, I was in Saigon. That was my first six weeks. Then I got an assignment near Da Nang. We went up there to clean out a nest of Cong in one of the villages . . ." He went on to describe his transfers from one war zone to another. He spoke dispassionately, using names she had never heard as if she should know them, Camranh Bay, An Khe. . . . She detected a frightening note of conviction in his voice. He spoke of duty, responsibility, and commitment, and the words had a chilling ring of familiarity to them. "Ho Chi Minh broke through, though, and trapped us up there in the jungle. For a while, we thought we were goners. But our guys came over with napalm and threw us a Chinese fish fry." She saw pleasure peek through his pride and thought, at the same instant, of September in Montefalco. "And then I got stationed in the DMZ."

"I see." She tried to think of a neutral innocent question to ask, but could not. All she knew of his past four years was a troubled senior year in boarding school, his unexplained absence from Charles' deathbed and funeral, and his sudden announcement that he had enlisted in the army.

He had turned away to watch the TV, which pictured a crowd milling in a street, carrying the proverbial antiwar placards. He turned up the sound. The announcer's voice described an antiwar demonstration that had taken place that afternoon in Los Angeles.

"Look at that!" He pointed. "Priests and nuns! They've got priests and nuns out in the street now!" Anger surged up through his amazement. "What do these guys think we've been doin' over there, whistling 'Dixie'? Jesus!" The announcer went on with his description of Johnson's appearance at a Los Angeles hotel where he was met with the largest antiwar demonstration in that city's history.

"Angelo," she ventured.

He said something about heroism and betrayal and the difference between the homecoming he had gotten in San Francisco and homecomings of soldiers from the Second World War.

She was thinking of the homecoming she had planned, a joyful reunion when they would exchange all the missing pieces. But the missing pieces were all painful, she realized, and the rest was only small talk.

He punched the off button. "Sorry. You were saying?"

She tried again. "Tell me about San Francisco."

He saw the silliness of her effort, smiled, and shook his head. "Let's not talk about me. All I've got is war talk. Let's talk about you." He joined her on the sofa. "I hear you've taken over the business."

"Yes." She sat back, relieved. "But only the legal side of it."

"You must feel proud of yourself."

"Proud?"

"I mean, all those years you put into studying. A single woman running her own business—I always knew you'd end up an independent woman."

He had not, of course, been around during those last painful months of Charles' life when the responsibility for his care had fallen on her. "It's a long story, honey. This isn't the time for that." She sat forward. "Tell me, have you eaten? Did you get dinner on the plane?"

"A massacred chicken breast, a dollop of mashed potatoes, and a slab of jello you could 'uv nailed to the wall." He winked. "As a matter of fact, I'm starved."

"Good. I'll fix something. Let's go into the kitchen. I've got lots of goodies in the fridge." She stood up and led the way through the dining room into the kitchen, grateful for the reprieve. The army, Charles' death? There must be something pleasant they could talk about for his first hour home. She turned on the light and began rummaging in the fridge as he came in behind her. "What would you like? There's cheese, eggs, a fresh pâté, and even bagels. You used to like bagels."

"I'd like to talk about what happened."

"When?"

He sat down at the kitchen table. "That last year when I was away at boarding school."

She took out everything within reach. "I'll tell you everything tomorrow, sweetheart. This isn't the time."

"I want to know now, Mom. Not tomorrow or the next day. You haven't changed a bit. You're still the master of postponement."

She lay an armful of things on the table. "What do you want to know, Angie?"

"How did he die?"

"Peacefully. He died quite peacefully."

"In the hospital or at home?"

"In the hospital."

"How long was he sick before he went to the hospital?"

"Four months, almost five."

"Is that when you took over the business, or did you wait until he died?"

The question struck her like a stone. She stepped back, breathless. "What do you mean by that?"

"It's time you told the truth, Mom. You were ambitious, and you wanted to have control of your own life. I've always known that about you."

"That is not true."

"Don't get me wrong. He encouraged you."

"You weren't there, Angie. You don't know. He asked me, *begged* me to take over the firm. He was sick for months, he knew he was going to die. He wanted the firm to stay in family hands. I was the only one he could turn to."

"If he was sick for months, if he knew he was going to die, why didn't he ever bother to tell *me?*"

She drew a breath. "Is that why you didn't come home at the end?"

He nodded, evasively. "What was the point? He didn't phone me or write to me for five months. I didn't learn about it until it was too late. When you decided to involve me, he was already in a coma."

A light broke in her mind at the far end of a long tunnel. She said, "Go on."

"Let's not kid ourselves. He may have had a thing for you back when he married you, but I was just along for the ride." He forced a smile. "Don't get me wrong. It wasn't that he didn't care. I don't mean that. He was generous, he gave me everything I needed or wanted. But let's face it—what he had for you was one thing, what he had for me was something else."

"You're wrong, Angie."

"He told me himself! I remember what he said a long time ago, he said there were all kinds of love. He said some was in the blood, and some was in the heart. Even as a kid, I knew what he meant."

"And so when he got sick and didn't tell you, you decided his problem was only between me and him. You decided to enlist in the army."

"Something like that."

"You were wrong, Angie." She thought back to all the things both she and Charles had kept from him. "He learned he had cancer in January, when he went for a routine examination. He kept it secret even from me for a while. Then it began to show. He told me, finally, but he made me promise not to say anything to you. He knew it was terminal, and he wanted you to finish your senior year without worrying. He didn't tell anyone at the firm, either. He kept on working as long as he could, until they forced him to go to the hospital. It was then he begged me to take over the firm. He imagined you would enter law school and take over one day from me. He made me promise not to tell you anything until he reached the end. It was too late, though, by the time I called you. Overnight, he had gone into a coma."

He peeled back the wrapper around a wedge of cheese. "Okay. Then why didn't you bother to explain the man to me back when I was a kid?"

The word *postponement* came to her, and with it the memory of darker secrets left buried. *I was raped.* She had let Charles go to his grave with that one lie. "I couldn't."

He smiled. She knew what he was thinking. "Where did you bury him?" he asked. "In Connecticut?"

She nodded. "Yes."

"With the Fitzgeralds?"

"Yes." He lay, of course, next to Silvanna, but that was Charles' own painful secret, and she had promised.

CHAPTER 3

I

"Ankommende Passagiere des Lufthansa Fluges vier und fünfzig . . ." The smooth female voice went on with the announcement over the intercom.

Carrying his suitcase, Kruger made his way toward the exit lead-

ing to the front of the Munich air terminal. It would be afternoon
when he reached his parents' house.

Outside, he hurried through the crowd along the entrance toward
the first Mercedes in the taxi queue. "Munich, please. I'd like to go
to the Bogenhausen section." He caught himself and repeated in
German, "I'd like to go to Munich, to Bogenhausen."

"Jawohl, Herr Kaplan."

He got in, pulling the bag with him. The driver, a middle-aged
man in a brown cloth cap and horn-rimmed glasses, pressed the
meter button and swung out into the airport traffic. Kruger sat back.
He had not visited the Munich airport for twenty-six years. And
only once during the war. As a soldier, he had always traveled by
train. "How long is the drive?"

"A half hour, depending on traffic."

"If you can hurry, I'd appreciate it."

"You have a Bavarian accent, Father. I take it you're not from
Munich, though."

"No. Well, yes. I'm originally from Munich, but I live in
America." He wished he'd kept to English. After twelve years of
separation from his parents, he wanted to ride in silence and think
about what lay in store for him. Busy with traffic, the driver, thank
God, kept silent. Kruger thought, Mother may be at the hospital
with Dad. I can keep the taxi waiting and drive on to the hospital if
no one's at home. His mother knew neither the flight he had taken
nor the hour when he would arrive. After her call four days ago,
when she told him that Walter was very sick, there had been endless
preparations to make: his passport had expired, and a replacement
had to be found to help Father Auden, who would take over St.
Luke's in his absence. He had been forced to wait until the last minute to book a flight.

Kruger had known that his father was not in good health for three
years, since 1964, but he had known nothing about the nature of the
disease, cirrhosis. His mother had never said anything about a drink-
ing problem, at least until four days ago. He had prayed through the
night on the flight over that he would find his father lucid enough to
talk. There were many things he had left unsaid and undone over
the years.

"So you live in America, Father?" came the inevitable question.

"Yes. In California." Before leaving, he had decided to answer all
questions about his reasons for staying away from Germany truthfully. If questioned by his father, he would now tell the truth. All of
it, if necessary.

"You've lived there long?"

"Since 1947."

The driver glanced back through the rearview mirror. Kruger waited for the next question. At the Passport Control in Frankfurt, he had prepared himself for any eventuality. Not knowing if he was listed in Germany as a war criminal accused in Italy, having no knowledge of what Montefalco had discovered in the aftermath of the war, he had resigned himself to the possibility of being arrested at the very outset of his return. The passport authorities had said nothing.

"You moved there after the war, Father?"

"That's right."

"You were here in Germany during the war?"

"Here. Then in Norway, France, and finally in Italy."

"You fought?"

"Yes. With the Wehrmacht." The answer came easily. He had given it before in America. That much he had given.

"Me, I was Panzer. You were probably with Kesselring, no?"

"Yes."

"The field marshal, I hear, died in prison."

"No. He went to prison, but he was freed in 1952. He died a free man." The thought of it, remembering his two reprisal orders, brought back a familiar anger. *Authority from the top down.* And from the bottom up?

They reached the outskirts of Munich: rows of uniform suburban houses built since the war, ugly efficient imitations of the familiar childhood *Bayerische.* He saw a road sign indicating Passau. Passau was the town where his father's bicycle factory was located. He thought of his father's beginnings: the Baumann bicycle shop. Since ordination, when he learned by innuendo what had happened to the Baumanns, he had kept silent on that subject in his letters home to his mother, knowing the mute pain she had borne since the war. And who was he to accuse his father? Over the years, during Germany's long period of soul-searching after the war, he had assumed that his father would disclaim his involvement with the Nazis, foolishly pragmatic as it had been, and refuse to acknowledge the responsibility he had for the fate of the Baumanns. Those were things they would talk about before the end came.

The skyline of the city came into view through the bright haze of industrial pollution: the paired rounded domes of the Frauenkirche's twin towers, the Gothic spires of the old City Hall, the Rathaus, and the top of the Maximilianeum, the Bavarian Parliament building.

Though destroyed in the war, the city had been rebuilt exactly as he remembered it.

"You recognize it?" asked the driver.

"Yes." All the way across America, all the way across the Atlantic, he had wondered what his feelings would be when he saw the city of his birth, the city where everything good and evil in his life had begun. He felt neither pleasure nor pain, but something in between. A sad nostalgia. As if he had come back to an incomplete event—something endlessly unfinished and avoided. The beginning point of a long voyage around a circle. He saw in the distance the Ludwigsbrücke over the Isar River. "On second thought, driver, can we make a quick swing through the center of the city and come back to Bogenhausen on the Luitpoldbrücke?"

"Sure, Father. Why not."

The route was familiar. They passed the Deutsches Museum on its little island in the Isar. As a teen-ager, he had often gone with his Hitler Youth friends to the museum to see the collection of state-approved art Hitler had hung there to glorify the Nazi aesthetic.

"The Isartor." As they crossed the ornamented Ludwigsbrücke, the driver pointed ahead toward the ancient city gate with its twin romanesque towers and its fresco celebrating the Emperor Ludwig's face-saving return to Munich after the defeat at Ampfing when his enemies sided against him with the Pope. His mother had told him the story as a child to illustrate the fate of great men who use their power to thwart the will of God. She had made the analogy when Hitler came to power as chancellor and began his oppressive moves against the Church and Munich's Kardinal Faulhaber. In the Marienplatz, the tower of the Neues Rathaus loomed overhead, forbidding as always.

He saw the busy Kaufingerstrasse and the little side street where the Baumann bicycle shop had stood, and in the distance the clustered rooftops of buildings where his parents' working-class tenement had been. The buildings there now looked new. They passed the little street leading to the great Frauenkirche, and he got a glimpse of its twin towers. A glimpse, too, of the scrawny little boy in short pants accompanying his mother to evening benediction services.

He sat back, feeling like a man who had wandered into a hall of mirrors to stand in the center and see himself reflected before and after to infinity.

At the corner of the Prielmayerstrasse he saw the gray Palace of Justice and the skinny brown-shirted teen-ager who had stood on the sidewalk with his father and waited for the Führer's open automobile to pass on its way to the Parliament building. He heard the roar again as the Führer swept by with his escort of SS men and remembered how disappointed he had been at seeing a little man in a pompous top hat instead of a big man like Bismarck or an old gray statesman like von Hindenburg.

He looked down at his black cleric's suit and wondered at the distance he had traveled from the sidewalk on the Prielmayerstrasse.

"You have a family here in Munich, Father?" asked the driver.

"Yes. A mother and father."

They started along the famous Englisher Garten on the Prinzregentenstrasse where, as a child, he had spent Sundays with his parents to escape the squalor of their tenement. The thought of Hitler lifting his father out of hopeless squalor had burned like a candle in the darkness of that last year in Montefalco.

"Geibelstrasse, Father?" the driver asked as they crossed the Luitpoldbrücke into Bogenhausen.

"Yes." He checked the street number he had scribbled on the piece of parish stationery.

"I take it your parents are well-off."

"My father makes bicycles."

"Bicycles are popular here. What's the name?"

"Kruger."

"Ah! Krügercycle! I know the brand, they're very popular here in Munich. He must be rich."

"Yes, I suppose he is." Baumann: the name came back again like a dormant unfiled criminal charge.

The driver turned into a street lined with imposing one- and two-story manor houses. At the next intersection they swung right into the Geibelstrasse.

Kruger gave the street number.

The numbers printed along the solid two-story houses descended. They pulled up in front of a two-story house built in the traditional Bavarian style. White plaster with a wooden gabled roof. On the second floor, a touch of his mother's taste, there were pots of geraniums set out on a small terrace.

"Nice," said the driver. "Very nice."

Kruger counted out the deutschmarks he had exchanged in Frankfurt for dollars. "Thank you. I appreciate your tour." He pushed his small bag into the street.

"Have a nice stay, Father."

"Thanks." He saw a black Mercedes Benz sedan in the driveway and recalled his plan to have the taxi wait until he checked to see if his mother had left for the hospital, but there was no need for the taxi. His father drove a black Mercedes. He went through an iron gate into the front yard. On the ground floor, curtains were drawn across both windows. He set his suitcase on the stone porch and pressed the bell button next to the heavy lacquered door. A chime sounded far off in the house.

The door opened on a young woman dressed in a maid's uniform. *"Ja? Was ist . . . ?"* She saw his Roman collar. *"Herr Kaplan Kruger?"*

"Ja. I am he."

As the girl stepped back, drawing the door open, the question in her face gave way to bewildered reticence. "Come in, Herr Kaplan," she went on in German.

He knew. The realization swept by him with a draft of stale pipe tobacco from the darkened foyer. For a moment, he could neither move nor speak. The girl waited, her eyes lowered to the floor. He lifted his suitcase and went inside.

The girl prolonged the little task of securing the latch. "Your mother is in the parlor, Herr Kaplan." She kept her face averted.

He lowered the suitcase to the floor, searching for something to say to free the girl from the burden of telling him that his father was dead. "Through there?" He pointed to a door.

"Yes, Father. Leave your bags, I will take them up." She curtsied with her eyes still lowered.

"Thank you." It took, it seemed, forever to reach the open door at the end of the hallway. His feet made a soft thump on the padded floral runner in the hallway. He wanted suddenly to turn and go back, but that—the notion of escape—was absurd. He stopped at the door and looked into a big, ponderously furnished room. His mother rose to her feet from a huge leather armchair. He hurried toward the tiny figure. She made small broken sounds as she rose. He wanted one of them to say something, but neither spoke. The light from the window behind his mother obscured her face as she lifted her hands to greet him. "Mamma," he said.

"Son."

She looked smaller than he remembered. "Mamma," he repeated. He saw a glimmer of momentary joy and relief blaze out through the pain in her exhausted face. For a moment, in silence, they held each other.

"Papa died," she said finally.

It sounded as if she had announced something Papa had simply *done.* He rested his chin against the top of her head. Her body felt like a small child's. "When, Mamma?"

"Last night."

Last night. Last night was both too soon and too late. Too late to recover what had been avoided and lost for twenty-six years, too soon for him to get here with the help and comfort he could offer as a priest and as a son. It was not that he hadn't tried. Between the call and his coming, there had been things he had to do.

She took a deep breath and stopped crying. "Karl." She drew back. She had aged more than he had expected. The skin around her eyes was wrinkled and translucent.

"Are you all right, Mamma?"

"Yes, *Liebchen.* I'm all right."

The words tumbled from his mouth before he could think. "I tried to come in time, Mamma, I tried. But it was impossible."

She touched his mouth with her fingertips, reading his thoughts. There was no sign of accusation in her face, though. "I know you tried. It can't be helped, *Liebchen.*"

He realized for the first time that they were not alone in the room.

"Karl—" She stepped back. "I want you to meet your father's friends."

He turned to find a middle-aged couple standing beside the fireplace mantel. They were well dressed and poised, and looked embarrassed by their intruding presence. "Herr Kaplan." The man bowed.

"Herr and Frau von Scheffel, this is my son, Karl," his mother said, "he has just arrived from America."

The man stepped forward and offered his hand. He was in his early seventies, with a round pallid face and a full head of meticulously groomed white hair. "Herr . . . ?" Kruger realized he had not listened to the name.

"Von Scheffel." The man smiled. His colorless gray eyes appeared enlarged by the thick lenses of his glasses. "I am pleased to meet you, Herr Kaplan. Your father often spoke of you."

Frau von Scheffel, equally stiff in her beige summer dress, stepped forward. "Herr Kaplan Kruger." She offered her hand. "I am Frieda von Scheffel." She smiled cautiously. "Permit me to offer our condolences. Your father was a dear friend of my husband's." A large diamond glinted on her proffered hand.

"Thank you, Frau von Scheffel." Kruger felt suddenly resentful for the intrusion.

"Your father and Herr von Scheffel had business together," said his mother, and he thought he detected a note of apology in her voice.

"Your father and I were friends for almost twenty-five years," von Scheffel said. His accent was Bavarian, and he pronounced his words with the clipped precision of the educated aristocracy. "He was a fine man. I admired him very much." The expressionless eyes darted to Frau von Scheffel.

"Thank you, Herr von Scheffel." Kruger recalled his father's political allegiances twenty-five years before.

"He often spoke of you, Herr Kaplan. He was very proud of your accomplishments. Very proud, indeed." In von Scheffel's look and tone Karl sensed that the man was speaking of more than his priesthood.

"Elizabeth." Frau von Scheffel had stepped forward to take his mother's hand. "We must leave you, my dear." She went on in crisp Berlinese German, talking of the funeral arrangements. Kruger studied her face: brittle and aloof under the smile, condescending in its expression. Frau von Scheffel turned without altering the smile. "We came, Kaplan Kruger, to pay our respects to your mother. We shall meet again, I'm sure."

"Frau von Scheffel." Before he realized what he'd done, he acknowledged the woman with a bow that did not belong to a priest.

"We must talk again, Herr Kaplan," said von Scheffel, returning the bow.

Karl retreated behind English. "Certainly, sir."

"Frau Kruger." Von Scheffel bowed again deferentially and guided his wife to the door. He moved, Kruger saw, with that familiar stiff confidence of Germany's old military aristocracy.

When they were gone his mother lowered herself wearily into one to the two leather armchairs.

He sat down opposite her. "Are you all right, Mamma?"

"Yes. I'm only tired. I did not sleep last night."

He tried to think of a painless opening but came up with only a guilty apology. "The passport took time, Mamma. I got it only yesterday with the help of the cardinal's office. There was no way for me to—" He left off.

"You did what you could, Karl."

The questions, he realized, were up to him. It was not her nature, even with his father, to speak her mind. He said, "Tell me what happened. How did he die, Mamma?"

"Peacefully. He died peacefully." She seemed relieved.

"At what hour?"

"A little after nine. I was with him when the end came." She found her momentum and went on to describe in simple dispassionate language the last days and hours of Walter's life, the slow deterioration of cirrhosis, the need finally for hospital care, the use of drugs in the last days and hours to ease the pain.

While she spoke, his thoughts circled around the question that had plagued him for years: whether his father would die as he had lived, indifferent to the Church. "Did Papa know I had not come?" he asked when his mother finished.

"No."

"What do you mean?"

"Toward the end, he was delirious. Father Probst, our young pastor, visited him yesterday afternoon. He stayed with Walter a long time. He gave Papa the last sacraments and heard his confession."

A feeling of relief came over him, but it was relief mixed with the guilt of failure. He would now, of course, never know what the state of his father's soul had been at death, nor what if any were the sins left unforgiven. "Did Papa say anything? I mean, about me? Did he say anything in particular about me?"

"I don't know what he said to Father Probst. But last night, just before the end came, he thought you were in the room with me." She looked down at her folded hands. "He said, 'Remember me, son. Remember the good times.'"

"Is that all?"

"Yes. He was confused by the drugs."

For a while, neither of them spoke. *The good times.* There had been good times in the past, Kruger thought. A mind in the last moments of drugged delirium often turns in on its own private memories. He had been at enough deathbeds to know that. He said, "I gather the funeral arrangements have been made."

"Nothing is final."

"I'll say the funeral Mass myself and perform the burial rite."

"Yes. He would want that."

"Have you . . . ?" He had asked the question many times before of other people. "Have you chosen a casket, Mamma?"

"No. Not yet."

"We'll do that together."

"Yes. I need help." Her voice collapsed and she began to cry.

Karl left his chair, knelt down, and embraced her. "Everything will be done right. Leave everything to me, Mamma."

She nodded. "Twenty-six years, Karl—why?"

"It couldn't be helped, Mamma, I had no choice."

After a while, she drew back. "You look tired, *Liebchen*. Go up to your room and lie down for a while."

"I think *you* should lie down."

"No. I want to sit here. Why don't you go up and take a bath? You've been on an airplane all night."

"All right." Her suggestion was like a temporary reprieve. "I won't be long." He retraced his steps down the hallway and took the staircase to the second floor.

He passed the first door down the hallway: his parents' bedroom. He looked in. Like the rest of the house, it was furnished with comfortable, solid, middle-class taste—like the bedroom of a *Bürgermeister*.

He moved on. In the years he had been absent, they had obviously reached the limits of their worldly dreams. The thought of it dismayed him. *This* was what his father had fought and struggled for?

At the second door from the end, he paused again. The window shades in this room were drawn, but he saw a huge desk, bookshelves, a glass cabinet, and photographs along the walls. His father's study. His mother had written only last year that his father, now retired, spent most of his days puttering in this room. Kruger walked in. The sweet stale odor of pipe tobacco permeated everything. The long bookcase against the wall was crammed with old magazines and newspapers. He went to the desk in front of the window. It was too large for the room. It had obviously been moved here from his father's office: the desk of a magistrate or a rich industrialist. Perhaps a little too grand for the director of a bicycle factory.

Something caught his eye in the glass case against the wall. He moved closer. There were things displayed on the shelves. It was difficult to see through the yellow film of nicotine on the glass. He leaned closer. Objects, papers, bric-a-brac. He saw a small dagger on the top shelf and recognized the silver handle at once: the token emblematic dagger awarded to the elite of Hitler's SS.

He held his breath and felt his blood run cold.

Next to the dagger, an old passport with a tiny *Hakenkreuz* printed at the center of the cover.

"Papa," he whispered.

And next to the passport, a stack of old letters and envelopes tied together with a blue ribbon. His own letters from the war. He recognized the yellowed stationery.

He felt suddenly dragged down by his own weight. He staggered forward and caught hold of the case to support himself.

The second shelf. The blood rushed to his face.

The graduation photo he had brought home from *Offiziersschule* in 1941. He moved closer: second row, fourth from the end, smiling stiffly, his Wehrmacht officer's cap pulled down over his forehead to give himself the air of fierceness.

He felt suddenly light-headed, dizzy.

Next to the photo, an old pistol. He knew the make at once: a Luger. On the handle was a tiny inlaid *Hakenkreuz*——what at home they called the swastika. He remembered where he had heard that word for the first time: from Anna Miceli in the summer of 1944. It was she who had told him what the Americans called his German national emblem.

Only certain elite had been given pistols inlaid like that with the swastika.

He forced himself on and guessed what it was before he even looked: a medal framed under glass in a flat wooden box. The Iron Cross First Class he had won in 1943 in Italy and finally sent home from Vergato for his father to keep as a memento.

It's all here, he thought, closing his eyes, letting his head rest against the glass.

An image of his father on his deathbed with the zealous but ignorant young priest in attendance came to mind. Their pastor would not have known what questions to put to the dying man.

He gave in to a feeling of hopelessness that seemed to embrace everything: the past, the present, and the infinite future. He thought of the things he could have left undone at St. Luke's to have arrived yesterday. "Oh, Papa." He grit his teeth and covered his face, letting the thought he had kept at bay sink in his mind: the delay, the postponement, the avoidance stretched back twenty-six years; and the responsibility followed behind into eternity.

Thou art a priest forever.

He reached out in his mind for an escape, an absolution, and gripped a single word: *faith. As you get older, Karl, you will discover that the Providence of God has to work in the most appalling conditions.* The words had burned like a candle in the darkness of faith these last years.

He drew himself up from the cabinet.

I have seen it myself many times before, he said to himself, grasp-ing at straws, the power of God's grace and mercy, in other deathbed confessions.

Remember me, son. Remember the good times.

II

"Do you like this place?" Anna asked.

Angelo looked around the restaurant. Predictable, he thought. The kind of elegant New York French place his parents had always patronized: somber, staid, for the quiet old money. "It's great," he said. "You come here a lot?"

"Sometimes. Usually for lunch when I have clients to entertain."

Angelo sipped his second Cinzano and soda, surveying the blue-rinsed women around the room. "Is this one of Dad's old places?"

"No. It was opened only last year." She touched the lapel of his new blue suit. "You look wonderful tonight, sweetheart. The suit is beautiful."

"Thanks. You look pretty great yourself." He liked her in that black summer dress. She had worn it for dinner once before. He liked her dark hair when she wore it long and loose about her face.

"Is something wrong, Angie?"

"No. Why?"

"You look pensive."

She had never been able to read his moods or his mind. He said, "I was just thinking about the news in the paper this morning. They've bombed the DMZ again."

"I thought the United States called a truce the other day."

"Apparently Hanoi doesn't believe in truces." He knew she was tired of their war discussions. In the last two weeks since he had come home, they had talked about Vietnam a lot and had long since come to an impasse. His mother stirred her cocktail, refusing to take the ball. He said, "So what's new at the office?"

"We won the U.S. Army—McCallum case. McCallum agreed to settle out of court, if that's winning."

"You must feel great."

"It was going to be a long fight."

The McCallum was a case inherited along with everything else from his stepfather. "You must be pretty good."

"Yes." She smiled. "I am good."

"Dad said you'd never make a great lawyer. I guess he was wrong there."

"I didn't say great, Angie. I said good."

He changed the subject. "By the way, I took you up on your offer and ordered another suit from your tailor."

"Good. You're beginning to look like yourself again."

"I also used your charge account at Saks and bought some more shoes." She had arranged with various stores for him to charge clothes.

"I told you to buy whatever you need, darling." She touched his hand affectionately. "You're going to need a whole new wardrobe."

He knew, of course, where she was leading. He said, "I also bought four pairs of jeans and some boots."

"I said *whatever* you need." She sipped her drink. "By the way, I spoke this morning to Dean Folsom at Columbia."

"Do you think they've got breadsticks here?"

"You realize you have three years of undergraduate work ahead of you."

"There's no hurry."

"You're twenty-two."

"I told you, Mom, I haven't decided what I'm going to do." She had dropped the question of career on him several times in the last two weeks, but he had so far avoided the answer, not knowing yet if he would re-up or not.

"I think it's time we talk, Angelo. You've been home for over two weeks, and we've had no time together. When I leave for the office in the morning, you're asleep. When I come home at night, you're dressing to go out. It's like—" She hesitated. "It's like living with a stranger."

"Okay. Talk."

"The day after tomorrow is Saturday. We could rent a car and drive out to the country."

"Sure." He hoped she meant the house in Connecticut where he had spent weekends as a kid. "Why not."

"Tell me something, sweetheart."

"What?"

"Where do you spend your time when you go out at night?"

He had prepared himself for the question. "I go walking. I like to take walks. I got used to walking in Vietnam."

A peculiar look came into her face. She knew he was lying. "Yesterday the maid came to me with a pint bottle of liquor and some matchbooks, wanting to know what to do with them."

"We used to buy liquor like that in Saigon. It's easier to carry that way." He added, feeling familiar traps closing around him, "I bought it to keep in my room."

"You're old enough, I guess, to buy liquor in any form you like. I was referring to the matchbooks. One in particular. From a bar called the Metropole."

"Oh. That dive." He felt relieved to see the waiters approaching with their food. As they handed the plates around, murmuring little waiter things about the freshness of the veal, the beauty of his mother's Italian *funghi porcini,* he recalled the Metropole bar on New York's West Side where he had met the oriental girl named Sharon, the girl he had thought looked Vietnamese but turned out to be Filipino.

When the waiters had gone, his mother said, "I think you should be careful of places like the Metropole. I once had a client who frequented that bar." She sliced through the huge steamed mushroom on her plate. "He went there for the prostitutes."

"I wandered in, I had a drink, and I left." He sliced the end of his steak to see if it was as rare as he had ordered. "This looks great."

"Good." She waited while the waiter uncorked and poured the champagne, then said, "There are decent, very attractive girls in the East Side singles bars, Angie."

"I know. I've checked them out."

"You're a handsome boy. There are plenty of nice girls in New York. You could meet any one of them, if you wanted."

He thought of Lan Tien, the Vietnamese girl he had dated in Nam. "I've got a girl friend."

She looked surprised. "I didn't know."

"We've been steady now for—oh, three years." Angelo busied himself with the steak, filling his mouth. His mother had always said not to talk with his mouth full.

"Why haven't you introduced me?"

He shook his head, pointing with the fork to his mouth, thinking in the interval how he would introduce the subject of Lan Tien, a lost but useful cause. "I can't," he said finally, "at least not yet. She's in Vietnam."

His mother lowered her knife and fork to her plate. The surprise in her face was more than he had anticipated, more like shock.

He said, "Her name's Lan Tien. She's great. You'll like her."

She stared at him and said nothing.

He swallowed. "You've got the wrong impression of the Vietnamese, Mom. They're great people when you get to know them."

"It's not that, Angelo."

"Then what?"

"You've—" She sat back. The color had drained from her face. "You've left Vietnam."

He saw that he was already trapped by his alibi. "So what? The war's not going to last forever. When it's over, maybe she'll come to America." He reached for his glass of champagne, trying to work out all the implications of his next dangerous commitment before he spoke again. Lan Tien was there, he was here: whatever he chose in the future to do or not to do was his business. Meanwhile, she was a perfect excuse to avoid the "nice girls" his mother knew in New York. He said, "We're going to be married when the war is over."

There was no reaction whatever. She went on staring at him blankly. Then he saw something curious: she was staring not *at* but *through* him—at something very far away, it seemed.

"*Mom.*" He laughed. "She's very nice. I promise you'll like her."

She murmured something in Italian under her breath. He heard only the words *la guerra* and *la bestia:* war and beast. He did not speak good Italian.

"What?"

"Nothing. An old Italian expression my grandmother used in the war. There's no translation."

The maître d'hôtel, a pompous little Hungarian refugee in a tailored tuxedo who had fussed over his mother with too much familiarity when they came in, approached their table. "Madame Fitzgerald, is anything wrong—the table, the food?"

"Everything is fine, Gregory."

"I was concerned, madame. You seemed displeased."

The little man obviously pampered his rich regulars. He had made a point of seating them at the restaurant's epicenter. Angelo broke in, "It's great, man."

The Hungarian penguin bowed and withdrew. "Forgive me for intruding, madame."

The champagne bubbles were settling. Angelo lifted his glass. "I didn't mean to shock you, Mom. Anyway, the war will go on for a while. It'll probably be years before I see her again." He smiled and touched her champagne glass with his own. "Cheers."

She lifted her glass. "Cheers." The smile she forced only accentuated the fear in her big brown eyes.

They sipped together, stiffly, in silence.

He thought, all I want is a little fuckin' space of my own to breathe in! Jesus! I'm not a *kid* anymore! He said, "I'll tell you what. We'll rent the car, just you and me, and drive up to Connecticut. I'd like to see the house again. After that . . . after that, I'd like to drive by the cemetery and see Dad's grave."

CHAPTER 4

I

Kruger reached the foot of the coffin, sprinkled it again with holy water, and returned the silver instrument to the font. He opened the German translation of the *Collectio Rituum* to continue the graveside service. "From the gates of hell . . ."

"Rescue his soul, O Lord," came Father Probst's response.

Kruger glanced toward his mother, seated under the green canopy next to the gravesite. In the last few minutes, she had not lifted her eyes from the prayer book in her lap. Her face under the black brimmed hat was an expressionless mask. He went on with the burial service. "May he rest in peace."

"Amen," responded the small crowd of mourners under the canopy. Except for the distant cousins seated on either side of his mother, he knew none of them. He lifted his voice. "Lord, hear my prayer."

"And let my cry come unto Thee." The von Scheffels, he saw, and the five pallbearers who had carried his father's coffin out of the church and from the hearse to the gravesite, made no effort to respond. They stood apart from the mourners, just outside the canopy. On the ride over to the cemetery, his mother had explained his father's pallbearers. "They are members of a veterans' organization your father belonged to here in Munich."

"Let us pray." He began the prayer for mercy. He had said it a hundred times before in English, but never in German. He read it from the *Rituum,* occasionally glancing up at the faces of the six top-hatted pallbearers. "Businessmen," his mother had said. One of them, a short plump elderly man with a smooth baby face, leaned toward von Scheffel and whispered something. Von Scheffel looked surprised and turned to glance back over his shoulder in the direction of the automobiles parked below in the cemetery drive. "Thus

Your mercy may unite him with the company of the choirs of angels in heaven, through Christ Our Lord," Kruger said, ending the prayer.

"Amen." His mother's voice was audible over the others.

He stepped toward the casket and made the sign of the cross over his father. The summer sun beat down on the gray metal coffin and its spray of white chrysanthemums. Father Probst had told him before the service began that the flowers had been sent by *friends of your father*. "Eternal rest grant unto him, O Lord."

"And let perpetual light shine upon him."

"May he rest in peace."

"Amen." The response sounded strangely uncertain. For the last two days, his mother had chosen to keep silent about the things in his father's study. The door to the study had been kept closed. "May his soul and all the souls of the faithfully departed, through the mercy of God, rest in peace." He had meditated all last night on this prayer. Unlike his own human mercies had once been, God's were infinite.

"Amen." Louder than the others, his mother's response sounded like a plea.

It was finished. He closed the book and nodded toward his mother. As the mourners began to rise, he said to Father Probst, at his side, "I'll accompany my mother home," and handed the parish ritual book to the young priest.

"Yes, Father."

Kruger joined his mother under the canopy where his two cousins, the Seidels, were helping Elizabeth to her feet. "Mamma." He embraced her, then guided her toward the far side of the canopy, and as they reached the end of the casket, his mother made the sign of the cross.

"Frau Kruger." Herr von Scheffel and his wife stepped toward them. "Frieda and I wish to offer our condolences."

"Thank you, Herr von Scheffel." His mother shook the man's hand but seemed anxious to move on.

Kruger removed the black cope he was wearing and signaled one of the two altar boys to come forward. "Please return this to Father Probst for me, son."

"Yes, Father."

"My dear Elizabeth." Frau von Scheffel kissed his mother. The gesture and her words were forced.

"Herr Kaplan Kruger." Von Scheffel drew him aside. "I would like for you to meet an old friend of your father." He motioned for one of the pallbearers to come forward, a thin, sallow-faced man in his late sixties. The man removed his top hat. "Herr Müller was one of your father's closest friends, my dear Karl," said von Scheffel.

The man's German sounded like gravel on concrete: *"Mein Beileid, Herr Kaplan Kruger."* Müller offered his hand. The condolences he offered sounded perfunctory.

"Thank you, Herr Müller." The man's hand was soft and clammy.

"Your father and Ernst were friends for over twenty-five years, Karl," said von Scheffel, encouragingly.

Ernst Müller: the name struck a distant but familiar chord. Kruger tried to think back where he had heard the name before.

Müller was rasping on about his father: ". . . and perhaps, while you are here in Munich, Herr Kaplan, you will honor us with a visit. Your father, you know, served as president of our veterans' group from 1950 to 1959." He added with pride, "Der Verein der Alten we are called."

The Club of the Old Ones, Kruger thought, feeling a chill on his sweating face.

At the mention of the name, his mother took hold of his arm. "We must go, Karl. I'm very tired."

"Excuse us. We'll talk later, Herr Müller." Without waiting for a response, he led his mother through the mourners gathered on the lawn outside the canopy, ignoring condolences as they passed. She seemed unsteady on the mown grass. He held and guided her down the hillside toward the Mercedes limousine at the curb. People moved aside for them to pass. Twenty feet from the car, he caught sight of a man dressed in a tweed suit standing off to the side between the tombstones, staring at him. The man smiled and made a gesture of acknowledgment with his hat.

Kruger took a second glance at the Nordic sunburned middle-aged face. He slowed, staring, and saw the face under the hat merge with the image of a boyish blond face under a Wehrmacht corporal's cap. "Mamma." He came to a dead halt.

"What is it, *Liebchen?*" She saw what he was looking at but only seemed mildly puzzled.

Reiger. The name came falling through his mind like a stone. Corporal Hans Reiger. His communications officer in Montefalco: the man who had transcribed and sent all the radio messages between Montefalco and the OKW.

"Karl?" his mother asked.

He had last seen the man twenty-three years before—the night before he deserted and fled south behind American lines. "That man, Mother."

"What about him?"

Reiger had moved away down the hillside toward a small sports-car parked at the curb. His mother did not know Reiger, he saw. Why here? he thought. Why to Papa's funeral?

Reiger got into his car, started the engine, and drove off.

"It's nothing, Mamma." He led her toward the waiting limousine.

Inside, neither of them spoke as the driver pulled away. The air conditioning began to purr through the ventilator, gradually cooling the soft dark interior. Kruger watched the driver as they curved down the hillside through acres of lawn and gravestones. The limousine, his mother had said, was a courtesy provided by Herr Scheffel and his friends.

Reiger. He was alive. But why here? And the others? Ernst Müller? Der Verein der Alten?

He spoke at last. "Mamma?" But there was no response. He saw that she was staring vacantly at nothing, lost in her own thoughts. "Mamma?" he asked again.

"Yes, *Liebchen.*"

The driver passed through the big iron gates and swung out into the road leading toward Munich. "That man who spoke to me—"

Again, she seemed not to hear him.

"Mamma?"

"I'm listening, son."

"He said his name was Müller, Ernst Müller."

"Yes."

"He was a friend of Papa's?"

She nodded. "He owns a factory here in Munich that makes farm machinery. He and your father had business ties."

"Von Scheffel said he had known Papa for twenty-five years."

She nodded. "Yes."

"I know the name Müller, Mamma. Papa spoke of an Ernst Müller a long time ago. That weekend when I came home from the military academy."

"He is the same man. He was a very important official in the party during the war."

Overhearing his mother, the driver looked up through the rear-view mirror.

Kruger lowered his voice to a murmur. "And the others? Von Scheffel and the other pallbearers, were they . . . ?"

"Your Papa owed everything to those men. His business, every-thing." She saw that the driver was listening, covered her face, and began to cry softly. Kruger drew a deep breath and looked out through the tinted window at the rolling Bavarian farmland stretch-ing off as far as the eye could see. "You should have stayed in America, Karl," she said, "you should not have come back."

II

Between Westport and Trumbull, they left the Merritt Parkway and turned south on the highway leading to Monroe. "When we get to Long Hill, keep your eyes open for the turnoff, honey, I always miss it," said Anna.

"It's about a mile past the Huntington turnoff." Angelo pointed toward the skeletal remains of girders and corrugated steel. "What happened to that tractor factory?"

"I don't know. It was here last January. It must have burned."

"You don't go up for weekends anymore, do you?"

"Now and then. Not often. It's a long drive, and I don't like doing it alone." More than the drive, though, after Charles' death she had hated staying alone in the house. She had spent only one weekend there in the last two and a half years; the rest of the visits had been only for the day, to make sure that the caretaker she had hired in nearby Stevenson was doing his job.

"If you don't use it, why don't you sell it?"

"It's been in Dad's family a long time. It wouldn't be right to sell it."

"Why? Our weekends in Connecticut belong to the past. That's all over."

"*Angelo,*" she admonished.

"That's the turnoff ahead." He pointed.

"Right. I remember."

She turned into the country road leading north to Stevenson. As they passed into the familiar rolling farmland, the hot sultry flatlands gave way to the cool forested parkland northwest of Indian Well. Angelo, she saw, sat watching the familiar landmarks of his childhood pass: the small country store at the Indian Well turnoff where, on their drives up from the city, he had always forced Charles to stop for fish bait; the old clapboard motor lodge nestled in the forested park where they sometimes, on Saturday evenings, stopped for fresh trout dinners. A mile beyond the lodge, she turned into the country lane winding through the old Fitzgerald property.

"It's paved," Angelo said.

"Yes. They paved it two years ago. Thank God. Remember the rains?" The road had been impassable during the heavy spring rains.

"I liked the dirt one better. It looks too public now."

"I know. But childhood country dirt roads belong to the past, Angie. We have to let go." Her insinuating use of his own remark irritated him, but he kept silent. They passed the Froelich's weekend prefab cottage. Beyond the Froelich cottage, their house came into view, nestled in a small grove of maple trees at the top of a gentle slope, a modest but substantial two-story house built of sober gray fieldstone in the first quarter of the nineteenth century.

"The fence needs painting." Angelo pointed to the white wooden fence bordering the property.

Charles had repainted the fence in 1959, four and a half years before his death. The biting Connecticut winters had blistered the white paint. "I'll phone the caretaker when we get back to the city and have him tend to it," she said, turning in before the iron gate. "Will you open the lock?" She took a ring of keys from her purse. He got out, unfastened the padlock, and swung the gate open.

When he returned, he said, "The rungs on the gate are bent. Someone ran into it."

Probably the hippies who had moved in up the road, she thought, but said nothing. Angelo had come home from the war hating hippies. She started up the slope to the house, dreading what they might find after two years' negligence, and swung around the gravel turnabout to the plain wooden front door. The shutters across the facade were closed, a stark reminder of her absence. "I closed the shutters the last time I was here. There were robberies in the neighborhood last year."

"You should have used the reverse strategy. In Nam we learned not to advertise our retreats." He got out.

For a moment, bewildered, she sat wondering where all this anger was coming from. He had loved the house as a kid, but at seventeen, when he entered boarding school, he had abruptly announced that he had outgrown it.

She got out and followed him toward the barn, an ancient wooden structure that had served in recent years as a storeroom. Charles had neglected the barn after he sold Angelo's childhood Shetland pony. The red clapboard sidings had long ago faded, and the white wooden fence Charles had built as a corral for the pony had collapsed. Angelo surveyed the damage, then turned away without speaking.

Anna caught up with him at the corner of the house. "Angelo—!"

"Which key is it?" he asked, cutting her off.

"The big gold one with the tape on it." The door was jammed, frozen into its frame by the winter dampness. He struck it with his shoulder. "Your caretaker hasn't been inside all winter," he said. The door gave way. She followed him into the house to the living room. The morning breeze through the front door stirred the stale odor of mildew in the room. "Jesus," he muttered, "the room stinks." He threw back the curtains over one window, unlatched the shutter, and opened the window.

"I'm sorry, Angelo. I didn't . . ." She left off as light flooded the room. It was filled with furniture, the pieces that had always been here and the pieces she had shipped up last winter when she redecorated the apartment. Angelo continued along the wall, opening the two remaining windows on the front of the house.

"There. That's better." He turned. "You should have—" He saw the furniture clustered like furniture in an antique store. "So this is where it all went."

He had spoken about the furniture that first night home, but had never asked what she had done with it. "When I redecorated, I stored some of the things up here, Angie."

He moved around the room, touching some of the pieces: the antique commode, the two eighteenth-century French armchairs, the breakfront which had always stood in their New York dining room. He touched the pieces, she saw, that Charles had inherited from his mother-in-law in Italy. "You shouldn't have moved this stuff up here," he said, "it's too damp up here."

"Yes, I see." The veneer had begun to peel from the commode. "I'll have them moved to a safe place in the city."

"The fact is, you really didn't want them, did you?"

"It was a temporary move. I didn't realize . . ."

"I don't believe that. You never really liked this stuff to begin with."

"I moved everything here on the spur of the moment, Angie. I needed a change." She thought of the loneliness and guilt that had hounded her after Charles' death. The overnight decision to redecorate, triggered by the prospect of Angelo's return, had been as much for herself as for him.

"A change from what?"

She thought of the compromises Charles had made with himself over the years to be with her and after his death her haunting feelings of past selfishness. "I was alone in the apartment with these things. I needed to forget."

"That figures."

"Now what does that mean?" They were back suddenly to that first night at home.

"These were Dad's things, Mom, not yours. There's scarcely one thing left of Dad's in the apartment, did you know that?" His anger swept by her like a moving wall.

"Yes, Angie. I know."

"Why?"

"I . . . I needed to think about the future. Your future. These things belong to the past."

"Come on, Mom. I'm not a child anymore. I'm twenty-two years old!"

She moved toward him. "What are you saying?"

"I'm saying I *know*. You don't have to keep pretending with me."

"What do you know?"

"The poor guy's *dead,* Mom! So what difference does it make *now*. Admit it!"

"*It?*"

"Don't get me wrong, now. I'm not saying you did anything wrong. I know you guys worked it all out between you. But let's face it, the poor guy came out holding the short end of the stick, didn't he?"

She came to a dead halt next to an armchair, infuriated by the evasive accusations. "What are you talking about, young man?"

He backed away, reading challenge into her anger, evaluating it. "Why do you think I came back here? Back home, even? You've told me *some* things. Now, I want to know some more things. Like back in the beginning, back in Italy, when you got married. You married the captain to escape the war, didn't you? You had another man's baby to raise, you had me to raise, and you needed a way out, isn't that right?"

She glanced away. The room around her had shrunk. She seemed to be standing in a dollhouse, with Angelo huge and life-sized against the opposite wall. She said, mechanically, "That isn't true." But the force of truth was not in it. Memories came flooding in on her, too many, too soon, for her mind to sort through.

He said, "As I say, don't get me wrong. I think you worked it all out from the beginning. Dad knew what he was getting into. All I want to know is, did you love him when you married him?"

"No." Her throat closed around her tongue.

"And he knew it?"

"Yes."

"But he went ahead anyway?"

"Yes."

"He knew you loved the guy before him, Lamberti, my real father, but he went ahead anyway?" His eyes widened with amazement.

She said, despising the half-truth, "Yes."

"I see." He nodded, thoughtfully. "I guess that explains why I was in his *heart,* but never in his *blood.*"

"No. You're wrong."

"Come on, Mom. I've had a long time to think about this. I was the other guy's son. The one Dad knew you really loved. I *look* like *him.* How could he love me when I always reminded him of the other guy—the one he'd lost out to?"

"You've worked this all out for yourself, Angie, but you're wrong." She watched him turn away toward the wall. "You've misread us both."

He chuckled. "You even got rid of his favorite painting of you."

She saw what he was staring at: the small oil portrait that had hung in the New York apartment for twenty years. The portrait of Silvanna Agnoletto-Patini, Silvanna Fitzgerald.

Like a key, she turned the truth in her mind, and a small door seemed to open for her. "You're wrong, Angie. The portrait is not of me. It was never me." He turned toward her, slowly. "Your father and I always told you it was me, but it wasn't. It is his first wife, Silvanna." She left the statement lying where it fell like a feather in the silence.

His cheek twitched. "I don't believe that."

"Then I will show you a photograph of Silvanna when we get back home tonight."

He swallowed thickly, foundering. "Even so, he loved you."

"Yes. And I loved him, too. Maybe not the kind of love you think of for a normal marriage, maybe not the kind you needed as a child. But it was the best we had under the circumstances. It's true, for Charles you were always another man's son. We couldn't change that. But I was always another woman, and we couldn't change that either."

He moved to the window and looked out, pensively. "What was he like?"

Her pulse fluttered. She knew who he meant. She rummaged in her mind for one of her parental evasions. They had worked well enough in his childhood, but were now hopelessly inadequate. "We knew each other for a very short time, Angelo. It was wartime. Things happened very quickly. I was very young. It was a long time ago—." She broke off abruptly before she went out the other end of truth into another destructive lie.

"I really look like him, don't I?"

"Yes."

"Funny. Here I was—with only the present to live in. And there you and Dad were—with only the past. You guys should have told me. That wasn't fair."

Anna recalled that relentless theme of her days as a parent: her obsession that the future belonged to Angelo, having lost her own to the past. "It's hard to know what's right to tell a small child."

He chuckled. "You used to tell me how the Big Bad Wolf got into bed with Little Red Riding Hood. And it wasn't even wartime for the Hoods."

"I'm sorry." That, too, sounded hopelessly inadequate.

"Do I remind you of him?"

"It was a long time ago," she said with bitterness, realizing, of course, they were talking about two entirely different kinds of men.

"Faces remind you, don't they? I mean, like a girl I came across last night in one of the East Side singles bars. She reminded me of my girl in Vietnam, Lan Tien. It must have been hard to forget all those years when you were looking at me. No wonder I got all the love."

She saw that they were running parallel to the worst horror of all. She changed the subject. "This girl, this Vietnamese girl—do you love her, Angelo?"

He shrugged. "I don't know. I don't think I know what that feels like yet. For me, love is only what you feel when you miss someone. Like Lan Tien. Like both dads. As a kid, that's all I learned from you. Love is only a feeling of missing." He closed the shutters and the window in front of him. "I miss her, that's all."

"There's time. Give yourself time."

He moved along the wall, closing the other shutters and windows. "You mean, time by itself heals everything?" She dared not answer the question. He went back along the wall, pulling the curtains closed.

"I had the caretaker paint the upstairs bathroom," she said, "Would you like to see it?"

"No. I've seen enough. I want to drive over to the cemetery. I haven't seen where you buried him."

"He's where he wanted to be. With Silvanna." She followed him out and waited by the car while he bolted the front door. Instead of heading for the passenger door, he came toward her where she stood at the driver's door.

"I'll drive," he said, tossing her the house keys.

"But you have no license, Angelo."

"Yes, I do. I have my military license. If it's good over there, it damn well ought to be good over here."

CHAPTER 5

I

We've drawn a new line of defense, Papa. We call it the Caesar line. Everything's going well. And last week, Papa, I was awarded the Iron Cross First Class for my service to the Reich here in Italy. I was told by my commander that my promotion to captain is now almost certain. Tell Mamma I'm healthy. I know she worries, but I'm much more worried about you both in Munich. We heard yesterday that the English bombed Munich again. Is it true? Mamma is right. You would be safer in the country until the war is over. But I guess you have bicycles to worry about for the troops. We must not lose faith in Germany's future victory. The Führer has promised victory if we stand firm at this hour of trial. We will triumph, Papa, I'm sure of it! Do not lose faith! Be certain of it!

> Your loving son,
> Lieutenant Karl

And across the bottom of the letter, as always, he had scribbled:

HEIL HITLER!

Kruger returned the frail yellow page to its envelope and picked up another written farther up the boot of Italy, from behind the Gothic Line. The paper had gotten cheaper and thinner as the war dragged on. This letter, like most of the others, had been written to his mother. She, not his father, had been the one to correspond.

August 1944

Dearest Mamma:

Word has probably reached you and Papa about the surrender of Florence to the Allies. Everything is well with me, despite the setback. Since my transfer to Tuscany, I've been given command of a small unit. I think the war here will be won by units like these, ordinary soldiers who remain faithful and obedient to the will of our Führer. Tell Papa that our Italian front is secure. Tell Papa we will win. He must believe that! It is already destined! We can't fail!

The next line had been scratched out. By then, August of '44, he had begun to doubt the old Nazi propaganda. The letter abruptly changed tone:

Mamma! Something wonderful has been happening to me! I will tell you all about it when I see you!

He sat back in his father's swivel chair. He had written the letter one afternoon when he returned from a meeting with Anna Miceli in the Adele Ravine. They had made love again that afternoon, and afterward had talked again of marriage when the war was over. When he returned to headquarters, he had written to his parents for the first time about the change taking place in himself. He had not dared, of course, to describe either the joy he felt or its cause, for letters were carefully censored by German authorities for careless remarks about supplies and positions.

He replaced the letter in its envelope and sat back. The evening breeze through the window behind his father's desk carried a sweet fragrance like jasmine into the study. When he entered the study a half hour ago, he had forced the window open to get rid of the stale odor of pipe tobacco. The window had not been opened for a long time. The collection of memorabilia spread out on the desk under the fluorescent lamp looked strangely macabre. A dog barked somewhere off in the quiet residential neighborhood. Just after dark, when his mother finally went to bed, he had taken a walk through the Bogenhausen to the Isar River, trying to unravel the tangled threads of his father's story. On the drive home that morning, he had not questioned his mother further in the presence of the chauffeur; nor afterward, when they were alone, did it seem right to return to the painful subject so soon after the funeral. His mother had refused to have a traditional Bavarian wake, and he now knew why. She had abhorred his father's friends and had only a few of her own. She had gone to bed when they returned. Later, he had taken a walk, then returned and gave in to the dreadful knowledge that the answers to his questions were waiting for him in his father's study.

The letters. He flipped through them again. All the letters he had written home during the war, from the time he entered *Offiziers-schule* until the time he last wrote home in late September of '44 to send his Iron Cross to his father. He had sent the medal almost as an afterthought, for by then the decoration had become meaningless to him. His father had kept the letters folded in their envelopes in chronological order, tied up with a blue silk ribbon like love letters. He had obviously read and reread them many times over the years. In the beginning, he had written like an idealistic young boy, filling his letters with the memorized phrases of Nazi propaganda, the kind of stuff he had learned in the Hitler Youth. Then later, as the war dragged itself up the boot of Italy, there were signs of hopelessness and despair. He had written *The Führer visited us today. He was magnificent!* when he was twenty-two. He had written *If we surrender now, it is not the Reich that will fail, but the German people themselves* when he was twenty-six.

The only bright hopeful notes were the occasional references he had made to the *wonderful thing* that had happened to him.

He sat forward and rested his head in his hands. He had not let himself dwell on the image of Anna's face and body for years, for so long, in fact, that they were difficult to summon back. But the image was there, just under the surface of his memory, as vivid as if she had just walked out of the room.

He closed his eyes. It was wrong for him to stare like this at her naked body. Even the face brought with it forbidden thoughts and desires: the bodily pull backward on his soul toward human love and sex, which, in Anna, were inseparably one and the same. She looked up at him from the tablecloth spread across the pine needles, smiling, a little frightened, nervous and beautiful in her youthful nakedness. He was dangerously near sin to toy like this with the image of her and he recognized and acknowledged the peril. It would take but an instant now to relinquish the will and say *yes* to the evil behind the lost remembered good.

Anna opened her mouth to speak. The soft afternoon light wavered across her face and body. Her mouth formed words, but he could not remember what she had said that afternoon: he could only summon up a feeling indelibly stamped in his body: hope, love, and a boundless sense of completeness—of having come finally to rest.

"Anna," he whispered, feeling the downward drag of an irrevocable loss that seemed to cover his entire life stretching forward, day by day, through eternity. A soldier, then a priest: however much he had tried throughout his life to approach some kind of perfection, he would never again approach that simpler perfection which had once been within his reach. *Better to marry,* he thought, *than to burn.* He had never been either soldier or priest completely. He was really the most wretched of men.

"Karl?" His mother's voice came from the door, barely audible.

He lifted his head, quickly. She stood in the frame, backlit by the light from the hallway. She wore a dressing gown. Her thin gray hair had come undone and fallen in wisps about her face. "I thought you were asleep, Mamma."

She came into the room, her eyes darting over the objects spread out on the desk top. "I tried," she said, "but it's no use. It's too soon to sleep."

"I know." He felt ashamed of what lay spread out across the desk. It was too soon to confront her with this darker side of her grief.

She absently fingered the collar of her dressing gown. "It's all there, except for your uniform. He kept that in the closet."

"Mamma," he pleaded.

Her voice sounded suddenly very small. "I knew you would find Papa's things. I didn't want to hide anything. I left them as they were."

He got to his feet. "Go to bed, Mamma. We'll talk about it in the morning."

"No. We'll talk now. I'd feel better if you knew everything."

"Then come sit down." He started around the desk.

"I'll sit here, son." She backed away and sat down in a straight-backed chair near the wall. He remained standing. There was a long strained silence as she searched for a place to begin.

"I don't understand, Mamma," he said finally. "Why did he keep all this stuff? The war ended a long time ago."

There was a faint sigh. "Not for Papa. For Papa the war never ended." She hesitated.

"Go on. Tell me."

"You remember what our life was like before the war—in the years between the two wars?"

"Yes. Of course."

"You wouldn't understand Papa, unless you had lived with him from the beginning. He was a proud man. He always wanted to succeed at something. When he came back from the war in 1919, you were a baby. He had never seen you until then. He came back to a Germany that was destroyed. He could not find work. He was hopeless. You were the only light in his life. For the next twenty-three years, nothing changed. He was not an educated man, and he was not talented. Then came Hitler." She sighed. "You know the rest of that. Papa joined the Nazi Party in 1940. You went to the military academy in '41. You came back home only once. You did not see how Papa's life had changed for him because of Hitler. When it ended, he was a successful owner of a bicycle shop. He was a little man in the party, so they left him alone after the war. He and most of his friends. But for Papa, it was like 1919 all over again. This time, Papa refused to believe that Germany was going to be humiliated and destroyed again. He could not bear the idea of being punished again. He began to drink." She left off, fingering the collar of her dressing gown.

"Hitler was a monster. It was he who destroyed Germany."

She looked at him and asked, "Did you think that at the time?"

The question silenced him. He shook his head.

"Neither did Papa. He was a good man. He was not like the others. Müller and the rest."

"And the Baumanns? Did he know what became of the Jews who had owned the store?"

"The human mind is strange, Karl." She lifted her hand and formed in the fluorescent light the shadow of a dog's head on the opposite wall with her closed fist. "Remember?" It was a game she had played with him as a child. "You see what you want to see. Did you know about the Jews?"

"I was in Italy, Mamma. There was very little news from home. We heard only rumors from soldiers who had been on the eastern front."

"Did you believe them?"

"No."

"There was no news here, either. Only rumors. A few believed, but most did not. By then, the bombings had begun. They told us if we didn't fight back, we would be destroyed. The old nightmares came back to Germany. When it was over, we felt like we were waking from a nightmarish sleep. At first, the truth they told us was too horrible to believe."

He turned toward the Nazi memorabilia. "But why *this*, Mamma?"

She began to cry softly. "Papa drank because he did not want to believe what Germany, what the Nazis, had done. At first, he drank to forget. But he could not forget. It was all around him. In 1964 he turned over the management of his business to von Scheffel. After that, he never went out. He spent his time here at home, working in the garden, sitting in his study with his—with his things. He died of cirrhosis because he drank, Karl." She covered her face. "But it was not his fault. By then . . . by then, he was insane."

When he finally spoke, his voice shook uncontrollably. "Why didn't you tell me, Mamma? You could have told me."

"You were in America. You had your own responsibilities. Besides, it did not happen all at once."

"I'm a priest! I could have helped him!" He thought to himself, but I did not. I didn't even come in time for the end.

"Once, when he was himself, he made me promise not to tell you. He didn't want you to come. He wanted you to remember him as he was." The words came back to him: *Remember me. Remember the good times.* She said, "For Papa, you were a war hero. He used to tell me you were the one man, the one soldier, who had ended the war with honor."

A gust of wind billowed the white lace curtains, stirring the wisps of hair around her face. The sweet fragrance in the air was suddenly nauseating to him. He slowly sat down at the desk. "I was no hero, Mamma."

"You were to Papa."

Something immense gave way inside him and fell like a wall blown away by a bomb in a silent newsreel. He looked at the token emblematic SS dagger before him on the desk and said, "I didn't end the war with honor. I ended it with the worst of them. I murdered innocent people." In the silence that followed, he dared not look up. Yet, the spoken admission of his crime after all these years left him with a strange feeling of weightlessness. He went on, "I executed fifty innocent Italian civilians, Mamma." When he looked up, she was sitting rigidly in her chair, with her face paralyzed into a vacant question. "It happened in September of 1944. In Montefalco. I was —" He started to say he was twenty-six, but realized there was no room now for mitigating excuses. "We were behind the Gothic Line. I was in command of the garrison holding the Reno Valley." He quickly sketched for her the backdrop of the time, the chaos and confusion behind German lines, the orders and counter-orders from the High Command, his decision to retreat, the order to stay and collect the shipment of supplies from the north. The murder of his soldiers by partisans, he said, had been the result of his decision to obey. He spoke calmly and simply, without ornament, for a lifetime of self-examination had printed the facts plainly in his mind. He told of his six-month affair with Anna Miceli and his hope of marrying her after the war.

In the minutes it took to tell his story, his mother sat without moving. Only once, when he finally told of Kesselring's order to carry out a military reprisal execution of civilians, did she react: her mouth parted. His decision to obey, he said, had not been made in the heat of passion. It was a choice made in the face of conscious moral repugnance and therefore fulfilled all the conditions of a mortal sin of murder. He told her when he stood in the square and gave his soldiers the order to fire, he knew what he was doing. And he knew what he was doing when he gave the *coup de grâce* to the two men who had not died. "Then came an order to retreat." His voice broke with the remembrance of hopelessness and guilt. "It came that same day. After I had killed fifty innocent men. For Kesselring—my superiors—what I had done was meaningless. Murder meant nothing to the German High Command. After that, I lost all belief in Germany and the war. All I could do was try to save the lives of my soldiers and the lives of other people in Montefalco. Anna's life. I could not change what I had done. I went north with my men to the mountains. A month later, I deserted and surrendered. You know the rest, they sent me to the prison camp in America." He looked down, feeling old waves of guilt wash over him. "I confessed my sins to a priest in Italy. He gave me absolution. But I don't know if he heard me. He was an old priest. I think he pretended to hear, but he was deaf. I confessed again in America, to the prison chaplain; but by then there was no way to go back and make reparation. He absolved me. I never told the civilian authorities. Until now, I don't know if I have yet been charged with any crime in Italy. I think they believe I am dead. Nothing has ever been said." He clasped his forehead with both hands, wanting to cry. "After the war, I was afraid. For myself. For you and Papa. I was afraid to come home."

His mother said, "Like Papa was afraid to *leave* home."

"I asked to be sent to France. I knew I couldn't help the dead. I could only bring help to the living. I thought I could make up for the evil by doing good. That's why I became a priest." He gave in to the impulse and shaded his eyes. It felt good to cry after so long.

His mother's hand came to rest on the back of his head. Startled, he looked up. She was beside him. The shock in her face had dissolved, leaving behind a look of well-tried compassion. "You could have told us everything," she said.

"I could have. But I didn't." He glanced at the rusted Luger on the desk and thought of the night in Montefalco when he turned the barrel of his own pistol into his mouth. He had drawn back that night from one damning mortal sin—suicide—but had lived on to commit its unforgivable companion: despair.

"Karl." She touched his face. "'Look at me.'"

He did so. His mother's eyes widened with fear. "What you did was terrible. But it was done. You cannot change it. God has forgiven you." She looked at the gun.

"It isn't enough. God's forgiveness isn't enough." Out of long habit, he locked the fingers of his consecrated hands together. He thought of his father's escape into alcohol and madness and saw, suddenly, a reflection of himself.

"Then what *is* enough?"

"I should have stood trial like the others."

"But you didn't."

"No."

She drew a long breath. "In the beginning, Papa drank. In the end, he—"

"I've lived with it so long that I've grown used to it." He felt suddenly helpless, like a small boy.

"Karl." She grasped his face with both hands and lifted it. "What will you do?"

"Nothing, Mamma. I'm a priest. If I confessed, if I went to trial, there would be a scandal. More sin," he added helplessly. Pain shot across her face. Her eyes spilled. "The sin is endless, Mamma."

She drew him forward, pressed his head to her stomach, and held him tightly. "You must leave Germany. Go back to America. You must never come back. If you do, they may arrest you."

He turned his face into the fabric of her dressing gown and wept.

"Do you understand?" she said. *"Never."*

II

They drove south on the Merritt Parkway and took the first Bridgeport exit north of the city. A short distance from the parkway, the commercial area gave way to a quiet, graceful suburb of tree-lined streets and turn-of-the-century mansions set back on meticulous lawns. They passed a gray, somber Gothic Episcopal church. "Down there," Anna said, pointing toward a metal fence bordering the church property, "where you see the two columns. That's the entrance."

Angelo turned into the asphalt lane leading through the cemetery. "Where now?"

"Take the left fork. It's just around the bend. Near those trees at the foot of the hill."

"It's beautiful." He scanned the rolling lawns and huge shade trees.

"Yes, sweetheart. They take very good care of things." She pointed again. "Just here. We'll have to walk up."

Angelo parked the car. Anna led the way up the neatly mown lawn of the hillside through the tombstones. A hot fragrant breeze rolled down through the trees, smelling faintly of wilted funeral wreaths. At the top of the slope they reached a cluster of tombstones and statues set apart behind a plain metal fence. "Are these all Fitzgeralds?" he asked.

"Yes. They all belong to Dad's side of the family." Not only had Angelo not come to Charles' funeral, she realized, he had also never visited the Fitzgerald gravesite. She followed him through the swinging gate, removing her rosary from her purse, a habit she had acquired from her mother and grandmother years before in Montefalco when they visited the Miceli graves at the cemetery of San Tommaso. The habit of the rosary and her sudden thought of her father and brother always came together like links in a mental chain. She pointed. "He's there, honey, just above his parents." She led him between the tombstones to the area of more recent burials. Two plain white marble stones lay apart from the others in a small plot set aside by Charles for himself and Silvanna. Two vases of fresh summer flowers rested in the Bermuda grass at the foot of both stones. She had engaged a local florist to replace their flowers once a week.

"I should have brought something," Angelo said, approaching the grave.

The guilt in his voice, she knew, had nothing whatever to do with flowers. He had come three years late. She stood back to let him have the grave to himself, sensing his need for privacy. He carefully avoided the graves and knelt on one knee to read the inscription on Charles' tombstone. She knew it, of course, by heart: *Charles W. Fitzgerald. Born September 16, 1915. Died December 12, 1964. A loving husband.* Below that, in long-hand scroll and in quotes: *"Più bello che si può."* There was a small cross below that and the letters *R.I.P.*

Angelo looked back at her, *"Più bello che si può?"*

"It's a saying about Florence. It doesn't translate well, but it means they made things as beautiful as they could."

He nodded and turned away to the tombstone again. She pretended to finger her rosary. After a moment, she heard a soft broken sound. She kept her eyes averted, not daring to intrude on what she knew was his private and, until now, unarticulated grief. He had never been able to show feelings in front of her, save those of anger and rebellion. They had never enjoyed the kind of intimacy necessary to share open grief. His reticence was a trait, she had long ago concluded, that he had inherited from his German father; it was certainly not from the Italian side of his family. The constrained sound of his crying died away. Uncomfortable with her motherly embarrassment, she waited for him to regain his composure. He rose to his feet. "Better late, I guess, than never," he said.

She wanted suddenly to close the space between them with an embrace: to hold him. She said, "It wasn't your fault, Angelo. He knew that."

He started by her, looking preoccupied. At the gate he said, "Are you ready?"

"Yes. Whenever."

He passed through the gate and let it swing closed behind him. She followed, apprehensive, trying to decipher the confusing signals emanating from his behavior. The visit to the gravesite seemed incomplete, like their visit to the weekend house. He began ambling down the slope toward the car, weaving a zigzag path through the tombstones. She followed. Presently, he drew up and waited for her to reach him. "About college," he said.

"College?"

"I'm going to wait on that for a while."

"You're not a child, Angelo. You're free to do as you wish."

"Good. I'm glad you said that." He continued ambling down the slope. "That makes things easier for us both."

She could taste the dread. "What things?"

His words came out so fast, so easily, that they sounded quite natural and harmless. "I was going to tell you later this weekend, but now's as good a time as any. I'm going to re-up."

Downwind, she could taste the morbid odor emanating from the wilted floral displays. When she finally spoke, the word splintered. "Re-up?"

"Re-enlist. I've decided to go back into the army." He kept his slow easy stride. "This time, I'll be upgraded to captain. It's almost automatic. Particularly, if I ask for another tour in Nam." The words kept coming from his mouth, but she heard only the tenor of guilty evasion in his voice. He sounded like an artless criminal babbling before the jury. "That way, I'll probably reach major by the end of the war. Plus—I'll be able to track down Lan Tien while I'm there—while there's still time." He looked back, seeing he'd left her behind. "Come on, Mom," he said, relinquishing his evasion with a deprecating smile, "you must have at least suspected."

She thought of the cruel games children are wont to play. She walked toward him, fumbling to gather her rosary into her purse to gain time. How could she have suspected when his whole effort these last two and a half weeks had been to evade her, when his whole energy had been given to elaborate deceptions? She walked slowly. By the time she closed the space between them, her shock, confusion, anger, and fear were distilled into one obvious and simple question, and she asked it with a raw feeling of nakedness. *"Why,* Angelo?" He saw that her question covered more than mere re-enlistment.

"Why? What do you mean, why?" He was stalling. "I *like* the army. It's good for me. I belong there."

"Belong?" She choked on the anger.

"Yeah! *Belong!"* He raised his voice to meet her challenge, then began walking again toward the car. "I feel good in the army. I was happy in the army. I need it."

She distilled her horror into a single word. "Vietnam?"

"Vietnam—wherever. I like soldiering. It suits me. I mean, I was happy in the army, for the first time I was *happy.* Does that make sense?"

"No."

"Don't get me wrong, now. I'm not saying I wasn't—I'm not saying you and Dad didn't . . ." He let his absolution blow away on the breeze.

I'm not saying you did anything wrong. All I want to know is, did you love him when you married him? I guess that explains why I was in his heart, but never in his blood. They were both, she knew, thinking the same thing.

He went on, "I'm saying I feel like I accomplished something there—in the army. Like I did something for myself for a change. Like I earned what I got. They don't *give* you *anything* in the army."

"Love?"

He chuckled. "I thought we covered that subject."

For me, love is only what you feel when you miss someone . . . love is a feeling of missing.

She said, appalled, "You miss Vietnam?"

"I miss the feeling of accomplishment. I can't explain it. I mean—" He looked off, groping for the right words. "The feeling of power.

Like what I did—what I chose to do—I did myself. Nobody did anything *for* me. I did it all myself. And that's power. That gives me a feeling of freedom."

"Killing people? That's freedom?"

"Depends on the reason you do it. War is different. In war—in Vietnam—you *have* to do it, you're supposed to do it. That's what you're there for, to win. Life and death—it's a different kind of game when you're in a war."

"Angelo!" She took hold of his arm and pulled him to a halt. "I was in a war. I know what war is. I saw it."

He considered her statement, then spoke to her as if she were a naïve and sheltered child. "I know you did. I understand how you feel, I do. Your dad, your brother, your husband, my father. But see, you aren't lookin' at it like a soldier. Like maybe my dad saw it differently."

She released his arm. "It was a hideous meaningless bloodbath!"

"Maybe so. But we—you and I—we wouldn't be standing here rich and free if there hadn't been a war." He turned away toward the car.

She started after him again, foundering for a way out. "It isn't the same, Angelo. We have lost the war in Vietnam. If you die fighting in this monstrous war, you will go down for a useless defeat."

"You mean, like the Italians in your war went down for an American victory in Italy?"

"Worse!"

"Like my father went down, my *real* father?" He smiled.

The words collapsed on her like a wall. She said, breathlessly, "You don't understand."

He shook his head, smiling, and winked at her. "You see, you're not really consistent. One of the first things I remember as a kid was your telling me my real daddy had gone to God in the war. He was a soldier, you said, and he fought in the war and gave his life for his country. You told me he was a very brave man. A hero. And you said God took care of heroes." He playfully jostled her shoulder. "So just think of that when you worry. I just want to be like the man you loved—my father. A hero."

He went down the hill to the car.

V

1972

CHAPTER 1

I

"Is everything okay, honey?"

"Everything's fine."

"And Sarah? Is she well?"

"Sarah's fine."

Anna shifted the receiver. "What about the baby? How's little Piero?"

"Piero's doin' fine."

As usual, Angelo gave nothing away on the phone; but this time, his voice sounded strained. She said, "Tomorrow's your second anniversary. I wanted to phone today, in case I missed you on Monday. Happy Anniversary, darling."

"Thanks."

"Be sure to tell Sarah."

"I will. How's California?"

"Warm, sunny, and smoggy." She felt grateful for the small spark of interest. "Anything would be better than New York at this point. And Connecticut? How's the weather up there?"

"Cold. We've had a cold spring."

"Lent's always cold. Just pray you don't have another big snow. Have you fixed that heater yet?"

"Yes, Mom." He sounded impatient.

She quickly backed off. "I'll finish up here in Los Angeles on Wednesday and be back Thursday."

"That's your first time in L.A., isn't it?"

"No, honey, I've come out on business several times."

"I forget. I was out there in '70. But that was San Francisco."

"Yes. I remember." She remembered the phone call from San

Francisco where they had sent him to be processed out of the army
for the second time. Two weeks later, he came home. Occasionally
in conversation he wandered back to the war. Anything could trigger
the topic. Dr. Sykes had cautioned her against letting him dwell on
the war. "By the way," she said, "did the woolies fit?"

"Did *what* fit?"

"The sweater I sent to Piero."

"Oh. Yeah. It fit fine. Thanks."

"He's growing so fast, it's hard to know."

"Right."

She could tell he wanted to hang up. "Anyway, tell Sarah 'Happy
Anniversary' for me."

"I will. Thanks."

"I'll phone when I get back."

"Right. We'll talk later."

"Good-bye, darling."

" 'Bye, Mom."

Anna returned the receiver, feeling as always after a conversation
with Angelo like a squirrel racing inside a wheel. The brown suit she
had hurriedly put on was wrinkled, but would have to do. She had
awakened after eleven to discover she had set the clock last night,
but not the alarm.

She dialed down to the hotel's front desk.

Their second wedding anniversary, she thought. Funny how fast
time flies.

A man's voice came on the line. "Front desk."

"This is Mrs. Fitzgerald in room four-one-four. Does the hotel
have a Catholic Directory there at the desk?"

"A what, ma'am?"

"A directory that lists the local Catholic churches here in Los Angeles."

"Oh. Yes, ma'am, I think we do."

"Good. I'm coming right down. I want to make a noon Mass in
the neighborhood, so if you look for it in the meantime, that would
help."

"Yes, ma'am."

She hung up, checked her purse for the keys to her rented car,
and hurried out. Waiting for the elevator, she glanced at her watch:
11:25. She liked the Château, nestled high up in the hills above the
city, but its elevators were the slowest in Los Angeles. She had arrived on Friday, two days ahead of her meeting, and had spent the
weekend relaxing. She thought of Angelo in Connecticut. He and

Sarah would probably spend the afternoon watching a football game on television. In the last two years since he had taken over the house, his life had become monotonously predictable. But country life suited him. Charles would have been glad, too. After a difficult six months at home, Angelo had met and married Sarah in 1970, and that winter they had moved to Connecticut.

The elevator arrived, and she started down.

The spring of '69 had been the worst period. He had come back from his second Vietnam tour a full-fledged captain to announce he was giving up his army career. His passionate commitment to the war in Vietnam had somehow backfired. He arrived home withdrawn, apathetic, and deeply depressed. For two months he refused to speak about Vietnam. Finally, she prevailed on him to see a psychologist, and his sessions with Dr. Sykes seemed to help. Three months later, with the consent of Sykes, he asked to move up to the Connecticut house, and she readily agreed. Though his trust fund from Charles was quite adequate, he found a carpenter's job in nearby Stevenson to give himself the freedom of self-support. Within four months, without any advance warning, he had met and married a young Connecticut girl, and six months later, in July, she gave birth. A month after the marriage, when she finally met Sarah, she found her charming, simple, and utterly devoted to Angelo. To her surprise and delight, they had chosen the name Piero for their son.

The elevator door finally opened. Anna hurried to the old-fashioned reception desk. "Good morning. I'm Mrs. Fitzgerald."

"Right." The young man bent down under the reception desk. "I think I've got what you're looking for, ma'am."

She glanced at the clock above the pigeonhole key box: 11:29.

He brought up a thin paperbound book. "This it?"

"Yes." She blew away the dust from the cover.

"We don't get many requests for that here at the Château." The boy smiled.

"Oh, I'm sure if you looked hard you could find a few RCs in Hollywood besides Bing Crosby," she said, thumbing through the book, looking for church listings by area.

He laughed. "Now, I *could* direct you to a decent synagogue over on Crescent Heights."

She smiled, found the area listings, and ran her finger down the page. "West Hollywood. North Fairfax, is that nearby?"

"Sure. Just two blocks from here."

The last midday Mass was scheduled at 11:30. She had missed that already. She moved her finger down the page. Sweetzer. Driving through the city yesterday, she had passed North Sweetzer. "St. Luke's on North Sweetzer," she said, checking the schedule of Sunday Masses: 12:00.

"North Sweetzer's probably your best bet. That's three blocks west of here."

"Good." She started to close the book as something caught her eye. Looking down the page again for the listing, she felt an old but familiar sensation of sickness in the pit of her stomach.

St. Luke's
Sun. Mass 6:30–8:00 . . .

She skipped down the schedule of Masses.

8764 M. Sweetzer
Pastor: Monsignor Karl Kruger

"Something wrong, ma'am?"

She read it again: Monsignor Karl Kruger. Over the years, she had often come across the name. It was a common German name.

"Ma'am?"

"It's nothing." She returned the directory and said, absently, gesturing, "The man's long dead."

Outside, heading for her car, she paused out of habit to check her face in her compact. Kruger. The name still had its force. But she had learned from experience the folly of hatreds harbored. Hatred, she had learned too late, was like love, a flame, as Charles used to say, in the heart ever burning.

II

She was late for Mass. She had taken a wrong turn off Sunset Boulevard, found herself at a dead end, and had to backtrack.

She parked in the lot next to the big modern brick church and hurried toward a side door. This is silly, she thought, hesitating nervously at the door. The man's been dead for twenty-seven years.

She went in.

Caught between the bright midday sunlight and the dim light inside, her eyes could only make out a blur of shadowy figures kneeling in the last pews. She moved quietly to the last pew, grasped the wooden support, and turned toward the sanctuary. The priest facing the congregation behind the altar had bowed. He was nearing the Consecration. The green vestments he wore obscured the shape of his body, but she could see in the bright sanctuary lights that he had short dark hair with hints of gray. There was a movement in the pew as people shifted down to make room for her. "Thank you," she whispered and groped her way in. She had forgotten to genuflect.

This is utterly silly, she thought, and made a nervous perfunctory genuflection on the kneeler. As she rose, she saw the priest raise himself from his bow before the altar. It was impossible to judge the man's height from this distance. She knelt down. The nervousness, the vague feeling of dread—they were understandable. She thought of Livia's letter at the end of '46 announcing Kruger's death and searched the back of the pew for a prayer book. She found one and opened it.

Over the PA system the priest's voice broke the silence. "Bless and approve our offering, make it acceptable to You, an offering of spirit and truth."

Spirit and truth. She held the book and stared at its page. The low guttural voice with its musical lilt, the soft-edged foreign accent were familiar.

"Let it become for us the body and blood of Jesus Christ, Your only Son, our Lord."

She heard the familiar roll of the "r." Impossible, she thought. She tried to remember Livia's unequivocal words in the letter. She wanted—but suddenly could not bring herself—to look up.

"The day before He suffered He took bread in His sacred hands . . ."

The voice was unmistakable. An image came back: Kruger's face, sheltered from the bright sunlight by the bill of his officer's cap, laughing as he teased her in lilting German.

". . . and looking up to Heaven, to You, His almighty Father, He gave You thanks and praise."

She forced herself to look. The priest had lifted his face toward heaven, prayerfully. Under the bright altar spotlight, his features were difficult to discern at this distance. Her eyes had still not adjusted to the light. But the jaw and the nose . . .

The priest then lowered his gaze to the altar. "He broke bread, gave it to His disciples, and said . . ." With a show of reverence, he bent toward the altar with the white wafer in his fingers, preparing to say the words of the Consecration.

For one instant, she let go of her disbelief. *This!* she said to herself, thinking of the two years after the war before Livia's letter came, I thought of everything but this: a *priest!*

"Take this, all of you, and eat it. This is My body which will be given up for you." He slowly genuflected before the consecrated Host.

My body. Her disbelief came back with the long-repressed image of another Kruger kneeling over her, half-naked on the floor of the Adele Ravine. It was impossible, a priest.

She shuddered, thinking, I kept silent. For twenty-two years, I kept silent: silent after the war, thinking he was alive, silent after Livia's letter, thinking he was dead. She had said in the beginning, *I will never allow myself or my child to become anyone's victim. Ever again.* She had broken all other vows for that promise—for Angelo.

"Take this, all of you, and drink from it. This is the cup of My blood, the blood of the new and everlasting covenant . . ."

Another image suddenly blinded her vision: Kruger in his military uniform, standing obdurately in the center of the crowded Piazza Nazionale. *"Feuer!"* a voice shrieked.

But at the altar the voice was a slow, measured murmur: "It will be shed for you and for all men so that sins may be forgiven."

She heard the long *raffica* of machine-gun fire echo from the walls of the piazza as her father and brother spun crazily backward, their clothes riddled with bright vermilion spots.

"Do this in memory of me." The priest slowly genuflected before the consecrated Blood.

The curse she had sworn that night in the rain outside her parents' house pierced her memory like an arrow. She watched the priest lift the chalice for the congregation to see and worship the Blood within it.

A tiny sound, muffled behind her hand, broke in her throat. The man on her left turned to stare at her. The priest lowered the chalice to the altar and repeated his genuflection. Anything but this, she pleaded to herself, *anything.*

"Let us proclaim the mystery of faith," he said.

The congregation responded, "Christ has died, Christ is risen, Christ will come again."

She had run from him first in life, then she had run from him in death. She thought of the price paid for that escape over twenty-eight long years: by herself, by Angelo, by Charles . . . by her mother, Livia, *Nonna* Adelaida, and said again to herself, this is impossible!

"Father, we celebrate the memory of Christ, Your Son." The priest went on innocently murmuring the words of the Mass.

She leaned forward, suddenly convulsed by a spasm in her body.

She wanted to scream, but there was no breath to form the sound with.

"Ma'am," said the man next to her, "are you all right?"

She found her breath and nodded. "Yes. It's nothing." She waved him away and sat down in the pew. As the Mass went on, she sat staring at the floor. For twenty-three of those twenty-eight years, since 1947, believing that he was dead and could not reach back from the grave to harm the living, she had kept the truth to herself, at first harboring it in her heart, like a sharp deadly sword; then later, in her memory, like a bitter mistake she alone had made and could not go back to rectify.

"Through Him, with Him, in Him, in the unity of the Holy Spirit, all glory and honor is Yours, almighty Father, for ever and ever."

Glory? With a feeling of hopeless grief, she sheltered her eyes with her hand, remembering Angelo at the cemetery. *You see, you're not really consistent. One of the first things I remember as a kid was your telling me my real daddy had gone to God in the war.*

Her mind emptied. She sat listening to the voices of the priest and the congregation, trying to think what she could do. She could think only of Angelo, Sarah, and the baby in Connecticut, struggling to hold onto their share of a costly peace. It would have been better, she thought, if he had simply died.

"This is the Lamb of God who takes away the sins of the world. Happy are those who are called to His supper."

The congregation responded, "Lord, I am not worthy to receive You, but only say the word and I shall be healed."

The German records show that Kruger died at the end of October near Vergato. She now remembered Livia's exact words. But there was no mention of any further proof.

She looked up. The voice, yes. But years had passed. At this distance, the features: she thought of the reprieve that would come if she was wrong, and she felt suddenly hopeful. Here and there, people began to rise, preparing to approach the sanctuary for Communion.

She would know, of course, if she got close enough—if they came face to face. The thought of Communion from his hand sent a chill of terror through her. But she had no choice.

She stood up, left the pew, and joined the line of communicants in the aisle. The priest approached the communion rail, followed by an altar boy.

"Body of Christ."

The closer she got to the rail, the more familiar the sound became. She found herself wishing there were more communicants ahead of her, wanting to postpone this most monstrous of all revelations. He reached the far end of the rail as she started toward the place left vacant for her. She dared not look at his face directly, not yet, but she saw him glance at her as he came back along the rail. She knelt down, sensing that his gaze was on her as he passed by with the altar boy. His passage stirred the air around her face.

"Body of Christ." He started again at the end of the rail, moving toward her. She drew in air, trying to slow the pounding of her heart. In the corner of her eye she saw the unmistakable jaw, the sharp line of his nose: Angelo's jaw, Angelo's nose. The brown hair was beginning to gray. She knew exactly how old he would be now: forty-six.

"Body of Christ." He was two communicants away.

"Amen," came the response.

She found herself wondering if she had aged as little as he.

The altar boy passed by and held the patent under her chin. She held her breath and lifted her face. She saw, at first, only green vestments coming toward her. An eternity seemed to pass between lifting her eyes and seeing his face. The mouth, the nose, the chin—her recognition was instantaneous. And the eyes. They stared down at her, wide with the horror of his own recognition. Angelo's, their son's eyes: as blue as the day she last saw Kruger's eyes in the Comellini *ammasso* on the Via Benedetto.

He hesitated, holding the tiny wafer for her, then spoke.

"Body of Christ," Kruger forced himself to say. She went on staring at him for a moment. Anna. He was not mistaken. She was older, but the beauty had remained indelible. He realized, holding the sacred Host, there was nothing he could do or say but what the ritual demanded. He repeated the words, "Body of Christ," feeling the edge of an inchoate grief slice through his heart.

"Amen." She opened her mouth. The hatred that blazed up in her huge brown eyes took his breath away.

He placed the Body of Christ on her tongue.

She closed her mouth and looked down. Her cheek twitched, and he thought he saw pain take the place of hatred.

He moved on, knowing his face was now an open map of the guilt and shame he felt. A waiting parishioner watched him, puzzled by the brief exchange with the woman stranger in the brown suit. He picked a Host from the ciborium and said, "Body of Christ."

She had, in the meantime, stood up.

"Amen."

He placed the Host on the man's tongue and tried to imagine what lay ahead for him. He had never made any real provisions or plans. When he looked back in her direction, she was gone.

III

Monsignor Kruger turned into the rectory driveway. The light is almost gone, he thought, looking through the windshield at the limpid blue twilight. He had tried to get home well before dark, knowing that Anna would either contact him by phone or confront him personally at the rectory. As he hurried to the rectory's side door, he saw a light burning in the kitchen window. If Anna had phoned or visited, Father Auden would know.

Father John, his young assistant pastor, was preparing dinner in the kitchen. "Father Karl!" John greeted him jovially.

"Hello, Father John." Kruger went to the sink to wash his hands.

"How was the game?"

"It was fine. We won."

Auden went on to congratulate him as he flipped his omelet in the skillet. Anna had been nowhere in sight after the twelve o'clock Mass, and he had been forced to go on with parish business as usual for the rest of the day, attending a football game between St. Luke's High and one of the local Catholic prep schools.

"By the way, were there any calls for me?"

"A few." Auden slid the omelet from the skillet to a plate. "I put the list of messages on your desk. A woman called this afternoon, but she wouldn't leave her name." Kruger started for the door into the hallway. "She said you knew who she was," Auden added. "I asked her for her number, but she wouldn't leave that either. She said to tell you she'd be in the lobby of the Beverly Hilton Hotel at eight-thirty tonight." He looked up. "She sounded kind of worried."

"What else did she say?"

"Nothing. I asked if she was in trouble, if I could help, but she said that *she* wasn't the one in trouble. She had a foreign accent. Do you know her?"

"Yes. Her name is Miceli. Anna Miceli." He hesitated, wondering if he should tell John everything. After all, they were each other's confessor. But for the young man's sake, he would have to prepare him. "I knew her twenty-eight years ago. In Italy. In a town called Montefalco."

Auden left off salting his omelet. "I didn't know you'd been in Italy."

"Yes. During the Second World War." He had long ago told John about his serving in the German Army during the war, but had never elaborated. Young people John's age thought all German soldiers were stereotyped Nazis, having read only about the famous men in the war and seen them as villains in the movies. "I was stationed in Italy."

"That's so? I didn't know." Auden cut into his omelet.

He ventured one step further to prepare the young priest for what would inevitably follow. "I commanded a Wehrmacht unit during the German occupation of Italy. We were stationed in Montefalco, Signora Miceli's hometown."

"What happened, did you become friends or something?"

"Yes. You might say that." It was enough for now. He looked at his watch and saw that two hours remained.

"Are you going to meet her?"

"Yes." The Hilton was a twenty-minute drive from the rectory. This time, the least he could do for Anna was to be punctual.

CHAPTER 2

I

Anna chose one of the upholstered easy chairs near a plate-glass window overlooking the street, a chair that gave her a full view of the hotel entrance, and sat down. The clock on the wall above the reception desk said 8:16.

She shifted her purse in her lap, trying to compose herself. After Mass, she had remained in her hotel room for the rest of the day, weighing the human against the legal options. As always, uppermost in her mind had been Angelo: the effect that a public criminal charge would have on the boy. First, she had investigated the possibility of criminal charges. After several phone calls to colleagues familiar with international criminal law and procedures, specifically Italian and German laws regarding war criminals, and a phone call to a university professor familiar with ecclesiastical law, she had defined the legal options.

She opened her purse, fidgeted with the notes she had made, then closed the purse.

If she filed charges in Italy, it would take weeks, maybe months, for the news to filter back to America. There would be time to prepare Angelo. In the meantime—

She started up as she saw a man come through the entrance, feeling the panic return, but he wasn't Kruger, and she sat back down. In the meantime, she would begin where she *had* to begin: with Kruger himself. She forced herself to concentrate on her mission. For this, their first meeting in twenty-eight years, there were things she would say and things she would not say, I am here to accuse him, she affirmed, not to defend or explain myself. She would—she had to—exclude all personal feelings from the issue of criminal charges. That much, at least, she had learned over the years as a lawyer. She pulled at her sleeve. Nothing in her appearance or her manner, she had decided, would lead Kruger to conclude that she was one of those proverbial Italian women who, *sedutta e abbandonata,* returns to revenge an unrequited passion. Her accusations and charges would be of murder: mass murder. For the time being, she said to herself, until such time as evidence required it, I will say nothing about my father and brother, and nothing about Angelo.

She saw that she was sitting too rigidly in her chair and shifted herself. To forestall any misconceptions as to who she was (he had last known her as a nineteen-year-old impressionable peasant girl), she had chosen a tailored gray suit and had coiled her hair into a chignon, careful to look like the exacting businesswoman she had since become.

The big hand on the clock moved forward: 8:24. She tried to accept the fact that she was frightened, but could not.

She checked her own watch and tried to turn her thoughts to Chuck Furgeson preparing to fly out tonight from New York to meet with the McDonnell-Douglas people tomorrow in her place. She had told her partner that personal matters had come up, and they required her immediate return to New York. She would fly from there to Italy and open the case against Kruger.

Kruger was there. She winced, seeing the small white square of the Roman collar across the lobby a few feet from the entrance. She stood up and felt an impulse to move, to signal him with a gesture, but any gesture now would look like a concession. She wanted him to know that she now held all the power. He caught sight of her and started forward. He walked a little stiffly, just as he used to walk through the streets of Montefalco on his regular afternoon outings. His face showed nothing more than bewildered amazement. Ten yards away, he stopped. For a while, they stared at each other, each waiting for the other to make the first move. Against the surrounding noise of the lobby, the stillness of the space between them was electrifying.

She saw him swallow and muster his courage. "Anna." The name seemed to fall from his mouth.

She took a slow, deliberate breath, thrown off guard by the note of feeling she had heard, then forced the word that came from her mouth to sound like an indictment. "Yes."

He made a small gesture with his right hand. "You're well, I see. I'm glad." He seemed to realize how idiotic his statement sounded.

"Did you expect otherwise?" She made no effort to hide her sarcasm.

Flustered, he said, "No. I didn't know."

Didn't know. The old familiar excuse of ignorance. There is much you don't know, she thought. "I'm not only alive, but I'm well, *Lieutenant*."

He nodded, perplexed and embarrassed.

Again, they were silent. She forced back another rush of panic. He moved his hands as if to concede her point. She reflected on the riddles hidden up to now under their words and looks, the mute indecipherable language of twenty-eight years of separation. She recalled how easy it had once been, when they were lovers, to read his mind. She had expected to see wary evasion in his face, but saw, instead, only guilt and shame. "A priest," she said, finally, remembering those two wretched years of suspense after the war. "I thought of everything but that."

"I—I was ordained here in California in 1955."

"And now you're a *monsignore*." This time, her sarcasm hinted at feelings of hatred.

"Yes."

She hesitated. The open readiness of his replies had rattled her confidence. She stammered, "It's hot in here. I must sit down." He saw the confusion behind her non sequitur, and she flushed.

At that instant an elderly tourist couple passed by. The woman acknowledged his Roman collar politely. "Good evening, Father."

He nodded and smiled. The man's shame, she saw, was real and brought a blush to his face.

This is absurd, she thought, prolonging her choice of a chair to compose herself, recalling her choice of the hotel lobby to ensure safety. She thought back to the months at San Paolo watching the convoys of German PWs pass by on their way south, waiting for the day when she might recognize him among the prisoners. She would have sacrificed the safe secret of her pregnancy to point him out to the Americans as the Butcher of Montefalco (she gripped her purse, waiting for the unsuspecting couple to get beyond earshot), but that was before Charles and before Angelo had come into her life. This —a businesslike meeting in the lobby of a Hilton hotel—this was not at all the kind of scene she had once imagined. She forced herself to say, "Sit down, Monsignor Kruger."

He chose the chair opposite, separated from her by only a low coffee table. The close proximity shattered her brief composure. There was an odor of bath soap from his body. She remembered his meticulous habits of cleanliness. She thrust the thought away and hurried to her memorized list: "I take it—you came here after the war."

"I was a prisoner here during the war. I returned at the end of 1947 and entered the seminary. I've been—" He sighed. "I've been a priest here in Los Angeles for seventeen years."

The same artful candor, she was thinking as she hurried on. "I assume you know why I called you here tonight."

"Yes."

"I also assume you knew this might happen, one of us might find you." In her effort to disguise personal feelings, she was sounding like a scolding employer.

He nodded, then qualified his admission. "But only by accident. I knew German records had listed me as killed in action."

This time, his candid admission took her entirely by surprise. She blundered ahead, "Nonetheless, you undoubtedly made plans for what you would do if you were found."

"No. I have no plans."

"I see." She knew she was so far making a fool of herself. She tried to take a different tack. "I take it you're now an American citizen."

"Yes."

"The movements of an American citizen, you realize, can be traced anywhere in the world."

"I've no intention of going anywhere, Anna."

The familiar use of her first name, together with the realization that he obviously knew all the angles, angered her. Bill Pritchard had been quick to point out that Kruger's American citizenship would protect him from immediate extradition. She drew herself up. "Let's not waste time, Herr Kruger." Her voice shook as she spoke. "You committed the war crime of mass murder in Italy in 1944."

He looked down, defeated, and nodded again.

She sat forward and suddenly lost control of her voice. "Did you think we had forgotten?" It skittered off shrilly.

"No."

She could not contain the momentum of her anger. "Did you think we had not bothered to look for you?"

"No."

"Then what? Did you—did you think you'd be safe here hiding behind your American citizenship? Behind your Roman collar?" He shook his head. The anger kept coming, rushing up like water from a *sorgente calda;* and with it, tears broke in her eyes. "Did you think *time* would heal the wounds?" She saw by his expression that she had betrayed herself and tried quickly to cover. "You are not beyond the statutes of any limitation, Herr Kruger."

"I didn't try to hide, Anna. I knew I was listed as dead. I"—he hesitated, cornered—"I went on thinking that no charges had been filed."

The realization that he thought her appearance at Mass that morning was something she had planned silenced her. When she finally regained her composure, she said, "You're mistaken. No charges have been filed as yet. My appearance at Mass this morning was an accident. I am a Catholic. I came to hear Mass. I live in New York, not in Los Angeles. I found your church by accident when I—" She backtracked, realizing she was saying too much. "No charges have been filed, but it makes no difference. You will be charged in Italy with war crimes and crimes against humanity. And with conspiracy to commit those crimes."

"I see."

She sighed, realizing she had passed the crucial hurdle. "I presume you know how many men you murdered," she said, giving in to a small corner of her feelings.

"Fifty."

The abstract number brought to mind her father and Piero. "At least—" The tears came back. She swallowed. "At least, unlike some Nazi criminals before you, you *know something,*" she said, trying for sarcasm but succeeding only at pain. He made the familiar gesture of locking his fingers together. He had often done that when she teased him about his German obsession with rules and regulations. "I will speak plainly, Herr *Monsignore*. The Italian Government will be informed that you are alive and living here in California. I am a practicing lawyer." She took a calming breath and went on, "I will return to New York, prepare the charges, and then go to Italy and personally open the case against you." She remembered Pritchard's caution. "Moreover, I have already informed my colleagues here in the United States of your identity and the charges against you." She left out the fact that she had sworn Pritchard to secrecy for the time being to protect Angelo.

Kruger seemed pained by the implication. "I understand, Anna."

Anna. This time, the familiar gentle way he said the name, given his ignorance of Angelo, stung like a serpent's bite. "You understand nothing," she said. "To you, I am Mrs. Fitzgerald."

"I see." Disappointment wavered in his eyes. "Then you have married?"

He had taken her again by surprise, and she was trapped. He was leading her to a precipice. "My life is not in question here. Yours, on the other hand, is. For instance"—she hurried on, grasping for anything on her list before he could speak—"does the Church know what you did in Montefalco?" The ecclesiastical expert, Dvorjetsky, had introduced a whole list of canonical questions.

He had heard the tremor in her voice and questioned it with a look. "No."

"When you came here and applied to the seminary, did they not ask you about your past?"

"Yes."

"And you told them nothing?"

"No charges had been filed." His face turned crimson. "I said nothing."

The realization came to her: the moral and spiritual damage he had wreaked in the souls of innocent Catholics to maintain his masquerade. "Seventeen years. You are beyond forgiveness." She knew, though, that she meant twenty-eight years, and the forgiveness was hers.

He kept his eyes lowered and made no move to respond.

This time, his submissive acceptance of the truth was like a slap in the face. She thought, it is *he*, not *me*, who is under scrutiny here! She sat forward, feeling her anger detonate into rage. "Tell me *this*, Herr Oberleutnant," she challenged, "do you know what they call you?"

"They?" He seemed frightened.

"The people of Montefalco. Do you know what they call you?"

"No."

"Il Macellaio di Montefalco is what they call you!" This time, the force behind her suppressed tears overwhelmed her. An image of her father and brother dead in the square tore through her mind; and behind it, Angelo's face decimated by incurable anxiety and depression. *"Macellaio!* Or have you forgotten what that *means* in Italian?"

"Butcher," Kruger murmured. Tears flooded her face. There was a moment of suspended silence. He slowly sat back, wondering at the fury of her attack. But how could he question it? He had murdered friends, perhaps close friends, twenty-eight years ago. He had simply never imagined that the flame of her hatred would burn so hot after so long. He thought again of his other betrayal and wondered if the wells of hatred were deeper than he had ever imagined.

She regained her control and sat upright in her chair. "If you refuse to return willingly to Italy, we will bring charges against you here in America on the grounds that you withheld information from the immigration authorities. Whether the charges were filed or not, you knew you violated the Rules of War and were liable to charges of murder. You will be tried here in America, deprived of your citizenship, and then extradited."

"I understand. You don't have to explain the law to me. I know what I have done, I know why you called me here tonight, and I know what you intend to do. I did not come here to justify myself. What I did in Montefalco was a crime. Everything you accuse me of is true." He drew a breath, knowing that in this he could not be reproached, and said, "Except one thing. I did not become a priest to hide behind a Roman collar."

"I don't believe you."

It was an insignificant thing, but he said it anyway. "I did not change my name, Anna."

She weighed his little defense, and he knew before she spoke that she had rejected it. "You knew when you became a priest what might happen, even here, halfway around the world. You knew it, and yet you took the risk."

It was true. He opened his mouth to speak, to explain the motives behind his choice—the need to make reparation for evil with good —but realized motives were useless in the face of cold legal facts. Instead of responding, he made a lame gesture with his hand.

She said, "Then you will have to take responsibility and blame for that as well." Behind her anger, behind her hatred, there was now a loathing kind of contempt. "You have betrayed everything." But the loathing gave way as her hatred had given way, and her face collapsed under the helpless weight of pain. "Everything. Both in this world and the next. You are the worst of them all."

Her knife sank into the heart of the matter, the center of his darkest fears for his future—not in this world, but in the next.

She stood up. "There are other things to be said. But for now, it is enough that you know you will be charged, arraigned, and tried."

He asked, knowing she had been careful to avoid touching on their relationship, "Please tell me one thing, Anna. How long after I left did you look for me?"

"Long enough." Her face altered, exposing a soft vulnerable wound.

"I thought someone might one day happen along and recognize me. But never you."

"You mean, you thought I would never leave Montefalco. You thought I could go on staying in—" She broke off.

"No. I thought others had been hurt worse than you."

Shock detonated in her face. "I was there. I saw it."

"I know you were there. I know you saw it all. Montefalco was small."

She was rattled again. "I knew them—all from childhood." She turned to retrieve her purse from the chair.

"What I did to those men in the square was one kind of crime. I can be charged with that crime and tried. What I did to you was another kind of crime. There is no court of justice for that, Anna. Save yourself."

She swung around, frightened. "Those men were innocent! You arrested innocent men, you lined them up in the square, you did not even take time to question them!" The accusation was true, but he saw something larger than fear in her face.

"Please, Anna. Tell me the truth." He got to his feet, clumsily. "There's more to this than what I did to your friends in the square that afternoon, isn't there? I promised to marry you after the war was over. We both—" He stopped short at the thought of love, remembering his priesthood.

She started away. "I have nothing more to say to you."

"I've told you the truth," he said, checking an impulse to follow. "Please do the same."

She drew up, but kept her back to him. "My personal feelings have nothing to do with the charges against you."

"I know that. I know what I did to your friends. But twenty-eight years is a long time to go on hating a man as much as you do."

She turned. Tears streamed down the wreckage of her face. *"Mostro,"* she said. *"Mostro schifoso."*

"Why, Anna?" She was nineteen when he left. Even the hatred of rejected love could not have endured this long, this strongly.

"You arrested people indiscriminately. You did not even bother to question them. To you, those men were *numbers!"* Her voice carried across the lobby, and people turned to stare. "They had no *names* to you, they were *numbers!* I was there! I saw it all! They were cattle to you!" She let go of something held back and wept, openly. "A quota you had to fill! I watched you! They were not just friends you killed. It was my father and my brother."

For a moment, isolated in the open space where he stood, he could only stare at her, understanding, but not comprehending what she had just said.

"Do you understand now, Herr Kruger?" She backed away.

He tried to nod, but could not even do that much.

She saw she had attracted an audience. She backed off a few more paces. "If I were you, Monsignor, I would learn how to pray." She turned and walked swiftly toward the door.

II

Monsignor Andrew Halpern, a thin little man who always seemed to be racing ahead of his cassock and purple sash, darted into the outer office of the cardinal's residence where Kruger sat waiting. Halpern had been the cardinal's assistant now for eight years. He hurried toward the alcove where Kruger sat in a straight-backed chair. "Good morning, Monsignor Kruger. Forgive us, we're behind this morning."

As long as he had known Halpern, they were always behind at the cardinal's office. "Good morning, Monsignor." Kruger stood up.

"Please come." Halpern motioned for him to follow. "His Eminence will see you right away." Kruger hurried to keep pace down the hallway to the cardinal's study. "When you called last night," Halpern said, "I wasn't sure we could squeeze you in, but since it's an emergency, I put you in between Bishop Clairborne and the Diocesan Building Fund. He has an appointment with Mr. Belmont's committee at ten-fifteen," he added as they reached the study door.

"I'll be as quick as I can, Andy."

Halpern was gone before he finished the sentence. Kruger knocked.

"Come in, come in!" came the cardinal's hearty voice. The curtains in the study had been drawn back from the three big windows, filling the long room with sunlight. At the far end of the room, Cardinal Boyle sat behind the plain wooden table that served for a desk. "Monsignor Kruger! Come in, Karl! Close the door and come in."

"Good morning, Your Eminence." Kruger closed the door softly and moved toward the desk.

"Monsignor Halpern says you phoned last night and asked to see me this morning." Boyle gestured. "Sit down, Karl."

As usual, the cardinal had skipped formalities. "Thank you."

"What's on your mind?" Boyle sat back. When the matter to be discussed was grave, it was the cardinal's way to appear relaxed.

"What I have to tell you will take time, Your Eminence. The problem is very serious."

"All right." Boyle smiled. "Take your time. For you I have all the time in the world."

Kruger settled himself in the straight-backed leather armchair. "What I have to say comes, I'm afraid, late. Seventeen years late." Boyle's eyes widened behind the lenses of his glasses. "You know that I was a German citizen when I immigrated to America in 1948." The cardinal nodded. "You know also that I served in the German Army during the Second World War." This time, there was no response. "Let me go back to the end of 1947—when I applied for the seminary and was interviewed about my past life." He came to the hard part.

The cardinal's face was now an expressionless mask. "Take your time, Karl."

"In the interview I was asked if I had knowledge of any impediments that stood in the way of my being a priest. I said no. Looking back, I probably should have said yes. I wasn't sure then, so I gave myself the benefit of the doubt." He took a breath, realizing he was rushing to get to the painful part.

Boyle nodded his understanding.

"In 1944, I was captain of a Wehrmacht unit occupying a small town in Italy . . ." As he narrated the skeletal facts leading up to the reprisal, the cardinal's face became leaden. "In retaliation, I was ordered to carry out a military reprisal execution of ten male civilians for every soldier shot. Six soldiers had been shot, five had died. I—" He swallowed the mucus in his throat. "I obeyed. We arrested fifty civilian men from the village. A few hours later, we carried out a public execution in the town square." He paused, feeling as if he had just crossed a deep gorge walking on a tightrope and reached the other side. There was no reaction from the cardinal beyond a small gesture for him to go on. The stone in his episcopal ring glinted. "In the months leading up to the execution, I had known a young girl from the village." He now retraced his steps to weave his affair with Anna Miceli into the story of the execution, for the two were inseparable. "Yesterday, by accident, she came to Sunday Mass at St. Luke's. Last night, she confronted me in the lobby of the Beverly Hilton Hotel. She said no charges were filed after the war because German war records showed I had been killed following my retreat from Montefalco. Since I last saw Signora Miceli, she has married, moved to America, and she now practices as a lawyer in New York City." Small beads of perspiration glistened on the cardinal's upper lip. "Last night, she told me something I had not known before this. Among the men I executed that morning were her father and her brother. She had given up her search for me in 1947, when she was told that I had died, but now she intends to go back to Italy, file charges against me before the Italian War Crimes Bureau, and begin the legal proceedings to bring me to trial in Italy." He left off, trying to think of facts he might have left out. Except for those of motive and circumstance, he had confessed everything. He sat back and waited.

It took minutes, it seemed, for the cardinal to react. He lifted the telephone receiver and pressed a button. "Monsignor Halpern, please," he said. When Halpern came on, he said, "Andrew, I don't want to be disturbed now. When Mr. Belmont and the others arrive, tell them something urgent has come up. I won't be able to meet with them today. Give my apologies. In the meantime, no calls, please." He hung up and looked down, thoughtfully. There was no hint of censure or anger in his steel-gray eyes. It was the face, as always, of an aging chairman of the board, a cautious and experienced diplomat in a black and scarlet cassock, wearing the episcopal cross and ring and the scarlet *zucchetto* of a prince of the Church. Presently, he moved again. This time, he rose and slowly walked to the open window across the room. Kruger thought how small the man had become in these last seventeen years. Boyle was seventy-four now, and his hair had turned white. At the window, he stood looking out with his hands clasped behind his back. The mozzetta over the shoulders of his cassock stirred in the breeze. An eternity of minutes seemed to pass. Then he spoke in a voice that was curiously distant. "Tell me, Karl. Why did you want to become a priest to begin with?" He had, of course, gone straight to the heart of the moral question of conscience.

"I wanted to make up for the evil I had done by—by doing good." It sounded childishly innocent.

"At the time you performed the execution, did you think you were guilty of a grave sin?"

"That's still difficult to answer. I knew that murder, of course, was a grave sin. I debated the question with myself, but I could not separate my personal from my military duty. I came to the conclusion that what I was doing was an act of war and therefore legitimate. In my mind, I transferred responsibility for the act to my military superiors. But that was a rationalization for what I knew in my heart was wrong."

"The human mind and the human soul are complex instruments, Karl. The question of your guilt under the law and the question of your guilt in God's eyes are not the same. You understand that, I'm sure."

"I think I am guilty under both, Your Eminence."

"I see." He was silent for a moment, then said, "Did you ever confess to a priest what you had done?"

"Yes. Twice. Once in Italy after I deserted and again in America while I was a prisoner of war."

"But not after you immigrated and entered the seminary?"

"No, Your Eminence."

Boyle moved back to the desk and sat down. "I ask you these questions for several reasons. For the past as well as the future, we must separate the moral and religious questions from the secular legal questions. They are humanly connected and will influence our future actions, but they are spiritually separate. I asked those questions because I have known you to be a good priest for seventeen years, and your record seems to confirm your motives for becoming a priest." He sat back. "I will leave aside, for now, the issue of your original failure to inform us of what you had done. That is a question of conscience that belongs to the past. You are now an ordained priest, and there are very serious issues at stake for both you and the entire Church. Have you given thought to what lies ahead for both?"

"Yes, Your Eminence. I will be charged with war crimes, I may be extradited to stand trial in Italy. In the eyes of the court, I will be tried as a former Wehrmacht soldier, but in the eyes of the public, I will be a priest on trial for mass murder. There will be grave scandal." He thought of the sermon on responsibility and penance he had delivered only yesterday.

"I see you've given the problem some thought."

"I have."

Boyle smiled thinly. "Then you understand that our first responsibility is to protect the spiritual welfare of the Church that you represent. We must try to prevent that scandal."

"Yes."

"Are you aware that the Vatican has faced this problem before?"

He nodded. "A few years ago, a German bishop was accused of a similar crime while he served in Italy as a German soldier. He was, I remember, never brought to trial. He was asked by the Vatican to retire."

"The international uproar and scandal over the case caused grave spiritual damage to Catholics all over the world."

Kruger sighed. "I recall wondering at the time if the man thought he was guilty under the law, and if so, how he reconciled his personal moral responsibilities with those of his priesthood."

"You read my thoughts, Karl." The cardinal smiled again. "I know the mind of the Vatican in this matter. Your first responsibility is the spiritual good of the Church. Ironic as it may seem, the good of the many comes before what you may suppose is your own good. It may not have occurred to you before, but there are subtle forms of self-abnegation and spiritual forms of martyrdom. You may be called upon to exercise the virtue of blind obedience."

A small door of escape in the back of Karl's mind slammed closed. He said, "I understand."

The cardinal spread his hands and touched his fingers together. The blood-red episcopal ring on his finger glinted again. "Did the woman in question say when she would leave for Italy?"

"No. Soon, I imagine."

"You said she's a practicing Catholic?"

"Mrs. Fitzgerald attends Mass on Sundays, that's all I know. And she's an Italian."

"Is she aware of the consequences for the Church in opening this case?"

"She accused me of hiding behind my Roman collar and using the Church to evade responsibility."

Boyle lowered his eyes. "You had an affair with this woman."

"Yes. In Montefalco. Twenty-eight years ago. I promised to marry her after the war."

"And she's aware you did not know who her father and brother were?"

"Yes."

The light from the windows glinted from the cardinal's glasses, obscuring his eyes. The lean face was calm though, the manner businesslike. "Officially, of course, the Church cannot interpose itself between the woman and her decision to prosecute you. There can be no hint of official ecclesiastical pressure, for that would jeopardize her freedom of conscience." He nodded and smiled to confirm the truth of his statement. "On the other hand, there's no reason why you yourself should not try. As a matter of fact, you are the only person who would likely have influence with Mrs. Fitzgerald at this point."

Kruger looked up and said with a feeling of dread, "She has nothing but hatred for me now. Not only as a man, but as a priest."

"Time has a way of calming feelings so that reason can decide. As a lawyer, she will know what I mean."

"It's too late for that, Your Eminence. Twenty-eight years too late."

"We must try. We've no other option, Karl. I cannot order you to visit her, I can only suggest it."

Kruger hesitated. "What do you wish me to do, Your Eminence?"

The cardinal's response was immediate and businesslike. "I will trace Mrs. Fitzgerald's whereabouts in New York for you. You have my permission to go to New York and meet with her, if you can. The rest will be up to you."

Kruger nodded.

"I would recommend that you leave at once. Tell your assistant, Father Auden, nothing about this matter. Tell him that I have given you permission to leave town on—on confidential matters. In your absence, he will assume responsibilities as pastor of St. Luke's."

"Yes, Your Eminence."

The cardinal looked at his watch. "When you return, we will take up the matter of your pastoral responsibilities and that interview you had back in . . . ?"

"1947."

Boyle pushed back his chair. Kruger took the cue and stood up with him. "In the meantime, my dear Karl, let us both pray that good will finally come from all of this. I will remember you in my daily Mass until you return." He moved around the desk and offered his hand.

Kruger started to kneel and kiss the episcopal ring.

"No, Karl." Boyle grasped his hand and shook it firmly. "After this long, we are friends and brothers."

CHAPTER 3

I

Luisa Miceli removed her daughter's toasted bread from the kitchen grill. "If she's to visit the Moreras this morning, you will have to drive her."

"Anna's wasting her time with the Moreras. They'll sign her witness papers, but they won't give money for his extradition." Livia Pirelli sat down at the kitchen table and poured herself a cup of her mother's strong black coffee.

"She has to try. In any case, she has no car. You must drive her."

Livia saw that the toast was burned, as usual, on one side. She and Alfredo had given her mother an electric toaster last year for Christmas, but Luisa always insisted on her old-fashioned stove. "Mamma, why don't you use the toaster?"

"I don't like those electric gadgets you use." Luisa set the dish of toast on the table.

"It's after seven, what time does the *marchesa* get up?"

"Anna was up late last night working on her legal papers. She'll get up when she wants." Luisa poured herself a cup of black coffee and sat down.

"You're not going to eat breakfast?"

"It's Lent. I'm fasting."

Livia began scraping the burned side of her toast with a table knife. "American women, I hear, get up in time for what they call *brunch*. The rich ones, at least." She had driven in from Pisa Thursday evening, and both mornings afterward Anna had gotten up well after eight.

"Your sister is tired. She's been through a lot this last week."

A door upstairs slammed. Livia made a face thinking of Anna's week in comparison to her own last twenty-eight years.

"Fix your hair, you look like you've slept in it."

"Fix my hair? For whom, Mamma? Anna? Besides, I *have* slept in it." She buttered her toast in silence. Out of the blue, after twenty-eight years, Anna had arrived in Montefalco three days ago and become an instant celebrity with the news she brought. Not only was Il Macellaio alive, he had become an American citizen, a priest

—indeed, a *monsignore*—and was the pastor of a California church. She had come back, so she announced, to collect evidence and witnesses for the charges she had already filed in Bologna. "You'd think she was some rich foreign celebrity the way she sweeps through town," Livia taunted. "Yesterday, she told Tedeschini—she told the chief of police—that she wanted him to organize a public meeting and talk to the survivors himself."

"So?"

"She doesn't understand these people. They'll agree to appear as witnesses at his trial here in Italy, but that's it. His extradition from America will cost a fortune, it will take forever, and it probably won't work anyway. He's an American citizen, and besides—he's got the Vatican on his side."

Luisa went to the stove and lowered an egg into the pot of boiling water. "Today, sometime today, I want you and your sister to sit down and talk. If you have a problem with Anna, then you must tell her and not give vent to it with petty squabbles. Do you understand?"

Livia backed off, angrily spooning sugar into her coffee. "If she needs a car, Mamma, she can have it. But I will not drive her around like a chauffeur. I'm forty-six years old. I am not her little sister anymore."

The truth was, though, that Anna was and had always been her mother's favorite and, even after learning of her affair and child, Luisa felt that she could do no wrong.

Upstairs, the toilet flushed.

Her mother stood by the stove, timing the *marchesa's* three-minute egg. Her mother said, "I wish you would support Anna, instead of opposing what she's trying to do here."

Livia's coffee splashed across the table. *"Oppose?* Who do you think has been protecting her all these years?" She recalled the blame she had gotten from her mother for Anna's actions when she finally revealed the entire story back in 1955 at the time of *Nonna* Adelaida's death.

"This is a nightmare, Livia, for all of us."

"The nightmare, as you call it, has just begun! You wait and see, the Vatican is not going to let her go through with her plan. And when Montefalco finds out the *whole* truth, her case is going to backfire—not on *her,* she can go back to America, but on *us,* who have to go on living here in Italy."

"That man killed your father and your brother, Livia," her mother said with sudden vengeance, "have you forgotten that?"

"No, Mamma. I haven't forgotten. But what do you think will happen when the Moreras, the Vianellis, the Faggionis, the Lancettis —when Montefalco finds out our Anna was the Nazi's whore, and that she had his child?"

Her mother removed the egg from the boiling water. Anna's affair with Kruger was a subject they had studiedly avoided all these years. "It was a long time ago. She was a child."

Anna passed the four framed holy pictures in the hall outside her bedroom. They had been there for as long as she could remember: Santa Lucia on her tomb, headless; San Francisco smiling at his cloudless heaven of birds; San Cristoforo with the Christ Child waist-deep in the river; and the Madonna with her Child, youthful and serene. The pictures under the glass had faded but were, like so many things in the house, unchanged. Except for a few decorative additions and a few modern conveniences—a telephone, electric lights, a proper bathroom, and a television set—the house was the same as she remembered it from childhood.

Downstairs, her briefcase and papers lay on the dining table where she had left them the night before. She had stayed up late working out a strategy for gathering witnesses and evidence. After a few hours' sleep, the plan seemed even more sensible than it had last night. She paused at the table to arrange the pages of her notes. Of the six families she had so far visited, she had found twelve living witnesses to the *rastrellamento*. They had all agreed wholeheartedly to the question of an Italian trial, but when she raised the question of contributing to the legal costs of an extradition trial in America, she had come up against doubts and hesitations. She had decided last night to use her own law firm for the American extradition procedure and bear the principal costs herself.

On her way into the kitchen, she quickly ran through the list of people she would visit that day: the Moreras, who had lost a father in the reprisal, and the Turattis, whose father had been a close friend of her father. "Good morning, Mamma," she said and kissed her on the cheek. "Livia." She acknowledged her sister at the table and took her place opposite.

"Good morning." Livia eyed the dark blue dress she was wearing. "That's a pretty dress."

"Thank you." Anna smiled. "Do you think it's modest enough for old Carmela Turatti?" Carmela Turatti, Giovanni's elderly invalid widow, would be the one who decided how far the Turattis would involve themselves. She had chosen the dress remembering Car-

mela's outspoken disapproval of those short-hemmed dresses girls
had worn throughout the war.

"The Turattis? I thought you were seeing the Moreras this morning."

"I am. And the Turattis this afternoon, after I meet with Signore
Tedeschini at the police station."

"You're wasting your time with the Turattis. They will sign your
papers as witnesses, but Ricardo Turatti controls the purse strings,
and he won't give you a single lira for your American trial."

Luisa handed Anna a plate with an egg and cheese and toasted
bread. "Ricardo will do what his mother tells him to do."

"Thank you, Mamma," Anna said.

"You seem awfully cheerful this morning," said Livia.

"I found a solution to the problem of financing the extradition."
She poured herself coffee.

"You seem to think it's going to be easy bringing your"—Livia
rerouted herself—"bringing that Nazi priest to trial."

"I never said it would be easy. Justice, in my experience, is rarely
easy." Livia made a face at the reference to her career. There were
unspoken jealousies of both her wealth and her career that she had
detected in Livia these last few days.

Luisa stepped in. "If you're going to drive Anna to the Moreras
this morning, Livia, you must get dressed."

Livia had worn her terry-cloth wrapper to breakfast. She had gotten fat over the years. There were jealousies in that, too.

"You expect these people will give you money for his extradition,
but they won't," Livia said. "They're too practical. And they can't.
They're too poor."

"I've already said I'll pay for it myself. One way or another, the
man will be brought to trial in Italy."

Livia studied her face for a moment. "And when do you plan on
announcing the big secret? Before or during the trial?" She smiled,
challengingly.

There was sudden silence in the room, punctuated by the faucet
drip in the sink.

She had intended to raise the question of her affair with Kruger
and the question of their son tonight at dinner. There were important legal and tactical reasons why she should delay the public confession of her personal connections with Kruger, aside from those
touching Angelo himself. "My personal relationship with Kruger is a
separate issue altogether. It has nothing whatever to do with the
criminal charges against him."

"That's a legal nicety," said Livia.

Her mother interrupted. "Go upstairs, Livia."

"No, Mamma," Anna said, "let her say what's on her mind."

"My question isn't exactly legal. It's more—what? *Human.*"

"Go on." Anna felt last night's pain in her neck return.

"I just wondered. You told us you met with Kruger in that hotel in Hollywood."

"Los Angeles."

"Whatever. You told us you read him the charges you were going to make in Bologna."

She recognized the look in Livia's face. They had shared everything as girls, even their most secret feelings. "That's correct."

"You didn't tell us much else about the meeting. For instance"— she smiled, toying with a piece of buttered toast—"did you finally tell him that he killed Papa and Piero? You never did tell him here, you know. He left Montefalco never knowing about Papa and Piero."

Anna's tongue felt thick in her throat. "There was no opportunity here to tell him. And yes—to answer your question—yes, I told him about Papa and Piero in Los Angeles."

Livia nodded, making a show of thoughtfulness, toying with her now. She knew the next question before Livia let it fall like lead in the silence. "And did you tell him he has a son living in—where is it? Connecticut?"

Anna rose to her feet, fumbling to move the heavy chair. She looked toward her mother with an admissive kind of pain, then left the room.

II

Hugging the riverbank, the train rounded the curve just north of town and lurched over the junction of a siding between the outlying buildings of Montefalco. Kruger gripped the support rail across the carriage window to steady himself. Through the evening fog rising from the river, rows of new cube-shaped buildings came into view. A quarter of a mile north of town he saw the ragged mountain slope behind the Miceli farm.

There was a sudden screech of old brakes as the train rocked along the station platform. The crowd of tourists bound for the spas of Montefalco pushed forward in the corridor, forcing him against a large Italian woman. She looked back at this foreigner behind her in a sports shirt and flight jacket and cursed.

The setting sun had cast a long shadow down the western side of the valley. The old town was the same as he remembered it at this time of evening: a congestion of old stone and stucco houses with terra-cotta roofs. Higher up the slope, the Romanesque tower of the church of San Tommaso still dominated the town. For the first time since he had decided to continue on to Montefalco, he felt frightened.

In the deepening twilight a few electric lights were coming on. The last time he had seen Montefalco, it was shrouded in a wartime blackout. The depot building was new. In place of the ramshackle structure he remembered, there was now a white clapboard building ornamented with quaintly carved eaves. As the train came to a halt, he retrieved his suitcase and inched his way toward the carriage door. He looked at his watch: 4:37. Last night in Bologna, when he decided to follow Anna all the way to Montefalco, he had carefully checked the train schedules to allow as little time as possible for the visit. Less than two hours remained for him to accomplish his mission and return to the station for the night train back to Bologna at 6:24.

He raised the collar of his flight jacket. By now it was certain that Anna had announced her discovery to the townspeople. By now his name would be on the lips of every native of Montefalco, and some would remember his face.

He stepped down to the asphalt walkway and followed the crowd to the station, feeling suddenly like a criminal revisiting the scene of his crime, and, like a criminal looking for the cathartic freedom of mental re-enactment, he had rationalized his motives for coming.

He let the waiting-room door slam closed behind him. The little room was empty. The tourists who had preceded him had continued through the depot to a tourist bus parked outside. He looked around for a coin-operated locker. His plan had been to check his bag at the station and reclaim it on his return, but there were only two vending machines in the depot.

"*Buona sera,*" a man called from the ticket window.

"*Buona sera.*" Kruger walked toward the chubby middle-aged face framed in the small grilled window. It was not a familiar face to him. The right age, perhaps, but not a face he remembered. "I've just arrived on the Bologna train," he said in English. "I'd like to store this bag at the station for a short time. I'm catching the six twenty-four back tonight."

Unconcerned, the ticket agent produced a tag with a string attached. "Put the top part on your bag, keep the bottom part, and put the bag down there on the counter. You can reclaim it when you come back."

Kruger did as he was told and started to the front door of the depot.

"By the way," the agent called after him, "if you decide to stay overnight, there will be an additional charge!"

"I won't be staying, thank you." Outside, there was a familiar smell of sweet damp air blowing from the direction of the river. Except for a single car, an old Fiat with a makeshift taxi emblem on top, the parking lot was deserted. Its driver sat sleeping at the wheel. He awoke as the whistle signaled the departure of the train. Kruger spoke to him in Italian. "Excuse me, signore, are you free?"

The man sized him up with a glance. "Depends." He was young, in his early twenties, with a rough bullish face dominated by a thick nose. "Where're you going?" He had already started his engine.

"To a farm on the other side of the river, just north of town."

"Get in."

The inside of the taxi smelled of stale wine and tobacco. As they swung from the parking lot, the driver asked, "Which farm?"

"It used to belong to the Miceli family."

"I know the one." He swung into the Via Garibaldi. Kruger recognized the small shops lining the street above the river. The driver turned on the headlights and illuminated the metal frame of the bridge spanning the Reno River. He was a little drunk and looked ill-tempered at being aroused from his sleep. "The Micelis," Kruger ventured, cautiously, "do they still own the farm?"

"The old lady owns it. You here to see the old lady?"

"Yes. And her daughter." He studied the man's profile for a reaction. There was none.

"You here from Pisa?" They swung north on the main road leading out of town. Kruger realized the man meant Anna's younger sister. "Or the other daughter? The one who lives in America," the driver added.

"No, America."

"Where're you from? You don't sound American."

He pretended not to hear.

"You here to take the waters?"

"No. I'm here on business."

The driver looked back, suddenly solicitous. A sour-sweet odor of stale wine swept by on the wind. "What hotel are you in, signore?"

"I'm not staying. I'm leaving on the evening train to Bologna."

The driver turned back to his wheel. They had reached the edge of town. The road traversed a small pasture. "My cousin and I came here from Naples to open a hotel. If you change your mind, it's the Lombardi. In the new part of town."

"Thanks." In a field on the far side of the river an ancient *casa colonica* came into view. Kruger instantly recognized the stone mill tower attached to the farmhouse. The farm had once belonged to the Caselli family. During the war, the Casellis had been adamant Fascists and had collaborated with the occupying German Army. In recent years there had been grim stories of brutal postwar reprisals carried out against Italian collaborators. "That farmhouse," he said, "the one there with the tower—who owns it now?"

"The Ravello family. They own all the farmland on that side of the river."

"It used to belong to the Casellis."

"Caselli? Never heard of them."

The man was too young, of course, to have lived through the war. If the locals were now talking about what had happened here in 1944, he was obviously indifferent to their stories.

The cliffside over the river fell away to a gentle slope of pasture land bordered by a dense forest. Anna had said that the land once belonged to her family, who had been wealthy titled *padroni* in this part of the Reno Valley in the years before Mussolini's rise to power.

"You say you're taking the night train back to Bologna, signore?"

"Yes. The six twenty-four."

"How will you get back into town? Walk? It's not possible." He slowed, scanning the roadside for the turnoff to the Miceli farm.

Kruger realized he had overlooked the question of transportation back to the station. An hour and twenty minutes remained. "If you leave me at the farm for an hour, and then come back, I'll pay you for the hour and double your fare."

The driver made a slow left turn into the dirt road. "The fare one way is twelve hundred lire. The hour will cost you another two thousand."

It was ridiculous, but he had no choice. "Agreed."

"In advance."

Kruger took out his wallet and counted four thousand in lire bills. The ancient Fiat inched up the road, which was overgrown with weeds from disuse. "Here." He handed the bills over the seat. "Stop here. I'll walk the rest of the way."

The bills vanished into a cigar box on the front seat. The driver stopped and gunned the motor to keep it running.

"Remember!" Kruger got out quickly. "One hour! I must make that train, do you understand?"

"*Sì!* One hour! Don't worry, signore!"

He started up the slope toward the Miceli *casa colonica* cradled against the side of the mountain. A single light burned in one of the ground-floor windows. The taxi's headlights swept across the pasture, momentarily illuminating what looked like the remains of a barn. The pasture itself, now overgrown with weeds, had once been the grazing land of the Miceli's mule. The waist-high stone wall skirting the pasture had collapsed long ago into rubble. He thought of Anna's father and brother. Since their deaths, the farm had obviously been left untended. The last of the twilight lingering along the crest of the mountain cast a soft lavender reflection from the hills on the eastern side of the valley.

The pounding of his heart, he realized, was not from the exertion of his climb, but from fear and dread. The light in the ground-floor window came from the living room. Someone moved across the window, a woman with long dark hair. He drew up in the gravel drive fronting the house, feeling his doubts return. He had debated the question of going on to Montefalco for the last day and a half, since learning in Bologna that the charges had been filed. The cardinal had said to follow Anna to New York, persuade her to change her mind. But he had said nothing about Italy.

The silhouette passed across the window again. Anna, he was sure. She was here. He let the air run from his mouth and felt relieved. He raised the heavy iron knocker and let it fall. Its thud resounded inside the house. He started to lift the knocker again, but heard the sound of a woman's voice calling. He took two steps backward. A bolt slid back. A plump, dark-haired woman opened the door, gathering the folds of a blue dressing gown to her body. She stared at him, squinting out warily into the darkness. "*Sì?*"

"*Buona sera, signora.*"

"*Buona sera.*" The woman threw the greeting back like a challenge.

"I'd like to speak to . . ." He hesitated. The name stuck in his throat. ". . . to Signora Fitzgerald." He had wanted to say Miceli.

For a moment, the woman peered out at him, trying to identify him in the faint light. She opened the door a little farther and the light touched his face. She registered the shock of recognition with a horrified twitch, stepped back, and grabbed hold of the door. She tried to speak, but choked on the word, *"You . . . !"*

Anna called out from the back of the house. "Livia?"

"Please," he said. "Please tell her that I've come to talk." He repeated his statement silently to himself, and it sounded absurd. "I'm Father Karl Kruger," he added. His own name suddenly struck him as something shameful and monstrous.

Anna's sister grabbed hold of the doorjamb with her free hand and gaped at him with horror. "Anna . . . ?" Her voice quivered away, out of control.

"Who's there, Livia?" Anna called impatiently.

He saw her emerge from a door at the far end of a big room. She wore a dark dressing gown. She came toward the front door with her hands raised behind her head, preoccupied with securing her long dark hair with a ribbon.

"No!" Livia shouted. "Stay back!"

Across the living room Anna saw Livia turn from the door with a look of horror. Behind her, in the darkness beyond the door, stood the shadowy figure of a man. For a moment, holding her hair raised with the ribbon, she did not move. The man took a step forward, and the light struck his face. "Anna," Kruger said.

She let go of the ribbon and it fluttered to the floor.

"He has come, Anna," Livia gasped.

She saw Kruger's arms and hands move: a gesture of appeal. He wore civilian clothes, a short jacket, a sports shirt, and dungarees.

"Please, Anna," he said, "I've come here to talk." The word *talk* sounded idiotic, thinking of the distance he had come.

Livia started to close the door, but Kruger caught and held it open with one hand. "No!" she cried. "You will not! Anna! Call the police!"

"I did not come here to harm you, Anna," Kruger said. "I came to talk."

Anna's shock passed. "Livia!" She hurried forward. "Get back. I will deal with him myself."

Kruger said, "I came from America to see you, to talk with you. I have only a short time, Anna. I must go back to Bologna tonight."

She pushed Livia aside and opened the door wider. Dressed in civilian clothes, he looked—and the thought of it electrified her—like an older version of Angelo, but much leaner.

"Anna? Livia?" her mother called from the kitchen.

"Keep mother in the kitchen," she said to Livia, staring through the door at Kruger, who had stepped back into the gravel turnaround. "Don't let her come out here."

"Anna!" Livia exclaimed.

"Do as I say, Livia!" She left the foyer, went outside, and closed the door behind her.

"Anna," he said, his voice compounding the chill from the night air that ran through her body.

"Why—?" She had to get her breath to speak. "Why did you come here?"

"To speak with you."

The poverty of the reply left her speechless. Neither of them moved for a moment. She said, "To . . . give yourself up?"

"To talk." He shook his head helplessly. "I have . . . I have something to ask you." He looked suddenly foolish, standing in the gravel clearing with his shoulders slumped.

There was an angry outburst of voices in the living room, Livia shouting at her mother to keep back from the front door.

"My mother knows you're here. She knows who you are."

"I'm sorry. There was no other way to reach you."

She closed her mind to the appeal she heard in his voice and, leaving the doorway, started across the gravel turnaround. "Follow me," she said cautiously, keeping her distance. "I don't want Mamma to meet you."

He followed her. Where the road sloped down near the woods, she turned around and saw him silhouetted against the light from the living room window. He had stopped twenty feet from her, giving her, she realized, the security of distance. She was shaking, though whether from fear or the cold night air she could not tell.

"Anna," he said again, "I haven't come here to harm either you or your family."

"You will be arrested," she said, "you know that. When they learn you're here, they will arrest you." She thought of endless extradition proceedings awaiting them in America and the sudden and unexpected boon his presence in Italy afforded the prosecution.

"I came less than an hour ago. I will leave when we've talked."

"Talked?" she asked, amazed. "You came all the way here to *talk?"* She heard and, at once, regretted the note of mockery in her voice.

"Yes," he sighed. "I came to ask you—beg you—to reconsider your decision to prosecute me. I'm a priest. If you continue—"

She interrupted: "You're *mad!"*

He went on. "If you continue what you are doing, it will bring harm, terrible harm, to the Church." It sounded like a speech he had prepared.

"You came here to Italy to tell me *that?*"

"Yes. You're a Catholic, Anna. I'd hoped by now you'd have had time to think it over. The Church . . . the Church has enemies. You know what they will say . . ." His hand, hanging at his side, went out in another helpless, foolish gesture of resignation. She took a deep breath, thought of the useless lengths he had gone to in daring to come here, and felt her anger and outrage give way to something unexpected: pity. In the intervening days since Los Angeles, she had steeled herself against every inroad on her feelings but that. She said, "I find it hard to believe you came all the way here to Montefalco to argue for the Church."

"It was my duty," he said softly. "If I go to trial, it will not be a former German soldier they will try but a priest. The scandal," he added, "will touch every Catholic."

"Did it occur to you that I am not responsible for the damage you *have done* and *will do* to the Church?"

"Yes."

"You knew what would happen if you were ever found, you knew that when you became a priest!"

He nodded. "I told myself in the beginning it would never happen. I rationalized everything. I lied to myself. I convinced myself that the good I could do as a priest was worth the risk." Again the words sounded like a memorized speech.

"You gambled, in other words, and you lost."

"Yes."

In the momentary coda of silence and over the buzz of crickets in the nearby grass came the sound of Livia's and her mother's voices from inside the house: angry, frantic shouts.

"How did you know I was in Montefalco?" she asked.

"I went to New York. You told me you lived and worked in New York. I phoned your home. Your son was there—for the weekend, he said. He told me you'd left for Italy on a business trip—to Bologna. He gave me the name of your hotel in Bologna."

When her paralyzing terror had passed, she asked in a voice that betrayed that vulnerable soft center she had kept hidden in Los Angeles, "You spoke to . . . my son?"

"Yes." He was silent for a moment. His breath punctuated the damp cold air. Suddenly he spoke in Italian. "I didn't know you had a son." The sound of Italian from his mouth cut like a knife.

She thought back to the Adele Ravine and the afternoon she

promised to give him a son. That was in August, three weeks before he murdered her father and brother and then deserted her. The pain she had hidden under righteous anger all these days, since finding him alive after all these years, suddenly closed in on her. She turned her face toward the darkness, fearing he would see the light reflected in the tears watering her eyes, and, leveling her voice with professional courtroom detachment, said, "Yes . . . I have a son."

He nodded again, this time with a look of preoccupied resignation, and then said, "Did you know that a priest can absolve everyone else but himself from sin?" His Italian had even improved over the absent intervening years.

"Why . . . why did you really come here?"

"To ask your forgiveness," he replied, adding quickly as an afterthought, "and to prevent scandal."

She considered his reply, thinking how much there was to forgive: the murder of her loved ones, broken promises, twenty-eight years of forgetfulness. He had become a priest and left her alone to raise a son who had been born in the predestination of his own damnation. Feeling the hard-edged bitterness return, she said, "I've already opened the case against you. I've already charged you before the military authorities in Bologna. It's out of my hands."

"They told me the charges had been filed when I went to the War Crimes Bureau there."

She pressed again, aware that she wanted to hear the reply she anticipated but dared not supply. "Then why would you bother to come?"

He stumbled clumsily, revealingly, in his reply. "They said . . . they said you would need evidence . . . and witnesses. I thought maybe—"

"I see." She retreated back to the familiar ground of a prosecuting attorney. "The evidence lies in the graveyard. You knew that. And as far as witnesses are concerned, there are many survivors in Montefalco." She could not help adding, "You knew that, too."

He said without further hesitation, "I need your forgiveness, Anna. For what I did to your father and your brother, for what I did to you. For everything."

She held her breath until the blood rushed to her face. In the lighted window of the living room she saw the figure of Livia pass by, heading, she imagined, toward the phone. Delayed by shock, a realization leapt forward in her mind. She let the air go, breathed, and said, "How did you get here—to the farm?"

"By taxi."

She thought of the revenge she had inspired in the townspeople these last few days. "You fool! Did anyone recognize you?"

"No. The driver was too young, too drunk to know me."

She knew the Tuscan temper, the instinct of these people for swift revenge. They would not wait for an arrest warrant, once they knew of his presence, and they would not let him leave Montefalco either free or alive. "You were"—and the thought of it truly amazed her now—"mad to come here!"

"I know," he said, conceding with another lame gesture. Angie was wont to make similar gestures when she cornered him in his little deceptions. "The train to Bologna leaves soon. Unless I'm stopped by the police, I'll leave just as I came."

"If these people find you, they will kill you, and if they kill you without benefit of a trial, it will be no better than the justice you handed out in 1944." She saw a crack appear in her furious five-day apostolate of justice, saw her mother draw Livia back into the lighted frame of the window. She started quickly toward the house, keeping close to the woods to avoid passing near to him. "Go," she said, "go quickly. Take the path by the river. You haven't much time." Another recollection brushed by her mind: It was the same path she had taken that first time she followed him out of town on one of his afternoon walks, the path on which she had contrived to meet him for the second time in the winter of 1944.

"Anna!" he called after her, but she moved on, wondering how she would explain to her mother and sister the opportunity she had let slip through her hands.

"Anna!" he called again.

But thinking of the absurd renunciation of his appeal, his brave but foolish appearance alone at night here in this most dangerous of all places, she could not let herself stop.

Behind her he murmured something after her in Italian as she reached the gravel turnaround. She thought she heard the word *forgiveness* again. She stumbled in the loose gravel. If there had been any triumph at all in discovering him alive in America, he had leveled it with his abject, almost childlike, humility. Crossing the turnaround, she passed the same place where she had stood that night when her mother and Livia prayed inside the house over the riddled bodies of her father and brother, the same spot where she had stood to watch the convoy of his trucks pass by on the road north to Vergato.

She remembered the vow she had sworn that night, the curse she had brought down on him for the son he had given her and then abandoned.

In the grass next to the grove where he had stood a twig snapped. He had started back down the hill.

Leaving yet again. It came up, twenty-eight years of bitterness, hurt, rage, hatred, and frustration; twenty-eight wasted years—her most precious womanly years—of fighting the memory of his loss. "Go!" she screamed out into the darkness. "Go back to America! You are damned!"

CHAPTER 4

I

Another light broke before his vision. Kruger stirred, feeling a throbbing ache. The black hole below him seemed to fall away, seemed part of a different place and time.

Anna's voice called up from the darkness receding from him, and he tried to reach down and grab hold of her, but it was merely a voice and not a body that was falling away into nothingness.

He opened his eyes, lingering in the fuzzy haze between darkness and light, wondering where he was, for there was something blue—a pale blue wall—beside him where he lay. And he lay, he suddenly realized, in a large lumpy bed that was not his own bed. His head rested on a pillow that smelled of mildew. His vision focused. Lace curtains billowed at an open window filled with a soft, rose-colored light. The first clear thought that came to him was: dawn.

He sat up on the bed. His neck ached as the blood raced to his head. He looked around and remembered: Montefalco, the fourth-floor room in the Hotel Montecatini. Slumping down, he tried to retrace the sequence of last night's events. After Anna left him, he had walked down the hill. Instead of waiting for the taxi, he had walked on toward town. Time was running out. The walk back, which somewhere turned into a run when he realized that the taxi would not return, was now only a blurred impression of moonlit darkness, a race (endless it seemed) against odds calculated in seconds, and a feeling of emptiness so large that even God seemed small in it. On the outskirts of town he had heard the whistle echo down the valley and knew that he had missed the train—knew that he would now be forced to spend the night in Montefalco. Somehow, he had no longer cared what happened to him, and when he walked calmly into the station, the ticket agent was already closing up for the night. He had inquired about the owners of the Hotel Montecatini from the agent and had learned that it was managed now by a family not native to Montefalco. Reclaiming his suitcase, he had walked up the Via Garibaldi into the old town, making no attempt to disguise himself from the people passing in the street. He had passed through the Piazza Nazionale to the hotel in the Via Benedetto. At the desk (the same desk that had served the Fascist receptionist in 1944) he had registered in the hotel ledger, indifferent to the possibility that the young clerk might know the name, even indifferent to the clerk's request for his passport and his assurance that he could reclaim it in the morning. The boy had then escorted him to a room on the fourth floor: the very floor he had formerly occupied with the other Wehrmacht officers. To the room that had once been the home of Sergeant Rudolf Oster. Alone in the room, he had stretched out on the bed in the darkness, feeling again like a murderer come back to the scene of the crime. He had lain there until the early hours of the morning, twisting the knot of his conscience, unable and unwilling to sleep for fear of what now lay ahead for him in the days, weeks, and months to come.

Through the open window came the distant toll of a church bell. He recognized the harsh clang: the bell in the tower of San Tommaso announcing Sunday morning Mass. He swung off the bed and stood up. But of course there was no church in Montefalco where he could say Mass. On the other hand, if he hurried (and if he wore secular clothes) he could reach San Tommaso before Mass began. He splashed his face with cold water in the familiar sink against the wall. He had seen Rudolf Oster wash himself at this same sink, he remembered, looking around the room. The walls, though repainted, and the old metal light fixtures attached to the walls, were the same. He dressed and, as an added disguise, took from his suitcase the cheap white vinyl cap that he had bought yesterday in Bologna to protect his face from the sun. With that, and his sunglasses, he would look, for all purposes, like any other holiday tourist.

In the corridor outside he paused before the door to the room he had once occupied as a commandant. Though repainted, the door was the same: he remembered its original varnished stain with a shameful feeling of *déjà vu*. Inside the room someone was washing at the sink. He suddenly remembered that night following the execution when he returned to the room to gather his belongings for the retreat from Montefalco: the night he placed the barrel of his pistol into his mouth and coldly calculated the advantages of suicide. Last night, running back to town along the moonlit path, that same impulse to escape through suicide had come over him, but this time he had seriously entertained the temptation, knowing as a priest the awesome penalty for that final and unforgivable sin. Anna's words *You are damned!* had sounded in his ears, and in the heat of the moment, he had heard another voice reasoning with him: being already among the damned, my suicide will be meaningless to God. You cannot compound damnation.

In the lobby downstairs, he found the night clerk asleep behind the desk and tiptoed quietly out. The street was deserted. He turned in the direction of the Piazza Nazionale. The metal blinds were still drawn in front of the shops. He passed the building where Signora Comellini had run the lucrative Fascist dry-goods store, the *ammasso*. It was now a modern drugstore. He thought of the Fascist Caselli family.

Sunday Mass had begun, and he was late. He hurried on, wanting, but not daring, to run. The station clerk had told him that the first train to Bologna would leave that morning at 10:25. Over four hours remained. He remembered the passport with its photo pasted conspicuously in the flyleaf: the photo taken in 1967 when he returned to Munich for his father's funeral. The face was unmistakably that of the infamous German commandant, the Butcher of Montefalco. In moments of vanity, he had sometimes prided himself on the lingering youth of his face.

He reached the northwest corner of the Piazza Nazionale. Except for an old man sweeping the cobblestones near the post office, the square was deserted. He turned up into the narrow Via Santa Lucia and felt in the pit of his stomach a sudden coil of nausea. It came not from hunger, but from revulsion: the sight of the Municipio, the building where he had maintained his offices and issued the order for the reprisal. The two-story stucco houses lining the street looked the same as he remembered them twenty-eight years before: even the laundry dangling on lines stretched between the houses. Nothing had changed.

II

"Go in peace. The Mass has ended," said Father Canavese from the altar. The stoop-shouldered pastor of San Tommaso bowed toward the cross and left the sanctuary with his two altar boys as the congregation spilled into the aisles.

Anna, Livia, and their mother stood waiting in one of the center pews for the congestion in the aisle to thin. The crowd at the eight o'clock Sunday Mass that morning was made up of locals and out-of-town tourists, Italians and foreigners. Moving along the center aisle, Captain Luigi Tedeschini, Montefalco's portly middle-aged chief of police, caught sight of Anna, smiled, and gave an officious little bow.

Anna returned the smile and nodded.

"Hypocrite," Livia murmured.

She ignored her sister and glanced impatiently at her mother. The argument with Livia last night over phoning the police had gone on until the small hours of the morning, and she was too tired now to respond to her sister's baiting. Luckily, she had reached Livia before she could phone the station. Livia had denounced her for allowing Kruger to leave Montefalco, and when she heard the Bologna night train go by, and learned she had been tricked, a whole new argument had broken out. In the end, Livia had been forced to concede that arresting Kruger in Montefalco would be tantamount to executing him without a trial, and that would be no justice at all.

As Anna followed her mother and Livia into the aisle, she glanced again at the statue of the Sacred Heart in the vaulted shadows across the church. After twenty-eight years votive candles still burned at the foot of the statue.

Stalled for a moment at the congested church doors, Livia leaned back and said, "I hope you haven't forgotten how to pray."

"Move on, Livia, you're blocking everyone's way." *If I were you, Monsignor, I would learn how to pray.* Her words that night in Los Angeles came back to her. She had lain awake all last night, praying that he had made his train and left safely, praying that in the weeks to come, when she returned to face him in America, she would not succumb again to that unwanted pull in the heart.

"I hope for your sake Tedeschini never finds out," said Livia, moving out into the square.

If he did find out, if she was questioned, it would be very hard to go on talking of extraditions. Last night Livia had said, "No one's going to believe you let him escape so you could bring him back alive to stand trial. Your motives are quite transparent, Anna."

Observing her crossing the sunlit Piazza San Tommaso, some of the locals nodded respectfully. There was Ursula Auriti, wife of one of the executed *contadini,* Maria Bruzzno, the wife of Matteo Bruzzno, once Montefalco's blacksmith, and the *contadini* Lucco Cassla, Duccio Morera, and Gianni Vianelli, three of the few young men left in Montefalco, all men whose fathers had died in the reprisal. There was also Paula Bosco, the wife of Gianni Bosco, Montefalco's tailor, who had run the shop after her husband's death and gone blind over the years in the process. There was the Faggioni family, who had lost their father and subsequently their farm, since there was no adult male left to do the work.

Anna hurried through the crowd toward Livia's car, parked at the edge of the cobblestone square. Livia and her mother had dropped back to talk with friends. She would wait for them at the car.

"Signora Fitzgerald!" Carmela Turatti came hurrying toward her. In her late sixties now, Carmela was an old-fashioned woman who clung to strict local traditions. Her husband, Leonardo, had been a close friend of her father's, and the two men had played cards together at least once a week. Leonardo had died in the square with her father. "Anna, wait." Carmela took hold of her arm and led her aside. "Signore Spisani explained to me yesterday this business of extradition." Spisani was Montefalco's young local attorney. Anna did not trust him. "He says it will cost a fortune to bring the *Macellaio* to trial in America."

"Yes. But it's unavoidable." She kept moving toward Livia's car, feeling the first signs of panic.

"Spisani says the man's American citizenship is legal since we did not file charges against him after the war."

"That's debatable, Carmela. The American courts will decide." Still another crack appeared in the crumbling wall of defense for her motives in both calling for extradition and trial and for letting him escape.

Under the black kerchief around her head Carmela's dark crafty eyes narrowed. She rubbed her wrinkled chin and said, "Spisani brought up something you haven't mentioned to any of us before, Anna. The possibility of reparation money from the German Government."

Anna stopped dead, speechless.

"It's something you must consider, my child." Carmela smiled. She was missing one front tooth. She went on. "Don't misunderstand me. Justice is the main thing. But these people are poor. You must understand the practical side. I speak not for myself, but if you want these poor people to contribute money for an *American* trial, there must be hope of recovering it."

"No. I will not use reparation as a motive, Signora Turatti. And I'm surprised you would suggest it." *Justice is the main thing.* She heard in the words the echo of her own voice.

"You've been away a long time, Anna, and time has a way of healing wounds. Here in Montefalco the young people control everything. Let's be practical, they have forgotten."

"Tell the young people of Montefalco that I've decided to finance the American legal proceedings myself," she said, repressing her anger, "and all I will need from Montefalco are witnesses for the Italian trial."

"Nevertheless, Signore Spisani says—"

"Never mind what Spisani says. I don't want to hear the subject mentioned again, Carmela."

The old lady shrugged. "It's out of my hands."

"Good day, signora." Anna walked quickly to Livia's car, thinking back a week to the original momentum of the wheels of justice she had set in motion, glad she had sought refuge last night in the old habit of postponement, glad, for whatever reason, that he had gone.

III

Kruger adjusted his sunglasses and took a copy of the Sunday morning Bologna newspaper displayed in the rack against the wall. The tobacco shop where he had stopped on the busy Via Risorgimento along the riverside was crowded with tourists buying postcards and souvenirs. The old woman behind the counter had lost her temper and was shouting at the young girl assisting her. He took a handful of lira coins from his pocket, listening to the woman's familiar voice. "No," she was shouting, "that card is two hundred lira! The others are three hundred!"

He edged his way between two English tourists waiting their turn to pay. "Excuse me." Behind the counter, the woman's wrinkled face was startlingly familiar. He held up the paper, put four hundred-lire coins on the counter, and turned away. *"Grazie."* He knew the woman but not her name. She had often visited the Municipio during the occupation to plead for concessions on behalf of her husband, who ran Montefalco's pharmacy.

"Signore," she called after him, "wait! You have overpaid!"

He pretended not to understand and hurried off down the street. This was the second time since he had left San Tommaso after Mass that he had recognized a local face. He continued along the sidewalk opposite the river, heading toward the Viale Filipetti. After the six o'clock Mass, he had decided to spend the remaining time between Mass and the train's departure walking through town, instead of returning to the Montecatini. During Mass he had had second thoughts about the passport held overnight by the hotel management. By now he had begun to fear his name, nationality, and passport number would have been turned over to the local police. There was the chance someone at the police station—or even at the hotel—might have recognized his face or name.

He turned up the narrow residential Viale Filipetti into the old town. From here it was a ten-minute walk back to the Montecatini. He looked at his watch: 9:15. An hour and ten minutes remained till the train left. Again, he wondered if it would be better to leave his passport and suitcase behind in Montefalco and replace the passport in Milan, say, or even in Rome. On the other hand, if charges had been filed, would they be registered at the various American consulates before he could replace the "lost" passport?

He slowed his pace uphill, relieved at least to have left the main thoroughfare along the river. Passing the Via Garibaldi earlier, he had seen a police car crossing the bridge with two officers inside. They were scanning the pedestrians walking along the bridge, but that meant nothing in a little town crowded with foreigners.

Halfway up the hill, he turned into the narrow Via Ospedale. From here he could take the Via Mazzini and avoid crossing the crowded Piazza Nazionale at the post-office end of the square. There was no way back to the Montecatini, save circling the entire old town, without passing through the piazza. The Via Firenze led into the square at the Municipio end, and he could easily reach the Via Benedetto from there.

Three shops down the Via Mazzini he saw a familiar sign over a storefront window: BOSCO. *Sarto.* Even the sign itself had not changed over the years. Gianni Bosco had been one of the few men he recognized that morning in the square. He had owned and operated the tailoring shop here in the Mazzini during the occupation, he and his wife, Paula. He had recognized Gianni among the victims too late to intervene. Not only that, nothing had been said about selecting hostages on the basis of innocence or guilt.

As he reached the shop window and looked in, he saw an elderly woman bent over a table, cutting fabric. Under the overhead lamp her profile appeared quite old. Her hair was like combed cotton. He remembered the tailor's wife, who had always remained quietly in the background when he paid calls to have his uniform mended. This woman was far older than Signora Bosco. As he started to move on, the woman looked up to the window. In an instant, behind the thick-lensed spectacles, he recognized the lined face of Paula

Bosco. The skin was like crumpled parchment. The woman craned her head to make out who stood at her window, but her eyes, enlarged by the lenses, were glazed with a translucent mucus, and the pupils were milky white.

He moved on quickly, stunned by the change in Paula's face, knowing at once the reason for her ravaged appearance.

The realization was slow in coming. He drew up at the corner of the Via Firenze and stood staring down at the cobblestones. The women in the Via Gamberini stringing laundry over the street, the woman in the tobacco shop, Paula Bosco: the town was inhabited by women! The evidence had been there all morning—in church, in the streets—he had seen only a few young people and even fewer children. The inhabitants of Montefalco were *widows*. The conclusion he had thus far kept at bay bewildered him.

He turned up the Via Firenze toward the Piazza Nazionale, walking at a swift even pace, thinking now only of the 10:25 train and its escape.

If these people find you, they will kill you, and if they kill you without the benefit of a trial, it will be no better than the justice you handed out in 1944.

He thought of Cardinal Boyle's directive on Monday. *I cannot order you to visit her, I can only suggest it.* In retrospect, his disobedience in coming all the way to Italy seemed like the action of a madman! He thought again: the criminal come back to the scene of his crime.

And with that, he entered the square and saw, first, the Municipio on his left. They had restored the building. He kept moving, grateful that the crowd was concentrated at the opposite end of the square, near the post office. But across the square, the Via Benedetto was crowded with tourists. He saw scorch marks on the Municipio *campanile* where it joined the roof and remembered the night Oster set fire to the building and burned all the official records.

He raised his cap to wipe away the sweat from the brim and saw a police car turn into the square from the Via Garibaldi at the far end. He drew up as the car moved along the north side of the square in the direction of the Via Benedetto.

Fear swept ahead of reason. He could not reach the Via Benedetto ahead of the police car, and if . . . ?

Turning away, he proceeded along the south side of the square. In one of the shop windows he saw the police car turn along the facade of the Municipio. It was making a tour of the entire piazza. He passed the old Banco Commerciale. It was now called the Banco di

Roma, but the building was the same: the old Palazzo Berticelli, which had once belonged to Anna's family in the days before Garibaldi. He remembered the women who had stood there that morning, watching him execute their husbands and fathers.

The police car gained on him as he reached the southeast corner. Mechanically, he ambled toward the crowd milling in front of the post office. In the crowd he would look like the other foreign tourists. They had rebuilt the post office, as well. He remembered the flames that had poured from its windows and ignited the roof.

The police car drew alongside as he passed near the place where Oster had stood. And the machine guns were over there—he dared not look—in that open space.

He melted into the crowd gathered at the wall of the post office. Behind, the police car passed, threading its way through the people. He took a breath, and felt suddenly dizzy, realizing he had held his breath all along the post office.

People stood near the wall, staring at something, then passing on. He moved closer and saw the object of their curiosity: a rectangular bronze plaque set into the post-office wall. He saw that he stood on the exact spot where he had given the *coup de grâce* to the unknown Italian deserter.

A trickle of sweat ran down his forehead and dropped across the lens of his sunglasses. The police car turned into the Via Garibaldi. He felt suddenly foolish. He stepped closer to the plaque. The bas-relief inscription was tarnished with age. In Italian, the locals had written:

> In memory of the innocent victims of Nazi
> war atrocity who died here in reprisal execution.
> September 1944.

Two columns of names were engraved on the plaque: Abruzzo, Gian-Carlo, Abruzzo, Pietro Luigi . . .

The names of his victims were listed alphabetically.

Baldini . . . Cremonini . . . Crespi . . .

He had never bothered to remember the names of the local Italian men.

Grizzeli . . . Gallo . . . Lombardi . . . Machiavelli . . .

The young deserter he had condemned to death by default, the man he later shot with his own pistol.

Miceli, Angelo Salvatore . . . Miceli, Piero Luigi.

Anna's father and brother. He did not know even now which

name belonged to the father and which to the brother. A huge leaden weight sank in his gut.

They were cattle to you! A quota you had to fill! I watched you! How could he blame her for twenty-eight years of relentless hatred?

He closed his eyes and tried to breathe, but the space around him was airless. He thought of the long journey he had made to come back and stand here in the very spot where his flight from himself had begun: soldier then, and now priest.

Letting a little rope out, and then pulling it back in. The appalling . . . the inexorable cruelty . . . of God's Providence.

He reached up absently, removed his sunglasses, and wiped the sweat from the bridge of his nose, feeling a curious stillness come over him: as if he had come full circle to a point of rest. He remembered a similar feeling in Munich six years before, when he toured the city of his childhood beginnings on his way to his father's death.

He opened his eyes, realizing he could never go back and recover what had been lost here. Nor could he rest in the same blind peace he had labored to earn for seventeen years as a priest.

In the same breath, two thoughts came to him: *there are spiritual forms of martyrdom* and *you are damned!*

He stood for a while, trying to imagine a Providence which could allow a man to damn himself for eternity to protect the larger good, but he could not imagine it, and knew suddenly the human answer to the question of why he had come back to Montefalco.

He turned away to the north side of the square and began weaving through the milling crowd toward the Via Benedetto. The clock in the Municipio tower read 9:43. *You may be called upon to exercise the virtue of blind obedience.*

He caught sight of an old woman in a black skirt, shawl, and kerchief. She had stopped to look at him, holding a basket of food. She was small, not more than five feet tall, with tufts of white hair protruding from the kerchief. Their eyes locked. He realized he had absently removed his sunglasses to read the plaque.

The old woman made a strange, superstitious gesture with her right hand and took one step backward into the path of an oncoming tourist. The man jostled her, but she seemed not to notice. In her dark wrinkled face he saw shock dissolve into terror. She made the sign of the cross.

He backed away, angling across the piazza. She pointed at him, tried to speak, but could only make a stammering noise, and was momentarily lost in the crowd. He continued away. She appeared again, emerging from the crowd in front of an outdoor restaurant, still pointing at him. *"È lui!"* she cried, wagging her finger. "It's *him!"* But the crowd around her did not understand and only looked amused and puzzled. *"Guardate!* Look! Look!" she shouted, catching the attention of some Italian locals. "Look!" she stammered, then began to hurry after him, pointing. The contents of her basket, oranges and lemons, spilled out, bouncing across the cobblestones. "Stop him!" she shrieked. "It's *him!"*

He reached the open space in the center of the piazza. People on both sides of the square began to turn and look in his direction.

"It's the *tedesco!"* the old woman cried, bearing down on him. *"Il Macellaio!* It's *him!"*

He realized, seeing the crowd gathering, that it was useless to think of returning to his hotel. He thought of the train in forty minutes. Something skittered across the pavement and struck his leg from behind. He saw that he was surrounded on three sides by six young boys with a soccer ball. They had not been in the square when he entered.

"Stop him!" the old woman shouted. "He killed my Paulo! It's him!"

He started across the Via Firenze side of the piazza.

"Lucio!" one of the boys called to a boy whose foot rested on the soccer ball. The boy laughed and called out something in a strange dialect. He was not a native of Montefalco. He kicked the ball, it shot across the cobblestones and was caught by the foot of another boy. The boys followed, circling him. They were not more than twelve or thirteen years old, street urchins dressed in dirty ill-fitting dungarees and T-shirts. The tallest of them kicked the ball close to his feet. The game caught on, and the other boys called to each other as they circled, laughing.

He began turning as he walked, trying to avoid the ball, aware that the crowd had stopped to watch. Two local *contadini* began to move forward. The old woman went on shouting, "Stop him! He's the Butcher! Don't you know him?"

The ball struck his feet from behind. He stumbled and fell face-forward to the pavement. The impact of his hands against the cobblestones shattered his sunglasses. He left them where they lay and got to his feet, looking around at the crowd massing along the three sides of the piazza.

The old woman shouted at the crowd, *"Il Macellaio!"*

Her voice galvanized two more young *contadini,* and they joined the others.

"Lucio! *Il ballo! Qui!"* There were catcalls from the young boys and laughter. He realized they were not only too young to know what they were doing, they also didn't care. They ringed around him, following his progress across the square, firing the ball at his legs.

IV

Anna turned from the Garibaldi into the Piazza Nazionale and braked, stalled by a crowd watching something in the square. She saw, first, a group of young boys in front of the Municipio, kicking a soccer ball, then saw a man trapped in the boys' circle, racing, stumbling, dodging the ball. "Oh my God," she said, recognizing the man's dungarees and flight jacket. Over the murmur around her a woman's shout filled the square: *"Il Macellaio!"* There were *contadini* converging on Kruger at the southwest corner of the square. She thought with horror of the night train to Bologna.

Old Maria Pucetti appeared, shouting, pointing to Kruger as he vanished down the Via Firenze. *"Il Macellaio!"*

Contadini, a dozen of them, began running after him.

For an instant she sat with her hands riveted to the steering wheel. Livia's retort last night when she forbade her to phone the police ricochetted through her mind like a sharp stone: "Let them kill him! An eye for an eye, Anna!"

"Damn him!" she shouted. She struck the steering wheel with both hands, threw the car into gear, and swung toward the Via della Republica, calculating her chances of reaching him before the *contadini*. The Republica ran parallel to the Firenze. She swerved right into the shop-lined Via Mazzini, racing between parked cars. "The fool!" she exclaimed. "He promised to leave!" Passing the dead-end Via Ospedale, she saw him turn from the Via Firenze and race toward her down the Mazzini. For the moment luck was with her. She drove in against the sidewalk and blared her horn. "Get in!" He stood gaping at her. She shouted in English, "Damn it! Get in!" He did as he was told. She threw the car into reverse and raced backward. "Get down!" she yelled, swinging forward into the Via Ospedale. He stared at her with astonishment. "Do what I tell you! Get down!" As she steered between the parked cars, he turned around and lowered himself into the small space under the dashboard. "Keep your head down!" She careened into the Viale Filipetti and started downhill. "They would have killed you!" she exclaimed, shifting into first gear to help brake her descent. She came to a halt at the Via Risorgimento and took a deep breath. "I warned you this would happen. Why didn't you leave?"

"I missed the train."

The silly childish answer silenced her. She waited for a truck to pass, then swung north toward the Via Garibaldi and the bridge over the Reno. "What the hell were you doing in the Nazionale? Have you gone mad?"

"I went to Mass this morning. After Mass, I was afraid to go back to my hotel. They have my passport. The next train out is at ten twenty-five. I went walking. I got trapped in the square."

She swung east across the bridge. "Which hotel?"

"The Montecatini."

The hotel he had lived in during the occupation. "Dear God."

"It's almost ten twenty-five. Take me to the station. I can still make the train."

"And your passport? What about that?"

"I'll deal with that later."

"You can't leave Italy without it," she said, thinking ahead to the options opening for her: an arrest in a safe city.

"So far, there's no warrant for my arrest. I'll go to a consulate in one of the cities."

Over my dead body you will, she thought. At the far side of the bridge she saw a police car parked at the station and remembered there was always a police car at the station when the crowded daytime trains arrived. Instead of turning into the station parking lot, she continued up the Via Garibaldi into the east end of town. "You can't leave on the ten twenty-five. There's a police car at the station."

He sighed and dropped his head against the seat. "This is absurd."

"Absurd is not the word, Monsignore." She kept pace with the traffic moving south and looked around at the rows of ugly concrete buildings erected since the war, trying to think what to do with him. She could hide him for a while, notify the Bologna authorities, and have him transferred to a safe prison outside Montefalco. But there was no place here in town to hide him. She glanced down at the Butcher of Montefalco, the monsignor, the ex-soldier, her former lover and the father of her son doubled up under the dashboard of her sister's car and suddenly wanted to laugh.

"I want you to take me to the police station," he said.

"If I take you to the police here in Montefalco, you won't last an hour. Montefalco is not Bologna. Those men back there in the piazza—they would rather kill you here than try you in Bologna. The police would not be able to stop them."

He lifted himself. "There's no other choice, Anna."

"Keep your head down, dammit!" They were approaching the south end of town. "Give me time, I'll think of something." But she could not, for the moment, focus her thoughts on anything more than the present ludicrous farce. The crest of the Adele Ravine appeared over the roofs of the buildings.

"Go back, Anna," he said, "turn around and go back to the police station."

"Do you think I planned this?" she shouted.

"You don't understand." He hesitated. "I've changed my mind. I'm not going to leave Italy, I'm not going back to America. I want you to turn me over to the police. I'll explain to the people here what I want to do. They won't harm me."

She looked down at him under the dashboard, silenced. Given what he had said last night, what he had just said made no sense. She looked away and kept driving. They passed the old tobacco shop that had once been the last building at this end of town. She said, "I'll find a place to hide you for the time being. You can't go back to Montefalco. I know those men. They will kill you. Like their brothers killed the Comellinis and the Casellis after the war. They're mountain people. For them, revenge is the same as justice."

Ahead, the ragged crest of the Adele Ravine looked the same after all these years. She thought of the places that lay beyond to the south, then it came to her. She smiled to herself, realizing she had long ago arranged the perfect place to hide him. "When we get to where I'm taking you," she said, "you'll stay there until I decide what to do. If you leave, if you are seen by any of the locals, they will kill you. Do you understand?"

"Yes."

His agreement was too easy to believe. "You have no passport and no transportation out of this valley. If you try to escape, you will be found. Moreover, as soon as the police know you're here, they'll start looking—with or without a warrant."

"I will not try to leave or escape, Anna." He pulled himself up and sat back in the seat.

She shifted down to second to climb the slope leading to the crest above the ravine. "You knew before you left Bologna that it was useless coming here." He did not respond. She saw that he was staring off absently toward the ridge above the ravine, toward the place where the path had once been. "You knew it was useless, didn't you?"

"Yes."

"Then why?" She instantly regretted the question.

"Let's just say it was my duty as a priest to come. I had to try."

Last night he had said "I need your forgiveness, Anna." Forgiveness? She kept her eyes averted from the ravine ahead, feeling anger and bitterness return, thinking again of what he knew, the death of her father and Piero, and what he did not know, the son he had given her.

I've changed my mind. I'm not going to leave Italy. She understood now, but said nothing. They had reached the crest of the road overlooking the wedge-shaped ravine. She saw him turn to look down at the trees—the pine and acacia grove—below. An image flashed through her mind: the two of them naked together on the tablecloth under the trees. She swallowed, revolted by the image.

"It hasn't changed," he said. "It looks the same."

"Perhaps. But appearances deceive." They started down the far side of the ridge into the valley. High on the bluff of the next hillside, the convent of Santa Cecilia came into view. "It was really duty, wasn't it?" she said. "You followed me here because it was your duty." She knew before she asked the question that she was testing his truth as a priest against his truth as a man. She regretted the question.

He hesitated. "Yes."

"Duty—" Her voice broke on the word. "Duty was your excuse before. It was your duty when you shot my father and brother. It was your duty when you shot fifty innocent men. You left here doing your duty as a soldier." She braked on a downward curve. "And you came back doing your duty as a priest. Have you ever in your life done your duty as a man?"

He said nothing.

Swinging free from the last hairpin curve, she shifted into third. The road hugged the river's edge for the next half mile. "You will be safe where I'm taking you," she said. "Meanwhile, I'm going to make arrangements in Bologna to have you transferred to a safe prison. Do you understand?"

"Yes."

"You cannot leave this valley, and you cannot leave Italy."

"I understand."

His passive submission was maddening. "I take it you know the rules. You will be tried before an Italian military court. First, you will face a Vatican hearing. If the charges against you appear justified in the ecclesiastical court, they will strip you of your priesthood."

"I know the rules, Anna."

Her voice shook with anger, and she knew that it had nothing whatever to do with war crimes. "Then you know you will not be tried as a priest. You will be tried as a man."

"I understand."

She swung into the dirt road leading uphill to the convent. "I take it you remember the Convent of Santa Cecilia."

"Yes." He looked surprised.

"And you remember Father Alessandro, the pastor of San Tommaso?"

"Yes."

"He's chaplain here now. He will let you stay with him at the convent rectory until I return." She threw the gear into first on the steep grading. "This is the last place in the valley they will think to look for you."

He looked at her for the first time since they had set out. "I don't understand. They're bound to come here. They'll put two and two together and know we're only repeating ourselves."

She swung around a hairpin curve, realizing what he meant. "They know nothing about us," she said. He stared, astonished. She recalled what she had said to her mother last night after the argument with Livia. She repeated her argument. "What happened between us has nothing to do with the charges against you."

"You're wrong, Anna. You must tell the police what happened. If you don't, they will use it against you—not against me." He sounded like a priest admonishing a penitent. "You must tell them the truth."

This first spoken admission of his intentions to go to trial silenced her. She swung around another curve. Tell them the truth? she thought, picturing herself announcing to the town that she had come back to prosecute not only the murderer of her father and brother, but also her former lover and the father of her son. "And what is the truth?" she asked.

He thought for a moment, then replied, "You were young at the time. I . . . I seduced you. I was the military commandant here, and . . . and I seduced you. You were not responsible for what happened, Anna."

The lie she heard in his voice frightened her. She said, "Was that really what happened? You seduced me?"

"They can't hold it against you. It was a long time ago. It happened to many girls in the war, Anna."

She reached the convent grounds at the top of the hill. "You mean, just another wartime romance."

"Yes." This time, the lie was plain. The sunlight through the windshield blinded her for a moment. He went on, compounding the lie, trying to reinforce his foolish reprieve. "I was responsible. I started it—remember? Tell them it lasted only a short time, and then I left you. Tell them the truth."

She drove past the huge wall fronting the convent cloister. She thought of his truth and her truth and the chain he had innocently left around her neck to bind her to him for twenty-eight years. "I'm afraid the truth is much larger than you think."

"What do you mean?"

I need your forgiveness, Anna, the words came back. She turned at the corner of the convent wall. A father and brother murdered in ignorance? *It lasted only a short time, and then I left you.* A brief wartime romance? Stretching charity, that she could conceivably forgive. But a son born under the curse of willful and blind obedience to an inhuman and murderous duty, that even God could not ask her to forgive. Following the convent wall toward a small whitewashed stucco cottage set apart from the cloisters in a grove of pine trees, she finally answered his question. "It doesn't matter what I mean. It will change nothing." She drew up before the low laurel hedge around the convent rectory. The front door opened, and the elderly Father Alessandro came out on the tiny porch. He looked far older than his years. He left the porch and walked up the flagstone path toward the car, limping. His left arm swung free at his side like an appendage that did not belong to his body. He seemed to recognize Anna behind the wheel and stopped, surprised. His face brightened, he smiled, and waved.

"He looks much older," said Kruger.

"He suffered a stroke ten years ago and had to leave San Tommaso. He's half paralyzed now. They put him to work as chaplain to the nuns." She opened her door. "Wait here. I will talk to him."

Kruger watched Anna hurry toward the old priest. She met him halfway down the path, the priest greeted her warmly, and listened intently while she spoke. Kruger recalled the pastor's hatred of everything he had stood for during the war. Alessandro had made no secret of his loyalty to the partisan cause. On the morning of the execution, he had come to the Municipio to plead for the lives of the hostages and offer himself as an exchange for all or even one of the victims. His pleas had been in vain.

Anna gestured to the car. The priest looked up, shocked, and in the bright sunlight the little color there was in his face drained away. Leaving Anna, he started toward the car. In spite of the limp and the paralysis of his right side, he carried himself erect, with dignity. His eyes betrayed no clue to his feelings. He would have been, Kruger realized, the priest who had buried the dead after the execution. As Alessandro approached the car, he was aware only of a burning feeling of shame. He thought of his own quixotic priesthood and wondered if the saintly old parish priest knew as yet that the Church, in ignorance of his past life, had elevated him to the spiritual honors and responsibilities of the *monsignori,* and he was now, in the eyes of the Church, once again superior to the old priest in office. The thought of the misplaced honor made him suddenly feel small.

The old man reached the gravel clearing where the car was parked. He stared at him through the windshield, then nodded and smiled. Limping, swinging his paralyzed arm, he came around the car to the passenger door. "Monsignore Kruger," he said. His speech was slurred by the paralysis of half his face. He extended his good left arm and opened his hand, palm upward. The rich Florentine sound of his Italian had not changed. "You are welcome. Come."

CHAPTER 5

I

Anna rummaged in the bread bin and brought out one of her mother's biscuits. She had not eaten since breakfast. On the drive back from the convent, she had stopped in at the Montecatini, only to learn that the police had come to the hotel a half hour before and collected Kruger's passport and bag. She heard Livia answer the phone again in the living room.

"It's Captain Tedeschini again. It's the fourth time he's called," Livia said from the kitchen door.

"Tell him I'll phone him back. I haven't eaten all day, and I can't talk now."

For the last four hours, every time someone called, she had

repeated the same statement. If Kruger was found, he would be taken to Bologna to a military prison and held until the bureaucratic red tape of charges and warrants caught up with the facts. But knowing Italian bureaucrats, that would take days. She had said nothing more, stalling for time until she could reach the Bologna military authorities herself and arrange for Kruger's safe passage out of Montefalco.

She put the biscuit on a plate and sat down at the kitchen table, feeling exhausted.

She had phoned the chief of military police in Bologna several times, but so far had not gotten through. It was Sunday, they had said. The chief had gone fishing. On the other hand, it was doubtful if Tedeschini could be restrained from searching for Kruger until tomorrow morning. The whole thing was beginning to look like an *opera buffa*.

Livia came back into the kitchen. "He said to tell you that he's issued a local warrant and they're going to search for Kruger. He says there's no way the man could have left the valley in the last six hours."

"He can't issue a warrant. The case is beyond his jurisdiction."

"I didn't argue with the man."

"How does he know he's still here? There are lots of ways he could have left. There was a train at ten twenty-five. And another one at one-fifty."

"Tedeschini says not." She ambled to the table. "How do you know the train schedules?"

"I hear the trains. They're rather hard to miss."

"Where did you go after your meetings with the Moreras and the Turattis this morning?" Livia sat down at the table.

"I had business in town."

"For four hours? Franco Turatti phoned about noon. He said you never showed up."

"I had more important things to do."

"They say Kruger was seen in the Piazza Nazionale at about ten this morning. He left the square and disappeared. Gianni Lancetti said he and the other *contadini* followed him out of the piazza. They looked everywhere, but couldn't find him. That's odd, don't you think, considering how small the town is?"

"What are you suggesting?"

"You found him, didn't you?"

"Don't be ridiculous."

Livia studied her face for a moment. "Your face always looks the same when you lie, did you know that? When we were young and you lied about Kruger, I could always see it in your face. You haven't changed."

Anna got up and left the table to put distance between them. "What would I be doing with Kruger, may I ask?"

"Saving him. Gianni and his friends were going to kill the man. You used my car and took him somewhere. To hide him."

Anna sliced through the cheese and nicked her index finger. She dropped the knife and looked at the tiny red welt of blood.

"You see?" Livia said. "When you lie you get nervous and make stupid mistakes. You've seen him, haven't you? You were with him all morning."

She realized it was useless. Having been party to her adolescent deceptions, Livia could still read her mind like a map. "Yes. I was in the square. They recognized him. Maria Pucetti recognized him. They were going to kill him. That's not the kind of justice I have in mind for him."

"Where did you take him?"

"To a safe place. Tomorrow, I will notify the military police in Bologna. I'll turn him over to them, but not to Tedeschini."

"In other words, you're starting all over again."

Anna sucked at her finger. "I'm doing the only thing possible under the circumstances."

Livia laughed, mockingly. "You haven't changed a bit."

"I know Lancetti and his *contadini,* they will kill him rather than wait for an uncertain trial."

"And when Tedeschini, when the *contadini* find out that you were responsible for his escape, where do you think they will put the blame?"

"They can blame whomever they wish." Anna hurried out the kitchen door.

Livia followed her into the living room. "And when they find out you had an affair with the man—that you have a son by him—who do you think will be blamed for keeping your secrets all these years?"

"You need not concern yourself with taking blame for anything I have done, Livia." She busied herself gathering up papers on the dining-room table.

"It's *enough,* Anna! I have lived all my life with your deceits!"

At Livia's shout, Luisa hurried down the stairs into the living room. "What's going on here?" she demanded, frightened.

"She didn't go to the Moreras or the Turattis, Mamma," said Livia. "She lied. She was with Kruger this morning. She found him and took him someplace in my car. To hide him."

"Anna?" Her mother questioned with disbelief.

"They would have killed him!" Anna turned to the telephone.

Livia followed. "Why don't you tell the truth for once?"

She started to dial the number in Bologna, but could not remember all the digits.

"I want you to go to your room, Livia," Luisa said.

"I'm not a child, Mamma!"

Anna dropped the receiver onto the phone. "I told you, he will be taken by the military police, not by Tedeschini."

"You came to Italy to bring him to trial. Now you've changed your mind. You've seen him twice now, and you've done nothing."

"I've charged him under the law, and he will be tried under the law."

"The *law.*" Livia laughed, contemptuously. "This obsession of yours for the law. It's a pretense." Anna picked up the receiver to dial again, not knowing what number she wanted. "You've lied to yourself for so long you no longer *know* the truth! You didn't come here for justice! You came for revenge!"

"Livia, please don't," their mother pleaded.

"She's *mad,*" Anna said, breathlessly.

"Mamma doesn't understand that you could love and hate the man at one and the same time—Mamma doesn't understand what revenge is. But we do, don't we?"

Anna fumbled with the notepad by the phone, searching for the Bologna number.

"Did you finally tell Kruger about his son?"

"Angelo is not involved."

The telephone began to ring.

"Where did you hide your lover?"

"He is *not* my lover! I will not tell you!"

The phone rang a second time.

"The Adele Ravine?"

Again, the phone rang.

"Santa Cecilia?"

The phone rang a fourth time. "They will kill him," Anna murmured.

"It would be better for both of you if they did."

The phone rang a fifth time, then was silent.

II

High in the convent belfry the old *campanello* gave one more feeble clang, then went silent, leaving the Angelus unfinished. Father Alessandro crossed himself and chuckled. "That would be Sister Veronica pulling. They take turns with the bell. Sister Veronica's old now, she never has the strength to finish."

Kruger smiled. Far off down the valley another bell began to toll the evening Angelus. He stood surveying the priest's chestnut orchard in the garden slope behind the rectory. Father Alessandro had planted the trees over the last ten years, and the tallest were only shoulder-high. None would bear fruit in the old man's lifetime. The clank of the distant Angelus ended, leaving only the faint whistle of wind in the twisted pine trees to define the cloistered silence of the hilltop. Kruger said, returning to their conversation before the Angelus rang, "And Signora Bosco?"

"She kept Gianni's shop. She became a very good tailor herself. But she's almost blind now."

"And Signora Comellini, the old lady who ran the *ammasso*— what became of her?"

"She was lucky. She left Montefalco right after the Americans came and moved to Milano. The *contadini* captured her daughter, her husband, and her son, though. Her daughter had married a German soldier and had given birth to his child. The Americans found their bodies up there near Monte di Granaglione." He pointed to the peak beyond the western flank of the valley. From here one could see all the way north beyond the Adele Ravine, beyond even Montefalco. The sun had just set behind the hills, and the valley already lay obscured by deep shadows. From the northern side of the Adele Ravine came the groan of an engine, and then the headlights of a big truck appeared over the crest.

Kruger said, "Anna told me she would come back before dark."

"In any case, I think you will be safe here for the night." The old priest started back to the rectory. "Come, Monsignore, it's getting dark. It's hard for me to keep my balance in the dark."

Kruger joined the old man shuffling up the hillside. "If the local police do come, Father, I should turn myself over, don't you think?"

"That depends, Monsignore."

"Please call me Karl." The title *monsignore* had an embarrassing, almost feudal ring to it in the old man's half-paralyzed mouth. Kruger breathed in the sweet odor of pine. For the first time in a week, he felt close to the frontier of peace. He said, "If I had known a week ago what I know tonight, I would have been able to salvage something."

"What do you mean?"

"My priesthood, at least. They might have left me with the right to say Mass, if nothing more. This way—" He left off. The old priest took out a handkerchief, wiped the saliva from the paralyzed side of his face, left the conclusion hanging in the air, and shuffled on toward the rectory. "I'd like to ask one more favor from you, Father, before she comes."

"Certainly."

"I want to make my confession."

Alessandro nodded. "We can do it here—now—as we walk." He dug into the pocket of his cassock. "In fact, I even have a stole with me. I keep it in my pocket. The nuns—they like to confess at the strangest times." He looped the purple stole around his neck to keep it from blowing away in the wind, then murmured the opening prayer.

Kruger made the sign of the cross. They walked slowly, side by side. He said, "Bless me, Father, for I have sinned. My last confession was eight days ago, last Saturday." He paused, feeling like a small boy confessing his first mortal sin. "In the last week, Father, I have committed three mortal sins." He recalled his morning abstinence from Communion and his paralyzing fear of approaching the parish priest of San Tommaso to ask for confession. He listened to the old priest's labored breath and took hold of his arm to help him up the rugged slope, then went on, "In choosing to come back to Italy, I acted in disobedience to the wishes of my superior, Cardinal Boyle. I came here without his permission. I believe that was a serious sin of disobedience."

Alessandro nodded.

"Second, I committed in my thoughts the sin of impurity." This, he realized, was the most difficult of the sins to confess. He wondered how much Father Alessandro already knew of his relationship with Anna, whether she had years ago confessed her own sins to the old priest. "My reasons for returning to Italy were not for the good of the Church. There is a woman here in Montefalco . . ." He went on to explain, without using Anna's name, his affair with the woman twenty-eight years before and the fact that he had unwittingly executed both her father and brother. "I came back to ask her forgiveness. Last night, after seeing her, and again today, I committed the sin of impurity in my thoughts. Twice."

Alessandro reached the small garden surrounding the rectory. He stood looking out across the valley and the mountains beyond. "I understand," he said, wiping his mouth again with the handkerchief.

"Finally, I came close, perhaps even committed, the sin of despair. Last night, after seeing the woman, after realizing that the crime I had committed here would follow me for the rest of my life, I entertained the thought of suicide for the second time in my life. This time, I seriously considered it. And the consent of my will—my will to die—was, I believe, as good as the action. The only thing that prevented me was cowardice."

After a moment, Alessandro gave a sigh. "Despair, of course, I mean the loss of hope and the denial of God's charity, is possible only when faith and trust have gone."

"Yes. Exactly. Then you see my predicament, don't you?" The old priest nodded. The wind went on hissing in the pine needles overhead. "I don't trust my faith anymore. Faith asks me to obey the voice of the Church, to trust blindly in the judgment of my superiors. My conscience, on the other hand, tells me I must in justice go to trial for what I have done."

Alessandro dabbed at his mouth again with the handkerchief, looking off fixedly toward the darkening valley. "Speaking priest to priest," he said, "I need not, I hope, admonish you on the subject of God's infinite mercy, Monsignore."

"No." Kruger heard the note of doubt in his own voice.

"What more can I say?" The priest raised his good left hand and gestured helplessly. "You know all the questions and all the answers as well as I."

"Yes, Father."

"For your penance, Karl, say ten Our Fathers and ten Hail Marys, and pray to God for the grace to trust Him again." The knotted stole fluttered up around his neck. "I will give you absolution now." He began the prayer and raised his left hand in the sign of the cross as Kruger said the Act of Contrition. When they finished, Alessandro said, "You ate very little lunch. You must be hungry."

"I'll walk awhile here in the garden, Father, and say my penance." He glanced off toward the Adele Ravine. "If Anna comes, ask her to wait for me."

"Yes." The old priest smiled. "A few more minutes should not matter now."

III

Anna left Livia's car parked in the Via Garibaldi. A crowd of townspeople had gathered in front of the police station in the Via San Vitale. She kept to the darkened side of the street, out of the light. Among the people she saw Carmela Turatti, Giorgio Vianelli, and Lucco Cassla, people who had refused up to now to take part in the American extradition procedure. The rest were *contadini* and women, sons, wives, and daughters of men who had died in the reprisal. They were arguing among themselves, and as Anna reached the station entrance, she felt the roiling heat of blind mob violence. She turned to the door, quickly.

Young Sergeant Lavallo, Tedeschini's deputy, looked up, startled, from the reception-room desk. "Signora Fitzgerald!"

The young sergeant had been a boy at the time of his father's death. She had known his mother. "Those people out there, Roberto," she said, "why have you let them gather like that? What's going on?"

Lavallo got to his feet. "We can't stop them, signora. We can only demand they stay in the street. Word got out that Kruger's hiding somewhere in the valley."

"I want to see the captain, Roberto."

"I'm afraid he's busy, signora." She walked briskly to the open door into Tedeschini's office. The room was filled with cigarette smoke, she saw, and his voice was audible. "Signora Fitzgerald!" Lavallo started to intercept her, but she reached the office door before he could stop her.

The squat balding chief of police sat behind his old-fashioned desk with the telephone crooked in his neck, smoking nervously. He looked up, astonished. "Yes, yes," he said over the telephone, motioning for Anna to sit, "I'll telephone Bishop Cavallotti myself. . . . In the morning, yes. . . . Thank you, Monsignore." He hung up. "Ah! Signora Fitzgerald!" He pushed himself up, smiling with forced cordiality.

Anna closed the door. "What's going on out there, Captain? What do those people want?"

"Nothing to worry about. Please—sit down." She remained standing, and he went on. "The people got word of Kruger's escape. There's a rumor going around that he's still here in the valley. They came to demand we conduct a search." He started around the desk to intercept her as she crossed to a suitcase lying open on a table. "Here, signora. Please sit down."

Anna ignored him. She saw underwear, shirts, and a black cassock. "You took his things from the Montecatini, I see."

"You'll be pleased to know we found everything, signora. His suitcase and his passport."

Anna recalled her demand two days ago that Tedeschini speak to the people about helping with her extradition proceedings. She said, "You know you have no authority to arrest the man here in Montefalco, don't you, Luigi, since no warrant has been issued in Bologna." She turned from the table and crossed to Tedeschini's desk. She saw Kruger's green American passport lying among the papers on the desk.

"I spoke with Major Sanzio, the chief of military police in Bologna," Tedeschini said. "I explained the situation. Since the warrant has not been issued, he tells me he can do nothing. He suggested we deal with the matter ourselves in the meantime."

She sat down in the chair facing the desk. "You mean, stretch the law."

"Sanzio says the warrant of arrest can be issued tomorrow morning when the offices open. In the meantime, as the Americans say— a bird in the hand." He sat down, reached for a cigarette, and gave her a little smile of complicity. "The question now, of course, is where the man is hiding. I'm convinced he's still here in the valley somewhere. There are only two routes out of the Reno." Her cold intractable stare confounded him, and he hurried on. "This morning, after he escaped, I notified Vergato and Spedaletto, and they posted roadblocks. So far, nothing has turned up, but we're sure he's hiding in the hills. He knows them well. He hunted partisans there during the war, they tell me." He lit the cigarette. "Rest assured, signora, if he's here, we'll find him." His eyes bulged as he drew on the cigarette.

"I came here, Luigi, to ask that you let Kruger leave the Reno unharmed. To ask that you allow the police of Bologna or Pistoia to arrest him. He cannot leave Italy without"—she glanced again at the passport—"without his passport. If you arrest him here, if you jail him in Montefalco—even overnight—those people out there—the *contadini*—will never let him leave here alive."

Tedeschini's mouth twitched under the thick black moustache. "Nonsense. You've been away from Montefalco too long, signora. This is a modern town now. You exaggerate the danger."

"I exaggerate nothing. You're not a Tuscan, Luigi, you were not here in '44. You know nothing of what these people feel."

The captain sat back, amazed. "You puzzle me, signora. I don't understand. You were the one who filed charges against this man—you were the one who initiated the entire proceeding."

"Nonetheless—"

"You were the one who demanded these poor people give money for his extradition. And now that he's here . . ." He shrugged.

"My purpose is to see that the law is served, Captain. To see that he stands trial. I have no use for the justice of mob violence."

Tedeschini puffed nervously on his cigarette. "You expect me to do nothing?"

"You have his passport. He cannot leave Italy. He will be arrested before he leaves the Reno Valley."

"Assuming he's still here."

"You know as well as I do that he is."

The small dark eyes narrowed, scrutinizing her face. "What do you mean, signora?"

She thought of the irony now in Livia's accusation. "I want justice, not revenge, Luigi."

He let the cigarette smoke curl up his face. "The fact is, signora, I am an elected official here in Montefalco. Elected by"—he gestured toward the door—"by these people. If I let the man go free, if I make no effort to find him . . ." He stood up. "I'm sorry."

"I see." Anna also stood up, calculating the options that now remained. Her eye rested on Kruger's American passport.

"I've already issued a warrant for Kruger's arrest." Tedeschini left the desk and walked to a map tacked on the wall. "An hour or so ago, I ordered my men to search every house in Montefalco. If they don't find him here in town, they are to search the farms. I assure you, once he is found, every precaution will be taken to ensure his safety." As Tedeschini proceeded to describe his plan for searching the valley, Anna opened her purse. It would, she calculated, take ten minutes to reach the convent and another half hour to clear Tedeschini's zone of jurisdiction. With her back turned toward the captain, she took the passport and dropped it into her purse. Tedeschini tapped the map with his finger. "From there," he said, "they will head south to Spedaletto."

"Forgive me, Captain, I must go now." As she reached the door, the telephone in the outer office began ringing. "I have things to buy for my mother before the shops close."

"I will, of course, keep you informed, Signora Fitzgerald." He seemed relieved.

"Yes, please do." Young Lavallo was on the phone when she stepped into the reception room."

"Yes, Signora Pirelli," she heard him say, "she's with the captain right now." He looked up to see her heading for the front door. "Signora Fitzgerald," he called after her, "it's your sister. She wants to . . ." Anna was through the door before he could finish.

IV

Pairs of headlights fanned through the darkness, first one, then another. In the distance, two automobile engines strained up the hill.

"Go beyond the wall." Father Alessandro pushed Kruger through the rear door of the rectory into the moonlit garden. "There's a gate at the bottom of the garden. Hide outside the walls in the ravine until they've gone."

"If they question you," Kruger said, "tell them the truth."

"Go! Quickly!"

He broke into a run down the slope, dodging between the chestnut trees. At the foot of the garden he passed through a grape arbor and reached a high stone wall. In the light of the half-moon he felt his way along the wall to a heavy wooden gate. Unopened for years, it had rotted loose from its hinges. He rammed the boards with his shoulder, the gate opened, and he found himself on the far side of the wall in a dense grove of overgrown trees. Beyond the wall, there were voices. Flashlights fanned the darkness. For a moment, he stood weighing the balance between surrender and escape. He thought of the ludicrous chain of events in these last twenty-four hours—missed trains, accidental encounters in the streets of Montefalco, Anna's sudden appearance in the Via Mazzini, the convent sanctuary with Alessandro—and he wanted suddenly to laugh! He had come here in disobedience, and God was playing jokes with him!

Nearby, in the orchard behind the wall, someone shouted. A flashlight beam cut through the trees overhead.

Father Alessandro had agreed with Anna. If he was found here in Montefalco, the *contadini* would kill him. Without hesitation, he lunged forward, then realized too late that the ground under his feet was not level. The rocks gave way and he slipped down, rolling head over heel. In the next moment he found himself lying in the shallow bed of a gully. He knew at once where he had come to: the dry bed of a mountain *torrente.* Overhead, a frightened bird fluttered up through the trees. Like all the *torrenti,* the gully would follow the slope of the hill down to the river. He got to his feet.

Through the thicket and behind the wall, the shouts came closer.

He began moving downhill, following the gully's dry clay bed, feeling his way slowly through the darkness.

V

Anna's headlights swept across the white wall of the convent cloister as she reached the crest of the bluff. The grounds outside the cloister were deserted. She rounded the northwest corner of the wall and her headlights fanned across the facade of the rectory. On the drive out, she had passed no police cars. Don Alessandro hurried out as she pulled to a halt. She left the car motor running, jumped out, and met him on the flagstone path. "Where is he, Father? What's happened?" She saw from the expression in the priest's face that her fears had been realized.

"The police came." Alessandro tried to speak quickly, but his words were garbled by the paralysis of his mouth. "I told him to hide—there—down in the ravine below the garden." He pointed. "They searched the grounds. They did not find him. I told them he must have gone south toward Spedaletto." He sighed. "When they left, I called to him. I went to find him. But he—he's gone. He has not come back."

"Gone where?"

"I don't know. The mountains. He talked earlier about the *burroni*—the places where the partisans hid when he was here during the war. He knows the mountains."

The *burroni* were the ravines cut into the mountainsides around Montefalco. "Which *burrone?*"

"He did not say, Anna."

In the moonlight she could see the ridge of the Adele Ravine less than a quarter of a mile away. She said with a strange feeling of amazement, "Never mind, Father. I know which one." She started to turn.

"Anna!" The old priest caught her arm. "The police—they know you helped him. They know you brought him here to the convent. Tedeschini phoned while the police were here. He ordered them to arrest you, too."

"My sister told him," she said, "my sister's responsible."

"Your sister? I don't understand."

"I can't explain." She started back to her car. "If he comes back, Father, tell him to wait for me here."

"Anna! You must not look for him!"

She kept moving, though, thinking of Livia's betrayal. *Mamma doesn't understand that you could love and hate the man at one and the same time—Mamma doesn't understand what revenge is. But we do, don't we?* The backwash of twenty-eight years' resentment for carrying *her* burdens. Livia had learned well.

She found her sister's flashlight in the glove compartment and tested the batteries. Alessandro stood watching, bewildered. She threw the car into reverse and swung backward to turn, thinking of the laughable ironies of chance and circumstance, the possibility of ending where they had begun.

VI

Kruger rested against the boulder, taking deep breaths to slow his racing heartbeat. The climb up the ridge and the descent down into the Adele Ravine had once been an easy task for him. He rested his head against the damp mossy stone and looked back into the darkness at the wedge-end of the ravine. He would be safe here for the time being. Anna had said the police knew nothing about their use of the ravine years before.

The underbrush looked denser now and the trees much taller than before, but the ravine itself was unchanged. Nearby, the river water swirled around the rocks along the bank. As always in early evening, a mist hung over the water. That was the same. And the sweet woody odor of pine was the same. He remembered how soothing the wild natural smells here had once been. He had sat with Anna by the river many times, listening to the peaceful sound of rushing water.

His heartbeat slowed, and he felt a sense of calm return. Pushing free, he sat down at the water's edge.

His options now: to wait here in the ravine until morning or walk back into town tonight. There was no way out of the valley, save the highway and the paths through the mountains. If the police knew he was still here, then the *contadini* probably knew, and they would watch the mountain paths.

Odd, though, that the police came to the convent. Anna had said it was the last place they would think to look. Could she have changed her mind and told them? Wait at the convent, she had said, I will come back before dark.

He picked up a small pebble and tossed it into the black swirling water. It vanished noiselessly.

No. She would not have done that. It was purely accidental.

He threw another pebble and it, too, vanished noiselessly into the darkness.

He smiled. Maybe God has lost patience with me. The cardinal said one thing and I did another. Maybe God has simply lost patience and let go of the rope.

He took a still larger pebble and threw it, but it, too, disappeared into the rushing water, as if into nothingness.

Amazing, he thought, how ludicrous things can become when God lets go of the rope and things fall from Providence to chance. Boyle had talked about spiritual trials, God's kind of trial; and now, having pushed God too far, there would not even be the absolution of a human trial.

You were mad to come here! If these people find you, they will kill you, and if they kill you without the benefit of a trial, it will be no better than the justice you handed out in 1944.

Funny, after seventeen years as a priest, I should have known better than to gamble with God. I have gambled with God for Anna, and I have lost the forgiveness of both.

He recalled that night in the Montecatini after the execution. I did it here in Montefalco once before, gambled and lost both. With Anna and another god.

He picked up another stone but did not bother to throw it.

Those young *contadini* who chased him that morning, the old woman who screamed at him—after so long, their rage was in the blood now.

He dropped the stone and got up, feeling suddenly weary. The walk back to town was not a long one. He was merely postponing things here. I will take the railroad tracks along the river, that's the shortest route. I'm familiar with the way, God knows: it hasn't changed since the night I walked back to town with Anna to meet another—he smiled—a perhaps more heroic death.

He started across the rocks toward the woods, then stopped and looked around, wondering if he had imagined a noise back in the underbrush behind the grove. Nothing. He started again, then heard a limb snap. A bird—a black *corvo*—fluttered up from the trees, startled, and winged its way into the darkness across the river. When he turned back, a flashlight beam cut through the darkness behind the grove.

He thought, grasping for straws, not like this—a victim of meaningless circumstance—not as long as I have some choice.

He looked to the river, weighing his chances across the thundering rapids midstream, then realized again he was merely postponing the inevitable.

The underbrush cracked behind him. He turned. The flashlight beam came to rest on his face. In the blinding light, he blinked and waited. The light went out, but the blindness stayed with him. The underbrush at the riverbank moved and snapped. There were small panicky female sounds; and then, before his vision came back, he saw someone emerge from the grove. He said, recognizing the woman's outline, "Anna?"

It was ludicrous how far chance could be stretched.

He stood riveted to the rocks, recognizing her, but refusing to move. She stumbled forward over a loose rock. "Karl!" The sound of his Christian name, thrown out without thinking, startled her. She, too, stood riveted.

He came to her in the darkness, murmuring something to himself.

"Hurry," she said, still panting, out of breath from the race down, "you must leave. At once."

He stopped a few feet away. "How did you know?"

"Don Alessandro—he told me—he said you went—you went to the *burroni*—I knew which one."

"You came down alone—in the dark?"

The question was idiotic. "I had to! You can't stay here! The police know, Karl!"

"How?"

"Never mind how. Alessandro told them you went south, but they'll figure it out, they'll come back. You've got to leave!"

He shook his head. "It's pointless. There's no way out of the valley."

"There is. I have my sister's car. I'll drive you to Bologna myself."

"If they find us together, they'll arrest you, too."

"They will arrest me, anyway. They know. The *contadini* know, too. They'll form search parties, they'll look for us both now."

He considered what she had said. "Go back home, Anna. The *contadini* have no reason to harm you."

"My sister told them! Everything!"

With ignorant obstinacy, he refused to move. "That was a long time ago. They can't still hold that against you. Go back home. They'll harm you only if they find us together."

She realized they were racing in circles. He knew nothing of what Livia had told them. "You don't understand. I can't go back, not tonight. They know that I tricked them. I lied to them."

"That was twenty-eight years ago. They won't hurt you just because you hid me at the convent!" he pleaded.

"You don't understand! You don't know what they did to Ursula Comellini!"

He stared at her, perplexed.

Across the river, a flashlight beam suddenly cut through the darkness. "Paulo!" a voice called.

"The police," he said.

"No, Karl." She began to cry. "The *contadini.*"

He sighed, looked down, and dug his hands into his pockets. "Go back, Anna. Do as I say. This is the best way—for everyone. Believe me."

"You will die if you stay here!"

He nodded. Then for an instant they stared at each other, both realizing she had said the words once before. She remembered: the Comellini *ammasso.* The afternoon he offered her family transportation out of the valley, the afternoon she came face to face with the opportunity to tell him about the child and lost it.

"Paulo! Mario!" It was Antonio Faggioni's voice. "This way! Over these rocks!" His flashlight came to rest on the opposite bank.

She grabbed hold of his hands and pulled them from his pockets. "This time, we will both die. They've come here to kill us both."

"But why?"

She shook her head, pleading. "Trust me. For once, trust me."

Another beam inched its way toward them on the riverbank.

He acquiesced and let her lead him across the rocks into the safety of the grove. The flashlight passed the place on the rocks where they had stood seconds before. A man cursed in the darkness on the opposite bank. As they passed the spot in the grove where they had made love twenty-eight years before, he tried in his mind to reach out to the ludicrous limits of human chance but saw, instead, the amazing limits of something else—the other thing.

My sister told them! Everything! You don't understand! You don't know what they did to Ursula Comellini!

Father Alessandro had said that Ursula Comellini had married a German soldier and had given birth to his child. The *contadini* had killed her after the war.

He pulled her to a halt in the darkness under the trees. "Anna. I want to know. Now. Why do they want to kill you?"

She began to cry, openly, as she had cried that afternoon in the Comellini *ammasso*. But this time, it was not a child he heard in the darkness, but a woman. She moved closer, but he still could not see her face.

"Ursula—they killed her because—because she had a child. A German's child . . . When you left here, I was pregnant. . . . You have a child . . . a son . . ."

CHAPTER 6

I

She drove without headlights, and there was only the light of a slip of a moon to steer the car by. Neither of them dared to speak. Down the hairpin curves leading from the ridge into the valley she kept waiting for headlights to appear from the opposite direction. Don Alessandro had said the police had turned south when they left the convent. A quarter of a mile beyond the convent, she ventured, finally, "We'll go south through Pistoia and then take the road back north through the Futa Pass to Bologna. We can't risk going through Montefalco." He said nothing, nor had she expected him to. Ahead, two bends down the road, headlights moved toward them through the trees. She let up on the accelerator.

He read her mind. "There's a dirt road ahead."

She had seen it already, a small road angling off up the hillside. She braked and turned from the highway. A hundred feet up the road, she swung off and came to rest in a small grove of trees and cut the motor. They sat in silence, waiting for the car to pass, each waiting for the other to speak. Karl rolled down his window. The only sound was the monotonous rasp of crickets outside.

He was the first to speak. She knew, before he asked the question, what it would be. "Why didn't you tell me?"

The habit of silence and hatred, she realized, was so old that it was very hard to break. She did not even know where to begin. She said, "I wanted to keep . . . I had to keep the personal issues separate." She knew, of course, that she had meant the silence of years before, in the beginning, not this last week's silence, but she stumbled on nonetheless. "I told myself that the criminal charges had nothing to do with—" She left off, grateful for the sound of the approaching car, grateful for a last postponement. The headlights fanned across the highway below as the car rounded the bend. But neither of them, she realized, was now in the least afraid. For a while, there was silence again, as he waited patiently for her to go on. Then she said, "When you left me here—in September of '44, when you left me behind—I was pregnant." The word made her neck and ears ache. She closed her eyes, looking for words that would not carry the bitterness and hatred she had felt for twenty-eight years, but there was no way to avoid either. "I did not know at the time. I wasn't sure. Then you left. And it was too late. I gave birth to your son in 1945." She had so long imagined the announcement as an accusation and indictment that the telling of it now seemed like an afterthought. It left her with a strange feeling of emptiness, as if Angelo's birth had been something they had both missed. She covered her face, wanting but unable to weep.

Mamma doesn't understand that you could love and hate the man at the same time—Mamma doesn't understand what revenge is.

He breathed out a single word: "God."

She lowered her hands. "I have hated you for twenty-eight years. I came back here telling myself I wanted justice. But I didn't. I wanted revenge."

"I killed your father and brother."

"Not for them. For myself."

Her statement—her confession—silenced them both. Leaving her headlights off, she started the motor and reversed into the dirt road. The highway was deserted when they reached the foot of the hill. She turned south toward Spedaletto.

"Where is he?"

"In America. He lives in Connecticut."

"What month of 1945?"

"June."

He considered the month for a moment. "He would be twenty-seven years old now."

"Yes. He was born here in Italy. In Florence." A feeling of relief came over her like the relief of confession, and she went on, "After you left, I stayed in Montefalco until the Americans came. Till November. By then . . . by then, I was beginning to show. I couldn't stay." The story came out piecemeal—her marriage to Charles Fitzgerald, their move to America with the boy, the explanation of the Italian soldier she had invented to protect herself and the boy, her alibi, which became in later years a nightmare labyrinth from which she could not escape. As she spoke, she saw that she had left out whole sections of her life—the misery of the DP camp, the years following the war when she lived for the day she would find and denounce him, the relief she had felt to finally learn from her sister that he had been listed by the Germans as killed in action—but there was too much to tell in so little time. They reached the outskirts of Spedaletto. "I never told the boy who you were," she said. "He thinks his father died in the Second World War."

"And your husband? Where is he?"

"Charles is dead," she said, ashamed to announce it as an afterthought.

He looked at her. "You didn't say."

"He died in 1964."

"I'm sorry."

She thought she detected a note of relief in his voice. "It wasn't a perfect marriage, but he was a good man."

"Did you love him?"

"Yes and no. Love like we—you and I—had was impossible."

He nodded. "I never tried again."

His admission left her speechless, and for a while they drove again in silence. She turned on her headlights as they drew up behind a truck. They neared the village and the valley began to narrow abruptly. Spedaletto was the last village before the Porretta Pass.

"We bombarded Spedaletto," he said.

"Yes. And we rebuilt it after the war."

The truck slowed to a crawl across the narrow stone bridge to the eastern side of the river. They reached the commercial section of the small village. She checked both sides of the road for signs of police cars.

He said, "The boy . . . my son . . . what's his name?"

"Angelo. Angelo Piero Fitzgerald."

"After your father and brother."

"Yes." The truck turned from the highway into a service station. She sped up and passed a small roadside market and tavern.

"How you must have hated me," he said.

"Yes." She thought back over the years, marveling at the force of her obsession. "Love and hatred are the same thing. Two sides of the same coin."

"Like guilt and fear."

The last house in the village went by. The mountains closed in abruptly, forming a deep ravine rising up to the Porretta Pass. She crossed still another bridge, this one to the western side of the ravine.

"And the boy knows nothing about me?"

"Nothing. I told his stepfather before he was born that he was the son of an Italian soldier I had married in 1944. After that, I couldn't—didn't—retrace my steps. He grew up thinking his father was a war hero." She recalled the afternoon at Charles' gravesite when Angelo announced he had re-enlisted. "I told him the Germans had killed his father."

"He still thinks I'm a dead Italian?"

"Yes." She pressed down on the accelerator to begin the winding ascent up the Porretta Pass. The road threaded its way in a series of sharp curves sheltered from the moonlight by cliffs on either side. A dense mist from the nearby cataracts obscured the thrust of her headlights. Karl braced himself against the swing of the car. She was thinking of what lay ahead for him in Bologna, when she realized her reckless speed was pointless. They had gone beyond Tedeschini's jurisdiction. She let up on the accelerator. "Tell me the truth. When you left here, did you suspect I was pregnant?"

"No."

"Did you know I was in the square that morning?"

"Yes."

"Did it make any difference to you that I was watching?"

"Yes."

"But not enough to stop you."

"No. I knew what they ordered me to do—what I did—was wrong. I knew those men were innocent. I knew I would never see you again, and you would never forgive me. But I told myself I was a soldier, and it was my duty. Back then, duty came before everything."

"And afterward, did you ever change your mind? I mean, about duty?"

"I deserted near Vergato in October. I was captured by the Americans. I changed my mind, yes. But it was too late to change anything else."

"So you became a priest."

"Yes."

She slowed to meet an oncoming car. "Why?"

"Guilt, to begin with. Then, later, I told myself I could make up with good for the evil I had done."

"Did you?"

"No."

She considered the truth of his reply, then said, "Yesterday—today—I think I saw signs of a very *good* priest."

"I am an average priest, Anna." They were nearing the crest of the pass. Her headlights passed through a fog bank. "I disobeyed my superior in coming here. What you saw was a man."

"Doing his duty?"

"Yes."

Her headlights illuminated a roadsign ahead: Paso de Collina. "Then what kind of duty was it that made you come back?" She was sounding like an attorney questioning a defendant.

"You know the answer to that, you said it this morning on the way to the convent. Guilt and fear are just as blinding as hatred. I told myself I was coming to save the Church from scandal, but I merely wanted forgiveness."

"I see." She tried to imagine forgiveness, but it sounded like a foreign word to her. Like the habit of silence and hatred, the habit of revenge was so old that it would be just as hard to break.

He said, like an awkward afterthought, "And to see you."

They reached the summit of the pass. Thinking of the monstrous mistakes they had made here in Italy, his little afterthought brought tears to her eyes. "I brought you here for revenge, Karl, not justice. I should have left things as they were."

"You can maybe forgive me for what I did to you, but not for what I did to the others. There are the Cimonis—there's Paula Bosco, the Pucettis, and the *contadini*. There's Maria Pucetti, there's your mother and your sister. They have the right to a trial."

The road began its twisting descent down the southern slope of the pass toward Pistoia. That long-familiar feeling of urgency—of crossroads reached and choices to be made—suddenly gripped her. "Those people—the majority—they don't want justice. They want reparation money from the German Government. I heard them talking yesterday, and tonight they were talking again. They want money."

"Their motives for wanting a trial have nothing to do with justice."

He was right, of course. It was the weakest of arguments. She thought again of what awaited him in Bologna, weighing the good to be gained against the good to be lost. "Your archbishop was right. Trying you now for what you did as a soldier will only destroy what you have done as a priest."

"I think God will manage."

"How? You've already judged and sentenced *yourself*." She

braked on a curve, remembering what she carried in her purse. The dark Tuscan plain appeared below through the hills. She thought, thirteen years of practicing law. This will be the hardest case of all. "Answer this question, Karl," she said, "answer it as a priest. Can a Catholic—can a man—commit a sin in order to accomplish something good?"

"Why do you ask?"

She braked again, stalling for time. The twinkling lights of Pistoia came into view below. "Please answer the question."

"No. The means does not justify the end."

She knew she was arguing now outside her competence, from moral rather than civil law. She said, "It was a sin, wasn't it, for you to come here? A sin of disobedience."

"Yes."

"And by coming here without your cardinal's permission, you leave the Church no choice. You will lose your priesthood, won't you?"

"Yes."

"In other words, the right thing for you to have done was to ask permission from the Vatican to go to trial," she said, choosing her words carefully.

"It's too late for that now. . . . Yes, that would have been the right thing."

She braked behind a slow line of cars snaking its way down the cliffside. "Tell me this, then. If you had the choice to make again—I mean as a priest—would you first ask permission to stand trial?"

He shrugged. "I suppose so. But that's neither here nor there."

She could not, of course, stop the machinery of law here in Italy, but she could slow it down, play for time. They passed the roadside indicating Montecatini to the west. And, ahead, the roadside pointing to the Futa Pass to the east. She quickly calculated the amount in traveler's checks in her purse.

He pointed. "There. On the left. That's the shortcut to the Futa Pass. We can avoid Pistoia."

She took, instead, the right fork to Montecatini.

"Anna . . . ?" He looked at her, baffled. "You took the wrong one. We want to go east, to Prato."

"I know."

"It will take all night to reach Bologna this way."

"We're not going to Bologna."

"What do you mean, not . . . ?"

"We're going first to Lucca. From there, to Milano—to the international airport. To Mertinza." They passed the turnoff to Capo di Strada, the last exit south into the valley. She said, "I have money with me. You can take the next flight out of Italy. There's no warrant yet for your arrest. They can't stop you. Once you're out, you can connect with a flight back to America."

"Don't be foolish, Anna. I have no passport."

She smiled, comparing twenty-eight years to the infinitesimal space of two short days, thinking how easy it was to make choices when you let go of ignorance and selfishness. She opened her purse and fished out his passport. "Trust me."

II

They left the car parked in the unloading zone outside the departure terminal at Mertinza, the international airport west of Milan. At 1:15 in the morning, the terminal was all but deserted. Inside, they checked the electronic schedule, found a BOAC London departure at 1:46, and booked a single one-way seat with the only ticket agent working at that hour, a young Italian in his mid-twenties. Seeing the disheveled appearance of their clothes, the boy was at first suspiciously puzzled. Recent hijackings, Kruger concluded. Anna paid for the ticket with her traveler's checks.

"Your passport, Mr. Kruger?" the boy asked. Kruger handed him the passport with its American eagle seal on the cover. "You have no baggage, Mr.—" The young man broke off, taken back by the photo inside. Kruger glanced down at the passport photo and saw that he was dressed in clericals and a Roman collar.

He had forgotten about the photo. "No, nothing." He was listed, moreover, as "Rt. Rev. Monsignor Karl G. Kruger."

Anna saw his confusion and embarrassment. "Is there someplace open where we can have sandwiches and coffee while he's waiting?" she asked to fill the awkward silence while the young man took down the name and passport number.

"Yes, signora." The agent pointed with his pen. "There's a coffee shop near the departure ramp."

The boy returned the passport. "Here you go, sir." He smiled as if to acknowledge an intrigue. "I've—uh—listed you as *Mr.* Kruger on the ticket."

"That's fine." He blushed. Anna seemed amused by his predicament.

"Have a pleasant trip, sir." The boy handed him the ticket and the boarding card.

They walked in silence down the vast terrazzo-floored waiting area toward the departure gates. He tried to think of something appropriate to say, but there was nothing left to speak of except things that touched on his personal feelings.

Anna, too, seemed constrained by silence.

So far, he had asked only polite reserved questions about his son, calling him "the boy," not daring to claim the familiarity of "Angelo," but by the time they ordered coffee and sandwiches, he had thought of the last time, years before, when they had separated with essential things left unsaid. "The boy—Angelo. My son. Tell me what he looks like."

She seemed both surprised and relieved. She reached for her purse. "How stupid of me. I have a photo with me in my billfold." She removed a small photo from the plastic envelope inside.

It was a bad photo, the kind one purchased from a public vending machine. The boy wore an army uniform but no cap. The face was that of a handsome young soldier, grinning awkwardly at the automatic camera. The features were blurred, but the jawline, the nose, and the cheekbones looked strong. He had short dark hair. The eyes were light.

"It's the most recent I have," she said. "He took it himself in 1967. He sent it to me just before he left for Vietnam."

He steadied himself against the table. "He's got your hair and your cheekbones."

"The eyes are blue-green." She added, "He has your jaw. Stubborn."

He thought back twenty-eight years to the plan they had shared for a child after the war ended: he had wanted a boy, she a girl, but they had compromised with one of each. "He's married, you say?" he asked. The pain of lost years came back, this time with the sharper edge of grief.

"To a girl from Connecticut named Sarah. Piero has just had his second birthday."

"Funny." He smiled, awkwardly. "I mean, to think I'm a grandfather."

"Karl . . ." She sat forward. "When I finish here in Italy, I'll go back to New York. I will tell Angelo everything. He will want to meet you."

He nodded. "If it can be arranged, I'd like that."

The voice came over the PA system, *"Signori e signore, annunciamo . . ."* The woman announced the immediate boarding of the

BOAC flight to London in both Italian and English. "Passengers will proceed at once to Passport Control."

Anna said, hurriedly, "One thing you should know. He was in Vietnam twice. When he came back the second time, he wasn't himself. The war changed him."

He thought of the young men in his parish at home who had come back from Vietnam "changed," as she called it. He thought, too, of the changes he and Anna had suffered in their own war. "War has a way of doing that, doesn't it? The young are the ones who end up paying. For both sides."

"This war . . ." She hesitated. "His war was different from ours. Perhaps when you meet him . . ." She let the sentence die.

The voice over the PA was droning on. ". . . This is the final call for BOAC Flight Thirty-eight to London. Passengers holding boarding cards will proceed to . . ."

"It's time," he said.

"Yes."

"We haven't eaten." He pointed to the untouched food.

"I guess there wasn't time, after all."

He handed her the photo. "Here."

"No. You keep it." She smiled as she got up. "I have others."

"Your purse, Anna." He tucked the photo into his pocket and got up.

"Oh." She reached back to the table. "I'm so forgetful."

He saw her face waver between panic and resignation as she turned to the door. Over the years as a priest he had learned to read faces. She had wanted to say something at that moment of immense importance, but the opportunity had passed by. Forgetful? he thought, following her. Anything but forgetful.

They joined the fifteen or so passengers moving down the departure ramp toward Passport Control. Again, an impassable silence fell.

"Your passport and ticket," she said to fill the vacuum.

"I have them."

She reached into her purse and took out several American bills. "Here. You'll need money. Take this."

He remembered he had only a few American dollars left. "Thanks. I'll pay you back in America."

"Whenever. You forget, I've become a rich woman since you knew me."

He remembered the image of a very pretty small-town girl who prided herself on a few pretty clothes, who used to confide in him her secret fantasies of the big wonderful mysterious world beyond Montefalco. Again, as they neared the Passport Control booth, he had the familiar panicky feeling of missed connections: essential things left unsaid and undone.

"Remember what I said about an attorney," she was saying in a small shaky voice. "Whatever the Church decides, Karl, you will need experts in both international and Church law."

"I understand." He thought, this is not what either of us wants to say.

They came to a halt behind an Englishman in holiday ski clothes. On an impulse, seeing only seconds remaining, he said, "When you see Angelo—when you see the boy—" His face burned with both grief and shame. "Please tell him something for me. Just tell him I did not leave Montefalco knowing about him."

"I will tell him." He saw her eyes flood, but she kept her gaze on the Passport Control booth.

The man in the ski clothes passed through the booth. "You know the name of my parish. Write me," he said, starting to turn.

"Karl." She took his sleeve, and he turned back. "One thing more. The forgiveness will come. But it will take time."

"I understand." He left her and moved toward the officer in the booth. Waiting for the man to glance through his passport, he looked back at Anna. She stood apart from the crowd, watching. He moved on through the booth. A few feet along, he turned again to look back: a lot could be said, he realized, with merely a look.

The passengers at the booth blocked his view of the ramp.

Despite the years that had gone by, he was sure she would understand what he meant by a look.

He crossed to the far side of the ramp and craned to see, but she was gone.

VI
1972

CHAPTER 1

I

Cardinal Boyle paced the length of the study, pausing to raise the shades on each of the three windows, then stood and looked out at the gray February morning. He was small and fragile in his white clerical shirt and black trousers. "All in a week," he reflected aloud.

"Yes, Your Eminence," Kruger said. The old leather of the chair creaked. A second button began flashing on the cardinal's desk phone. In the last hour, he had taken no calls.

"You arrived in Montefalco on Saturday night, and you left on Sunday night?"

"Yes, Your Eminence."

"And you knew even before you went there that she had filed the charges?"

"Yes."

"One thing I don't understand, Karl." The cardinal folded his hands behind his back. "Aside from making a useless trip to Montefalco, why did you stay on after you saw her?"

He thought back to the beginning of the long narrative he had given Boyle over the last hour. He had left out the business of the evening Bologna train. "I missed my train, Your Eminence," he replied, feeling like a delinquent schoolboy, "there was only one train out that night, and I missed it."

"So you spent the night and toured the town the next morning."

"The next train was at ten twenty-five."

"And after she found you, she didn't turn you over to the police?"

"No."

"Between Saturday night and Sunday morning she changed her mind?"

Kruger shifted impatiently in his chair. He had gone through every detail of the events leading up to his return to America, save those of his and Anna's personal feelings. The cardinal was now arranging the facts in a more logical sequence. "Saturday afternoon, Your Eminence," he said, qualifying.

"And then she told you about the child—your son."

"Yes."

Boyle began turning the ring on his finger behind his back. It was a tic Kruger had noticed over the years when the prelate was angry. "I see."

"She had wanted to keep the boy out of it. There is no legal connection between the personal and the criminal issues."

"I understand the *human* disjunction, Karl." The cardinal raised the window two inches to let in air. "What I am concerned with now is the larger"—he turned from the window and walked toward his desk—"shall we say, the *spiritual* disjunction."

He returned to the original purpose of his appointment. He had spoken with Boyle last night when he returned home and told him at the outset that he wanted permission to stand trial in Italy. In their fifteen-minute phone conversation, he had drawn a broad outline of his present dilemma. "I came back," he said, "to ask your help with the Vatican. You are the only one with authority, Your Eminence, who knows me as a priest."

The cardinal took his time seating himself. The telephone light went on again, but he ignored it. He drew his chair close to the desk and said, "She let you leave Italy, knowing that extradition would afterward be very difficult."

"Knowing that I want to return and stand trial."

"And if the Church refuses your request?"

"I hope that it won't."

"I see." Boyle made a painful face. "The fact that you have a son does not help your case."

"I was a layman, a soldier, at the time."

"I mean your public image. The press and the media will make no distinction between what you *were* and what you *are*. They will use your priesthood against you." He smiled thinly. "A priest with an illegitimate child is always a good story."

"The child is twenty-seven years old."

"Nonetheless." Boyle opened a manila folder on his desk and made a note on one of the pages. "While you were in Italy, did you make contact with the ecclesiastical authorities there?"

"No. There wasn't time."

"Good. The Vatican does not like us to short-circuit the chain of authority." Boyle flipped through the papers in the folder and drew out a page. "In your absence, Karl, I phoned Cardinal Fiorelle, the Secretary for Canonical Affairs in Rome. I explained what I knew of your case and asked for a preliminary opinion on the Church's position in this kind of matter. The case, he told me, is very unusual. As far as he knows, there has been only one other case of a cleric holding ecclesiastical office who has been charged with war crimes. He emphasized that the principle guiding the Church's position is the well-being of the Church as a *whole.*"

"I do not ask to keep my office. I ask only for the right to exercise one of the powers of my priesthood, to say Mass."

"If you wish to keep any rights as a priest, you must be prepared to obey the Holy Father's wishes."

Kruger sat back, racing in his mind for arguments. They all led to the same end. He said, "I have committed a serious crime. I will not be free of my guilt until I stand trial in a secular criminal court. It's a matter of conscience."

The cardinal sighed and sat back. "I understand, Karl." He strained for patience. "You have responsibilities as a man and responsibilities as a priest, and in this case they do not coincide. Perhaps you should re-examine your conscience and see which responsibility involves the greatest good, the Church's or your own."

"The Holy Father knows there is no higher court than a man's conscience."

"Let me put it this way." The cardinal smiled again, this time pointedly. "Take a Catholic, any Catholic. What if, after careful self-examination, a Catholic comes to the conclusion that he cannot in conscience continue to believe, say, in the doctrine of papal infallibility? In that case, where does the Catholic in question look for a final court of appeal?"

"Faith," Kruger murmured.

"Just so." Boyle returned the page to the folder and sat back. An image flashed before Karl's mind: himself, at twenty-one, dressed in the uniform of a Wehrmacht cadet, standing at attention on the parade ground of the *Offiziersschule. I, Karl Gustav Kruger, swear by God this sacred oath, that I will render unconditional obedience to Adolf Hitler.* Across the desk, the cardinal went on talking: something about immigration, citizenship, and extradition. Kruger tried to listen, but could not free his mind from the thought of the widening space between him and Boyle. *Faith:* he said the word silently to himself, and it fell like a pebble on the surface of a pond, with shock waves rolling out in circles from the center. "Karl?" The cardinal's voice brought him back.

"Sorry. You were saying?"

"I was saying that it will be difficult for the Italians to win an extradition suit against you. The charges were filed long after your citizenship was granted."

"In my opinion, Your Eminence, that is merely a legal nicety. Charged or not, I have lived with the crime for twenty-eight years."

Boyle ignored the hint of anger in his voice. "I will submit your request, Karl, to the Vatican. I will use what influence I have. Your record as a priest for the last seventeen years will serve you well. In the meantime, until we know the Holy Father's will, I must enjoin you under your vow of obedience to do and say nothing publicly about this matter. This time, I trust you will obey."

"Yes, Your Eminence."

"Undoubtedly, the press in Italy and Europe will soon learn of the charges against you and your visit to Montefalco. The news will spread to the press here in America, to Los Angeles." He sat forward and reopened the folder. "I have made arrangements, meanwhile, for you to withdraw temporarily from the public eye." He drew out a page and perused it. "There is a small mission some miles from the town of Desert Hot Springs. The pastor is an elderly priest, Father Emilio Mendoza. I've known him a long time. I believe you speak Spanish, no?"

"Yes, but it's rusty."

"Father Mendoza's parishioners speak little English. You will remain there until the Vatican makes known the Holy Father's will. Father Mendoza will explain what your duties will be."

"My forty days in the desert?"

Boyle smiled. "Prayer and penance—what is Lent for?" He looked down for a moment, and the smile dissolved. "I take it, Karl, you know what the Vatican will do if they refuse your request and you disobey—if you return to Italy without the Holy Father's permission."

"Yes, Your Eminence."

"I have never in twenty years as archbishop here had to inform a priest that he has been laicized by the Vatican. If you go to trial without the Holy Father's consent, the Vatican will hold a trial *in absentia*. If you are found guilty of grave and publicly scandalous disobedience, you will lose your priesthood altogether, and all its rights and privileges."

"I understand."

Boyle pushed back his chair and rose. "In your absence, Father Auden will take over as pastor of St. Luke's."

"He is a capable young man." He rose, thinking of the sermon he had given two Sundays ago: *Faith, trust, commitment, responsibility—there is a direct connection between those Christian virtues and the virtue of penance.*

"He's had the advantage of a good example, so far." Boyle circled the desk and held out his hand, palm downward, indicating he would abide by formalities this time.

Kruger genuflected and kissed the blood-red stone in the episcopal ring. The cardinal's gesture was calculated, he realized, to remind him of his vow of obedience. As he started up, Boyle reached down, grasped him by the arm, and helped him to his feet. "Thank you," he said, embarrassed.

"I guess we're both getting on now." Boyle chuckled. They started together down the length of the room. "One more thing, Karl. This woman, the mother of your son, I gather despite everything that she still loves you."

The statement took him by surprise. "She has forgiven me for what I did to her. Yes, that is a kind of love. But she knows she cannot forgive me for what I did to the others."

"And you? What are your feelings toward her?"

"My feelings are irrelevant. She is a Catholic, and I'm a priest."

The cardinal nodded, pleased by the reassurance. "In other words, nothing has changed."

"Nothing."

"Good. I merely wondered."

II

A light snow had fallen overnight, but by two o'clock the next afternoon, when Anna left the office and finally located a rent-a-car with good snow tires, it had begun to melt, turning the Merritt Parkway and the secondary roads leading up to Stevenson into shallow rivers of slush. The drive up to Connecticut had taken an hour and a half longer than she had anticipated, and it was close to 5:30 when she pulled into Swenson's Mobil station near the Indian Well turnoff, two miles below the farm. While old Mr. Swenson filled the tank, Anna checked her makeup in the rearview mirror. She looked tired, but that could not be helped. For the last eighteen days, she had been like a squirrel again, racing inside the wheel. She had stayed on in Bologna for a week after Karl left, trying futilely to reverse what she had started. She had withdrawn financial support for the American extradition trial in an effort to block the Italian side of the procedure, but had failed when the people of Montefalco took charge of the American litigation. Spisani had informed her that the trial would go forward in America. She had returned to New York after a week to set the wheels of Karl's American defense in motion, contacting Pete Kramer, an expert in international law who had worked closely with Charles at the UN, to assess the chances of success in the extradition proceedings. Pete had gotten back to her five days later, saying he thought Karl's defense was probably fifty-fifty, considering the fact that the charges were filed long after citizenship was granted.

Anna paid for the gas with a credit card. While Mr. Swenson wrote up the ticket, they talked about weather. As far as snow was concerned, Mr. Swenson informed her, you never knew in the first week of March if this was the last one or not.

"Fifty-fifty," said Anna.

"Here you go, Mrs. Fitzgerald." Swenson handed her the ticket to sign.

"Has Angelo been down lately?" she asked.

"No, ma'am. Not for—oh, maybe a month or so. Sarah comes in, though. She's been buying the gas. Haven't talked to Angelo in some time." She could tell that Swenson knew more than he wanted to say. He tore off the receipt. "Good to see you, Mrs. Fitzgerald," he said, "it's been a while."

"Since December." She smiled and took the receipt.

"Tell Angie hello for me."

"I will. Thank you, Mr. Swenson."

She pulled out into the narrow highway. The slush would freeze tonight, making the drive back to town twice as dangerous. She turned on her headlights. She had forgotten how quickly the gray smoky twilight descended in the Connecticut hills. The sky and the snow-covered landscape were the same lead-colored gray.

She passed the old lodge and slowed for the turnoff to the farm.

Last night, when she phoned to ask if she could drive up for a visit, Sarah had answered. Angelo, she had said, was out at the barn. "But we'd love for you to come up."

Anna turned into the road leading to the farm. It was covered with an inch of closely packed snow, and her wheels spun. She let up on the accelerator and eased forward.

Last week, when she returned from Italy, she had phoned Angelo to say she was back, but made no mention of the reasons for her trip. It had taken a whole week to steel herself for this visit. What she had to tell Angelo was, she knew, merely the tip of a much larger iceberg, and she dreaded what she would find below the surface: the truth about his father, she suspected, ran all the way down into the boy's childhood.

She drew up at the gate. To her surprise, Angelo had replaced the metal gate with a white wooden one in the same traditional criss-crossed style as the fence. She got out, unlatched the gate, and left it open, not knowing yet if she would stay the night.

She would tell him when they were alone. Perhaps after dinner when Sarah put the baby to bed. As she turned into the gravel space before the house, she had one last sudden impulse to turn back— like an old reflex. She thought in the next instant of the stories that had already begun to appear in the Italian press, short inaccurate releases about the American Catholic priest who had once been a "Nazi" soldier (Karl had never been a Nazi) and who was now accused of war crimes by the citizens of a small town in Tuscany. In the last week the stories had begun to appear in other non-Italian European newspapers. As she knew it would, the story had ignited like a brush fire.

"Anna!" Sarah called from the house where she stood in the open front door with little Piero straddling her hip.

Anna got out. Sarah came toward her with the baby. "It's freezing, Sarah!" she called, hurrying to the house. "Don't come out!"

"Hi!" Sarah embraced her. She wore an old-fashioned kitchen apron over an ankle-length gingham dress.

"I got slowed down by the slush." She drew Sarah back to the door.

"You look great!" Sarah beamed.

"You, too!" They reached the foyer. "And look at little Piero! He's grown an inch, at least!" She hugged and kissed the baby, but he recoiled, frightened by this sudden invasion into his small world.

Sarah closed the door. "Come in and get warm. Angie's in the den watching the tube."

Anna followed her into the living room, removing her coat and gloves. Logs burned in the fireplace and the room looked invitingly cozy.

"Angie says you've been in Europe."

"Yes, I was there for almost two weeks." She felt an edge of panic. "I'll tell you and Angelo about it later." Far back in the house she heard the TV.

"Didn't you bring a bag?" Sarah took her coat.

"I brought a few things, but we'll leave them in the car till later." Anna stroked Piero's head. He was gaping at her with his hand in his mouth. There was no hint of recognition in his eyes. "Look at his hair! It's grown out dark!"

"Yes, it's going to be Angie's color." Sarah turned the baby for her to see, but he squirmed, recoiled again, and began to cry. "All right, all right." She nestled him on her hip. "I think he's hungry. I'll feed him and join you in a bit." She led Anna back into the foyer.

"You take care of Piero, and I'll go back and rouse Angie from his tube." She went down the short hallway to the rear of the house where Angelo had converted two small rooms into a single spacious paneled den. She stopped just outside the door. He sat with his back to her in an overstuffed armchair with his feet on a coffee table spread with magazines and newspapers. The evening news was on the TV, a report on the upcoming Nixon–McGovern presidential election, and the volume was deafeningly loud. "Angie?" she called.

Startled, he sat forward and dropped his feet to the floor. "Mom!" He looked nonplussed. "You're early!" As he stood up she saw in the flickering TV light that he wore grease-stained jeans held up by a black cowboy belt and a baggy flannel shirt open down the front. His hair had grown long again, down to his shoulders. He had gained even more weight since she last saw him in December.

She caught herself staring at his flabby belly protruding over the belt and said quickly, "Actually, I'm a little late, honey. I got slowed down in the snow."

"I must have dozed off." He moved around an easy chair to embrace her.

When she stepped into the room, she detected the faint but familiar acrid odor of burned marijuana under the odor of stale tobacco. "I should have phoned from the gas station."

He embraced her clumsily. His momentary proximity brought to mind the purpose of her visit. On an impulse, closing her eyes to the sudden pain she felt, she reached up and tried to press her hand against his hulking back.

He had pulled away, though. "Say! You look swell!"

"Thanks. I feel fine." She thought she also detected a faint smell of urine around him.

"You lost some weight over there in Europe!"

"I did, yes. A little."

"You look great," he repeated. "Did you see Sar and the baby when you came in?" He turned off the TV.

"Yes. The baby's grown. I hardly recognized him. And Sarah looks wonderful." She heard the lie in her voice. Sarah did not look wonderful, she looked strained and tired.

Angelo turned on a floor lamp. "Let's go up to the front. This room's a mess, and there's no place to sit." He gave an embarrassed laugh, indicating the only two chairs in the room.

"Any place is fine, honey." She scanned the room for the first time as she turned to follow. The drapes were drawn to shut out all the light. Then she saw it—hanging on the far wall in the corner next to the window: the small oil portrait of Silvanna Agnoletto-Patini. The sight of it (the only decoration in the room) left her with a feeling of uneasiness. In the hallway, heading toward the living room behind Angelo, she again smelled the tobacco and marijuana. Occasionally in the last year since his return from Vietnam, she had smelled the lingering aftermath of his habit. Fearing the backlash of his volatile and violent temper, she had said nothing about his escapes into drugged euphoria, hoping his dependence would pass with the birth of his child and its attendant responsibilities. He had gone on smoking, though.

"Sarah's been cooking all afternoon for you." He turned into the living room. "Sit there. That's comfortable." He pointed to the sofa, then crossed to the cane-backed French armchair at the far end of the coffee table and sat down.

"This is new." She indicated the velvet sofa as she sat down. Through the windows she saw that the twilight had almost gone. In the firelight, his eyes looked glassy and dilated. He turned away, observing her momentary stare, and shifted his weight.

"Tell me about your trip. Was it for business or pleasure?"

She could not, despite his discomfort, take her eyes from his face. There was a pallor in the skin she had never seen before, a dead blankness in his expression that gave him an unnerving look of absence and made a mask of the entire face. "It was neither, Angie," she replied, finally, to his question.

From the kitchen came the sound of the baby's laughter and Sarah's melodic voice, pleading with him in baby talk to eat.

Angelo looked at her for the first time since they had sat down, warily. "Did you see your mom?" he asked.

"Yes, I saw her." She recalled that he had never used the words *my grandmother*. "I saw my sister, too, your Aunt Livia. In fact, I saw everyone who was left in Montefalco."

"Was Montefalco changed?"

"Not much. More modern, maybe."

"Your mother, she must be what—in her seventies now?"

"Your grandmother is sixty-seven."

"Oh." He took a cigarette from a pack on the table. "Sar has a grandmother in her eighties."

She realized the empty questions and answers would go on like this until they had both run out of useless things to say about Italy. He had already sensed there was something ominous in store for him and was mentally preparing himself for a lecture. She also realized that it would take an act of will on her part, like a gigantic leap in the dark, to force herself to say what she had come to say, for her habit of avoiding truth, of postponing the ugly side of it, was a habit that had been with her all her life, and she still did not want to let go. "I came here this afternoon to talk with you, Angelo," she said. "There's something important I have to say." However clumsily, she had broken through the wall, at last.

He sat back and drew on his cigarette. "What about?" His posture became suddenly rigid, a reflex movement of defense left over, she suspected, from the nightmare of the war. "By the way," he hurried to add, "I spoke to a guy over in Stevenson. He's got some construction work coming up, on a new shopping center up there." He looked at her like a small frightened boy and gave her a nervous hopeful smile.

"It's not about your career, Angie. Your trust fund will support you for life." She thought of her endless harangues about his childish irresponsibility in relying entirely on money from Charles' estate to support himself and his family. Another piece of the puzzle fell into place. She felt a huge weight of grief sink within her, dragging with it what hope she had held for Angelo in its wake. In the next instant, her eyes flooded, and she said, "It's about me. Something I've done. I drove up to tell you something."

His voice, when he finally spoke, was shrill. "Shoot!" He gave a blustering laugh that did not conceal his panic.

"Not here, Angelo. Someplace private."

"Okay." He got reluctantly to his feet. "Get your coat. We'll go for a walk. I'll show you something at the barn."

Anna followed him into the foyer and took her coat and gloves from the closet.

"Honey," Angelo called back to the kitchen, "Mom and I are goin' out for a walk. How long before dinner?"

Sarah appeared in the hallway. "No particular time. We'll eat when you're ready."

Outside, only a faint gray light lingered along the horizon, but the snow reflected the light from the windows. The silence and the stillness over everything seemed magnified by the blanket of snow.

"I repainted the barn," he said, keeping a few steps ahead of her. "You can't see it in the dark, but I used the original red color. It looks great."

It was, she knew, a stalling diversion, for he was aware that the news she brought was something he would not want to hear. In the snow-lit darkness, the barn looked the same as the night Charles first brought her and Angelo up to Connecticut over twenty-five years ago. Angelo had been a small baby. "It looks lovely, Angie." He looked back, pleased by her response.

"I restored it," he said.

She continued down the slope behind him, trying to keep pace on the glassy surface of the snow. "Angelo," she said, "I don't know where to begin."

"You? A lawyer?" He laughed. "That's a first."

"This time—for the first time, I don't have a case to defend."

He waited for her at the bottom of the slope next to the remains of last year's vegetable garden. "Why don't you begin at the beginning?"

"Because"—she took his arm for a moment to steady herself— "there's no simple beginning." It was true: to tell the story from the beginning as she had lived it, as they had all lived it, was not to tell the real story. The truth of what they had been and what they now were lay beyond events, outside of either time or place or circumstance. It lay in themselves—dead center in the heart's darkness. They walked together slowly toward the white corral fence next to the barn. She said, "I went to Italy to file charges against the man who executed your grandfather and your uncle." She let her statement lie in the snow-muffled stillness. Their feet made soft crunching noises.

"Go on," he said, warily.

"I've told you only part of the story up to now. The part about the German occupation, the partisans, the murder of the German soldiers, and the reprisal that followed." She drew in a cold breath and forced herself to go on. "I haven't told you about myself. I was nineteen at the time. In January of 1944 I met the German officer in charge of the troops occupying Montefalco. He was twenty-six, a Wehrmacht first lieutenant. We"—she hesitated—"we fell in love, both of us, and we carried on an affair." Again, she let her statement fall between the crunch of their footsteps. Angelo said nothing. "That spring, and all that summer, we carried on an affair in secret."

She wondered at how much she had left out in that digested summary.

"You?" he finally said.

"Me." She went on, racing now against the mounting dread. "We planned to marry after the war. In September the Americans broke through the Gothic Line. You know that part of the story." As a child he had played American and Italian soldiers, she remembered, and he had pretended to attack what he called the "Gotham Line," confusing the name with a name from his comic books. "And then came the partisans. In retaliation, orders came to execute ten civilians for every soldier killed. The responsibility fell on my lover." They reached the circular corral fence. Angelo looked back toward the house where a light had gone on in the upstairs window of the nursery. "His name was—" She started over again. "His name is Karl Kruger. He's still alive."

"Jesus," Angelo said and shook his head.

It seemed she had said everything so quickly that he understood nothing. "We thought he had died in the war, but it wasn't so. I discovered him by accident last month when I went to Los Angeles."

There was no response. He seemed not to hear her.

"Like me, he immigrated to America after the war."

"And you went to Italy to file charges against him for war crimes?"

His instantaneous knowledge of the legal procedure surprised her. "Yes."

"California." He laughed softly. "Weird. You must have been relieved after all those years."

"Angelo, you don't understand."

"So you had an affair with a soldier—a Nazi soldier! What difference does it make?"

"Not just an affair."

He turned toward the corral fence and ran his finger along the snow collected along the top board. "Mom?" he said in a small voice.

"The man, Angelo, is your father."

There was no response. He went on raking the snow from the fence with his finger. The silence dragged on, magnified by the distant bark of a dog. His voice, when he finally spoke, skittered off in amazement. "My *father?*"

"Neither of us knew at the time of the execution, Angelo. It all happened so fast, neither of us knew for sure. I didn't really know for sure until after he had gone. We were young, Angelo. We loved each other. We were caught in the war. We were going to marry after the war." Nothing she was saying sounded right.

Angelo did not react.

"It all happened in a matter of days. The partisans shot six of his soldiers. The order came back from his superiors the same day. He didn't know, he didn't have the—" She hesitated between saying *the choice* and *the time* but knew there was no excuse in either. Instead, she said, "He did what they ordered him to do. Against his will. They rounded up men in the village, anyone they could find. He did not know they had taken Papa and Piero."

"What's his name?"

"Kruger. Karl Kruger," she gave his name again. "Karl Gustav Kruger."

He leaned against the fence. "Hey!" he called across the corral. "Bucky! Come here, fella!"

She felt a chill bite through her coat. From the darkness under the enclosed wooden shelter at the far side of the corral the head of a small Shetland pony emerged suddenly into the faint light. Bucky had been the name of the pony Angelo had had as a child, briefly. The way Angelo threw the name out, as if she knew already about this new pony, as if childhood was only yesterday, frightened her.

"Hey!" He reached over the fence and clapped his hands. "Come here, fella!"

"Angelo," she murmured. Far back in her mind something like the piece of a huge jigsaw puzzle fell into place.

"I bought him for Piero," he said, clumsily detouring from the subject. "He's only a couple of years old."

She took a step forward. "I thought he was dead, Angie," she said, "I thought it had ended years ago."

He hooked his arms over the fence to support himself. "And that story—the Italian soldier—that stuff about the Italian soldier who died in the war, what about that?"

"I was pregnant at the end of the war. When they questioned me in the DP camp, I made up that story. I was afraid they would think I was a German collaborator."

"The Army thought my girl Lan Tien was collaborating with the Cong," he announced, distractedly. He clapped his hands again. "Bucky! Here, fella!"

The ease with which his mind and mood leapt into a different space astonished her. Then she remembered the marijuana he had smoked. "Angelo," she murmured, wondering if he had attended to anything she had said.

"And Dad—I mean, Charlie—did he know?"

"Not the truth, no. When you were ten, I told him I had been raped by a German soldier. That's all he ever knew."

"Ten," he repeated, then seemed to withdraw fixedly into himself. She wanted to go to him, but he was beyond her reach. "Funny," he said, finally, "I always wanted to be like the guy you invented for me—a war hero." He suddenly leaned back, held onto the fence for support, and looked up at the sky. His mind seemed to take flight. "He was a neat guy, you know. You made him sound like a neat guy. Brave, selfless, tough, loyal—you name it." He stretched back, gripping the fence at arm's length, and began to rock back and forth as if keeping time to some inner music. "Charlie wasn't half that neat." The voice had become unnervingly boyish. "I always knew you loved the Italian more than Charlie," he added, then fell silent, rocking absently back and forth.

She gave up and watched him. The ache spilled into her eyes.

Suddenly, he pulled himself back to the fence and rested his forehead against the top slat. Then he murmured something to himself.

"What, darling?"

"I used to grieve for your loss when I was a kid," he repeated, "did you know that?"

"No, Angie. I didn't know that." The chill she felt was not from the cold but from a sudden and terrific horror.

"It's true." His voice was his own again. "I wanted to be like your Italian. But I always knew I could never match him. I always knew he belonged only to you. I tried, though. Did you know that? I tried."

She formed the word *yes* with her mouth, but could not say it because of the catastrophe she saw rolling down on her.

"I went to Vietnam twice. I tried," he said.

The pony came out of the shelter and snorted.

For me, love is what you feel when you miss someone . . . love is a feeling of missing. In her mind she let go of the fragile thread still holding him.

The pony came toward him over the snow, cautiously. He stood up and hooked his arms over the fence. "Where does he live?"

"Los Angeles."

He chuckled. "The City of Angels?"

She thought of all the self-redeeming explanations she had worked out to save Angelo and spare herself from indictment. She felt like a defendant worn down by evidence to naked questions and answers. "Yes," she replied.

"Is he married?"

"No."

The pony came up and warily stretched its nose to the fence, sniffing. "A widower?"

"No."

He stroked the pony's nose with the back of his fingers. "You did love him, didn't you?"

"Yes."

"And you still love him, don't you?"

"Yes."

The pony ventured closer. "You married, but he didn't. He must have loved you, too."

"Yes."

Angelo chuckled again. "A bachelor for twenty-eight years? Sounds to me like an obsession." He stroked the pony's forehead.

"He's a priest," she said under her breath.

"A what?"

"He's a priest, Angelo. A Catholic priest. After the war, he became a priest."

CHAPTER 2

I

The fact is, I don't believe I will be free until I receive the judgment of a criminal court of law. Kruger stopped writing. He was now an inch from the bottom of the page, enough space for a polite and encouraging conclusion. He smiled, thinking of the one-page limitation he had imposed on himself for the two letters he had written Anna in the last three weeks. It had worked. By limiting his space, he had forced himself to write only the facts and avoid all indulgence of personal feelings. He quickly scanned what he had written: the request that she not interfere if extradition procedures were launched against him, that she cooperate with the prosecution in both America and Italy, and that she tell the truth when the time came for interviews with the media. As before, he had been tempted to hint of his feelings toward her and their son, Angelo, but he had refrained. In both letters, he had asked her to keep Angelo out of the picture as much as possible. One day, he had said, they would meet, but not until the storm had passed. He signed the letter "Rev. K. G. Kruger," amused by the obvious overstatement of propriety. From the living room came the sound of the closing music for the four o'clock local TV news. Father Mendoza always watched the afternoon news. Kruger addressed the envelope to Anna's New York offices. The TV set went silent, leaving only the sound of the electric fan whirring on his bedside table. Like clockwork, Father Mendoza would collect his car keys and leave for the Marine base at Twenty-nine Palms to hear confessions at five o'clock. On his way, he would stop in at the post office in the village of Twenty-nine Palms and post the letter. Among the papers on his card-table desk he hurriedly searched for a stamp. Father Mendoza would not have time to buy stamps. On the window screen above the desk he caught sight of a lizard scurrying for cover. He had grown used to the little desert creatures during his stay at the mission, finding them everywhere, both in and outside the little clapboard rectory. He found the sheet of stamps and pasted one to the envelope.

Father Mendoza's bootsteps returned down the short hallway connecting the two bedrooms, the kitchen, and the living room, sounding like an entire army regiment on the thin hollow linoleum floor. Mendoza stopped at the open door of his bedroom. "I'm going to the base now, Monsignor," the old priest said. He wore short-sleeved summer army fatigues and looked, for all the world, like a tough but aging drill sergeant with his close-cropped white hair and neatly trimmed moustache.

"Do you mind mailing a letter for me, Father?" He made his way around the metal army bed lying between the card table and the door.

"*Mind,* Monsignor?" Mendoza laughed. "No, I don't mind." The priest took the letter and slipped it into his shirt pocket. After almost three weeks of sharing his small living space, Mendoza still hesitated to call him by his first name. It was the priest's way of maintaining some semblance of privacy. "By the way, there was no mention of you on the news today," Mendoza said. He spoke English with the lilting musical inflections of a native northern Mexican, which betrayed first impressions of the man's weathered wrinkled face. Behind the startling contrast of white hair and rough dark skin there was still another surprise in the priest's face: a hint of humor in the dark brown eyes that was an extension of the man's worldly street wisdom. So far, Kruger had learned only a little about the priest's background, that he was an authentic *mestizo,* half Mexican and half American Indian, and was proud of his mixture of native bloods. Once, in passing, Mendoza had spoken of his delinquent youth. As a young man, he had grown up in poverty in Chihuahua, the northern Mexican province. To break with the life he had been condemned to in Mexico, he had repeatedly crossed the border into the United States, and had spent time in American jails, waiting for transport back to Mexico. Finally, as a lesson to break his spirit, the U.S. authorities had sent him to prison on trumped-up felony charges. While there, he had met a priest working in the San Diego area. The priest had visited the prison regularly, and when time came for Mendoza's release, he had offered to sponsor the youth's immigration to the United States and eventually found Mendoza a job in San Diego. Six years after the priest first befriended him, Mendoza decided to enter the secular seminary and study for the priesthood. The priest again sponsored him. Mendoza had been a priest now for almost thirty years. He said, forcing a reticent smile, "As they say, Monsignor, 'No news is good news.'"

"I talked to Father Auden earlier," Kruger said. "Some newspeople came to St. Luke's looking for me. He told them I was on temporary leave."

"If they don't get an interview, maybe the noise will die down."

"Maybe."

"Not to worry." Mendoza chuckled. "The Mojave is a big desert." He left the hallway and crossed the small living room to the front door. "Mrs. Hamasake and her sister left some *chuletas* in the kitchen. I'll be back by eight. Eat without me if you get hungry."

"I'll wait." He followed Mendoza out of the house, letting the screen door slam behind him. The Hamasake sisters were two of the four local women who came regularly to clean house for the *padre*. For the sake of propriety, Mendoza insisted the local women always come in twos, and the Hamasake sisters took turns with two Indian women from the nearby Twenty-nine Palms reservation. Out of kindness, knowing that Mendoza did not cook, they always brought food and left it in the refrigerator. In the last three weeks they had doubled their already generous share of gifts.

Kruger stood on the concrete stoop in front of the clapboard rectory. On the way to his truck, parked between the converted barrack church and the rectory, Mendoza stopped to watch three jet aircraft streak across the sky high above the desert floor to the south. They flew in formation, tiny soundless specks, leaving three long white vapor trails behind in the cloudless afternoon sky. Above the ragged Palm View Peak southwest of Palm Springs they banked in formation, caught the sunlight on their wings, swung out vertical-winged in a wide curve, passed across the face of the sun, and leveled out toward Edwards Air Force Base to the northwest.

"F-one-elevens," Father Mendoza called back, and continued on across the bulldozed clearing to his pickup truck.

Kruger smiled to himself, watching the hulking enigma lumber to the truck. He had still not figured out the cardinal's motive for choosing to exile him to a parish like San Cristobal with a man like Mendoza. Here, surrounded by hundreds of square miles of desert and desert mountains, isolated on top of a small unremarkable hill in the middle of a vast stretch of uninhabitable land bequeathed by the government to the military and the Indians, Mendoza had created a parish, a ministry, and an apostolate out of the world's rejected waste. His parish was made up of transients, dropouts, and exiles. On the north, there was the Marine training base where boys learned the savage limits of human endurance and passed on to practice the art of war in Southeast Asia, among them a few practicing Catholics. To the south, the dry naked land of the Indian reservation, or what was left of that sad compensation. On the east and west, two small villages inhabited by pioneer exiles from the airless cities. In all, not more than seventy-five souls to care for and save. A handful came each Sunday to the mission, cooled themselves with paper fans through Mass, and then left in an assortment of old pickup trucks, vans, and secondhand cars. Mendoza had dispensed with every physical, emotional, psychological, and spiritual ornament in his ministry. Between him and God there were only his people.

Mendoza swung his truck back and sped off across the empty parking lot in front of the mission chapel. Kruger watched the green Toyota bounce along the dirt road leading from the mission to the two-lane secondary highway running east–west across the flat desert. The only sound around him was the wind whipping across the roof of the clapboard mission church next door. Though after four, the sun still sat high above the range of mountains to the west, but its narrowing angle to the earth had already lengthened the shadows of the hills to the south and filled the immense desert space with deepening colors. Mendoza's truck threw up a trail of dust that quickly dissolved in the wind. The mission sat on the leveled top of a low, perfectly rounded hill with an unobstructed view of the lower desert to the south and the Marine base and Joshua Tree Monument to the north. As the truck neared the highway, a white automobile turned from the eastbound lane into the dirt road leading up to the mission. The truck and the car stood side by side for a while and then separated. The thought came to him that press people from Los Angeles had discovered his whereabouts. The car started up the slope to the mission. But then why would Mendoza have allowed the car to pass? The car slowed in the soft dirt on the slope to the mission. He recognized neither the driver nor the passenger, a man behind the wheel and a woman in the seat beside him. As he turned to retreat into the house, the car reached the crest of the hill. Framed in a pastel scarf, the woman's face caught the sunlight through the windshield. He let go of the screen door and it slammed closed.

Angelo turned off the ignition. The man on the concrete stoop, his father, was exactly what his mother had described but not exactly what he had imagined. Like the priest in the car, he wore the familiar olive summer army fatigues, baggy trousers and an ill-fitting T-shirt. "He looks younger than I expected," he said.

"He has always looked younger than his years, Angie." His mother opened the passenger door to get out.

"What am I supposed to call him?"

She smiled. "Whatever feels comfortable." He was smoothing his hair with his fingers. She said, "You look great, honey, like your old self."

Worried about first impressions, he had compromised with her and let Sarah cut his hair shorter. His stomach was in a knot. He got out and followed his mother to the stoop.

She waited for Angelo to join her, then continued toward Karl. The look of shock lingered in his face. Smiling, she said, "We should have warned you, I know. I'm sorry."

Kruger saw that the boy was tall—at least six feet—and heavier than Anna had led him to believe. He wore a short-sleeved plaid summer shirt that looked too small on his big frame, corduroy dungarees, and tennis shoes. His dark hair, the color of Anna's hair, hung down to his neck and fluttered over his face in the breeze. Recovering himself, feeling idiotic where he stood above them on the stoop, he said, "Sorry." He started down. "It's a shock. I didn't expect you." He could not take his eyes off the boy, his son.

Anna saw Karl's expression and smiled again, her pride peeking through. "This is Angelo, Karl."

Karl approached the boy. For a brief moment, each looking at the other, each waiting for the other to say something, their eyes locked. *The boy's eyes,* Karl thought, *they're the color of mine.* A strange feeling of warmth flooded his face. The impulse was to embrace the boy, but he restrained himself and held out his hand. "Hello, son," he said. The words sounded conspicuously loud in the open space.

Angelo extended his hand. Though only a couple of feet, the distance he had to bridge to take his father's hand seemed immense. The word *dad* came to mind, but he judged it would sound weird. His face was crimson as he smiled foolishly, felt the strength of the man's grip, and said, "Sir."

His mother was saying, "I thought you should meet him, Karl. Now, rather than later. I didn't see any reason to wait. I found where you were by tracing the postmark on your letters."

Neither one of them was listening, Angelo saw. To break the ineluctable tension, to mask the feeling betrayed by his own lingering grip, he said, "There was only one Catholic church around Joshua Tree, sir. That's how we knew." He quickly made a mental note not to use *sir* again. It was a habit left over from the Army.

Kruger saw the boy's excruciating embarrassment. He forced himself to reach out and grip the boy's shoulder. "You're both welcome." The boy lowered his eyes, smiling through his confusion at this sudden physical acknowledgment. He added, "You're taller than you looked in your picture, Angelo."

"A little over six feet," Angelo said brightly and forced himself to look up. His father's eyes were the same blue-green as his, and the chiseled chinbone was his, too. "You're about six yourself," he ventured.

"Exactly." Kruger squeezed the boy's shoulder and gently shook him, wanting for the second time, but not daring, to embrace him. He said, "You flew here from New York, son?"

"We took a plane to Palm Springs, then rented a car. It was easy once we got to Joshua Tree."

Seeing the hint of shame in the boy's face, Anna stepped in. "It was my idea, Karl. I decided there was no reason for you and Angelo to wait any longer to meet."

"I'm glad you brought him." He turned back to the boy. "Real glad."

Angelo breathed. "Thanks. I was worried."

"Forgive me." Kruger laughed, looking down at his clothes. "I'm not quite *dressed* for the occasion."

"I still have my gear from Nam." Angelo laughed, thinking of what he wanted to say to this man ever since that night in the snow with his mother. "I sometimes wear it myself; the summer stuff's comfortable."

Kruger stepped aside, gesturing to the stoop. "This is home for the time being. It's not much, but come in." He followed them, recalling what Anna had told him in Milan about Angelo's Vietnam experience. *His war was different from ours. Perhaps when you meet him . . .*

Anna looked back and said quietly, "We won't stay long."

Kruger held the screen door open. "This is Father Mendoza's rectory. I take it you met him on the way in."

"He said he was the chaplain at that Marine base you've got here," said Angelo. "He gave Mom a letter of yours. He was on the way to the post office with it."

Kruger motioned for them to sit on the sofa, the one comfortable piece of furniture in the living room. "Please sit down. The sofa's comfortable."

"Thank you." Anna reached out and pressed Karl's arm encouragingly on her way to the far end of the sofa. She had made room for Angelo to sit close to his father, but the boy sat down in one of the aluminum straight-backed kitchen chairs at the end of the coffee table. He watched her move back to the other end, knowing her purpose.

"Can I get you something to drink?" Kruger asked. "There's fruit juice, soda pop, and beer." The offer sounded poor.

"Nothing for me, Karl." Anna smiled.

"A beer," Angelo said, "I'd like a beer."

"Sure. I'll get us a couple of beers." Kruger headed down the hall to the kitchen, grateful for a moment to collect himself. Beneath his shock there was a confused mixture of feelings: pleasure at the realization that he had, after all these years, come face to face with the son he had once promised Anna and afterward secretly longed for (he had often imagined the feeling of having a son, but nothing he had imagined even approached this strange sensation, nor could he define it) and mingled feelings of guilt, suspicion, shame—and even irritation. Had he been given warning, he could have prepared himself. He opened the refrigerator and saw only one bottle of beer on the rack. He had not even a whole bottle to offer. They would share it, he decided. He singled out his suspicion, uncapping the beer. Anna, of course, knew that he was only waiting for the Vatican's permission to return to Italy, and she had gone to great lengths to convince him to stand firm behind the safety of his American citizenship. He poured the beer into two glasses, filling one to the top. On the way back to the living room, he wondered suddenly if Anna might have cajoled the boy into coming now, instead of later, knowing she might succeed with his heart where she had failed with reason.

"Here, Angelo." He set the full glass of beer on the coffee table. The boy had lit a cigarette and was smoking nervously. Kruger took an ashtray from the TV set and placed it next to him.

"Thanks."

"Anna tells me you're married, son, and have a child." He took his place next to the boy.

"Yes—" Angelo stopped himself before he said *sir* again. "We have a boy."

"And you live in Connecticut?"

"Yeah." He flicked his ash. "Between Shelton and Stevenson."

For the first time, seeing the boy at close range, Kruger realized that Anna was right: The eyes and the chin had come from him, and the rest of the face, though fuller than he had imagined, was Anna's. He felt a sudden tinge of pride at the confirmation of their physical link. "Tell me about your son." *My grandson,* he thought.

"His name's Piero." Angelo glanced at his mother. "We named him after—" He stopped, caught in an embarrassing trap.

"After your uncle?" his father said, nodding and smiling knowingly.

"He's a beautiful child, Karl," Anna said, looking down with an ironic feeling of pride.

"And your wife, Sarah, do you have a picture with you?"

"No, sir."

"When were you married . . . ?"

Anna pretended to look for something in her purse while Karl searched for an opening into his son's confidence. The conversation went no further than a string of short questions and answers turning around Angie's life in Connecticut. Angelo, she realized, had not summoned the courage to say what she knew was on his mind. She sat forward and interrupted. "I've told Angelo everything, Karl." Her statement left a strange silence in the room, like a gaping hole. "I told him what happened in Montefalco, what happened afterward, everything." When neither seemed prepared to take up her lead, she added, "I also told him the reasons why I went to Italy to file charges, why you followed me there, and why you want to go to trial."

Kruger sipped his beer. "Then I guess you know I'm only waiting for the Vatican's permission to go back," he said.

"Yeah." The boy leaned forward, troubled. "She told me."

"The fact that I'm a priest, son, changes nothing. I did what they accuse me of." Kruger's face went hot and cold at the same time, and he looked down, feeling a new kind of shame. As a priest he had often listened to abject confessions of parental failure, but he had never experienced for himself the toppling feeling of its colossal fall.

Angelo said, "Mom got a letter two days ago from the Italian Government."

Anna stepped in. "My husband had a lot of friends in Italy. Government people. I made some phone calls, Karl. I received a letter from one of the Italian ministers. He reviewed your case. Because of the timing of the charges and the fact that you are legally an American citizen, there may be no grounds for extradition."

"I see." Kruger looked at his son, imagining the strange predicament they would both face if he remained a priest in America and they went on visiting each other in private for the rest of their lives. At one level, for a compromise, it would not be a bad kind of life. "The fact is, Angie, I'm not concerned with the problem of extradition now. Extradition or not, I want to go back of my own free will."

"But don't you see," Anna raced in hurriedly, "if the harm in going to trial outweighs the good, there's no moral justification for it!"

Kruger smiled. "I see you've been talking with Cardinal Boyle."

Anna sat back, disarmed. It was true. She had phoned the prelate twice to inform him of the legal situation in Italy. "You are a priest. Your responsibilities to the Church come first."

"Your mother thinks I'd be foolish to stand trial," Kruger said.

"Yes. I know."

"Is that why you've both come here?" Kruger asked, unable to disguise his disappointment to the boy.

"No, sir." Angelo fingered his beer glass, thinking back over twenty-seven-odd years to the time when he first remembered dreaming about the dead hero-saint who had been his father. The parallels he had drawn these last weeks between this man and the other and between himself and this one ran deeper than he even imagined. "I wanted to meet you." The tears that welled up in his throat were, he knew, from a place neither the priest nor his mother could dream of. He had spoken of it to no one save Sarah. "I thought you might go back to Italy before I had the chance."

"We had our separate reasons for coming, Karl," Anna said. "Angelo's reasons are his own. I told him what kind of man you are. I told him the truth about you. The fact is," she smiled at her son,

"I had lied to him for so long about his real father that he wanted to see and judge for himself."

Watching his son sit forward and drag on his cigarette, Kruger said, "He's a fine boy, Anna. Just like you said."

"Before you make your final decision, I wanted you to see for yourself."

"Mom," Angelo chided.

Kruger asked, "How old are you now, Angelo?"

"Twenty-seven. I was born in '45."

The realization struck Kruger for the first time. "Funny, you're exactly half my age. I was twenty-seven in 1945, when you were born." He saw a look of uneasiness come over the boy's face and quickly changed the subject. "Is this your first visit to Southern California?"

"Yes."

"It isn't all like this, you know. Desert."

"I've never seen a desert before." Angelo glanced from his father to his mother, realizing that if he was to say what he had come to say it would have to be in private with his father, and time was running out.

"Angie was thrilled when he learned you were staying in the Mojave Desert," Anna said, reading Angelo's expression. "He brought his camera."

"This is the best time to see the desert," Kruger said, "about a half hour or so before sunset." He took Anna's silent suggestion. "Do you want to get your camera and take a walk?"

"Okay. Yeah. I'd like that."

Kruger and the boy got up. Anna said, "You and Angelo go. I'll wait here." To preempt any argument she added, "I didn't bring any walking shoes."

"We won't be long." Kruger jostled his son affectionately on the shoulder. "You'll get some great shots of the San Andreas Fault from here."

The two men ambled to the front door. "You okay, Mom?" Angelo asked, opening the screen door for his father.

"I'm fine. Just be sure to get shots of each other."

Kruger turned on the threshold. "There's food in the refrigerator. Help yourself."

"Thanks."

Angelo let the screen door slam closed behind him. She heard them move off, talking of cameras and lenses. She took from her purse the letter the priest Mendoza had handed Angelo through the car window when they passed on the road. It was addressed to Mrs. Anna Fitzgerald at her New York office. She smiled to herself, opened the envelope, and removed the single sheet of stationery. Unfolding the page, her eye caught the last line above the signature: *The fact is, I don't believe I will be free until I receive the judgment of a criminal court of law.*

II

"There." Kruger directed Angelo's gaze toward two symmetrical foothills far off at the desert's southwest perimeter. "Between those two hills. Where you see that break in the desert floor." The San Andreas Fault ran off in a zigzagged line across the flat expanse of clay and sand like the rippled underground path of a burrowing groundhog. "The fault runs the length of California, almost."

"Jesus," Angelo said, then caught his profanity and glanced at him.

He smiled. "If you aim south, you can avoid the direct sunlight and get the fault farther out." He stepped back and watched the boy aim for a photo of the fault.

"The light's great." Suspended just above the mountains west of Palm Springs, the sun had spilled a brilliant pastel prism across the desert floor, transforming the vast space into a cratered moonscape. Silhouetted against the light, the boy's profile brought to mind the fanciful image of the son he had invented for himself years before. On the adjacent hill to the west, the living-room lights in the rectory had been turned on. Anna, of course, had arranged the whole thing, but he felt grateful for this chance to be alone with his son.

"What's that?" Angelo asked, pointing east toward a cluster of corrugated roofs isolated in a barren stretch of arid land.

"The Twenty-nine Palms Indian Reservation."

"Figures." Angelo smiled sardonically. "Looks like another one of Uncle Sam's payoffs. How do they make a living, pan for gold?"

The war changed him. Weeks ago, during the drive to Milan, Anna had spoken of the boy's bitter cynicism toward authority in general and the American Government in particular. She had hinted that something had deeply wounded him in Vietnam. "It's very hard for them," Kruger said. He thought, at once, of the boys at St. Luke's who had come back from the war with the same sense of bitter and cynical defeat.

"How's the view from that hill?" Angelo pointed east.

"You can get a good view of the Eagle Mountains from there."

"Do you mind?"

"No. Let's go." He led the boy down the hillside and across the dry bed of a ragged gulch washed deep into the crusty earth by the torrential desert rains. "We'd better hurry," he said, "the light's going." With the rapid cooling of twilight, a wind had picked up from the west, blowing gusts of loose sand up the hill. Angelo made a dash up the slope, ahead of him, and disappeared. When Kruger reached the summit, the boy had crossed to the far side of the table-topped hill and stood looking out across the vast stretch of scrubby desert toward the Eagle and Coxcomb mountain ranges.

"I'll take one of you," Angelo said. "Mom's making a collection of old photos. She'll want to add you to her rogues' gallery." He laughed, softly, but there was a hint of pain in it.

"Where do you want me?"

"There. At the edge. With those lights behind you."

Kruger did as he was told and took his place at the edge of the table top, facing southwest with his back to the lights of the Marine base. There was just enough sunset left for a couple of pictures.

Angelo moved sideways, searching for a desirable angle. "I guess you figured out why she wanted us to meet now, instead of later."

"It may be hard later, if I go back to Italy."

"No, sir. It isn't that." Angelo aimed and focused the lens. "She thought maybe if you met me, you'd change your mind and stay in America." He snapped the shutter.

"I explained everything in the letter Father Mendoza gave her." He started back across the table top.

"Wait! One more." Angelo maneuvered for a shot against the background of the mountains. He said, aiming, "Can I ask you a personal question?"

"Yes."

"Did you love Mom? I mean, back then." He snapped the shutter.

"Yes."

"And something else." He took aim again. "If you loved her, why did you do it?"

The shutter snapped. "You mean, the reprisal execution, don't you?"

"Yes."

The light reflecting from the boy's face was one of those strange desert colors, violet. "It was a choice at the time between duty and personal feelings. I chose duty."

Angelo looked up at two small air force jets streaking across the sky in the direction of Edwards Air Force Base. Angled high to the setting sun, they left behind pink vapor trails in the darkening sky. He said, "Did you think it was wrong, when you did it?"

"Yes. I chose duty above conscience. Why do you ask?"

Angelo ignored his question and pointed. "Those lights over there, sir—"

"The Twenty-nine Palms Marine Base."

The boy considered the answer. "Right. I forgot. You've got five military installations around here. There's Edwards Air Force Base and Fort Erwin."

"The Marine base and two sections of the China Lake Naval Weapons Center," Kruger added, sensing the boy was leading him to another question. "It's getting dark. We'd better go back. Your mom's waiting."

"Sure." As they crossed the tabled hilltop, the boy dropped back a pace. "Those bases were here during your war, too, sir," he announced.

"Yes. I believe they were." Kruger heard anxiety break through the voice. He realized the boy had been calling him "sir" for lack of anything comfortable. He slowed to let him catch up. "What's wrong, Angelo? Tell me."

"By the way, sir—what am I supposed to call you? I'm not sure what's right." His voice shook ominously.

They started down the slope into the dark gulch. "If it feels comfortable, Angelo, call me 'Dad.' I am, you know."

The boy laughed. "You're also a priest—a monsignor."

On an impulse, Kruger lay his arm across the boy's shoulder. It felt strange, this new venture of human physical intimacy after twenty-eight years, but quite natural and good. "I'm also a man, son. In God's Providence I became a soldier, a father, and a priest—all three. You see, God doesn't have a stingy imagination like us. He has made us in all varieties."

As they labored up the next hillside, Angelo said, "You've already decided what you're going to do, haven't you?"

"I'm waiting for the Vatican—for the Holy Father—to answer my petition. If I go back to Italy without the Church's permission, I'll lose my priesthood—everything."

They reached the hilltop. Kruger stopped to get his breath. Angelo moved away. "I think Mom's wrong when she says you won't gain anything by going back."

Kruger saw the boy stare fixedly toward the rectory on the next hill. "Why do you say that?"

"You said you did what you did—you killed those people—because it was your duty."

"A very misplaced sense of duty."

"Duty, nonetheless." The boy turned to face him. The wind gusted his hair back, leaving the face stark and colorless. He shoved his hands into his pockets, awkwardly. "I'll tell you something. But I don't want you to tell Mom. Ever."

"All right."

"I want you to promise—just like the promise in confession."

"I promise."

The boy thought for a moment, then said, "Your war was different from mine. You killed people out of a sense of duty." He swallowed, laboring with it. "In Vietnam . . . in Vietnam, I killed them for pleasure."

He was in Vietnam twice. When he came back the second time, he wasn't himself. The war changed him. He let go of the air in his lungs.

"Another difference . . ." The boy's voice wavered, faintly. "No one will ever accuse me . . . I'll never stand trial for *my* crime."

III

Kruger dialed the number from memory. As the phone at the Los Angeles end began ringing, his eye rested on the coffee-table ashtray. The boy had chain-smoked during his two-and-a-half-hour stay, and the remains were like the evidence of a soul in distress. He turned away, thinking of his own brush with despair twice before in his life.

The line connected and Monsignor Halpern's voice came on, "Archdiocese of Los Angeles."

"Monsignor Halpern, this is Karl Kruger."

There was an instant of surprised delay. "Yes, Monsignor. Good evening." Cautious, as always.

"I'm calling from San Cristobal, Andy," Kruger said. "I'd like to make an appointment to see His Eminence."

"You mean, here in the city?" Halpern asked, taken off guard by the abrupt request.

Boyle's instructions had been to remain secluded at San Cristobal until a decision arrived from the Vatican. "Yes, Andy. Unless His Eminence would prefer another place."

Halpern cleared his throat. "When would you like to see him, Karl?"

"Tomorrow."

"That soon?"

"Yes. As soon as possible." He smelled the lingering fragrance of Anna's perfume over the stale odor of cigarette smoke.

"Well, let's see . . . His Eminence has a full schedule in the morning. How about four-thirty?"

"Four-thirty's fine."

Halpern hastened to add, "Of course, that will put you back at San Cristobal pretty late in the evening, Monsignor." He was fishing for clues.

"Not to worry, Andy." He left it at that.

"How will you get into the city?"

Halpern knew, of course, that he had no car at San Cristobal. He explained his intention to get a ride into Palm Springs with Father Mendoza, take a bus into the city and a taxi to the cardinal's residence. "It takes about four hours from door to door, Monsignor," he said.

"I see." Halpern hesitated. "I only ask because of the recent calls and visits we've had from the press. I guess you know they've been trying to track you down."

"Yes. Father Auden keeps me posted."

"Perhaps you should make the trip in mufti—to be on the safe side."

"Yes, I'll do that." Outside, a truck door slammed.

"Good. Oh—by the way—we've had calls from your parishioners wanting to know if what they've heard on the news is true. I guess by now word has spread."

"Yes, Andy, I guess it has."

Halpern gave a small disapproving laugh. "He'll be expecting you, Karl."

"Thanks, Monsignor."

"Good-bye."

He replaced the receiver. There seemed to be a thousand little things to do between now and tomorrow, but they were meaningless for the moment. He thought of Anna's helpless look of dread when he saw them off at the car. She had said, trying to salvage her hopes, "I'm coming to California in June, Karl. Perhaps by then you'll be back at St. Luke's."

Mendoza came through the screen door carrying two shopping bags. He looked surprised to see him standing beside the telephone. "Sorry I'm late," he said, setting the shopping bags on the floor. "I stopped by at the base hospital. One of the boys has been injured."

"Was it serious?"

"Someone stabbed him in the stomach." Mendoza began removing the contents from the shopping bags, setting the things on the coffee table. The bags were filled with junk, the usual things people gave Mendoza for his Sunday five-cent garage sales. "He was selling drugs on the base. He must have cheated on one of his deals. He'll pull through." Mendoza started toward the kitchen. "Have you eaten, Monsignor?"

"No. I had visitors." He followed the priest down the hallway. "I gather you met Mrs. Fitzgerald on the way out."

"Yes. We passed on the road. They stopped me for directions." In the kitchen Mendoza began rummaging in the cabinet where the dry foods were kept.

"I didn't expect them. They flew here this afternoon from New York."

"That's what the boy said." The priest sounded neither surprised nor concerned.

"How did you know who they were?"

"The boy . . ." Mendoza smiled. "Your son looks like you."

"Yes, he does."

"They seem like fine people."

"She also said you gave her my letter."

Mendoza shrugged. "Why not?" He brought out a box of instant rice.

"She came here because she thought meeting my son might influence my decision."

"I see." Mendoza opened the refrigerator and rummaged.

Kruger ambled into the kitchen and stood next to the vinyl-topped table. "I'm afraid it backfired. I've decided to go back to Italy, Emilio, and stand trial."

"When?" Again, the priest looked neither surprised nor concerned.

"Now. I have an appointment with Cardinal Boyle tomorrow afternoon."

"The Vatican hasn't replied, has it?"

"No. It doesn't matter. Either way, I'm going. Up to now, I've only been gambling with the Holy Father. And with myself."

Mendoza took out the *chuletas* from the refrigerator. "I guess you know what he will have to do."

"We'll both do what in conscience we have to do. I'll stand trial as a layman."

"Do you know what you're choosing, Karl?" Mendoza asked, preparing the instant rice.

"What do you mean?" Mendoza, he realized, had used his Christian name for the first time.

"What's the penalty for a crime like that in Italy?"

"Life imprisonment. They don't have the death penalty in Italy." The priest turned on the gas oven. "Do you know what prison is like? I mean, for life."

"Only as a visitor."

"You won't know what freedom is until you've lost it. I know what I'm talking about, Karl."

"Lost it or found it?" He smiled. "There are different kinds of freedom, Emilio." He thought of what he had written to Anna that afternoon in his letter.

Mendoza chuckled. "There was a reason why Boyle sent you out here to San Cristobal."

"What do you mean?"

The priest opened the oven, set the dish inside, and closed the door. "Remember that priest I told you about, the one who sponsored me when I got out of prison? The one who, later, when I wanted to be a priest, got me into the seminary?"

"What about him?"

"Much later, years later, he told me something. He told me that he'd known all along that I had a vocation to the priesthood. He told me he had waited six years for me to make the choice for myself."

Kruger saw the playful twinkle in the priest's eye. "Boyle?"

Mendoza nodded. "He was chaplain at the prison where I was." He turned on the faucet to measure water for the instant rice. "When he phoned me to explain why you were coming to stay, he tipped his hand. He said out here in the desert you'd have time to ask yourself what Christ Himself would do in your predicament." He glanced back and grinned.

CHAPTER 3

General Augusto Cavallino, the president of the military tribunal, rapped the gavel. His voice fell like steel in the hushed silence. "And if there are further disturbances from the gallery, I shall have the courtroom cleared of spectators!" He had objected to a public trial. He had twice sat on public military tribunals judging cases of war crimes, and both trials had been marred by demonstrations in the gallery. The inflammatory press preceding the Kruger trial had aroused the public not only here in Bologna but in all the major Italian cities, and he had warned the government of the dangers of a public trial.

He glared down at the crowd of spectators from his place in the central courtroom of Bologna's Palace of Justice, letting the silence settle again, reminding himself of his determination to complete the Kruger proceedings before the Christmas holidays, a little over six weeks away. If disruptions continued, it could take months to reach a verdict. He leaned toward Major Pavoni on his right.

In the gallery a woman sneezed. Beneath the judges' bench, the defense and prosecution were ranged on opposite sides of the room. The defendant sat in a dock between two military policemen. Instead of the usual black gowns of a civilian tribunal, the three judges wore military uniforms. A head taller than the officers on either side of him, the president of the tribunal, General Cavallino, dominated the bench. His experienced, grave, and humorless face appeared lugubrious under the full head of carefully combed white hair. He was known, even by the general public, to be a man of uncompromising principles, a conservative force in Italian politics, and a military officer of the old school. Cavallino nodded to his fellow judges, Major Pavoni on his right and Colonel Ercolani on his left. He sat forward, opened the folio on the bench in front of him, and said, "I now call upon the prosecution to read the indictment."

A court reporter ticked out the president's words on a stenographic machine.

The prosecutor, Umberto Canavese, rose. He was a tall man for an Italian and he camouflaged his skeletal thinness under his voluminous black counselor's gown. Long accustomed to the procedures of military war crimes trials, he drew back the sleeve of his gown and checked his watch as he approached the bench. Among counselors, he had a reputation for logic, eloquence, and success. He carried a copy of the indictment prepared by the prosecution and submitted in advance to the court and the defense. He made a deferential bow to the bench. "May it please the court." He spoke confidently, with a Florentine accent as he opened the folio and read, "The Republic of Italy against Karl Gustav Kruger, formerly a citizen of Germany and an officer in the Wehrmacht section of the German Armed Forces." He looked toward the dock. "The Republic of Italy, by the undersigned, Umberto Giuseppe Canavese, duly appointed to represent the Italian Government in the investigation of the charges against and the prosecution of war criminals, pursuant to the charter of this tribunal and the Italian military code, hereby accuses as guilty, in the respects hereinafter set forth, of war crimes and crimes against humanity, and of a conspiracy to commit those crimes, all as defined in the charter of this tribunal, and accordingly name as defendant in this cause and as indicted on the counts hereinafter set out, Karl Gustav Kruger." He swung toward the spectators' gallery and continued. "Count one. The defendant, with divers other persons, committed war crimes in the town of Montefalco in the province of Emilio-Romano in the course of waging aggressive war by taking and executing hostages from the civilian population on September 14, 1944. These acts were contrary to international conventions, particularly Article Fifty of the Hague Regulations, 1907, the laws and customs of war . . ."

Kruger looked down at his folded hands. He had read the ninepage indictment when the prosecution filed it with the court. His defense attorney, Vittorio Burgati, had gone over both counts with him point by point to untangle the legal jargon. Three months ago, when the state appointed Burgati as his attorney, the issue of Kruger's attempt to cancel and then postpone the Montefalco execution had come up in the preparation of his defense. Initially, Burgati had hoped to base his case on those issues, but he needed evidence and witnesses. It was then that Kruger mentioned the name Hans Reiger. He informed Burgati that he had seen the man in 1967 at his father's funeral. Burgati had made several trips to Germany to look for Reiger. Later, without his knowledge, Anna had joined in the search. After three months they had all but given up hope of finding Reiger, and Burgati, falling back on his earlier intentions, had been forced to base his case on a premise that the reprisal was legal under international law and pursue the old mitigating argument of superior orders. In the past, so Anna had argued, cases of war crimes based on those two claims had rarely succeeded in any European court, but with the absence of Reiger as a witness, Burgati had had no choice. The trial, Kruger knew, was opening on shaky ground.

Canavese read on in the indictment. "On September 14, 1944, while acting as commander, he issued orders that fifty members of the male civilian population of Montefalco be arrested and held as hostages in reprisal for the deaths of five German soldiers under his command at the hands of Italian partisans."

It is true, Kruger thought, *stated in those terms, every word of the indictment is true.*

"On September 14, 1944, he was responsible for carrying out the order of execution of fifty male civilians by firing squad in the public square of the town of Montefalco, an execution witnessed by the population of the town." He turned to the gallery and looked out at Anna where she sat under the courtroom window. She looked pale. This morning she wore a dignified blue suit and a white blouse, and had knotted her hair behind her head. He closed his mind to the drone of Canavese's indictment.

In the seven months since he had returned to Italy as a layman, she had visited him regularly in the Bologna prison where he had remained, awaiting arraignment and trial. In America, between his decision to go to trial and the Vatican's official letter informing him that he had been deprived of his rights and offices as a priest and would henceforth live as a Catholic layman (there had been no grounds for excommunication, as such), he had not met with her. She had come to him on her own, after he committed himself to safekeeping in the Bologna prison, and offered to help with the preparation of his defense. He had refused her offer and begged her to fulfill her obligation to stand as a witness for the prosecution. Then, by accident, he discovered her collaboration with Burgati when his counselor questioned him one day about the Adele Ravine. Anna defended her involvement with the defense by arguing that Burgati was a professor of law at the University of Bologna and had little practical experience in courtroom tactics or presentation. Moreover, she violently disagreed with the compromise of Burgati's defense claims, insisting that he had not searched hard enough for the missing Corporal Reiger. She offered, in the end, to finance his defense herself if he would replace the court-appointed Burgati with a more aggressive and practical private attorney, but he refused.

Since then she had worked with Burgati, guided him, and continued her own search for Reiger in Germany, convinced that he was still alive. In September word leaked out about her meetings with Burgati, and the prosecution began to have second thoughts about calling her to the stand. Moreover, the reaction in Montefalco to her return to Italy was swift, and she was warned to stay away. This morning, this first day of trial, when he entered the dock and saw her sitting in the gallery, he had felt both alarmed and grateful, knowing she had braved the hostility of the spectators to demonstrate her support of him. Two days ago she had brought him a new gray civilian suit, shirt, and tie to wear at his trial.

"Count two." Canavese turned to the gallery. "The defendant wantonly burned public buildings in the town of Montefalco on September 14, 1944, without military justification or necessity. This act violated Articles Forty-six and Fifty of the Hague Regulations, 1907, the laws and customs of war, the general principles of criminal law . . ."

Anna saw Canavese turn to the dock to address the indictment directly to the defendant. Karl sat motionless, with his shoulders slumped. She would have to speak to him about his posture, for the deportment of a defendant in the dock was important. He *looked* like a guilty man. Canavese exploited his appearance, speaking in a voice edged with self-assured contempt. Though she had not had access to the written indictment, she had discussed the question of Karl's responsibility for the burning of the buildings in the Piazza Nazionale with Burgati. Karl had told Burgati that the order had been carried out by Sergeant Rudolf Oster, who issued it without his knowledge. As with most of Burgati's defense claims, the problem was one of evidence and witnesses, and Corporal Reiger alone could testify to Oster's insubordination.

"The order to burn public buildings in the town was issued the same night as orders were given to retreat. The burning of these buildings in no way contributed to the military necessities of the German Army and was intended as an act of punishment by the retreating army."

Anna read the headline of the Bologna newspaper in her lap: "Former Priest on Trial for War Crimes." Since the arraignment the European press had deluged the public with articles about the "former priest on trial for Nazi war crimes." She had passed a newspaper stand that morning to read the stories emblazoned across the front pages of the papers from Milan, Rome, Bologna, Genoa,

Florence, and Naples. The real issue of the trial, justice for the victims of the small town of Montefalco, had vanished under an avalanche of print exploiting the story of the so-called Nazi priest for every social, political, and religious issue now dogging the Italian people. She had warned Karl that the pressures surrounding the trial would inevitably influence the court's decision. She had begged him to dismiss his state-appointed attorney and seek private counsel. She had offered to pay the costs herself, but he had refused, insisting that the facts of his case spoke for themselves. In her opinion, the academic Burgati did not have a fighting chance against Canavese.

"Crimes are committed by persons," Canavese began the peroration of his indictment. "And while it is quite proper to employ the fiction of responsibility of a state or corporation for the purpose of imposing a collective liability, it is intolerable to let such a legalism become the basis of personal immunity. The court must recognize that one who has committed criminal acts may not take refuge in superior orders nor in the doctrine that his crimes were acts of states. Under the Italian criminal code, no defense based on either of these doctrines can be entertained."

Karl had lifted his eyes to stare at Canavese. Anna recalled three months ago in the visitors' room at the prison when the subject of the legality of his reprisal and the argument of superior orders came up. Karl had objected to Burgati's use of the old argument of superior orders, arguing that it had appeared in the defense testimony of every war crimes trial since Nuremberg and had no moral validity. Burgati, on the other hand, had pointed out that the legal dimensions of his case were not the same as the moral. Superior orders had been a deciding influence on him at the time of the execution. It could not be avoided in his legal defense.

Anna felt the familiar helplessness return. She had long ago realized why Karl had never, beyond an occasional guarded hint or a slip of the tongue, expressed feelings toward her other than those of simple gratitude and affection. He had already accepted the fact that he would be found guilty and sentenced to life imprisonment. To protect her from the mistake of investing hopes in him as she had done twenty-eight years before, he had decided to repress all the feelings he had for her as a man. Once burned twice shy. It had taken weeks for both of them to adjust to the fact that he was no longer a priest. For Karl, after seventeen years, the experience of living as a layman was painful and awkward. As a dedicated priest he had lost contact with the secular world of men and women together, and the sacrifice of his priesthood had profoundly lowered his self-esteem as a man. She suddenly wished Angelo had come to Bologna. It was she who had advised their son not to come, for fear the prosecution would exploit his presence at the trial.

"Wherefore, this indictment is lodged with the tribunal in Italian, English, and German," Canavese said, "each text having equal authenticity, and the charges herein made against the above-mentioned defendant are hereby presented to the tribunal." He made a formal, rather studied bow toward the bench. "Umberto Canavese, acting on behalf of the Republic of Italy." Closing his folio, he returned to the prosecution's table and sat down.

The preliminary procedures, the order convening the court, the swearing-in of the president, members, judge advocate, shorthand writers, and the interpreters, had taken over an hour. The reading of the indictment, twenty-five minutes. For a moment, while the president conferred with Pavoni and Ercolani, a tense silence fell over the courtroom. Karl still sat slump-shouldered. He looked exhausted and resigned.

As a murmur erupted in the spectators' gallery, Judge Cavallino called out sharply, "The courtroom will come to order!" then turned to Burgati. "If the counsel for the defense wishes to make any application before the accused is asked to plead, the court will hear what you have to say."

Vittorio Burgati got quickly to his feet. The contrast in appearance between Burgati and his opponent was immediate. He was a little man, a head shorter than Canavese, and his gestures were rapid and impulsive. He had a full head of unkempt black hair and wore tortoise-shell spectacles, which gave him an absentminded academic look. He addressed the bench. "I wish to make an application on behalf of the accused, Signore Presidente. The application is in regard to the testimony of witnesses for the defense." He went on to describe the importance of testimony from witnesses residing in West Germany. Given the lack of extradition agreements between Italy and Germany, it would be impossible to present testimony of Germans unwilling to come to Italy under existing rules. "On behalf of the defendant, I request that the tribunal authorize the testimony of these witnesses to be given by means of written depositions to be taken in Germany by the defense and presented as valid testimony in this court."

Anna felt relieved and encouraged by Burgati's precaution. He had not given up hope, at least, of finding their missing witness, Corporal Reiger.

Cavallino conferred with Pavoni and Ercolani, then spoke: "The tribunal will accept the testimony of such witnesses." He went on to say that the depositions must be taken in the presence of counselors for both the defense and prosecution, and the prosecution would have the right, after the depositions were taken, to cross-examine the witness, and such testimony of cross-examination would be received as evidence in court. Then he turned to Karl in the dock. "I will now call upon the defendant, Karl Gustav Kruger, to plead guilty or not guilty to the charges against him. He will rise and address the court."

He rose. Anna saw that the suit she had bought for him was too large, and the sleeves hung two inches below his wrists. Nearby, someone sniggered. He stood erect in the dock. He spoke, but his words were inaudible.

"You will address your plea in a voice audible to the court," Cavallino said.

Anna knew, at once, the reason for his murmured response. Privately, in his own heart, he did not believe in the plea he was forced to make.

"Not guilty," he said.

In the gallery a woman shouted, *"Assassino!"* The crowd around her broke into excited chatter.

Cavallino rapped his gavel. "Order! If there is disturbance in this court, those who make it will be forced to leave!" The chatter subsided. "The defendant will be seated."

Karl took his seat and folded his hands.

Cavallino looked at his watch. "It is now eleven forty-eight. The tribunal will adjourn until one o'clock this afternoon." He brought the gavel down.

In the next moment, in an explosion of noise, the spectators were on their feet, moving hurriedly toward the door. Anna waited until Karl was led from the courtroom and then joined the crowd spilling down the staircase to the ground floor. She kept to the crowd's fringe, relieved to see there was no one she recognized among the hundred or so people. Witnesses for both the prosecution and defense had been enjoined by the tribunal not to appear at the trial itself as spectators.

The ground floor of the huge Renaissance building was mobbed with people leaving for the lunch break. She pushed her way to the entrance and stepped out into the small sunlit square. She had no appetite, but there was a small coffee shop nearby where she could have relative peace for an hour. She darted through the traffic threading its way diagonally across the square, heading toward the street at the northeast corner. It was called the Via Garibaldi, and the coincidence of identical names with Montefalco's leading street had, since her arrival in Bologna, seemed strangely ominous.

"Signora!" she heard Burgati call as she reached the center of the square. He approached, blustering, heedless of the traffic, with his briefcase swinging and his gown blown back over his shoulder.

"Good morning, Anna." He seemed upset and distracted.

She nodded. "Vittorio."

He looked around as if someone in the crowd outside the courthouse might have observed him following her. "Something has come up. I need to speak with you."

"I'm on my way to a coffee shop in the Garibaldi." She took his arm. "Come. You can tell me while we walk."

He let himself be led. "This morning, before breakfast, I had a visitor. I never receive business calls at home, I have a wife and a child, I always make appointments at the university. The man appeared, unannounced!"

She smiled. A man of crotchety habits. "A bill collector, Vittorio?"

"The man came to see me about Kruger. He arrived from Munich and came to my door without as much as a phone call!"

She released Burgati's arm, suddenly alert. "What did he want?"

"He flew here from Munich to make a proposition to me concerning my defense. His name is Gunther Bohm. He's an attorney representing a Munich-based industrial firm. I don't know what firm, he wouldn't say. All he would say is that his employer sent him here to Bologna—to me—with an offer to finance the hiring of an additional private attorney for the defense." Burgati stopped and looked at her with laughing astonishment. "Imagine!"

"Did he say why?" she asked, knowing part of the answer already. People had been talking for weeks now about Burgati's line of defense.

"He certainly did! He was quite frank about it! He told me that Kruger should have the benefit of a private counselor more experienced in the practical side of war crimes procedures."

"I see." She took his arm again, thinking she could not agree more.

"I told the man, of course, that the decision was not mine to make, and he should have gone to Kruger himself. But the fellow knew of Kruger's refusal to accept private financial aid and said I should make the offer myself."

"Perhaps he knows of the offer Karl's mother made."

"Perhaps. At any rate, I told him the offer would be made to Kruger, but I myself would not be a part of it."

She thought, at once, of her long and fruitless search for Reiger. "Tell me, Vittorio, what was the name of the man's employer, this Munich industrialist?"

"He refused to say. He told me the man wished to remain anonymous." Burgati glanced at her with a knowing smile. "That's when my suspicions were aroused."

They had reached the Via Garibaldi. She steered Burgati in the direction of the coffee shop. "Go on."

"All I learned about the man was that he's a friend—*was* a friend —of Karl's father. That was the explanation this little Bohm fellow gave—a friend of the family." He chuckled, sarcastically.

"Is that surprising?"

"Not in itself, no. But I've had experience of these offers before. Every time there's a war crime trial in Europe, you can count on private and anonymous finance for the defense. It's no secret where the money comes from. There are a lot of rich men in the world who still keep the Nazi cause alive. You know about such organizations, I'm sure—usually innocent-looking veterans' clubs, that kind of thing. Germany is notorious for them."

"Karl was not a member of the Nazi Party, Vittorio," she said, recalling Karl's strange reticence when they talked of his father.

"So what? A verdict of innocent for any war crimes defendant is good publicity for their cause, no matter who the defendant is. They're crazy people, these Neo-Nazis."

"Did this Gunther Bohm know about our search for Hans Reiger?"

"I worked the conversation around to that. He had never heard of the man."

Anna let go of Burgati's arm. "You want me, I take it, to tell Karl."

"I would prefer that, yes. I think telling him myself would only further undermine his confidence in me."

She pointed to the coffee shop. "Would you like a coffee, Vittorio?"

"No, no. I have less than an hour to prepare my opening address."

"I will see Karl tonight and tell him about the offer."

"Thank you." He bowed. "And I trust you will tell him I think the money is quite suspect."

"I will certainly get around to discussing the Neo-Nazis with him, Vittorio, rest assured." She watched Burgati hurry back toward the courthouse, remembering the promise she and Karl had made in the beginning of his trial about secrets kept and things left unsaid.

CHAPTER 4

I

The window of his fourth-floor room in the Santa Croce prison swung open, letting the cold night breeze sweep in. There were no bars on the window of this room. Back in April, when he moved into the room, one of the fourth-floor guards had informed him that the room (more room than cell) was the one reserved for clerics accused of crimes and therefore, according to the rules of the Vatican Concordat with Italy, more comfortable than any normal prison cell. The guard had said he was quite lucky, being an ex-priest, to have been given the room by the warden.

Kruger stood at the open window, enjoying the rush of cold air. It would help him sleep, later. After seven months, he had even grown fond of the room. If a cleric—a real cleric, that is—came to prison, he would have to give it up, of course. Signore Dania, the warden, had assigned him the room only as a compensation for the fact that his imprisonment was, so far, self-imposed, since he had come back to Italy of his own choice. On the advice of the Italian authorities, he had agreed to lodge himself in a safe prison during the term of the trial instead of taking a room in a private accommodation. The advice had proved sound. The crowds around the Palace of Justice for this first day of trial had been hostile.

He leaned out the window. Beyond the dark space of the Giardini Regina Margherita, Bologna's big public garden, he could see the top of the Palazzo della Justicia and, farther north, the tower of the church of San Domenico. Since the preliminary hearings began, he had divided his life between the one and the other. From hearings and arraignments, he had gone to San Domenico for daily Mass, for though he had given up his priesthood, he had not abandoned his

Catholicism. Anna had almost daily joined him for Mass in the ancient church.

Outside the door to his room there was the rattle of his dinner tray being removed. To safeguard him from the other prisoners (patriotism ran high even here in Santa Croce), Signore Dania had ordered him to eat his meals in his room, thereby forcing the guards to shuttle back and forth between the kitchen and the fourth floor three times a day. The guards seemed not to resent the task, but it was a form of room service he could have done without. The meal that night had been the usual soup and pasta, but he had eaten little. The first day of trial had taken away his appetite. The prosecution had immediately called two firsthand witnesses, and the stories of their sufferings following the execution had corroborated his worst fears. Burgati's driving cross-examination of the witnesses, in an effort to substantiate his claim of military necessity, had been even more painful than the prosecution's examination.

The cold damp wind smelled of sulfurous industrial pollution. He closed and latched the window. The tray rattled off down the corridor outside, reminding him of Anna's visiting hour. You could keep time by the dinner trays, they came at six and were removed at seven, in time for visitors—if visitors came. Anna had not appeared for the last two nights and her absence had been a taste of what life would be like when the trial ended: the endlessness of hopeless expectations, living each day for one hour, knowing that she would come and go like the clockwork trays. She had promised to come tonight, though, and he would write letters to fill the waiting time.

He moved the gooseneck lamp from the chair next to his bed and set it on the small table. The room reminded him of other rooms he had occupied: his room at *Offiziersschule* and his room at St. John's seminary. The hard metal-framed bed, the wooden chair, the sink with its discolored mirror, and the single gooseneck lamp. The one luxury was the prie-dieu against the wall. The chair served for a bedside table. He moved it back to the little table and opened the three unanswered letters. One from Angelo, another from his mother, and a third from Father Auden at St. Luke's. He would answer Angelo's first. Angelo, on Anna's advice, had decided to remain in America for the trial; for if he came, he would surely be used as evidence for the prosecution's charge of irresponsibility as a soldier. The defense would argue that he was a dutiful soldier, but Angelo was a living witness to his military disobedience.

Outside in the corridor there were footsteps and he waited for the clockwork creak of the wooden floor. If the floor creaked, the guard was coming to his door. It creaked. A moment later, there was a soft tap.

Mario Savini, the night guard, stood in the corridor. "You have a visitor, signore," he said, buttoning his tunic. He gestured with his thumb over his shoulder and smiled. "The lady."

"Right. I'm coming." Kruger tossed the letters to the table, glanced quickly in the mirror, and went out. Following Savini to the staircase, he parted his hair with his fingers. His impulse was to take the stairs two at a time, but he held back behind the fat little man who labored down the steps one by one, wheezing. Counting the wasted seconds, he followed Savini along the first-floor hallway past the warden's office, the prison staff offices, and the prison guards' recreation room. The walls of the unpainted cavernous hallway were the color of dead moss. He wondered if the interior of Gaeta Prison, where he would spend the rest of his life, was as cheerless as that of Santa Croce.

Savini fished through a chain of keys and unlocked the door to the visitors' room. "It's five after seven, signore. So you have fifty-five minutes."

"Thanks." He stepped into the bare moss-colored room. Anna was seated, as usual, at the plain wooden table. The fluorescent light overhead always washed the color from her face.

She said, "Are you angry?"

"Worried." He wanted to circle the table and embrace her, but checked his impulse and sat down on the opposite side. "Two days. I missed you," he said, feeling he had earned his modest little confession. "I guess you've spoiled me." He let a delayed sense of relief wash over him.

She reached to the floor and brought up a straw basket. "I brought some gorgonzola and apples. And some pastries. The kind you like. *Mistocce.*" She set the little basket on the table.

"Thanks." He smiled.

"I forgot the toothpaste you asked for."

"It doesn't matter. I borrowed a tube from one of the guards."

"I couldn't come these last two nights. I had things to do."

He couldn't help saying, "You weren't in the courtroom this afternoon."

"No. Something—something came up."

"They called Aldo Baldini to the stand."

"I know. Burgati told me. He made a mess of the cross-examination."

"Why do you say that?"

"Aldo Baldini's father was the director of the bank when you were in Montefalco. Giovanni Baldini knew that you had tried to postpone the execution."

"Giovanni Baldini is dead."

"Burgati should have questioned Aldo about his father's meeting with you the night before the execution. I'm convinced he knows what took place."

"Burgati wanted Aldo to admit that the partisans were planning another attack on my soldiers."

"It was a useless line of questioning, Karl," she said, wearily. "Aldo was not more than fourteen at the time, and his father had no contact with the partisans. He will never prove the reprisal was a military necessity. Not to those three judges."

"He believes he can. Besides, he has no other argument."

"He does, though—your intentions at the time. Guilt must be based on the willingness to commit the crime."

"He can't prove that."

"Karl!" She gave up and sat back. "He hasn't really tried. He's using your case to test a theory of his own in a gray area of international law."

"I don't believe that."

"He's been writing articles on the Hague Convention rules for reprisal executions for years."

"He was appointed by the government. There's nothing I can do."

"You can ask for a change, you can replace him."

"I haven't the money to hire an attorney of my own, and I will not use yours or my mother's. We've been through this before."

"Karl." She sat forward. "There is other money available."

"Whose money?"

"Friends. Anonymous friends. Money has been offered to Burgati to hire a private associate attorney. He felt it might weaken your confidence in him if he told you himself. He asked me to speak to you. He told me this morning, and I spoke to him again this afternoon. A donation will be deposited in a bank here in Bologna."

"By whom? I don't have anonymous friends."

"I don't know."

"From where?"

She fingered the fruit in the basket. "The man who offered it to Burgati wouldn't give names."

"It's generous, and I'm grateful. But let's not kid ourselves. The money will be wasted."

This time, her anger was forthright. "If you want a guilty verdict, then tell the court! We can dispense with the trial!" He dropped his head against his hand, silenced. They were back again to where they had been countless times before. She went on. "What kind of verdict do you want, Karl?"

"A just one."

"Which means a verdict based on the law and not your personal sense of moral guilt. Do you believe you are guilty under the *law?*"

"I don't know." Burgati and Anna had both turned his brain over the last seven months like wood on a lathe.

"Then you must defend yourself."

She had argued this point a hundred times. He said, "Burgati has done everything he can to find Reiger. He's been through every record in Germany. There's no trace of the man."

"He may have changed his name after the war, Karl. There are other ways of tracing him. He may have left Germany, he could be anywhere. South America. A lot of them went there. You saw him at your father's funeral in 1967."

"I *thought* I saw him. I can't be sure."

"Try again to remember. Was he there alone, did you see him speak to anyone?"

"I don't know. It was only for a moment. We had just left the gravesite. My mind was elsewhere."

"You're sure your mother did not recognize him?"

"Positive. I've talked with her twice by phone. She had never seen the man before."

She appeared to weigh something in her mind for a moment. "You mentioned once that your father's friends were at the funeral."

He looked away to the clock on the wall—7:28. Both Burgati and Anna had repeatedly questioned him about people who had attended his father's funeral. Reiger, he was sure, had not stood at the gravesite with his father's Nazi friends. He said, "They were business connections more than friends. My father didn't have many friends at the end." He took an apple from the basket and turned it in his hand.

"What kind of business connections?"

"Bankers, industrialists. My father died a rich man."

"You didn't know the men?"

"Not personally, no. I went to Germany only once after the war."

"You said once that your father left you money in his will, but you gave it to your mother."

"I was a priest."

"Then your mother inherited everything?"

He saw by the look in her face that she was groping in the dark, but would not relent. "No." He hesitated. "Not everything."

"Who else benefited?"

He sighed. "My father belonged to a veterans' club. He gave some to the club."

"Veterans of what?"

"The war."

"The men, the friends at the funeral, were they members of this club?"

"Yes." He bit into the apple.

"Was Reiger a member?"

"No. I'm sure he wasn't."

"Why not, he was a veteran?"

"Reiger was a soldier in the Wehrmacht." He tried to swallow the morsel of apple, but his throat was like a closed fist.

"I don't understand."

"It isn't important."

"Is there something you haven't told me, Karl?" He did not reply. She reached across the table and lay her hand on top of his, gently. "Remember what you told me? We've no time left for secrets?"

He swallowed. It took moments for the soft pulp to slide free from his throat. He nodded, thinking to himself how bound up all their lives were: his with Anna's and Anna's with even his own father's. He sighed, saying, "My father was a member of the Nazi Party. Not an important member. Just average."

"Why didn't you tell me this?"

"It isn't important, and it isn't relevant to my case. I was never a member of the party. And besides, I promised my mother after my father died never to speak of it again."

"Tell me what you know, Karl. I will not break your mother's secret."

"He was a minor official. He gave money to the party, and they rewarded him with an honorary title. He wasn't active, but he believed in the party. He worshiped Hitler. It was the Nazis who gave him his bicycle business. They took it from a Jew and gave it to him for services rendered. He owed everything he had to the Nazis. When the war ended, he was still a believer. Not only him, but others, too." He gripped her hand. "The friends, the businessmen who came to his funeral, they were all Nazis. Still, in 1967. After the war, they formed a veterans' club. They still believe the Reich will come back one day. They hold their meetings openly, under the guise of old veterans' bashes. They contribute money to the cause. A lot of money, I think, disguised in all kinds of investments all over the world. It's mad, isn't it?"

She stroked his hand. "Reiger *was* a member, wasn't he?"

"He wasn't a member of the party during the war. He was only a Wehrmacht soldier like me."

"You recognized none of the men at the funeral?"

"Yes, two of them. A man by the name of von Scheffel. And another named Ernst Müller. I never asked or learned von Scheffel's first name. All I know is, he took over my father's business when— when my father began to drink. My father was an alcoholic. In the end, he went mad."

She sat forward, weighing her thoughts. "Tell me this, would your father's Nazi friends have any interest in the verdict of your trial?"

"I don't know. I haven't thought about it."

"Would a guilty verdict here in Italy affect the Neo-Nazis in Germany?"

He recalled what his mother had told him about the worldwide investments of his father's friends. "If they are interested, it would be only a question of publicity. They spend a lot of money to clear their reputation. Even today. Crazy, isn't it?"

"Perhaps."

"The money that was offered to Burgati, it comes from Germany, doesn't it?" he asked. She nodded. "In that case, the answer is no. Do you understand?"

"Yes."

"Tell Burgati I will have no part of it."

"I will do that, Karl." She gripped his hand again, tightly. "But I want you to do something for me."

"What?"

"Say nothing to Burgati about what we've discussed tonight. Say nothing about your father's membership in the Nazi Party."

"I don't intend to say anything. It's not relevant to my case. Anyway, why do you want me to keep my mouth shut now?"

She smiled, drew his hand closer, and softly kissed his fingers, smiling. "Trust me."

II

"The prosecution calls the witness Paula Bosco to the stand!" Canavese announced.

A murmur rippled through the gallery. Canavese folded his arms and stood waiting. The door behind the witness stand remained closed. At the bench the judges thumbed through pages, waiting.

Anna had not been present for the morning session, and Kruger saw she would be absent for the afternoon session as well. In these first eight days of trial, her attendance had been irregular. Her place in the crowded gallery today was occupied by a large woman wearing a red print dress. A group of young Italians stood against the wall at the back of the room. Seats came at a premium, and they were occupied mostly by middle-aged Italians, with a sprinkling of university students and newspaper reporters. He fingered the end of his tie, waiting. Paula Bosco had been named four days ago by the prosecution as a prospective witness. Her name on the list had not surprised him, but he had long dreaded her testimony more than that of the others. Back in February, in Montefalco, he had seen the visible scars of her suffering when he passed the Bosco tailor shop.

Presently, the small door in the paneled oak wall opened. Accompanied by a uniformed guard, Paula Bosco came out into the courtroom. She wore a matronly black dress and a heavy blue coat which, for a tailoress, looked old and frayed. The guard guided her to the witness stand and whispered to her. She nodded and felt for the railing. When she reached the fenced platform, she looked around the courtroom, but obviously saw only shadows. She appeared frightened.

Canavese and the court clerk approached the stand. "Raise your right hand, Signora Bosco. You will be sworn in."

The clerk called out the oath, and she repeated it, faintly. She was instructed to sit down.

"Signora Bosco," Canavese said, "please tell the court your full name, your place of birth, your present residence, and your occupation."

"I am Paula Maria Bosco. I was born in Montefalco, and I have lived in Montefalco all my life. I am a tailor."

Canavese eased her into the testimony with several questions about the Second World War: where she had lived in 1944, if she was married at the time, and her occupation during the war. She replied to his questions with single words, her thin voice barely audible in the huge room.

The president of the court admonished her, "You must speak up, signora, the court cannot hear your testimony."

She nodded.

"Signora Bosco," Canavese said, "can you identify the man seated in the defendant's chair opposite you?"

"Objection!" Burgati rose. "That question, Mr. President, is designed for pure effect. The prosecution is well aware that the witness is partially blind and cannot see the defendant."

"Objection sustained," the president conceded. Burgati resumed his seat, but the effect nonetheless had been achieved. There were murmurs of protest from the spectators.

Canavese moved thoughtfully toward the witness. "Signora Bosco, describe for the court your husband's political affiliations during the war."

"My husband's what? I don't understand."

"Your husband's political beliefs. Was he *for* or *against* the Fascist government of Mussolini?"

"Neither, signore."

"Neither?" Canavese feigned a look of astonishment. "How is that possible? All Italians at the time were either for or against Fascism."

Kruger knew before she spoke what the answer would be: he remembered Gianni Bosco's handicap from his visits to the shop. Canavese's line of argument that morning had been to show the random purposelessness of his selection of hostages for the execution. In the case of Gianni Bosco, the execution had obviously been meaningless. Embarrassed by the question, Signora Bosco lowered her eyes. She said, "My husband was almost deaf. From birth. He never learned to read. He could not understand such things as politics. In the square that day, he did not know why they wanted to shoot him." She covered her face.

Someone far back in the spectator's gallery shouted, *"Nazi murderers!"* The crowd took up the cry and broke into turmoil.

Cavallino began rapping his gavel. "Silence! Order! If there is not immediate silence, I will have this courtroom cleared of spectators!"

Burgati scribbled notes in the legal pad beside him on the table. Kruger felt sorry for the man.

CHAPTER 5

I

The morning of the eleventh day, the trial began with a steady drizzle, a cold wind from the Austrian alps, and a pewter-colored sky. Despite the weather's injustice, the indomitable demonstrators, the police, the news media, and the spectators returned. In the tiny square before the Palace of Justice the demonstrators milled in concentric circles behind police cordons. An hour before the proceedings began, they were already shouting slogans and waving hand-painted placards for the benefit of the sheltered portable TV cameras and the newspaper photographers. They were in place when the police car carrying the defendant drove up the Viale Giugno to the side entrance of the palace, and they shouted when the "Nazi priest" emerged from the car surrounded by police to be escorted into the building by his attorney.

The sight of the man, brief as it was, sparked the protesters' dampened spirits. The faction promoting the Italian Communist Party, the largest group made up of university students and unemployed Bolognese workers, was the first to surge forward. Placards defending the Italian Communist movement, placards protesting the return of Neo-Fascism in Italian politics, placards calling for the restoration of the death penalty for Nazi war criminals bounced in the air. Here and there among the Communist placards were hand-painted banners defending the new Italian terrorist organization, the Brigate Rosse. Their presence had been inspired by trial testimony in recent days concerning the partisan group of the same name that had operated in the Reno Valley during the Second World War. From the northeast corner of the square came the Italian Christian Democrats decrying, at once, both the "Nazi priest" and their political opponents, the Communists. They converged on the palace, and broke through the police cordon. For a moment, while the police reorganized and prepared to descend with truncheons, they appeared to be on the verge of a brawl with the Communist faction. Another splinter group milled in circles in the narrow Via Garibaldi. They carried the familiar time-tested placards protesting the presence of the Americans in Vietnam. The American "Nazi priest" had become in recent days the harbinger of all the evils of his adopted country, if not the world.

Inside the courtroom on the third floor of the palace, the noise of the crowd in the piazza outside was like the annoying background static of a mis-tuned radio station.

For this morning's session, knowing that the defense's strongest argument would be that of military necessity, Canavese had called witnesses from Montefalco who could testify that the war in the Reno Valley had already been lost by the time Kruger gave orders for the execution. To support his position, he had called Montefalco's former *postino,* Mario Brunetti, who had bicycled through Montefalco and the surrounding countryside for almost sixty years delivering the mail. Brunetti was part of Montefalco's landscape, like Monte di Granaglione or the church of San Tommaso. He had delivered mail before Mussolini came to power and had worn the postal uniform of several Italian regimes, including the Fascist, but everyone in Montefalco knew that his collaboration went no further than his clothes. Brunetti, now seventy-seven, as he proudly announced, had shrunk from a little to a tiny man since Kruger had last seen him. Canavese had examined him for over an hour, and by the time Burgati commenced his cross-examination, the old man's memory had been awakened to vivid and bitter recollections of the days and hours leading up to the execution. "Then let me put a question to the witness that he was asked before by the prosecution," Burgati said, turning back to Brunetti. The old man sat forward and cupped his hand attentively to his ear. "Approximately how many days before the partisan attack on Kruger's soldiers did the partisans launch a similar attack on German soldiers north of Montefalco?"

Brunetti considered the question. His wrinkled face twitched angrily. "Fifteen."

Kruger saw Anna turn to the elderly woman on her right and nod. She had appeared that morning with a woman she had once identified as her mother's best friend, Angela Guardini, who was not among the scheduled witnesses for the prosecution. The woman reacted to Anna's affirmation with a smile.

Burgati had made his point. There was a murmur in the spectators' gallery. He went on. "Fifteen days." He nodded thoughtfully, letting the number hang in the air. "In other words, the partisan band known as the Brigate Rosse had committed similar acts of murder and terror against the German troops stationed in the Reno Valley prior to the attack on Lieutenant Kruger's forces?"

"It happened in a village to the north, signore. The partisans set fire to a German fuel tank."

"I'm not speaking of *that* attack, Signore Brunetti!"

Brunetti went on, nonetheless. "The Germans shot twenty-five innocent people because of a fuel tank, signore! Is that a just reprisal?"

The point was made before Burgati could interrupt. The gallery erupted with cheers. Cavallino called for order. Kruger remembered the attack Brunetti spoke of and the reprisal carried out by the SS two weeks before the attack on his soldiers. For the Italians in the courtroom, it seemed useless to make distinctions between the SS and the Wehrmacht. They were one and the same thing: Nazis. Burgati steered the line of questions toward his thesis of military necessity. "Tell me, Signore Brunetti, at the time the partisans attacked the German convoy on September 13, 1944, were the German troops occupying Montefalco under military pressure from their enemies?"

Brunetti thought for a moment. "By then, signore, it did not matter."

"What did not matter?"

"Whether they stayed or left. By then, the war in Montefalco was already over. Everyone knew it was over. Even the Germans knew it was over."

"How do you know that, sir?"

"I was *postino* for the Germans and the *Fascisti,* signore. I delivered mail to the Germans. The soldiers *talked* to me. They told me it was useless to stay in Montefalco, it was over!" He looked at Kruger. "It wasn't to stop the partisans from attacking his soldiers that Kruger killed the people of Montefalco. It was to punish us for what the others had done."

Kruger looked at Burgati and, for an instant, their eyes locked, meaningfully. What the old man had said was true. He wondered how long Burgati would go on pulling at threads when it was clear that the entire fabric of his argument was unraveling. The law of reprisal executions had never, since Geneva and Nuremberg, been defined.

"I have no more questions," said Burgati.

"You may step down," the president said to Brunetti.

The old man seemed puzzled that his testimony had come to an abrupt end. As he started down the steps of the witness dock, a soft whisper began in the gallery.

"Mr. President!" Canavese stood up suddenly. "With the court's permission I would like to call an additional witness for the prosecution."

"Yesterday, Signore Canavese, you informed the court you would conclude the prosecution's testimony with the witness Brunetti." Cavallino made no effort to hide his impatience.

"I did so inform the court yesterday, Mr. President." Canavese left his table. "However, in the meantime, testimony has come to light which I believe is crucial. I respectfully request permission to summon an additional witness previously listed as only 'possible.'"

Cavallino conferred with the other judges. Kruger saw Anna start to rise, but she was restrained by Signora Guardini. She looked frightened.

"Very well, then," said Cavallino.

Canavese called out in a voice calculated to surprise the court-room, "The prosecution calls the witness Livia Pirelli to the stand."

At first, when the door opened and the witness appeared, Kruger did not recognize the plump middle-aged woman in a dark green suit. Then the name Livia came back to him, and with it the memory of the woman at the door of the Miceli farmhouse the night he arrived in Montefalco to visit Anna. As Anna's sister mounted the witness stand, he saw in her dark unmistakably Miceli eyes a look of mingled hatred and triumph.

The clerk approached the stand and instructed her to raise her right hand and place the left on the text of the Bible. She did so, staring all the while at Kruger. "Will you repeat this oath after me?" The clerk gave the oath and she repeated it in a calm clear voice.

"You may be seated," said Canavese.

Anna, Kruger remembered, had spoken of her younger sister and the possibility, unlikely as it was, that Livia would be called as a witness for the prosecution. She had warned Burgati that her sister's testimony in court might prove devastating to the defense. Burgati had tried unsuccessfully to block Livia's appearance on the stand.

Canavese paced for a moment, waiting for the restless stir in the gallery to subside. "Will the witness tell the court where she was born and raised?"

"I was born and raised in Montefalco and lived there until after the war."

"What was your maiden name before you married?"

"Miceli." Livia addressed her response to Kruger.

"Were members of your family among the hostage victims of the reprisal execution in September 1944?"

"Yes. My father and my brother."

"Were you the only surviving member of your family?"

"No. My mother, my grandmother, and my sister survived."

"Tell the court the name of your sister who survived."

"Anna Miceli, now known as Anna Fitzgerald."

Canavese turned from the witness box to address the entire court. "Before continuing my line of questions, I would like to remind the court of a statement previously made by the defense regarding the character of the defendant, Kruger. The defense previously stated that Karl Kruger *is,* and *was* at the time of the reprisal execution, a man—and I quote the defense—'a man driven by an exacting sense of duty and responsibility.' The defense, moreover, characterized the defendant as a loyal and dedicated soldier who, as commander of the German unit occupying the town of Montefalco, was—and I quote again—'faithful in carrying out his military orders.'" He circled back to the witness stand. "Can the witness recall by way of example any specific orders regarding contact between soldiers and civilians issued by the defendant during his tenure as commandant?"

Livia answered without hesitation. "Yes." She again looked directly at Kruger. "Shortly after he came to Montefalco, Kruger issued an order forbidding his troops and the townspeople of Montefalco to have any social contact."

"And was this order made public?"

"Yes."

Kruger saw Burgati quickly jot something in his notepad. Though the fact that he and Anna had had an affair in Montefalco during the war was commonly known by the people of the village, the facts of their relationship and the birth of a child had not yet surfaced in the trial testimony of either side.

"Tell the court what you know about the defendant's compliance with the order he issued to his soldiers."

Livia nervously fidgeted with the cuff of her coat. She then fixed Kruger with a punishing stare. "From January until September of 1944, Kruger carried on a secret affair with my sister, Anna."

It would now, he knew, all of it, come out. He looked off toward the spectators' gallery. The seat occupied by Anna only moments before was empty.

II

At 6:45 Vittorio Burgati telephoned again, and this time the operator at the Royal Hotel Carlton recognized his voice. *"Momento!"* She connected him immediately to Anna's room and let the phone ring. He flipped through the pocket directory lying on his desk, searching for an alternate number where she might be reached. He had phoned the hotel when he arrived home that afternoon a little after five. He had left messages twice with the hotel desk, but she had neither answered his calls nor picked up his messages. He hung up and sat listening to his wife and child playing in the next room.

"Vito?" His wife, Ginetta, stood at the door to his study, looking worried. "Will you eat now?"

He got up. "You and the baby eat. I have to go out now. I'll eat later."

"Is something wrong?"

"I don't know." He gathered his pocket directory and the keys to his car. "If anyone calls, take their name and number, and tell them I can be reached at the Carlton Hotel. Tell them to leave a message for me at the front desk, in Signora Fitzgerald's box."

Ginetta followed him to the front door. "It's raining, Vito. Can't it wait?"

He took his raincoat from the stand in the foyer and turned in the hallway outside the apartment. "I'll be back within the hour."

The drive from his apartment building near the university to the Carlton Hotel in the Via Montebello would take fifteen minutes in the rush-hour rain.

More alarming than Anna's departure that morning was her absence from the courtroom during the afternoon session. She had not been present when the prosecution, based on Livia's testimony and against previous witness disclosures, petitioned the court to call Anna to the stand, a petition he had failed to block. Cavallino had advised him to inform Signora Fitzgerald that she would be called to the stand following the testimony of Signora Pirelli, and by his calculation her sister's testimony would continue through the whole of tomorrow. With the intervening weekend, Anna would likely be called to the stand the following Monday. If her absence from court had alarmed him, the combination of her absence today and her remark last night had begun to frighten him. At last night's meeting to prepare for the approaching defense testimony, she had talked again about the Munich-based industrialist who had two weeks ago offered Kruger financial assistance for his defense. Last night she confessed to having spent time tracing down a certain Eric von Scheffel, who, she said, was a friend of Kruger's father and a member of a veterans' club in Munich called Der Verein der Alten. She had inquired if this Club of the Old Ones was among those he knew to be affiliated with the German Neo-Nazis. He had checked his files and informed her that it was, warning her at the same time not to contact the organization, having himself experienced in the past the malevolent pressure of similar "clubs." In the past, the price defendants had paid for favors from the Neo-Nazis had been immense. Kruger, he had reminded her, would have no part of Der Verein's assistance.

At the entrance to the luxurious hotel he left his car with a parking attendant. Inside, he hurried to the bank of housephones in the elegantly furnished lobby and called up to Anna's room. There was still no answer. He wondered if she might have gone to visit Kruger. Her visits had become almost nightly. He decided to leave a message for her at the front desk.

The night desk clerk greeted him affably. *"Buona sera,* Signore Burgati." The desk staff at the hotel now recognized him as a regular visitor of the famous Signora Fitzgerald. Anna's connection with the Kruger case had become an item of fashionable gossip at Bologna's most expensive hotel. She had been a guest there now for the last seven months.

"I'm trying to locate Signora Fitzgerald. It's very important. Has she checked in this afternoon?"

"I've not seen the signora all evening."

"May I leave a message for her?"

"Certainly." The clerk produced a monogrammed notepad, envelope, and a desk pen.

Burgati wrote, "Have tried to reach you all day. Please telephone me at home immediately. Burgati." He tucked the paper into the envelope, handed it to the clerk, and started toward the entrance.

"Signore!" The clerk held an envelope up and motioned him to return. "I just found this in Signora Fitzgerald's desk, signore."

Burgati tore the envelope open. The note was in Anna's hand, but written in a hurried crooked scrawl:

Am going to M. A hunch and a last resort.

She had underlined the last two sentences.

At all cost, delay opening your testimony until I return. Trust me.

Anna

He suddenly wished he were home in his study, poring over academic research, with nothing more unpredictable to face than the written page. "Women," he muttered, tucked the note into his pocket, and went out into the rain.

III

Kruger awoke from the dream with a start. He had been sweating. He felt a chill on his face and pulled up the blanket to his chin, listening to the rain pelt the window. The white walls of his room reflected the polluted amber glow of the city's lights. He tried to recollect the dream before it vanished, but remembered only that he had been lying in a bed—the bed in the Hotel Montecatini—and had worn a white alb and chasuble. For some reason, he had wanted in the dream to rise from the bed, but something had held him back. He had felt frightened and ashamed when he saw that someone was watching him through a peephole in the wall.

The wind drove the rain hard against the window. He could still smell his uneaten dinner in the room: the sweet odor of sausage and tomato sauce. He had eaten the bread, but had had no appetite for pasta and Bolognese sauce.

He thought of the unfinished letter to his mother. He had received a letter from her this morning asking if she should now destroy all his father's documents from the war. She had kept them up to now. He had thought about it and planned to write back, saying she should do as she pleased. The documents, as she guiltily called them, would not influence the outcome of his trial after today. In the letter his mother had again expressed her willingness to come to Bologna, but he had insisted at the outset that she remain in Munich, explaining the possibility of her being called to the stand to answer questions about his father's Nazi connections. As long as she remained in Germany, she could not be extradited. If the prosecution wanted her testimony, they could take it in deposition.

He thought of Livia Pirelli's testimony that afternoon. Anna had not been present for it. Nor had she visited him last night. After dinner tonight he had paced the room inventing reasons why she might not come: the weather, business with Burgati. And when seven o'clock passed, he had begun to imagine accidents on the slippery Bologna streets in the relentless downpour. He had imagined a fierce meeting between Anna and her sister after the testimony, but Anna had been absent during the whole proceeding. He had gone to bed at 8:30, trying to reason himself into accepting the fact that, after all, she *should* not come. The case had been lost before it even began, and he had begged her months ago not to tie her heart to a stone. He had tried to justify her absence with the argument of duty—this time to herself—but the old arguments of reason and logic had given way under the weight of feelings. Feelings he could no longer deny: loneliness and longing. In the end, he had simply accepted the fact that she would not come, and it would be like this forever, waiting out his life for the blessing of death in an endless repetition of disappointed expectations. Then he had escaped for a while into sleep.

The rain relented but went on softly pelting the window.

The dream had awakened him and the feelings had come back.

He drew the blanket down and sat up. That afternoon Livia Pirelli had described for the court how he had left Anna behind, pregnant. "As a result, she was forced to run away and spend the rest of the war as a refugee."

Anna had never told him of the misery she had endured after he left Montefalco.

He swung his legs from the bed. In his cross-examination Burgati had tried to salvage the old claims of duty and responsibility, but it was useless. The gallery had jeered and laughed at his questions.

The cold draft seeped through the bolted window. He had gone to bed wearing only underwear and a pair of heavy socks.

What Livia had failed to say was that they had loved each other, and the love, despite all the damage, had endured for twenty-eight years. There was some kind of fidelity in that, at least.

He reached out in the darkness for his watch on the chair next to the bed. He did not have to look where he reached, for he had always, since his seminary days, kept his watch in the same place on all his bedside tables. He was a man of small habits.

Nine-fifteen.

In their meetings, he and Anna had always sat across from each other at the table. On occasions, they had childishly ventured to hold hands, but never anything more intimate. They could have held each other, he was no longer a priest and no one was watching. But they didn't. And now they wouldn't.

He leaned forward, with his arms on his naked knees, and pictured her body on the pine needles in the Adele Ravine. Habit and belief told him at once that his mental picture and his rising desire were matters of serious sin. He had forgiven it in others a million times as a priest.

He tried, as he had in the past, to pray, searching his memory for a formal prayer of the Church that would serve a man like him who did not really want to rid himself of desire anymore. He looked up at the white plaster wall. Pray for whom? For Anna? For himself? And for what? God could not give back what they themselves had lost, and prayers of petition were for things that lay in the future. There were no prayers for things of the past, save those of forgiveness.

He looked down at his feet in the baggy prison socks and thought how comical he seemed for a former officer of the Wehrmacht, a former priest and dignitary of the Church. Except, who beyond God could now see him?

The rain hammered at the window.

He felt a wall break inside his gut.

No one will see, he thought, trying to give himself permission. No one at this hour will hear. Nonetheless, before it happened he covered his face with his hands.

IV

The directions Eric von Scheffel read to her that morning on the phone from Munich were exact, down to the description of the wooden lamppost, the numbered mailbox, and the little trimmed hedge in front of the house that distinguished the Volker *Reihenhaus,* as von Scheffel called it, from the other white-plastered working-class houses in this suburb of Innsbruck. She had paid for the taxi ride with the Deutschmarks she had bought between the Munich airport and the train station and got out. In the lamppost's yellow bug light she looked at her watch, 9:26, and thought of Karl in his Bologna prison. She pressed the doorbell and drew her coat close to her body. The Alpine night air was dry but bitterly cold. The door opened on a middle-aged man of average height with thinning gray-blond hair and a pleasant but featureless face.

"Ja?" He looked surprised, noticing first her foreigner's face and then her lightweight coat.

She spoke some of the few German words she had learned years before from Karl. *"Sind Sie Herr Volker?"*

"Ja." He smiled innocently and politely.

"Ich bin Anna Miceli." She used her maiden name, for if he remembered her at all, it would be as she was known during the war. Seeing that her name had rung only the tiniest bell, she added in Italian, "I am from a town in Italy called Montefalco."

The watery blue eyes widened. He stiffened, keeping his hand tightly on the doorknob. *"Ja."* The smile collapsed.

"I am a friend of Karl Kruger's. I've come from Bologna to speak to you about him."

"I'm—" He stepped back as the realization ignited terror in his face. "I have nothing to say. You have the wrong house." He started to close the door. "I cannot help."

She caught and held the door. "Herr Volker," she said, quickly, "I have not come here to make trouble. I need your help."

From the back of the house, a woman called out, *"Liebchen? Wer ist denn da?"*

He ignored the woman. "How did you find me?"

She lied, seeing there was no time to explain the complicated chain of events that had led her finally to Austria. "You are listed here in the Innsbruck directory."

He knew at once that her explanation was ridiculous. "There's nothing I can do for you. You have the wrong Volker," he added, trying to backtrack.

The woman called out again: *"Josef?"*

He asked, glancing back, panicky, "Why did you come here?"

"You know that Karl is on trial at this moment in Bologna, don't you?"

He saw it was useless and released the door. The woman appeared at the far end of a cozily furnished living room. She wore a bright flower-printed dressing gown. *"Josef? Wer ist denn da?"*

"Come in." He motioned, resignedly. "We have a visitor, Ilse," he said in English and closed the door. "This is my wife, Ilse." Anna saw that the woman was older than she had first thought. Her boyishly cut hair was the same gray ash-blond as her husband's. "This is Anna Miceli, Ilse. She's here from Bologna." There was a hint of apology in his voice.

His wife's athletically tanned face registered the word with shock. "Bologna?"

She knows, Anna thought. In English, she said, "I came to talk to your husband, Frau Volker. I mean no harm."

"Make some coffee, Ilse. I will talk with Frau Miceli." The woman hesitated. "Do as I say, Ilse." The woman gave her a frightened look and turned away. He pointed to an armchair near the fireplace, remaining standing until she sat down, then lowered himself into an orange upholstered sofa against the wall. A frugal two-log fire burned in the little grate. The imitation leather of the armchair felt stiff but warm. She thought: so this is what von Scheffel meant by a *Reihenhaus.* She said, "I am an attorney, Herr Volker, and a friend of Karl Kruger. More than a friend. I've come here on behalf of his defense."

"I cannot help."

"Yes, you can. Your name is not Josef Volker. It's Hans Reiger, so let's not pretend."

He was silent for a moment. "How did you find me?"

"Through a veterans' organization in Munich."

He knew at once. The watery blue eyes ignited again. "You mean Der Verein, don't you?"

"Yes."

"I am not a member of that organization."

"I know that. At first, I thought you might be. That's why I approached them to find you."

"I was never a member. And I was never a member of the Socialist Party, either!" he said with sudden vehemence.

She realized he meant the Nazi Party. "I know that, too. Let me explain." She backtracked. "Your name first appeared months ago in the preparation for Karl's defense when his attorney questioned him about the events leading up to the execution. Karl said you were the only person who witnessed his efforts to prevent the execution."

"That's not true. There was another. His adjutant, Rudolf Oster."

"Rudolf Oster is dead."

"I see." He seemed relieved.

"Karl said you sent his request to cancel and then postpone the execution to the High Command, and you were present at his meetings with Oster. I take it you know about the case."

"Only what I've read in the Austrian papers."

"The defense is about to open its case. At this point the evidence we have proves nothing—except Karl's guilt. Without you, the case is lost. Karl's attorney and I have searched Germany for months looking for you."

"I was never a German citizen."

"Karl thought you were. He saw you in Munich in 1967. He said you came to his father's funeral."

"I see." He looked away toward the fire. "So that's how you traced me through Der Verein."

"Yes."

"I was in Munich on business. I happened to read the obituary in the Munich paper. I knew Karl's father was in the bicycle business. I liked Karl. He was a good soldier . . . and a friend to me in Montefalco." He sighed. "I went to the funeral on the chance he would be there. I didn't know he'd become a priest. I'm not a Catholic. I would have spoken to him, but—" He looked up, frightened. "I didn't know his father was a member of Der Verein."

"Neither did Karl at the time."

"There was a man there I recognized. He—" In a sudden panic, he started to rise, then gave up and sat back. "I was in the Wehrmacht, but I was never political. Never! . . . I was a soldier—like Kruger."

"Take your time. We have until morning."

"After the war, I came back to Austria. I am Austrian. I have lived here in Innsbruck since the war." He hesitated. "I changed my name after the war. It was easy to do that back then. We Austrians . . ." He left the sentence unfinished. "I'm in the sporting-goods business. I travel in Austria and in Bavaria, and I specialize in ski equipment. My wife's a professional ski instructor, she"—he pointed to a framed medal on the wall—"she won a silver medal in the

Olympics." He saw that his argument had derailed. "There's a ski resort between here and Munich. In the Alps near Seefeld. I went there once to sell my equipment. The owner turned out to be a man I knew in the war. A Nazi. He's a member of Der Verein. He came here later and asked me to join the organization. I refused. He knew my real name, and they kept it on their files. He was the man I saw at the funeral."

Reiger's wife came through the door. Without looking at either of them, she placed a tray with two cups and a plate of pastries on the table. "There are cakes, if you are hungry," she said, then quickly withdrew. The logs sparked and snapped in the grate.

"Will you take cream and sugar?"

"No, thank you."

He handed her the cup. "Yes. I remember you now. Kruger pointed you out to me once in the streets of Montefalco. You were the prettiest girl in Montefalco, we all said. There were rumors that you and Kruger were meeting secretly. Rudolf Oster started them. He said you were having an affair."

"It was more than an affair. We loved each other very much. We planned to marry after the war."

He reached for the cream. "I see." Looking up, he said, "Then came the execution."

"He shot my father and my brother."

The cream splattered across the table. He stared, astonished, murmured something in German, then dabbed the spilled cream with a paper napkin. "Oster took charge of the execution. He made a list of the names. Kruger never saw the list. He did not know most of the people in Montefalco."

"He never knew what he had done until I told him. After the execution, we never saw each other again for twenty-eight years. Until I found him by accident in California. It was I who filed the charges against him in Italy." She told of her return to Montefalco, his sudden reappearance there, and his decision, finally, to stand trial. "I realized I had made a terrible mistake. I convinced him to go back to America and ask permission from the Vatican to stand trial. He wanted to keep his priesthood. He did not wait for the Vatican's decision. They defrocked him. He was convinced, and he's still convinced, that he's guilty. He does not think his efforts to prevent the execution change anything. Perhaps, morally speaking, he's right. But legally, it does. It makes the difference between a guilty and an innocent verdict. Do you understand what I'm saying, Herr Reiger?"

The use of his real name for the first time startled and frightened him. "I'm sorry. I cannot help. I cannot go back to Italy."

"Why? What are you afraid of?"

"Those people in Munich should have told you!"

"Told me what, Hans?"

"You don't understand—this is *Austria!*" He got up, saw her lack of comprehension, then sat back down. "When the war ended, we Austrians—we wanted to forget we had been a part of it. Hitler was Austrian. We wanted no part of him after the war, we . . . we wanted the world to remember the *Anschluss* as an invasion. But it . . . it really wasn't an invasion at all." He looked at her and said with sudden vehemence, "You have to understand what this means to *us*—to Ilse and me!" then gave up with a sigh. "When I came back, I had no job. People here knew I'd been an officer in the Wehrmacht, and they were afraid to associate with me. After a while —it took years!—after a while, they let themselves forget. I found a job. The job I have now—selling ski equipment. We have Austrian friends now. If I go back and defend a German war criminal—" He left off.

She said, "You are no different from me, Hans. You have been running and hiding for twenty-eight years."

"I did nothing! I am innocent!"

"I did nothing. I was innocent."

"I don't know what you did, but it isn't the same!" He looked toward the mantelpiece, where two photographs sat in ornate cheap gilded frames. "I have children! Sons! They know nothing! My wife knows, but my sons know *nothing!*"

She looked toward the mantelpiece: at photos of two young men in business suits, smiling. "It is exactly the same with me, Hans."

He hurried on, rattled, "They are both married, one lives here in Innsbruck, the other in Leinz. They have children, too! They are Austrians, and their children are Austrians!" He gave up, dropped his head against his hand, and said in a misery of shame, "My sons —I told them I spent the war behind an army desk here in Austria. They know nothing of Montefalco."

"And my son, I told him that I married an Italian soldier—a war hero. I told him his father died a hero in the war. That was better than a desk clerk, don't you think?" She sipped her coffee as Reiger gaped at her.

"What do you mean by that?"

"When Karl left Montefalco, I was pregnant with his child. Karl and I have a son, Hans. He's"—she glanced again at the two photos —"he's probably about the age of your sons. Until nine months ago, he never knew about Karl. When he was a baby, I invented a father for him. I lied to him. To hide my hatred of Karl, my bitterness and my sense of failure, I went on lying to my child for twenty-eight years. I invented a world for him to live in, and he grew up in that world of mine. But children, you know, can smell a liar like an animal can smell a coward." She smiled meaningfully. "My son grew up to be a liar himself, and he grew up hating the liar in me. Tell me, do your sons come to visit you much?" There was no response. She nodded. "Do they come to you when they're in trouble, Hans?"

"No."

"Our son grew up in a world I invented for him, and now he can't live in the real one. At least, that was true up to now. Nine months ago, I told him the truth. Everything. He came to me later and said for the first time in his life that he loved me. Odd, isn't it, what truth can do."

He said, breathlessly, pulling at his sweater, "If I go back, they can charge *me*, too! In Austria, I am innocent!"

"None of us is innocent, Hans. The only innocence any of us can salvage from war is legal innocence." She suddenly remembered that Karl had once said, in passing, that Reiger had the heart of a coward.

"I will lose everything." He looked around the room.

She wanted to say "You never had anything to begin with," but took a last gamble, a gamble with his Austrian sentiment. "You said Karl was a friend to you in Montefalco." He looked down, ashamed. "In what way was he a friend?"

"We had to choose an officer to lead the convoy—the one to Vergato. He called in all the officers and asked for volunteers. He knew Ilse had just given birth to Jürgen—my first son. When it came time to choose an officer, he sent me out to decode a message we'd received. I'd already decoded it. It was an excuse to have me absent when he asked for volunteers. The soldiers who went on the convoy the next day all died, except one."

"Friendship, then?"

After a moment, he said, "I have evidence."

"What kind of evidence?"

"Things. I have things. I don't want to discuss them with you, but I have everything I need for my defense."

"Then what have you to fear?"

He swallowed. "When are you leaving here?"

"Tomorrow."

"You can stay here with us for the night. There's a midday train tomorrow for Bolzano and Verona. I think we can connect from there to Bologna."

CHAPTER 6

I

Umberto Canavese walked past the witness box where Anna sat, thoughtfully tapping his pen. "Tell me, signora, did the accused, during his tenure as commandant, issue orders concerning personal contacts between his soldiers and the people of Montefalco?"

"Yes."

Kruger saw her nervously glance at him, then turn away. Canavese let the effect of silence take hold of the court. Saturday night, when Anna returned from Innsbruck with Hans Reiger, Burgati had given her a lengthy account of Livia's testimony for the prosecution and her replies to the defense cross-examination, and he was sure Anna had come fully prepared this morning to be questioned on their affair. Burgati had assured him that she would hold nothing back in her testimony before the prosecution.

Last night he had begged Anna to keep her promise and stand fast behind the truth.

Canavese said, "Will you describe the order I'm speaking of for the court?"

"He forbade personal socializing between the German soldiers and the local townspeople."

"Was this order made public?"

"Yes."

"And did it apply to all the soldiers and all the townspeople of Montefalco?"

"Yes."

"To himself?"

"Yes."

Canavese looked to the bench where Major Pavoni, the judge advocate, sat doodling with a pencil. "The defense has so far attempted to represent the accused as a soldier driven by a sense of fidelity to duty—almost, shall we say, a *religious* sense of fidelity. Would you agree with that assessment?"

Anna appeared uneasy for the first time since her testimony began. "Yes."

"Then with regard to the order in question, is it your belief that the accused abided faithfully by that order?"

Kruger quickly prayed she would answer truthfully.

"He did not obey the order," she said, angrily.

"Please explain how he failed to obey, Signora Fitzgerald."

The color had risen in her face. "I had personal associations with the defendant during his stay in Montefalco."

There was laughter in the gallery. He could tell that Anna was silently cursing herself as a lawyer for having let the man trap her so nakedly. *"Associations?"* Canavese smiled, twisting the knife. "Would you describe for us what you mean by *associations?"*

"We met in January of 1944, shortly after the defendant took command in Montefalco. I followed him on his afternoon walks. I contrived to meet with him alone. I was attracted to him."

Kruger looked up, amazed. They had met in the little bakery on the Via Santa Lucia. He had always thought that *he* had been the one to contrive the meetings. He felt a sudden sense of warm pride and pleasure, a delight that seemed out of place.

"And did you?" Canavese pressed.

"Yes. Subsequently, we had meetings."

"Secret meetings?"

"Yes."

"How would you characterize these meetings?"

Kruger sent out a mental message to her: *say* what the meetings were, what we had and did together.

She said in a voice like tempered metal, "I had an affair with the defendant. We became lovers."

The brief silence that followed was like the stillness of a vacuum.

Canavese said, "Tell the court what the results of this affair were."

She seemed to take hold of herself. She said, almost defiantly, "Love. The result of the affair was this—we transcended the barriers that the war had placed between us and we learned to love each other for what we were, not for what we had been *told* we were by our warring governments."

The answer ignited a murmur in the gallery. In the next moment Canavese silenced Anna's little momentary human victory. "Did you become pregnant with the defendant's child?"

"Yes."

He went on, quickly, "How soon before the order for the reprisal execution was issued did you become pregnant?"

"I don't know."

"A matter of months, weeks, days?"

"A week or two, I would imagine."

"Did you inform the accused that you were pregnant with his child at that time?"

"No."

"Why?"

Kruger caught Anna's eye and gave her a nod. He had felt her frustration as Canavese's web closed around her. "Because . . . because the Americans were advancing and I did not want him to remain any longer in Montefalco."

Canavese swung to face the courtroom. "In other words, by that point, it was clear to you, even a civilian, that there was no military advantage or necessity for the Germans to remain in Montefalco?"

Her reply was almost inaudible. "Yes."

"What?"

"*Yes.*"

Kruger thought of the clever use Canavese had made of this side of his personal as opposed to his military behavior. Fidelity to duty and military necessity—Burgati's two points fell like bowling pins under the single ball.

"How long did you believe it would take for the American troops to reach Montefalco?" Canavese drove ahead for his third victory.

"A few days."

"Yet the defendant ordered a convoy of his men to collect supplies for his garrison in Montefalco?"

"Those orders came from the commander of the German troops in northern Italy."

"But the defendant issued the orders in his own name."

"I don't know. I was not present."

Canavese steered around her escape into ignorance. "How long did the defendant wait after the convoy was attacked before he issued the order for hostages to be taken?"

"That night."

"In the *middle* of the night, you mean?"

"Yes."

"Was that order posted in public?"

"Yes."

"And how soon after the order was posted did the defendant carry out his threat?"

"The next day."

"In other words, the townspeople had only a few hours to turn over the partisans?"

"Yes."

"And did they?"

"No."

"As a consequence, what happened?"

Kruger saw that she had given up resisting Canavese's inevitable conclusions. She said, "Hostages were taken."

"How many?"

"Fifty."

"On whose orders?"

"The defendant's."

"From what section of the population were the hostages taken?"

"From the civilian males."

"Was any criterion used in the selection, or was it a random selection?"

"Random."

"In other words, he took them without consideration of their involvement, either direct or indirect, with the action carried out by the partisans."

Anna suddenly sat forward, alert to a small opening. Kruger knew where she was going before she spoke. She had long ago told him of her brother's membership in the Brigate Rosse, something he, of course, had been unaware of at the time. She said, pointedly, "I do not know what considerations were made in choosing the hostages. I do know that at the time of their arrest, two of the hostages were subject, under international military law, to arrest and execution."

Canavese covered his surprise by turning toward the dock. "Please explain."

"My brother, Piero Miceli, was among the hostages taken and executed." There was no hint in her voice of the bitterness she had carried for twenty-eight years. "My brother was a member of the Brigate Rosse. He had planned and participated in the ambush of the German convoy to Vergato."

Far back in the courtroom there was a sudden outraged cry, *"Traditore!"*

In the next instant, Cavallino brought his gavel down. "Silence!" He turned to Anna. "The witness will continue."

"The other hostage was a soldier. An Italian soldier who had previously confessed to being a deserter from Mussolini's army. As a deserter, he was subject to execution."

Canavese took two sheets of paper from the prosecution's table and approached Anna. "I have here a list of names, Signora Fitzgerald. Would you please read the list and tell the court if you recognize the names?"

She took the list and scanned it. "Yes. I recognize the names."

"You see two names in particular on the list. Angelo Miceli and Piero Miceli. Will you identify those names for the court?"

"They are my father and my brother."

"*Were*, signora," Canavese corrected. "They were among the victims of the reprisal execution, were they not?"

"That is correct." She returned the pages.

Canavese began a slow circle in front of the witness box. "How much time passed between the arrest of the hostages and their execution, signora?" he asked in a studiedly offhand manner.

Kruger recalled the point already conceded by both Anna and Burgati. According to international law governing the conditions for a legal military reprisal execution, sufficient time had to be given for the partisans to surrender before the hostages could be legally executed. Canavese had based his opinion on the evidence from previous war crimes trials and the usages laid down in the American and British Rules of Land Warfare. Anna, Kruger saw, knew where the question was leading.

She looked up at him, appealing now for his forgiveness. "A few hours."

"Speak up! The court did not hear your reply!"

"A few hours."

"How many hours would a few hours be, signora?"

"Four. Maybe five. I did not count the hours."

"Given the position of the partisans in the mountains, would it have been possible for them to comply with the defendant's posted warning before the execution took place? In your opinion, I mean?"

The meticulous wording of the question, obviously calculated to impress the tribunal, angered Anna. "No, it would not," she retorted. "On the other hand, it was not the defendant who set the hour for the execution. That decision was forced upon him by his adjutant, Sergeant Oster, and, ultimately, by Field Marshal Kesselring."

"That is your opinion and the opinion of the defense, signora," Canavese countered. "And there has been no evidence submitted to justify the court accepting that opinion as fact. Now—concerning the execution itself."

Anna looked at Burgati, appealing for help. The evidence she wanted, of course, was the testimony of Hans Reiger, though she obviously knew that its time had not yet come.

"Were you present during the reprisal execution in the Piazza Nazionale on September fourteenth, 1944?"

"Yes." Anna sat back, resigned now.

"Was the defendant present?"

"Yes."

"You saw him?"

"Yes."

"In what capacity was the defendant present?"

"He was the senior officer in charge. It was his duty to be there."

"It has been stated in previous testimony that a certain Sergeant Oster, the defendant's adjutant, actually gave the orders to fire. Is that your opinion?"

"Yes. Oster gave the orders."

"And on whose authority was Kruger's adjutant acting in so doing?"

"The Oberkommando der Wehrmacht," she snapped.

"And who present at the execution represented the so-called Oberkommando der Wehrmacht?"

She conceded the point. "The defendant."

Canavese continued his wide circle, walking very slowly. "Describe for the court what you saw in the minutes following the execution."

She said, quietly, "There were bodies lying on the street in front of the post office . . ." Her voice trailed away.

"Describe in *particular* what you saw the defendant do following the execution."

Kruger knew at once where the request would lead. Under examination, two witnesses had already testified to seeing him deliver the *coup de grâce* to two of the dying men. So far, the prosecution had not pursued the question further than the fact that he personally shot two hostages who had survived the machine-gun fire.

Anna sat vacantly staring into space for what seemed an interminably long time. Canavese let the silence hang like a pendulum on a fragile cord. At length, she said, "Not all the men had died."

"Go on."

"Two of the men . . . two were still alive." She said the words without any visible expression of feeling. Her thoughts, Kruger real-

ized, were directed toward the scene in the square, and the transfixed expression on her face suddenly frightened him.

"And the defendant? What did you observe him do?"

She knew, of course, what he had done, but they had never in all
this time together discussed that sad aspect of the reprisal. She
replied, "He went to them . . . where they lay . . . and he gave
them . . . he gave them the *coup de grâce.*" On her lips the euphe-
mism sounded harmless, like something someone might bestow on
another.

"Describe what you mean by the *coup de grâce.*"

When she looked up, there was grief in her eyes: not for the victims, he saw, but for him. "He shot them," she said.

"With *what* did he shoot them?"

She seemed both surprised and pained by the demand for elabora-
tion. "A pistol."

"Whose pistol?"

"His!"

Kruger realized Canavese was driving home to a particular point
not previously made. Anna's head turned as she followed Canavese's
circle across the floor. In the light falling over her shoulder he saw
something glint on her cheek. She had begun to cry.

"Can you identify for the court the two men the defendant personally shot with his pistol?"

"Yes," she murmured.

"Then please do so, Signora Fitzgerald. Identify the two men for
the court." Canavese swung to face her.

"The soldier . . . the Italian soldier . . . I don't know his name."

"And the other?"

Her lips moved, but the words were inaudible.

"Please speak up! The court did not hear your reply!"

"My father."

II

While Cavallino conferred with Pavoni and Ercolani, Burgati
stood waiting beside the empty witness box. Anna looked around
her in the gallery at the people talking in excited whispers.

Angela Guardini reached over and pressed her hand. "It will be
all right, Anna. Burgati will know what to do." She meant, of
course, the so-far mysterious evidence—the "things," as Reiger had
called them—that the defense's soon-to-be-called witness brought
with him from Innsbruck, the things he had refused to discuss with

anyone except Burgati. She had told Angela this morning about Reiger's imminent appearance on the stand, following her own calamitous testimony yesterday.

Karl went on sitting slump-shouldered in the dock. She knew it was not his fear of Reiger's mysterious evidence that had darkened Karl's spirits that morning during Burgati's opening speech but the lingering aftershock of her own testimony yesterday about her father. Last night she had visited Karl in prison and tried to explain why she had held back from him that one last truth. She had apologized, but the apology was as empty as she knew it would be. "I should have told you in Los Angeles," she had said, "and then afterward in Montefalco, but it seemed like just one more piece of evidence against you. And then, when you went back to America, I realized that I couldn't. I knew it would influence your decision. Like everything else I have dreaded in my life, I postponed the telling of it until it was too late."

Burgati went to Karl in the dock, whispered something, and Karl shook his head.

"What's going on?" Angela asked.

"I don't know," she replied. But she did— She knew, at least as far as Karl was concerned, what was going on. Karl had given up fighting after he had learned what he had done to her father. *What else have I done that I don't know about, Anna?* he had asked last night. And she had realized too late that the timing of her postponement, coming at the end of the prosecution's testimony, had been the turning point in the case.

Cavallino leaned toward Burgati, his eyes bulging like a frog's. "The court wishes to be clear about this, Signore Burgati. It is the intention of the defense to call only *one* witness?"

"With the court's permission, Mr. President." Burgati bowed respectfully.

Canavese sat back with a look of incredulous amusement at this unprecedented motion.

Cavallino asked, testily, "And have you finished your opening statements, sir?"

The question brought nervous laughter from the gallery. People turned to stare at her with knowing and amused looks of satisfaction. Even the laymen, she realized, understood what she had done to her lover with the announcement yesterday of his *coup de grâce*.

"Yes, Mr. President," Burgati said with horrifying confidence, "I have concluded my statements."

Cavallino's eyebrows shot up, amazed and perplexed. On his right, Colonel Pavoni stared off into space, bewildered. Major Ercolani fidgeted with one of the medals on his uniform. "Very well, then, you may proceed," said Cavallino.

Burgati addressed the court, smoothing the sleeve of his gown. "The defense calls the witness Hans Reiger to the stand."

Karl slowly and sadly lifted his head.

The man who came through the door behind the witness box accompanied by a guard was an older version of the man he remembered twenty-eight years ago: the trimmed ash-blond hair had thinned and grayed, the plain featureless face had filled out over the bones and the skin, still ruddy and tanned, and showed signs of age only under the eyes. Hans Reiger seemed flustered by the attention focused on him and groped his way into the stand, looking back to the guard for instructions. He glanced around to get his bearings. Burgati approached. Kruger recalled Reiger's self-effacing shyness, his habit of melting into a crowd, his cowardice in battle.

In a low voice Burgati instructed Reiger on the use of the earphones and microphone for the simultaneous Italian–German translation. He spoke to Reiger in German. "You will now be sworn in, Herr Reiger. Please remain standing."

A Bible was brought to Reiger. As he recited the oath, he looked toward the defendant's dock for the first time. There was an instant of shocked recognition. Anna was right, the man was terrified.

"You may be seated," said Burgati. Kruger looked again to Anna in the gallery. She forced herself to smile at him. Burgati asked Reiger for the usual brief description of himself.

"My name is Hans Josef Reiger. I was born in Austria. In Lienz, Austria, in 1920. I am an *Austrian* citizen," he repeated to the judges, lest they miss the fact in translation. "After the German occupation of Austria, I was drafted into the Wehrmacht. The *Anschluss* was in 1938, I was drafted in '40." His voice shook as his gaze wavered between Burgati and Canavese. "In 1942 I was sent to northern Italy. First to Milan. I had reached the rank of corporal. I was a communications officer," he hastened to add, "and I had had experience with electronics in Austria. In 1943 I was assigned to the Fourteenth Army—to the infantry—to a small unit north of the Green Line. You call it the Gothic Line. We called it the Green Line." He caught his own punctilious distinction and hurried on, "I was sent to join the unit occupying the town of Montefalco in September of 1943."

Kruger saw that it was his own riveted gaze causing Reiger's nervousness and he lowered his eyes. The names, the Wehrmacht titles in German, brought back vivid memories: . . . "communications officer" . . . (Reiger had operated his radio in the small room at the rear of the Municipio) . . . "third in command" . . . (above Reiger there had been Schreiber, and then his adjutant and his quartermaster, Oster) . . . "and I remained at that post until September of 1944 when we received orders to retreat from Montefalco." Reiger looked around to see if he had satisfied the request for a description of himself.

Burgati stepped forward. "During your term of duty in Montefalco, Herr Reiger, what were your specific duties as communications officer?"

"To transmit and receive all messages between our headquarters and other German command posts."

"Was it your office to send and receive all messages between the commander of your unit and higher authorities at the Oberkommando der Wehrmacht?"

"Yes."

"Who was the commander of the unit occupying Montefalco during the month of September 1944?"

"Karl Kruger."

"Describe for the court, please, the military situation in Montefalco in September of 1944."

He thoughtfully collected his facts, then began describing the Allied advance to the southern end of the Tuscan mountains, the breakthrough in the east toward Rimini, and the attack on Pistoia and the Reno Valley in the second week of September.

Burgati interrupted. "Before the Allies began to advance on Montefalco was there any military threat made to the troops occupying Montefalco?"

"Yes."

"By whom?"

"There were Italian partisans in the hills all around Montefalco, the Stella Rossa or the Brigate Rosse, as they called themselves, and they made continual attacks on the Germans stationed in the Reno Valley."

There was a murmur far back in the visitors' gallery. Cavallino sat forward, ready with his gavel.

"Go on, Herr Reiger," Burgati urged, "describe for the court the attitude of the German troops toward the Allied advance up the Reno Valley in the second week of September."

"We knew that the Green Line had not held; it would be only a matter of days before the Americans reached Montefalco. We knew that it would be useless to stay and defend the town."

Canavese sat forward, puzzled by Burgati's line of argument. Until now the defense had leaned heavily on the issue of military necessity to support the legality of the reprisal.

"We?"

"The officers, the soldiers—we all knew it was useless."

"And the civilian population, were they aware of the military situation surrounding them?"

"Yes. It was clear to everyone."

Burgati walked to the defense table. "Was there any communication exchanged between German headquarters in Montefalco and the Oberkommando der Wehrmacht at that time concerning your military situation?"

"Yes."

"Describe it."

Kruger knew at once what Burgati referred to.

"On September twelfth I sent a radio message to General Lemelsen's headquarters requesting permission to retreat and join with the 362nd Infantry north of Vergato."

"On whose authority was the request to retreat made?"

"Oberleutnant Kruger's."

From his papers Burgati took a manila folder and removed a single sheet of yellow paper that looked tattered and frayed at the edges. Kruger recognized the cheap wartime paper. "I have here a document which I will submit in evidence to the court." He crossed to Reiger and handed him the paper. "Will you examine this document and tell the court if you can identify it?"

Reiger glanced at it, quickly. "Yes. I know it."

"Please examine it to be sure."

"This is the handwritten message I sent to General Lemelsen's headquarters on September twelfth, 1944, requesting permission to retreat."

The stillness in the room was palpable. Kruger gaped at the paper in Reiger's hand, astonished.

"Is it a copy of the message or the original?"

"The original."

"In your own handwriting?"

"Yes."

"Will you read what is written on the page?"

Reiger read the words in German as the translator followed him in Italian. Kruger recognized his message to General Lemelsen.

When Reiger finished, Burgati took the paper. "Copies of this document will now be distributed to the prosecution and to the court, and I request that they be numbered and entered into the record." He returned to the defense table. An assistant rose and moved around the court distributing the copies to Canavese and the three judges.

"Did you receive a reply to your request from General Lemelsen, Herr Reiger?"

"Yes."

Again, Burgati took out another page; and again, Kruger recognized the paper. The same procedure was followed, the paper identified and read by Reiger, and entered into the record. So far, Burgati had made no effort to explain how Reiger had come to possess the originals of documents from the German files in Montefalco. Kruger recalled the night of the reprisal when he returned to the Municipio from the Montecatini to find the German files heaped on the pavement in front of the building. He had watched Oster set fire to the files while the Municipio itself went up in flames. He looked toward Anna. She sat bolt upright in the bench, looking astonished.

"Will you now tell the court how the defense came to possess these documents?" asked Burgati.

"I turned them over to you, Herr Burgati."

"When?"

"This morning."

Canavese read the document handed him by the assistant, outraged.

"And how did you come to possess these documents, sir?"

"I have had them in my possession since the war. Since September of 1944. I have kept them with me in Austria."

"But how did you come to possess them in the first place?"

"On the night of September fourteenth, Sergeant Oster ordered me to burn our files. He gave orders to burn everything that night, the files, the public buildings—"

Burgati interrupted, "We will take up the question of who was responsible for the burning of public buildings on the night of September fourteenth when we get to the second count in the indictment. What I want to know now is why you possess the originals of official German documents from the military files of Montefalco?"

"I . . . I stole them."

"When?"

"The night of the retreat."

"Why did you steal them?"

Reiger sat back, relieved and yet, at the same time, embarrassed by the admission. "We knew . . . I knew that the war was lost. . . . I knew there would be questions asked about what had happened in Montefalco . . . by the Allies. I was afraid. I was an Austrian, not a German, and I wasn't responsible for what the Germans had done. . . . The reprisal, I mean . . . I wanted the documents as proof that I had tried to prevent the execution. I sent messages to the OKW trying to prevent the killings. I wanted proof that our superiors had ordered everything. . . . All the orders, everything, came from above."

"In other words, you kept the documents instead of burning them as Sergeant Oster had ordered?"

"Yes."

"For evidence in your defense should the need arise?"

"Yes." Reiger flushed.

"In the reply you have just read from General Lemelsen, orders were given to the defendant to collect military supplies from the railway depot north of Vergato. Did the defendant obey that order?"

"Yes. The night of the twelfth, he called a meeting in his office."

"For what purpose?"

"To announce that a convoy would be organized to collect the supplies in Vergato the following morning and to choose an officer to lead the convoy."

"Were you present at that meeting?"

"In the beginning, yes. The lieutenant ordered me to return to my office and decipher a coded message."

"You were not present when the choice of officers was made?"

"No."

"Why?"

"It was Lieutenant Kruger's plan to have me absent when the choice was made. He knew that my wife had given birth to our first child. The mission would be dangerous, given the recent partisan attacks. I knew when he sent me from the room that it was merely a trick to have me absent when the choice was made. I had already decoded that message for him earlier."

"In other words, the defendant saved your life."

Turning toward Kruger with a look of shame mixed with gratitude, Reiger said, "Yes. He saved my life."

"Describe to the court what took place the following morning."

"Sergeant Schreiber led a convoy of five volunteers to Vergato. On the way back, a few miles south of Vergato, the convoy was ambushed by partisans. All six soldiers were shot. Only one returned. He was alive but seriously wounded."

"Five soldiers had been murdered?"

"Yes, five."

"And when did the defendant learn what had happened?"

"The afternoon of the same day."

"And what did he do as a consequence?"

"He ordered me to send a message to OKW headquarters, to General Lemelsen, stating that the convoy had been ambushed, all six soldiers had been shot, and the supplies captured by the partisans. He asked again for permission to retreat, saying there was no hope of defending the town without men and supplies."

Burgati went to the defense table and removed two more familiar pages from the manila folder. "Is this the message you sent on September thirteenth, 1944, to General Lemelsen?"

Reiger examined the page. "Yes."

"The original or a copy?"

"The original."

"Did you receive a reply from General Lemelsen?"

"No, sir."

"Did you receive any reply at all?"

"Yes. The request had been passed on by General Lemelsen to the commander of the entire German Army C in Italy, Field Marshal Kesselring. I received a reply from Kesselring."

"When did you receive the reply?"

"That same day. The night of September thirteenth, 1944."

"Is this"—he handed Reiger the second of the two pages—"is this the original of that reply?"

"Yes."

"Please read it."

Reiger read the familiar words: the order to remain in their defensive position in Montefalco and the order to take ten civilian hostages (there was the usual reference to Hitler's earlier hostage order) for every German soldier shot, to hold them pending the surrender of the partisans, and to shoot the hostages if the partisans failed to comply. To Kruger, the words sounded as if they had been written that very day: he remembered reading them at his desk in the Municipio, thinking with horror of the possible results for him and Anna.

Burgati went through the procedure again of issuing copies of the documents and recording them. There were angry whispers exchanged in the visitors' gallery. Kruger saw one of the reporters rise and hurriedly leave the courtroom. At the bench, Cavallino leaned toward the judge advocate on his right and exchanged a few murmured remarks.

"Following the reply received from Field Marshal Kesselring," Burgati continued, "what happened?"

"The Americans had reached Spedaletto. We knew it would be only a day or two before they arrived in Montefalco. There was no reason, other than punishment, to take hostages. We knew the partisans would not surrender, not with victory in sight. We knew the order to shoot the hostages was pointless."

Canavese, startled by the sudden confession of military uselessness, sat forward, waiting to see how Burgati would extricate himself.

"The defendant knew this?"

"Yes, of course."

Canavese's mouth parted. A murmur rolled through the room. Cavallino shouted, revealing his larger anger, "We will have silence in this courtroom!"

Burgati said, unperturbed, "What did the defendant do, knowing the military situation?"

"He ordered me to send another radio message to OKW, this time to Kesselring himself. He told the field marshal of the military situation, that it was pointless to either take or execute hostages. He had me quote the appropriate passage from the Geneva Rules of War regarding the conditions for a legal military reprisal. He requested permission to cancel the order for the reprisal."

At the defense table, Burgati produced still another yellowed page. "Is this your handwritten copy of the request sent on the evening of September thirteenth to Field Marshal Kesselring?"

"Yes."

"Look at it. Examine it before you answer."

Reiger did as he was told. "Yes. This is the original I wrote in the lieutenant's office."

Burgati gave him the second sheet he was holding. "And what is this document?"

"The reply I—the reply the lieutenant received from Kesselring."

"Please read aloud your message to Kesselring and then read his reply."

In a low voice Reiger began, "To Field Marshal Kesselring,

Oberkommando der Wehrmacht, September thirteenth, 1944, 17:15."

Kruger remembered the evening. He had missed seeing Anna, as they had planned in the church of San Tommaso. He had not known at the time that he would never speak to or see her again for twenty-eight years.

Reiger read Kesselring's reply. It had been received by Reiger, decoded, and presented to him within an hour after his request from Kesselring to cancel the reprisal. Kruger recalled the foolish debate he had afterward waged with himself over the choice between duty and conscience. ". . . and therefore, your request to countermand earlier orders is refused. In accordance with the Führer's directive, you will take and execute hostages in a ratio of ten to one. Heil Hitler. Kesselring," Reiger read.

Burgati took the two pages. "I would like to have these two documents recorded and added to the—"

"Mr. President!" Canavese interrupted, rising quickly. He left the table and approached the bench, red-faced with indignation. "I object to the introduction of such documents at this point in the trial! The rules of procedure in the charter of this tribunal state specifically that documents to be used as evidence by either party must be submitted to the court in *advance* of their presentation as evidence. The prosecution has had no opportunity to examine these documents prior to their introduction this morning. With due respect to the tribunal, I must state that these documents are inadmissible as evidence."

"Mr. President," Burgati said, mildly, approaching the bench, "also with due respect, I must point out that the rules of procedure cannot, in justice, apply here, strictly. As I stated, these documents did not come into the defense's possession until this morning. As they are essential to the testimony of the principal witness for the defense, and as the witness himself did not become available to the defense until yesterday . . ."

Kruger listened to the flood of legal jargon from his attorney, struck suddenly by the thought of how far he had come from the simple issues of moral responsibility and personal guilt that had driven him back to Italy almost eight months ago.

Cavallino conferred quietly with Pavoni and Ercolani while Burgati stood looking at the documents in his hand and Canavese angrily paced the floor.

No one, Kruger thought, has yet bothered to ask me about what choices I had that night before the execution. He recalled his long walk to the church of San Tommaso and the debate he had waged with himself.

There was a disagreement between Pavoni and the other two judges. Cavallino made a little gesture of dismissal to Pavoni and turned, disgruntled, toward the attorneys. "The tribunal cannot, given the nature of these documents, exclude them from the testimony on the grounds that their presentation is a violation of procedure. The documents thus far submitted will therefore be accepted as admissible evidence and recorded into the record. You may continue, Signore Burgati."

Burgati approached the clerk with the documents, then he turned to Reiger in the stand. "After the defendant received the second order from Kesselring, what took place?"

Canavese sat down, stony-faced.

Reiger thought in silence for a moment.

An image came to Kruger: himself seated in the confessional in the church of St. Luke's in Los Angeles. Countless times he had sat in judgment of the actions and choices of others. Always, in doubtful cases of mortal sin, the final verdict of guilt or innocence had belonged to the penitent, not to him. Always, he had asked the penitent himself to consider the conditions for mortal sin: sufficient reflection, grievous matter, and full consent of the will. If all three had been present at the time of the act, the penitent was guilty of mortal sin. Six, maybe seven, times in his seventeen years as a priest he had listened to the confessions of people who had murdered. To resolve their guilt or innocence, he had always asked them to weigh for themselves the three conditions. That night, alone in the church of San Tommaso, he had weighed them himself, and he had chosen to commit murder.

Reiger finally spoke. "The defendant, Herr Kruger, tried to delay signing the order. He knew, as we all knew, that the Americans would reach Montefalco within thirty-six hours. His adjutant, Schreiber, had been killed in the ambush that morning and had been replaced by the officer third in command, Sergeant Rudolf Oster. Oster was a Nazi—not just a soldier like most of us. A Nazi. On the evening of the thirteenth, I was called into the lieutenant's office. His new adjutant, Oster, was there."

Karl knew at once where Reiger's testimony was leading. He shook his head. Reiger was consciously avoiding eye contact with him. The meeting: Reiger had been there, had heard the argument with Oster, but he could not have known his mind! True, he had fought to postpone signing the order for the arrest, but he had known even then that duty would prevail over conscience, and he would ultimately sign the order. It was a game, the meeting, and he had merely been playing for time!

"The defendant, Lieutenant Kruger, tried to postpone signing the order of arrest. He argued there would not be enough time between the arrest of the hostages and the arrival of the Americans for the partisans to give themselves up."

Kruger dropped his head into his hand.

"He argued that the order could not be properly carried out under the Rules of War," Reiger said.

"*Bugiardo!*" someone shouted far back in the gallery. The epithet of *liar* seemed to frighten Reiger. The man standing directly behind Anna against the back wall of the courtroom continued yelling in the familiar Montefalco accent, "The bastard's a liar!" She turned to see Antonio Faggioni, the young *contadino* from Montefalco, lunge forward as Cavallino pounded furiously on the bench and shouted, "I order that man removed from the courtroom!"

"That man's a Nazi!" Faggioni bellowed. "He's lying!" Four armed guards descended and forcibly pulled him back. He was dragged yelling from the courtroom, "He's a liar! A liar!"

"Order! The courtroom will come to order!" Cavallino went on rapping the gavel until the uproar in the gallery subsided. Around her, Anna sensed the ominous tension of volatile rage.

"The witness will please continue," Cavallino instructed.

"As I say, Sergeant Oster was a Nazi." Reiger looked around, as if defending himself in the wake of Faggioni's accusation. "He was a fanatical Nazi, a member of the party. He . . . he argued that Kesselring's orders were to be carried out regardless of time, that Kesselring had ordered the reprisal, not as a warning for future partisan attacks, but as punishment for the last attack, and no delay was called for. He . . . he threatened to inform Kruger's superiors if the lieutenant did not sign the order at once as instructed." His voice trailed away weakly.

In the momentary silence, Cavallino and Pavoni exchanged doubtful glances. Canavese sat scribbling notes in a legal pad. Faggioni's outburst and accusation had had a leveling effect on the credibility of the witness. His account of the meeting would undoubtedly be challenged in the prosecution's cross-examination.

Burgati said, "You are testifying that the defendant's adjutant, Rudolf Oster, made threats?"

"Yes."

"How is it possible that an inferior officer in the German Army could have been a threat to an officer of higher rank?"

"The army was a network of Nazi informants. Oster was working for the Gestapo. All he needed to do was inform Kesselring of Kruger's failure to obey to have Kruger removed."

"And what would have happened?"

"He would have been ordered to shoot the lieutenant."

Anna saw Karl lift his head from his hand. He doesn't believe Reiger, she thought, seeing doubt rise in his face like a white flag of surrender.

"Did the defendant agree, then, to sign the order?"

"He dismissed Oster and me from his office, saying he would inform us of his decision."

"And did he?"

"Not at once."

"There was a delay?"

"Yes."

"With what results?"

"Sergeant Oster came to the radio room where I was. He ordered me to send another message, this one in his own name, to Field Marshal Kesselring stating that Kruger had refused to carry out the field marshal's order of execution. He asked permission to arrest Kruger, relieve him of his duties as commandant, have him court-martialed at once and shot, and to carry out the order of execution himself."

Burgati removed still another sheet of paper from the folder. "Is this your message that Oster ordered sent to Kesselring?" He again presented Reiger with the paper.

"Yes."

"Is it written in your hand?"

"Yes. And dated, with the hour indicated at the bottom."

"Did you do as Oster ordered and send the message?"

"No!"

"Why?"

Anna recalled Reiger's admitted motive for coming to Bologna, to clear himself once and for all of complicity in the murder of fifty innocent men. His chance, she saw, had now come, for he sat forward in his chair, suddenly agitated, and held up the paper for the judges to see. "I did not believe the reprisal was justified! It was not in my power to stop it, I was only a noncommissioned officer, I was not responsible for what my superiors did, I had no authority of my own!"

He must have sensed the pathetic vision he inspired in the courtroom, for he suddenly sank back and said, abjectly, "I kept the written copy of the order, but I did not send it."

Karl's gaze followed Burgati across the room to the clerk. During the recording of the document, his face remained fixed in shock.

"After Oster's visit to you in the radio room, what happened?" asked Burgati.

"Approximately an hour and a half later, he returned. He demanded to know why no reply had come to his order. I lied. I told him that the Futa and Giogo passes east of us were under heavy fire and messages were not getting through. Kruger had sent for Oster. Oster ordered me to accompany him to the lieutenant's office. He said he wanted me present as a witness." Reiger glanced at Canavese, misreading the prosecuting attorney's mute passivity, and stammered, "Oster was crazy! He was a fanatic! He wanted everything he did documented so that the Nazi Party—Hitler!—would know that he was loyal and obedient!" He looked around, terrified by the reproachful faces turned toward him. "Kruger signed the order. I witnessed him sign the order before Sergeant Oster."

Burgati took out another paper. It appeared even more frayed and torn at the edges than the others. "Is this the order Kruger signed?"

"Yes. That's the *original!*" Reiger said as if the paper was an authentic among fakes.

Anna saw that Karl had withdrawn into himself, mentally absenting himself from the room as he had done with her the previous night when she visited the prison to explain her reasons for silence about her father.

"After the order was signed by the defendant, who carried out the arrests?"

"Sergeant Oster."

"When did they occur?"

"The following morning." He waited for instructions.

"Go on." Burgati smiled, patiently.

"The order called for the arrest of ten civilians for every soldier shot. Soldiers were sent before dawn the morning of September fourteenth, and sixty civilian males were arrested in Montefalco and the surrounding countryside. You see, six soldiers had been shot," he backtracked to explain, "but only five had died. The hostages were taken to the military compound outside the town. At nine-thirty that morning—I remember the time, I was preparing to decode a message we had just received from Spedaletto about the American advance—at nine-thirty Oster came to get me. Lieutenant Kruger, he said, wanted to see me in his office. Oster ordered me to bring a copy of the Führer's order of September 1941 regarding reprisal executions. Oster ordered me to take *minutes* of the meeting"—he shot a look of calculated amazement at the three judges—*"minutes* of the meeting!" he exclaimed. "The man was *crazy!"* The judges stared, mutely. Reiger turned back to Burgati, "I was there to take down what Kruger and Oster said."

"The court understands. Proceed."

Reiger hesitated, collecting his wits. "They argued. The lieutenant —Kruger—insisted that they follow the letter of the law. He referred to the Führer's order of September '41 that Kesselring had quoted—ten hostages for every soldier killed. It stated that—*killed*. Only five of our men had been killed. Six had been shot, but five had died. Oster had arrested sixty hostages, ten for every soldier *shot,* not *killed!"*

Burgati interrupted again, patiently. "The court understands the figures. Tell the court what the defendant demanded of his adjutant."

For the first time in many minutes, Reiger looked directly at Karl. He said, "He demanded that they obey the Führer's order. He demanded that they execute fifty hostages instead of sixty."

Burgati moved slowly toward the defense table, letting the answer hang suspended in the silence. A pleasant sensation came over Anna like the restful ease after a refreshing breeze. She heard around her the urgent whispers of those who had not understood the German. Karl touched his forehead, shielding his face from view.

When Burgati reached the table, he said, "Did Sergeant Oster agree to the defendant's demands?"

"Yes. He objected, but he obeyed. He had no choice. Those were Hitler's orders."

Burgati removed the last remaining page from the folder and returned to the witness stand. From experience, Anna recognized the pattern of his movements and his silences. He had worked them out and timed them for this moment. The university academic seemed pleased with himself. "Are these the minutes, as you call them, of that meeting?"

"Yes." Reiger looked at the judges. "They are signed. Oster even *signed* them! He wanted proof that Kruger had been the one to reduce the number of hostages. He was convinced Kesselring would question him after the war; he was afraid he would not be promoted if he disobeyed the spirit of the law."

"This document will be entered as evidence, numbered, and

recorded." Burgati handed it to the clerk. "For the record, Herr Reiger," he added, almost as an afterthought, "answer this question for the court. If the defendant Kruger had not signed the order of execution, if the defendant Kruger had not personally conducted the execution, how many civilian hostages would have been shot?"

"Sixty."

"And how many, in fact, were shot?"

"Fifty."

"In other words, are we to conclude, in your opinion, that Kruger's participation in the reprisal execution in Montefalco on September fourteenth, 1944, resulted in his saving the lives of ten men?"

"Yes."

Close to Anna, two newspaper reporters rose quickly and started out of the courtroom. Before the wave of shock registered in the gallery, Burgati turned to Reiger in the witness box: "That concludes my questions pertaining to the first count of the indictment. Now let us turn to the second count concerning the burning of public buildings."

"Non e vero!" a woman in the gallery shouted. *"E colpevole!"* Before Cavallino could reach for his gavel, she had rushed down the aisle leading to the front of the courtroom. "He is guilty!" she screamed. "He is guilty! He killed my Paulo! My son!" At the center of the group restraining the woman, Anna recognized Maria Pucetti. "He is the *butcher!*" She screamed the epithet as though it rightfully belonged to Karl by the usage of twenty-eight years.

Reporters began pushing their way toward the door. The babble of voices around Anna, the contagion of impassioned shouts, persisted over the pounding of Cavallino's gavel.

It no longer matters, she thought with detachment, feeling the refreshing, and this time lingering, sensation of peace return.

CHAPTER 7

I

It had rained steadily for two days during the closing speeches of the defense and prosecution and the brief summing-up by Pavoni, the judge advocate. The familiar wooden armchair where Kruger had sat for almost three weeks felt damp and sticky that morning when he sat down. A few stragglers, delayed by the downpour, edged their way into the standing-room space of the courtroom. The spectators in the gallery looked disagreeably drenched. Kruger searched for Anna and saw her seated near his dock. She wore a brown raincoat over her shoulders, and her hair, drawn back from her face, had come loose in the rain. A single wet strand clung to her forehead, but she was oblivious of it. She smiled, nervously. He wanted to return the smile but could not share her confidence. He looked down at his damp bedraggled suit and thought back over the prosecution's cross-examination of Reiger. The question of criminal intention had been turned and turned until nothing more could be drained from it. He himself could have answered the questions in an instant. He had asked Burgati to let him take the stand, but Burgati had refused, saying he would only confuse the legal with the moral issues and resolve nothing.

Someone nudged his arm, and he turned to find one of the guards at the foot of the dock with a folded note. Surprised, he took the note. It had not, he knew, come from Burgati at the defense table. Then he recognized the paper. It was his letter to Anna from the mission in the California desert the afternoon she appeared with Angelo—the letter Father Mendoza had delivered as their cars passed on the road. He glanced up. This time, the smile she gave him came with a knowing nod. He looked at her letter and saw that she had circled the last two sentences: "Please try to understand my conviction. The fact is, I don't believe I will be free until I receive the judgment of a court of law."

The door leading from the judges' chambers opened. Cavallino, followed by Pavoni and Ercolani, filed in. The provost marshal stepped forward. "All rise! The courtroom will come to order!"

Kruger, together with everyone seated in the room, stood up. He quickly slipped the letter into his suit-coat pocket, stealing a second glance at Anna. She acknowledged his look with another smile. When Cavallino and the two judges had taken their places at the bench, the provost marshal instructed the courtroom to be seated and then announced the commencement of the day's proceedings. Cavallino had carried a single legal folder to the bench. He opened the folder and studied the page inside. The expression on his sober face revealed nothing. Kruger thought back to Cardinal Boyle's face across from him at the prelate's desk that afternoon in March when he announced his intention to return to Italy and stand trial. There had been the same thoughtful calm in Boyle's face, he remembered, the peacefulness of a mind comfortable in the responsibility of its decision and judgment. He had felt jealous of that comfort. "The court has weighed the testimony of both the defense and the prosecution," Cavallino said in a matter-of-fact voice, "and we have reached a verdict." He fingered the page in the folder, thoughtfully. The rain beat against the big window, softly. "I should like to say this to the defendant, the counsel for the defense, and counsel for the prosecution, and"—Cavallino looked out toward the visitors' gallery—"to all who have participated in or followed these proceedings. Much has been said here concerning the issue of both collective and individual human responsibility in the practice of war. First, let me say, behind every proceeding of this kind dealing with charges of war crimes, indeed, behind the entire body of law governing the practices of war in general, lies the shadow of another, larger question—the moral question of war itself. Undeniably, it is the common consensus among all right-minded men that war as such, in the abstract, is evil—an evil that we must live with as a weakness deeply rooted in our nature. As a consequence, the entire body of law governing the usages of war has always labored under the burden and shadow of compromise. A compromise, in the end, with man himself."

Cavallino paused to clear his throat. "Second, the issue before this tribunal is, however, not that of war itself, or even of one particular war, but the defendant's guilt or innocence in a particular *instance* of war. This issue is complicated by the fact that war is never waged by single individuals, but by many. Therefore, the individual's responsibility for particular actions cannot be entirely separated from the collective responsibility as a whole. In the beginning of this trial, for instance, there was debate over individual versus collective responsibility for actions carried out under orders of higher superiors. It is the opinion of this tribunal that the argument of superior orders is, at best, valid only as a mitigating factor in individual responsibility. It can never serve to free the individual from personal responsibility for criminal actions that he performs."

Cavallino sat back. "Third, and most difficult of all, the task of this and any war crimes trial is further complicated by the distinction that must be made between the individual's *demonstrable* criminal intention and the individual's personal and private conscience. Here again, the law labors under a larger burden, namely the burden of human morality, and it, in turn, labors in the shadow of compromise.

"Finally, before handing down the verdict of this court, let me say that the jurisdiction of this tribunal extends only to criminal actions and criminal intentions *demonstrable* under the law. Our judgment extends no further. The ultimate court of appeal is the individual conscience. And you"—Cavallino turned to Kruger—"the defendant, must look to yourself and to God for the final verdict of innocence or guilt." He sat forward and took the page from the folder. "The defendant, Karl Gustav Kruger, will rise now and receive the judgment of this court."

Kruger stood up. Someone far back in the courtroom coughed nervously. He had imagined up to now that the judgment and the verdict would come with more fanfare. He felt curiously calm, as if nothing of real importance was about to happen to him. For an instant, waiting, he tried to think of the difference between freedom and imprisonment, but the impending possible verdicts and sentences seemed like opposite sides of the same moral coin. He tried, then, to think of life with or without Anna, but realized he could not, he dared not, think further ahead than this single present moment of his life. The lines Anna had circled in his letter came to mind. The rain went on beating against the window like a thousand little fingers tapping.

"I wish to make it clear to the accused," Cavallino was saying, "that the findings of this court are final and not subject to review or challenge by any Italian or any international court." He leaned forward. "Signore Kruger, you were arraigned before this court charged with committing a war crime in the town of Montefalco on September fourteenth, 1944. I shall refer to that as the first charge. Moreward. "Signore Kruger, you were arraigned before this court charged with committing a crime against humanity in the same place and at the same time. I shall refer to that as the second charge." He sat up, swept the courtroom with his eyes, and said in a loud but calm voice, "The court finds you not guilty of the first charge and not guilty of the second charge." He closed the folder. For a moment, Kruger listened to the rain beating on the window.

Then a sudden sound shattered the silence, a choked muffled cry of pain that could have been either a woman's or a man's: he could not tell the difference.

He looked down at the floor in front of him, wondering why Cavallino's words seemed to have been spoken to someone not himself: why they gave him a feeling of relief on the one hand and incompletion on the other.

"You are therefore," Cavallino went on, "no longer the concern of this court, and you will now be removed by the provost marshal and held in safe custody pending orders for your release." He brought down the gavel for the last time. "This court is now adjourned."

II

Anna pulled the flaps of her beltless raincoat closer to her body. The rain, now a drizzle, had been coming down steadily for hours, relentlessly, since she arrived at the prison. The lining of her coat felt damp, and the damp sent a miserable chill through her body. She drew the collar up, tightening it around her neck, and turned her wrist to read her watch: 5:10. The light would be gone soon. From where she stood in the sheltered recess of the tobacco-shop door, the little door in the sooty prison wall across the street would soon be obscured by the darkness.

But there was no other dry place to stand on the street.

She had first waited in the trattoria down the street, seated at a window table where she could watch the side door of the prison from which the guard had told her Karl would emerge. When the demonstrators came with their placards, some fifteen or twenty of them, she had phoned the prison again to learn that the warden would not permit Karl to leave until the crowd dispersed. The *buffoni,* as the restaurant owner had called them, had marched for two hours, shouting anti-Nazi slogans, waving their sodden placards, until the small crowd of spectators they had attracted got bored and left. When the little trattoria began to fill with early diners and the management's patience with her wore thin, she had paid her bill, left, and moved her vigil down the street to the door of the corner tobacco shop. It had taken another hour for the demonstrators to give up, drop their placards in the street, and disperse. The cars that had passed had flattened the soggy placards to the pavement, and the rain had turned the cheap paper into mush. On some of the placards the printed tempera slogans had dissolved into colorful blurs and streaks which looked like the artwork of retarded children. Considering the passion and noisy conviction that had gone into their heraldry, the abandoned placards now looked merely pathetic.

Anna stared at the prison door down the street. She had, of course, said nothing to Karl or anyone about coming to the prison to wait for his release, nor had she left word at her hotel where she would be. She could scarcely make out the little door in the huge wall. He could come out, turn in the opposite direction, and she would never know. The thought of missed passages was all too familiar. Suddenly panicky, she left the doorway and hurried out into the rain. Mid-street, she stopped and stood among the melting placards, letting the rain beat against her face and run down her neck into the collar of her dress. There was no shelter over the prison door and no certain hour for his release.

The foolishness, the vanity of her inconsequential dilemma suddenly angered her.

Then she thought, *when I went into the tobacco shop for the candy, could he have . . . ?*

She turned back to the temporary expedience of the tobacco-shop doorway. Inside the recess, in the failing light, she caught sight of the reflection of her face: the face of a helpless frustrated eighteen-year-old girl in the body of a forty-six-year-old woman.

Eighteen: the number seemed to have come to her magically from the rubble of those selfish adolescent illusions. They had met two weeks before her nineteenth birthday. A realization came to her with appalling clarity: nine short incomplete months of planning for herself the design for a perfect future, and then . . .

She rested her head against the glass, listening to the relentless patter out in the street.

The greater part of her life, twenty-eight years of life, had simply fallen away. Running in blind vicious circles, blaming and cursing the present for what she had coveted and lost in the past, she had allowed a whole amazing world to pass by. She had been a slow learner.

Angelo, thank God, was still young.

Still, late as it was, there was a settling kind of peace in just *seeing*.

On the phone, the guard had told her that Karl would come out when the warden decided that the streets were safely cleared.

The ultimate court of appeal is the individual conscience. And you, the defendant, must look to yourself for the final verdict of innocence or guilt.

When she leaned back and looked at her face, the frustration and the helplessness seemed to have gone.

She thought of the strange designs they had made of their lives in order, by the simple accident of choice, to come to this: the door of a tobacco shop and the door of a prison.

She thought of Angelo, the unbroken link in all this time of their separation. He would phone tonight from Connecticut to learn the verdict.

Over the noise of the rain beating patiently on the street, she heard the sound of a man's voice, faintly, in the distance. Turning, she saw Karl's outline between two uniformed guards outside the open door in the prison wall. She thought he wore the suit he had worn during his trial and the striped tie she had given him. His suitcase stood next to him on the sidewalk. He shook hands with one guard, then turned, smiling, and shook hands with the other. The guards waved as he took the suitcase and started along the sidewalk in the direction of the tobacco shop.

Kruger paused, shifted the suitcase from his left to his right hand, then continued toward the intersection of the boulevard fronting the prison. Spots appeared on his suit. He shrugged. It didn't matter about the suit, really; the rain felt good on his face. He smiled to himself. He could walk for a while or—if he chose—he could wait at the corner and take a taxi, if one came; or instead, he could find a phone box and call a taxi: there were any number of things he could do—the choices were all his now.

Later, he would phone Angelo in the States and tell him of the acquittal, what it really meant. It was time now to talk with his son of choices. True, they had both done things, they had both made tragic choices, but those belonged to the past. Those things would never change. It was a matter now of simply learning to live with them. There was the present and there was the future—and those two belonged entirely to them. After all, the best God could ask of the worst or even the best of men was to live in the wisdom of hindsight, however sad that might be.

For now, he would find a nice inexpensive hotel convenient to Anna's hotel and phone her. The guards had told him, joking, that she had called repeatedly that afternoon asking when he would be let out. He would phone her when he found a hotel. They could then choose when and where to meet. He took a deep exhilarating breath. The air was cold but clean.

He caught sight of a movement in the dim light, someone leaving the door of a shop on the far corner. He looked again, and stopped. She stood on the opposite sidewalk: Anna, camouflaged under her funny rain gear. For a moment, arrested by shock and the sudden in-pouring of a terrific joy, he merely looked at her.

Then he circled the car parked at the curb blocking his passage and crossed the street. It was strewn, he saw, with the rubble of discarded placards: the placards that had floated up and down the street not an hour and a half ago. They belonged, it seemed, to the distant past, to something completely finished.

She came to the edge of the sidewalk to meet him.

He left the suitcase standing in the gutter and opened his arms.

They came together and held, like two souls converging at the end of long and separate voyages, coming to the end of one thing and the beginning of another.